*"LEAH CARRIES ON
IN THE BEST TRADITION
OF SCARLETT O'HARA."*

Publishers Weekly

For years she lived as an outcast with the man she loved. But now, far from the splendors and sorrows of war-sacked New Orleans, far from the wrought-iron balconies, the crystal chandeliers, and the tender, passionate moments she once had known, Leah faces intrigue, kidnapping, and an inescapable memory that turns her heart to flame.

Come with Leah, the lovely
heroine of DELTA BLOOD, as she
finds freedom at last—
at the river's end.

BARBARA FERRY JOHNSON
HOMEWARD WINDS THE RIVER

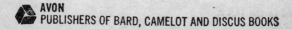
AVON
PUBLISHERS OF BARD, CAMELOT AND DISCUS BOOKS

HOMEWARD WINDS THE RIVER is an original publication of Avon Books. This work has never before appeared in book form.

AVON BOOKS
A division of
The Hearst Corporation
959 Eighth Avenue
New York, New York 10019

Copyright © 1979 by Barbara Ferry Johnson
Published by arrangement with the author.
Library of Congress Catalog Card Number: 78-62041
ISBN: 0-380-42952-7

First Avon Printing, May, 1979

AVON TRADEMARK REG. U.S. PAT. OFF. AND IN
OTHER COUNTRIES, MARCA REGISTRADA, HECHO EN
U.S.A.

Printed in the U.S.A.

For Jennifer Lee,
the newest little one to join the family
and
For all the many readers of *Delta Blood*
who have asked the question:
Which man did Leah choose?

Chapter One

THE BELLS IN the St. Louis Cathedral chimed the hour.

Their sound echoed throughout the Vieux Carré, the
French Quarter of New Orleans. Among the many who
heard them, the bells had a special meaning for three
people.

For Leah, sitting on a bench in Jackson Square, they
were a signal that the moment of decision was at hand.

For Baptiste Fontaine, looking out the window of a
house a few blocks away, they heralded a celebratory farewell to New Orleans before leaving for Belle Fontaine, his
plantation on the Mississippi River.

For James Andrews, pacing the floor of his hotel suite,
they were a reminder that only three hours remained before his steamboat departed for Indiana.

Leah opened her mesh reticule and took out two notes.
Slowly she unfolded one and began reading, scrutinizing it
letter by letter, phrase by phrase, like a child learning to
spell out his first words. She put it aside, picked up the
second note, and studied it intently, as if committing it to

1

memory, even though she already knew every word, every syllable by heart.

At the levee, a riverboat announced its departure with three farewell blasts. Startled, Leah looked up and gazed at the activity around her—a scene blurred and softened by her tears. Deliberately she ripped one note into shreds, then called to a small Negro boy standing nearby.

"You want to earn ten pennies?" She smiled at him, but her soft voice betrayed her inner turmoil.

He grinned and nodded excitedly, like a shiny new wind-up toy.

"Take this note to M'sieu James Andrews at the St. Louis Hotel. Take it straight to him. Hear?"

"Yessum, I hears."

"I'll give you the pennies now, but if you fail to deliver the note, I'll skin you alive."

"Yessum, I'se goin'. Now!"

In the small, elegantly furnished house, Baptiste propelled his wheelchair between packing boxes and through narrow channels marked by rolled-up carpets and leather trunks. All of the furniture was remaining behind so he and Leah could use the house whenever they came to the city. Leah loved the theater, and he knew the long days in the country might become tedious if there weren't a diversion now and then. With the war over, New Orleans would begin to celebrate Mardi Gras again; and even though he could no longer dance in the streets or follow the extravagant floats down Canal Street, he and Leah could stand alongside the parade route and watch. He must remind Benji to wrap the carpets and cover the furniture with dust sheets before they left. The part of Belle Fontaine they would be using for the time being was completely furnished, so there'd been no need to borrow from this house. In the packing boxes were linens, some antique bric-a-brac that Leah insisted she couldn't possibly do without, most of their silver, and their clothes. It would all fit into the wagon he'd hired to follow the carriage, so they wouldn't have to return to town until they really wanted to.

No, he and Leah could seclude themselves in their own Eden, away from the turmoil and hubbub of the city. He looked forward to sitting on the gallery, watching the boats move up and down the Mississippi and listening to Leah as she busied herself within the house. It would be a good life, quiet and idyllic, just what both of them needed after all they'd been through during the war.

Baptiste made one last tour of the rooms. Parlor, bedroom, nursery: each contained, like precious mementoes enshrined under glass, fragile tokens of past events. The house had already become less a home than a museum that sheltered poignant recollections of his and Leah's life together in it. He shuddered at the feeling of finality that clung like invisible dust to everything around him. He'd intended going to the kitchen to see how Benji—butler, valet, and friend since childhood—was progressing with the dinner. Instead he returned to the parlor and his vigil by the window.

As was his habit when thoughtful, Baptiste impatiently brushed back an unruly lock of curly black hair and smoothed his neatly trimmed black mustache. Where the devil was Leah? He slapped the arm of his chair. Then he reached for a long, black cigar. Thank goodness the wartime shortage of cigars was finally over: they were his one consolation during times of stress now that he could no longer walk off his frustrations. Leah was late! And she'd said she needed to do only a bit of last-minute shopping. Women!

At the hotel, James Andrews reached into the pocket of his tweed jacket and pulled out his watch for the third time in five minutes. He rechecked his trunk. He'd forgotten nothing. He ran his hands through his reddish-brown hair and relit his pipe. Opening a window, he heard the riverboat whistle. His own boat would be leaving shortly. Would Leah be on it with him, going to Indiana as his wife?

James had come to New Orleans alone for a brief vacation after the death of his wife, Zadah, and he'd fully intended on returning alone. He'd acquired the habit of having a single drink before supper at Le Coq d'Or, one of the more interesting bars. One night, that single drink had multiplied into four or five. His lawyer's instincts were alerted when he overheard two men in a concerned discussion of a woman of color on trial for murdering a Federal officer. Under most circumstances James had a modest, self-effacing nature; but when his strong, innate belief in justice came to the fore, he never hesitated to make himself heard. It was obvious these men were deeply worried about the young woman's receiving a fair trial.

After introducing himself to the two men and being invited to join them, he'd learned that one—Pierre De-Lisle—was also a lawyer, who was at the moment trying to convince his friend—Baptiste Fontaine—that the young woman would not be convicted. All the evidence was hearsay and circumstantial. What did Mr. Andrews think?

"I think I'd like to talk to the young lady. From what you're saying, I gather you're afraid the Union military judges will be prejudiced against her. That may or may not be. In any case, since I'm not a Southerner, I'd like to help, if you'll let me."

The first time James saw Leah, the woman accused of the murder, she wore a pale-gray gown with simple white collars and cuffs. Even so primly dressed and with her long black hair pulled severely back from her taut, fear-etched face, she was beautiful. There was a calm serenity about her as she walked into the room where he waited. Yet under her composure, he could sense a relinquishment of all hope and an acute despair that had drained her of all emotion.

At first James was only deeply moved by her plight, and he listened to her story with total professional objectivity. She was his client, and he would do all he could to get an acquittal. He did not believe her innocent of the violent crime, but he thought the violence had been done in self-defense. Yet she had persisted in denying that she'd killed Major Anderson while defending herself against his attempt to rape her. Nor would she swerve from that plea. And so James began to prepare her defense.

Seeing Leah every day and learning what her life had been as a free woman of color, as Baptiste Fontaine's *placée* or mistress, and as one of the many in New Orleans who suffered under the Federal occupation for over four years, he gradually fell in love with her. After the trial, at which she was found innocent, he remained in New Orleans to be near her. Over and over he'd tried to

4

tell himself that she belonged to Baptiste, that soon she would be leaving for the Fontaine plantation, but it was no good. He loved her and wanted to marry her and take her back to Indiana with him as his wife.

He had not been surprised at her refusal when he first asked her to marry him. He knew she had not been prepared for his proposal. Yet he also knew she was not unaware of his feelings for her. At last he received one promise from her: she would give him her answer before he left.

Still moving restlessly around the room, he had his thoughts interrupted by a knock at the door, and he hurried to open it. Expecting to see Leah, he was overcome with disappointment when he saw instead a little Negro boy panting for breath.

"Note for you, suh. De lady say hurry and I hurries."

"Thank you." James took the small, folded note and started to close the door. "Oh, here." He reached into his pocket and handed the boy several pennies. What was he purchasing with them? The words he wanted to read or a polite but sincere refusal? No, Leah would not clothe her answer in sugar-coated rhetoric. She would be honest and straightforward in her reply.

"Thank you, suh!" The boy sauntered down the narrow, carpeted hall, jingling the pennies in his pocket, and James quietly closed the door.

Dreading yet anxious to open the creamy white paper in his shaking hands, James walked to the window and began reading the fine, convent-taught script.

After the boy left, Leah remained on the bench for a few minutes. The Vieux Carré with Jackson Square and the St. Louis Cathedral—this was her home. Here she had been born and reared in the house owned by her father, Jean-Paul Bonvivier, but lived in by only her mother and herself. A house visited by her father when he could get away from his legal, white family. She loved this section of New Orleans with an all-consuming passion, a passion grown stronger under the cruel tyranny of Federal occupation. A quixotic passion, it could also flare into a hatred for attitudes she had often had to endure. Like all passions it was violent and at times almost self-destructive. It was then she fought with all the power in her to fend off chaotic despair and accept what she was even if she was never sure who she was.

She heard another whistle. Ships were again sailing to all ports of the world and up the Mississippi to the North. The North. She breathed in deeply and then exhaled slowly as if to rid herself of the pain clutching her heart. What did the North offer? Freedom or a new kind of bondage? Would she cast off the invisible shell of her heritage only to don a new one of fear and deceit?

From the time she knew what it meant to be an octoroon, Leah had been inflamed with one desire—to go North and "pass" as the wife of a white man. Though a "*free* woman of color," she had been reared a slave to the custom of *plaçage*, being the *placée* of a wealthy Creole. She was well trained for that position. Her mother, Clotilde, had seen to that. Wasn't her mother the *placée* of Jean-Paul? At times that all-engulfing, fiery passion to be free of her past had smoldered, banked with her contentment at being loved by Baptiste Fontaine. At other times, especially when forced to endure silently the indignities suffered by all free people of color, that passion had raged almost out of control.

In spite of having come to love Baptiste through long years of joy and sorrow, through the desperate years of the war and their fight to regain his plantation, she was not unmoved by James Andrews' proposal of marriage. Once more the embers were stirred up into the incandescent desire to go where no one knew who or what she really was. She could create a new identity for herself. She loved Baptiste, but was love enough? For days she agonized over the decision to go or to remain, until finally it could be postponed no longer. She had to choose between staying in New Orleans as mistress to Baptiste, the man she loved but could never marry, or going North as wife to James, whom she respected but did not love.

She had made the decision. Of one thing only was she certain: there would be moments of wondering about what might have been, but she would never let herself be destroyed by regrets.

Getting up from the bench, Leah made her way toward one of the gates of Jackson Square and mingled with the people sauntering along the banquette. Baptiste would be waiting, no doubt impatiently, for her to return. The late-afternoon sun was still hot and bright; she began to perspire under her light cotton gown.

"What in blazes took you so long, *chérie?*" As she entered the room, Baptiste clamped his hand down on one wheel and almost ran into a crate. "Damn this chair! Sorry, but I thought you'd never get here. Benji's fixed an early supper so we can leave for Belle Fontaine before dark."

He smiled at her tenderly and then to himself. Would she ever know how much he loved her? Perhaps tonight would show her. He'd ordered Benji to prepare a very special supper, with champagne and fresh strawberries smothered in whipped cream. Without Leah's help, the plantation would not be his to return to. She had not only labored in Federal offices to keep them alive during the war but had lent him her strength when he was ready to give up hope of getting his land back. It was she who had insisted they could find a way to pay the accrued taxes on Belle Fontaine when there was no money. And they had done it.

Leah didn't answer but looked around at the packing cases and luggage. *This is the day we've struggled toward for so long. This is the realization of the dream that kept me going during all those brutal, nerve-shattering, body-violating days in prison.*

She glanced at Baptiste sitting in the wheelchair. The war had put him there, had taken his legs and almost his life, but by some miracle it had not destroyed him. With his black, curly hair, neatly trimmed mustache, and brilliant smile, he was just as handsome as the day he rescued her from an overardent pursuer at the quadroon ball. She had not loved him when she became his mistress; but love had come eventually, wrapping itself around her and clothing her in contentment as his *placée*, the very thing she had sworn never would happen.

For a while it had been enough, especially with the decision to move to Belle Fontaine. Then James had walked into the prison and forced her to re-evaluate her life. Since she was a little girl, she had been moving toward this moment that meant total severing of herself from the past. Although she was frightened, she considered her decision irrevocable.

"I'm—I'm not going with you, Baptiste. I'm going North." She had mouthed the words, but had she spoken them aloud or only to herself? Unable to breathe, she stood rigid and waited for Baptiste's response.

For a moment Baptiste refused to believe what he'd heard. Yet somehow he had sensed it was coming, had had a premonition while he was planning the supper and ordering the best champagne to go with it. He'd thought James Andrews was in love with Leah, but he'd been afraid to question her about her feelings. He had been prepared, and at the same time had been unable to prepare himself, for her words.

"With James Andrews?" he asked in the same tone he might use to ask her if she'd bought a new hat.

"Yes." One small word, but the hardest she'd ever uttered. It was a period at the end of a sentence, the *amen* at the end of a prayer. It was final.

The room became deathly still and neither of them moved, paralyzed by the import of the moment, suspended in a catatonic state between then and now.

Baptiste wheeled his chair around. "At least you'll be safer than last time."

Leah cringed. His sarcasm was no easier to endure than a request to stay would have been.

"Is it what you really want, Leah?" His fingers shook as he lit another cigar.

At the sight of the cigar, Leah was momentarily overwhelmed with memories, memories of a night she had seen it glowing in the dark. That was the "last time" Baptiste referred to. When only seventeen, she'd fled north along the Natchez Trail and been captured by men planning to sell her into prostitution. Bound hand and foot, she'd heard hoofbeats coming along the trail and seen the glowing end of a cigar. Baptiste had rescued her and taken her back to New Orleans. In her mind his long, slim cigars became a symbol of him and his importance in her life. In time of stress he always lit up a fresh one, even if it meant discarding one less than half smoked. He'd done it again just now, and she knew what it cost him to ask her if going with James was what she really wanted.

"It's what I really want," she said quietly.

"You think marriage to him will give you more happiness than we've known together?"

"Please, Baptiste." She'd feared it would be hard, but nothing like the agony she now suffered. How could one judge what was happiness and what was not? It could not be weighed on scales or measured by a ruler. She only knew she had to get away and find out for herself. If she were wrong— She refused to think about that.

"Don't tell me you love him!" Baptiste thundered, then paused just as abruptly. It would do no good to lose his temper. He knew her too well. That would only make her angry. He spoke more gently. "I won't believe it."

"Not—not in the way I loved you, no," she said.

"Loved? When did it become *loved* instead of *love*? Yesterday? A week ago?" *It's true*, he thought. *It was never love, only pity from the time I was wounded.* He'd accused her then of feeling only pity for him, but when she'd insisted she loved him, he wanted so desperately to believe her he had thrust aside the doubts assailing him.

"Will it make it any easier if I say I still love you?" Leah asked.

"Say it, dammit, and I won't let you go."

"Then it best be left unsaid." Why wouldn't the pain go away? This pain that was squeezing her heart and crushing the breath out of her lungs. With each word spoken it became more intense.

"I'm not going to beg you to stay," he said.

"I know. I counted on that—your not begging, I mean. I couldn't have stood that."

At the moment she didn't dare look at him or she would break down. His wooden legs, shaped like human legs, were a cruel mockery of the flesh and blood they replaced. Better a shapeless peg leg that lied no lies beneath his slim trousers and polished boots. He reached up to touch the patch over his damaged eye, and she cringed. He continued to sit as straight in the wheelchair as if he were standing. Baptiste was a proud man. When she'd first known him, he had the arrogant pride of a wealthy, handsome Creole who had his choice of the most beautiful women in the Vieux Carré. She had not loved him then. Now it was a pride that white-hot pain, despair, loss, and tragedy had forged into an awareness of his importance as a man. And for that she loved him.

Baptiste suddenly turned his chair around so his back was toward her, and he gripped the arms of his chair. He loved her, and he was losing her.

"This—this is not a hasty decision, Baptiste. I've done a lot of thinking about it." He'd never know the hours she'd lain awake or the pain she felt in talking to him now. *Why didn't I write to him?* It would have been better than putting them both through all this. Because that would have been the coward's way, the easy way. She owed Baptiste more than that, even if it were an explanation he did not want to accept. "You'll be free now to marry—to marry Catherine Fouché."

"Catherine! Dammit, I don't love Catherine." His voice rose maddeningly. "She has no place in this conversation."

"Yes, she has. She'd make you a good wife. You should have children—" Leah choked back a sob at the irony that James knew and assured her it made no difference that she was pregnant with Baptiste's child. But Baptiste must never know. That was part of the pain, the most unbearable part, having to keep from him the fact she was taking his child with her. But to tell him would be worse, and at least she could spare him that torture. "Children who can bear your name," she said. "Belle Fontaine needs a mistress, not a *placée*." Strange, she thought, how in one sense those two words meant the same thing, but in another context, something completely different.

Baptiste lifted himself up as if to stand, and then, completely frustrated by his handicap, lowered himself down again and grasped the chair arms until his knuckles turned white. "I'm not going to let you go this easily," he said furiously. "Don't try to hide your feelings with all this talk of wife for me and heirs for the plantation. What we've lived through together can't just be put aside—as if it's old and out of date."

Oh, why do we go on like this? she thought. *Why don't I just walk out the door and put an end to this turmoil that is tearing us both apart?* "It is out of date. The war destroyed a lot of things and *plaçage* may be one of them."

"Being hidden away in this small house, yes, but living with me on the plantation—" It was this house and all the tragic memories. If she would just postpone her trip, go out to Belle Fontaine with him, he knew she would stay.

"Now you're the dreamer you used to say I was," Leah sighed. "We both were for a while. And it was a beautiful dream, but nothing more. It was as shining and as ephemeral as a bubble. Don't you see, Baptiste, you would be scorned by your friends. Even the future of the plantation and the sale of the crops might be affected." She didn't say it aloud, but she knew, too, that the former slaves might resent her, might not be willing to work for a man who kept an octoroon as a mistress. And Baptiste needed every one of them if the plantation were to succeed.

"We have many friends who accept you," he insisted.

"Here, yes, because it's been the custom. But not on the plantation. There's a difference between being your mistress and the mistress of your home. There'd be no social life at all if I were there. Wait," she said when he started to speak, "I know what you're going to say. That a social life is not important. Maybe you can say that now, but you'd feel differently once we were out there. Even if you didn't want to host dinners or galas, you'd miss your friends dropping by, especially during the holiday and hunting seasons. Remember what it was like during the occupation when you were forced to remain incommunicado here? You were miserable. But that was a Federal edict, something you understood the reason for. This would be different—no words spoken or written down, just an invisible veil of ostracism separating me from your friends."

Baptiste refused to admit that what she was saying was true. It couldn't be. His friends loved Leah and admired her for all she'd done to keep him alive after the tragic explosion had shattered both legs. And then during the occupation she had worked endlessly to keep food in their mouths. No, none of his friends would turn on her that way.

"Leah, look at me. If you can tell me you don't love me, I'll say no more."

Leah stood by the window and looked out at the early-evening sky, still lighted by the sun but covered with an almost imperceptible haze from the damp, muggy warmth

11

of the surrounding bayous. One of the strongest links between her and Baptiste had always been their honesty with each other. From the beginning she had been truthful about her intention to go North when she had the opportunity, nor had she told him she loved him during all the years when she knew it was what he wanted to hear and it would have been so easy for her to say it. If she had not then said she loved him, could she now, honestly, say she didn't and make the leaving easier?

Turning from the window, she ran and knelt by his chair. When she put her hands on the arms, he covered them with his. The pain was crushingly intense, and she knew she could not lie to him.

"I love you, Baptiste, but not enough—not enough to go on like this, to remain as your mistress but not as your wife. I have to go. I'll finally have a name. None of us— my mother, my grandmother—we never had a name. We only used someone else's. I never knew who I was. Now I will."

The pain that Leah suffered was none the less real for being more emotional than physical. Not so with Baptiste. For him the room became faintly but inescapably infused with a tense passion, as if it had been sprayed with an erotic perfume or aphrodisiac. The very presence of Leah, her nearness to him and now her wish to leave, had created an urgent desire to possess her completely. She was his and no one else had the right to claim her. The pain was intense and only within her embrace would it find release.

Suddenly, Baptiste's strong arms lifted Leah up and onto his lap. He was burning inside with an urge to kill James Andrews and a need to force himself violently on Leah, to show her whom she really belonged to. Furiously he wheeled his chair toward the bedroom. Once there, once lying beside him, she would respond as she always had. She would be his again.

Leah made no effort to move from his arms. She was fighting her own desire to be possessed by him as she had the night she agreed to become his *placée*. The pleasure she had known in his arms, the pulsating love that flooded through her each time they made love, the euphoria that pervaded her when they finally lay quietly in each other's arms—none of this could ever be described, but it had made her one with him. Now, it took all of her willpower to resist the urge to feel just once more the pressure of his body.

"Please, Baptiste," she begged. "If you make love to me, I might stay. But we'd both be sorry." She tried to bury her face against his chest when his arms refused to release her. "Let me go. Don't—don't try to hold me this way."

His only response was to cover her face and throat with kisses. When he reached her lips, his mouth was urgent and demanding. An unbidden moan escaped her as he unbuttoned the front of her gown and began caressing her breasts. Never had she longed for him as she did now. One word, one move toward the bed and she would stay.

Then, as suddenly as he had taken her in his arms, Baptiste released her and rudely pushed her from his lap.

"Now go, Leah. Right now. If it's your wish." It took all his strength to speak so cruelly, but at the moment his own pain was so intense he needed to see her suffer as he was suffering. He knew she wouldn't stay even if he'd forced her down on the bed and, in a sense, raped her. Not even if he'd aroused her enough to respond to him. It would have been only a pyrrhic victory, leaving him in more agony than he was now. No, let her go, but let her go hating and despising him.

He looked at her with steady, unflinching eyes. "Benji will take you in the carriage. To the hotel, I suppose."

"No—no." Leah was so shaken by physical and emotional turmoil she could hardly speak. She was furious with him for treating her this way, for arousing her to such a pitch of desire that she could hardly wait for him to take her and then discarding her like some wanton whore. He was despicable. And now—now he'd dared to imply that she was headed for an illicit rendezvous with James. Had he thought to stimulate her to the point that she would run right to James's bed? She deserved his reproaches but not this torture. In a fury, she turned on him, ignoring the grimace of frustration in his face and his hands clutching the arms of the chair.

"I have a hired cab waiting to take me to the levee."

"This house is still yours." He spoke more calmly than he thought possible. His treatment of her had given him

13

no satisfaction; if anything, it had merely increased his desire for her. But he loved her, and he couldn't bear to see her leave hating him as surely she must now.

"Thank you, but I don't think I'll ever return to New Orleans." He hadn't killed her love for him, but he'd made it easier for her to leave.

Please, Baptiste, no more words. She said it to herself, but she saw the same sentiment reflected on Baptiste's face. Words are for the dreams yet to come true, not for hopes that have died. She picked up her small, fabric-covered satchel. A carpetbag, it had given its name to the voracious horde that began swooping down on the defeated South even before the war was over. Now she was a carpetbagger in reverse, going to the North not for riches and illegal gains, but for a happiness that had eluded her grasp up until now.

Walking to the door, Leah motioned for the cabdriver to carry out a leather-bound straw trunk. She started following him and then paused. If she looked back, she would not leave. She did not need to turn around to see Baptiste sitting in the chair, his hands still gripping the arms. It was so silent in the room, she could hear Benji stirring something on the stove in the kitchen. It was time to go. She and Baptiste had not said good-bye, but there was no need to. The silence said it for them. Unhesitatingly she walked through the door and closed it behind her.

The cab moved slowly through the busy streets, among late shoppers hurrying along the banquettes and businessmen sauntering home after a convivial hour of drinking in bars. In Jackson Square nursemaids were exchanging one last bit of gossip while herding their charges or leisurely pushing a carriage toward the gates. To all of them, following a normal daily routine, it was the same as any other warm New Orleans evening. Unlike Leah, they had experienced no violent rupture in the well-established pattern of their lives.

Passing the cathedral and the famous Pontalba apartments, the cab headed for the levee. Flat-bottomed paddle-wheelers debarking passengers and offloading cargo from upriver were crowded among sleek clipper ships and foreign vessels with their delectable caches of coffee, tea, and spices from the Far East; rich silks, perfumes, shoes, and jewels from Europe; and more mundane but utilitarian goods like metal and glassware from the North. New Orleans was once again the busy port it had been before the war.

Among the people preparing to go aboard the river steamer *Louisiana Belle*, Leah saw James pacing back and forth, an anxious look on his face. She was later than she'd meant to be, and she wondered how long she'd kept him waiting. Telling the driver to stop, she leaned out from under the roof and called to James. If ever she had doubted his love for her, ever feared he would have second thoughts about having asked her to marry him, she didn't now as she saw the smile on his face at first sight of her. She smiled back, reassured now that she had not been wrong in choosing to go with him. To put the past behind her and make the transition easier, she hoped Indiana would be very different from New Orleans.

James hurried over to the cab and helped her down. As much as he longed to take her in his arms and hold her close, assuring himself that she was really here with him, he resisted the urge and merely continued to hold her hands.

"You're really here, Leah. I wasn't certain you'd come until I saw you in the cab."

"You didn't get my note?"

"You could have changed your mind. When you went home and saw Baptiste again."

"No, when I sent the note," she said, "I'd made my decision."

"But it wasn't easy, was it?" He couldn't see Baptiste letting her walk out of his life without an argument.

"No, but—I'd rather not think about it right now." Just as last year's cotton plants must be plowed back into the earth before a new crop can be sown, her life with Baptiste must be forever buried and allowed to disintegrate, not just wither away. Yet from the substance, from the enriching experiences, could come the courage and knowledge needed to help her marriage flourish.

"Or ever, Leah," James assured her. "Your life with Baptiste is none of my concern. I won't be jealous of the years you spent with him nor need you ever fear I'll ask about them."

"Thank you, James. How soon do we leave?" For years she'd watched these boats sail up and down the river, and always she'd tried to imagine what it was like to walk across the gangplank, stand by the rail as the ship pulled away from the land, and feel the slight undulation of the deck beneath her feet. At last she would see what the staterooms and the dining salon looked like. As excited as a child anticipating Christmas, she clutched James's arm. "How soon can we go aboard?"

James looked down at her glowing face. "I'd forgotten. This is your first trip, isn't it?"

"Yes, and I can hardly wait."

"Let me see about your luggage and we'll go right now. We leave in about half an hour. The first whistle has already blown."

He directed the driver where to take the bags and then led Leah toward the big stern-wheeler whose twin gold-crowned stacks were already sending out tentative puffs of smoke.

As in the pictures she'd painted in her daydreams, Leah stood by the rail and watched all the activity preparatory to embarking. Late arrivals pushed their way through those already waving good-bye to someone on deck. Here and there people were wrapped in tearful farewell embraces, laughing over a parting joke, or listening impatiently to last-minute advice. It was a motley crowd that boarded the boat: families with children who ran around the deck and threatened to fall through the rails in spite of parental chiding; many couples, young and old; men with legal-sized folders that identified them as entrepreneurs going North on business; and boisterous, roughly clad men who had come South on flatboats to sell their wares in New Orleans and were now returning home in style.

Leah felt the shudder of the deck beneath her feet as the engines were revved up and the great paddle wheel slowly began to turn. As soon as the *Louisiana Belle* was away from the levee and in the channel, the captain ordered full steam ahead and they were finally on their way.

People around Leah were waving and shouting to those

on shore. She let the excitement of the trip take over, and she looked up at James.

"There's nobody down there I know, but I feel like waving, too. Does that seem silly?"

"Not at all. Go ahead and wave. It's all part of the fun of being on board."

Gradually the voices of the people on shore lowered to a mere hum, and the brilliant colors of their clothes dulled into the bleak, monotonous sepia of a faded daguerreotype. Here and there a tinge of red or a flash of white was touched by the setting sun, but it was almost impossible to distinguish individual faces. All over the city, lights had been turned on in homes and on the streets. New Orleans was a city of brilliant, sparkling lights. In the distance a soft, rosy glow hovered over the Delta.

This is it, Leah thought. *This is the last I will see of New Orleans. I am bidding good-bye not just to a city of buildings and streets, but to a whole way of life.* She thought about René and Clotilde, her son and mother, buried in a single grave after they died during the horrible yellow fever plague. She had not returned to the cemetery often. Only the shells of who they had been were there; their essence, their real being had remained with her. Yet now, she felt as if she were deserting them, as if even that part of them she had clung to could not go with her but must remain behind in the place they had lived.

Suddenly Leah was jolted back into reality. On the shore but away from the crowds, she saw standing under a large tree the figure of a man leaning on crutches. He did not move, and she could not see his face, but she knew his eyes were focused directly on her. It couldn't be! Baptiste would never have followed her to the wharf. She closed her eyes against the sight. When she opened them, the figure was gone. It had all been her imagination, yet the experience was as real as if he'd actually stood there. She shuddered. Would he continue to haunt her like that, or was he assuring her that he, too, would remain behind along with the spirits of her mother and son?

Standing quietly beside Leah, James found it impossible to take his eyes off her. There was a flush of color in her cheeks now; and the distraught look, which had remained even after she was cleared of the murder charge, had fi-

17

nally begun to disappear. In the slight breeze, a few strands of her hair had been loosened from under her bonnet and were blowing gently around her face. After years of humiliation and suffering, she deserved a happier life than she'd ever known; and he would devote all of his energies to giving her that happiness. He loved her as he'd never thought he could love a woman, with an unselfish, almost dedicated commitment to put her needs first and at the same time a passionate desire to embrace her.

But that must wait; for the moment he could only stand near her and be captivated by her fragile beauty.

A Negro steward, in white jacket and trim black trousers, made his way along the deck announcing that dinner would be served in the dining salon in thirty minutes.

James touched Leah's arm. "I think we'd better go to the cabin and make certain your luggage found its way there."

The cabin. Mingled with her curiosity to see a stateroom was her apprehension about sharing it and sleeping with James. Although she was shaking inside, the calm, cool hand she put in James's gave no hint of her fears.

Leah stepped through the carved mahogany door, and she needed only one glance to know that James had reserved one of the largest and finest staterooms on board. There was nothing lacking for their comfort: a brass double bed, tables and chairs of gilt and lacquer, crystal-globed lamps, thick, plush carpeting, mahogany armoires, and a tall, hand-painted screen beside the ornately carved commode that concealed wash basin, pitcher, and jar.

"Oh, James, this is beautiful. I don't know what I'd envisioned, but it was nothing like this."

"We'll be on board for several days, and I wanted you to have all the comforts of river travel."

Leah moved from bed to chair to table and then to the armoire where her few dresses had already been hung. There was a suit for the days they would go ashore at various towns along the way, two simple dresses for days onboard, and a more elegant gown for dining in the evening.

Turning around, she found herself in James's arms. Not until that moment, not through all the days of the trial or

18

the clandestine meetings at the French Market had they done more than hold hands. Now, crushed against his chest, she felt his desire flooding through her just as during the dark and bitter days of the past weeks she had felt his strength flowing from his hands to hers. His was not a violent, tempestuous, passionate love, but a sturdy, steadfast love that would insure security and continuing support. There would be no dizzy heights of ecstasy, but in turn there would be no great pits of despair. Life would move along at an even keel that might at times be monotonous but could never be unsettled. And that, she thought, was what she'd been searching for all her life.

Holding Leah at first gently and then more tightly, James found it hard to believe she was really with him. In his dreams he had held her like this, but in actuality she had remained an intangible phantasm that eluded his touch. Now he felt her body, warm and desirable, pressed against him. She turned her face up toward his; and when he kissed her, for the first time since they'd met, he felt her lips part slightly. Her response was a surrender of sorts, but not yet an invitation. That would have to wait; her body began tensing in his arms, and he knew he had to give her time. She was not yet ready to receive him as her lover. There must be an emotional and physical hiatus, an ever-widening space of time and distance, between her past with Baptiste and her future with him.

Without wholly releasing her, James asked, "Would you like to change for dinner, Leah?"

"Yes, I think I would. I didn't take time while—while I was at the house, and I've been in this dress since morning."

James walked over to the commode. "There's warm water in the pitcher, Leah, and more in the second pitcher in the cabinet."

What she wanted most of all was to strip completely and bathe all over, to wash away the agonies of the day. A sponge bath would not be as satisfactory as relaxing in a full tub, but it might soothe some of the tension that had every nerve scraped raw. She supposed she could do it all behind the screen. She wasn't ready to undress in front of James.

"While you're changing," he said, "I'll do the same in

my cabin next door and meet you in the salon. Will thirty minutes be time enough?"

She could do no more than nod before he left, closing the door tightly behind him after suggesting she lock it securely.

Leah looked around the stateroom again; how thoughtful of James to reserve two rooms until they were married. Leah scolded herself mentally. Why had she supposed he would have it any other way? It was a rhetorical question with a very specific answer. While assured that James loved her, she had not assumed such respect. It was not something she'd ever really known—respect as a woman. But James had taken it for granted they should live apart until they were married; it was the only proper way to treat the woman who would be his wife. James would never know just what a great and generous act of kindness it was. She had been prepared to go to him before they were married, but he would not have it that way. His unselfishness gave her a new respect for herself.

Being in James's arms had not upset her, but she did feel the need to be alone for a little while and allow her anxiety to ebb. It was as if she'd been walking on her toes or holding her breath all day, and she needed time to regain her composure. Even a half hour would do it.

She went behind the screen and poured some of the warm water from the ornately flowered pitcher into its matching basin. Then she quickly stripped and put her soiled garments into her trunk. She picked out fresh undergarments and hose, and took her watered silk dinner gown from its hanger and laid it across the bed. Once more she stepped behind the screen and worked the fragrant bar of lavender soap into a lather. Standing on the soft, thickly piled rug, she bathed all over.

With all she'd been through that day, she almost forgot how hot and humid the weather was. Now, as she washed the perspiration off and rinsed in more tepid water, her whole body felt cool and refreshed. It was as if the water had not just washed away the dirt and grime on her skin, but had cooled down a burning fever inside her as well. She felt calm and at peace, if still somewhat exhausted.

James had said half an hour. There was time to take down her hair and brush it all out. Usually she pulled it straight back from her face. At one time its very straightness—an inheritance from both her white and Polynesian forebears—had seemed like a passport to success in the white world of the North, and she'd been especially proud of it. The one-eighth part of her that was Negro was visible only in her fawn-colored skin and the dark eyes that Baptiste said reminded him of amethysts. And even those as well as her high cheekbones could be traced to her Polynesian grandmother, her father's mother. From her white ancestors had come her slim nose, with only slightly flaring, aristocratic nostrils, and her thin but sensuously curved lips.

Now in the damp summer heat, a few tendrils of hair around her face wanted to curl; and she did not try to pull them back. Nor did she gather the rest into a tight chignon, but piled it softly in a large, loose bun that lay flat against the back of her head. Her face still showed the fatigue of the past weeks, and severity did not become her now.

So as not to become overheated again, she dressed slowly and took time to smooth the skirts of the dinner gown over her petticoats. Standing before the pier glass for a final check on her dress and hair, she took a long look at herself. Outwardly she appeared the same as always with her face softened a bit, perhaps, by the new hairstyle. But weeks of torture in prison, the trial, and the agony of indecision had taken the glow from her skin. If only she had some rouge. She pinched her cheeks and bit her lips. There, that looked better, not nearly so sallow.

Leah continued to look at herself and tried to fathom the depths that did not reveal themselves in the glass. She needed the days on the riverboat before the wedding to James and their arrival in Indiana for the slow metamorphosis that must take place inside her. "You are who you think you are." Both her mother and Sister Angelique had told her that when she sought to find her true identity. That the search was never successful she had learned to accept, and she had tried to create her own identity. Until today she had been an octoroon, a free woman of color. Now she must mentally bleach herself until she became white. She must always think of herself as white or this flight to the North would be tragic for both James and

21

her. The first flight had been aborted; this one must come to full term.

The half hour was up, and James would be waiting for her in the salon. Going out on deck, Leah saw that the sun had set and been replaced by a full moon in the clear night sky. For a moment she stood at the rail, breathed in the cool air off the water, and luxuriated in the breeze that brushed across her bare shoulders. It was a beautiful night, just the kind of night for beginning a new life.

Across the expanse of silver-flecked, black water, she could barely make out the shoreline. Giant water oaks and cypress came clear to the edge, their bulging roots washed by the huge, rhythmic waves of the frothy wake churned up by the riverboat's gigantic rear paddle wheel. Narrow when it left the boat, the wake spread as it surged toward shore into a triangle whose base was as wide as the river itself. In the dense, sub-tropical twilight there was little else to be seen; the land beyond was merely a darker extension of the water.

Suddenly Leah clutched the railing so hard her hands chafed painfully, and she had to bite her lips to keep from crying out. A freshly painted, pristine white gazebo stood near the river's edge like a solitary sentinel glistening in the moonlight. There she had rested for a few minutes when she fled North along the Natchez Trace, and there she had once planned to sit on warm afternoons and watch her child play on the sloping lawn. They were passing Belle Fontaine, where she had thought to live as Baptiste's mistress if never his wife. She felt herself going faint, and even as she gripped the rail tighter to keep from falling, she swallowed hard to control her nausea and an outpouring of cold sweat.

"Are you all right, Leah?"

She'd not heard James walk up behind her, but the sound of his gentle yet strong voice was calming and reassuring. She was not alone. She was with someone who loved her.

"I'm—I'm fine, James. Just a little weak—hungry, I think."

"Are you sure? Can you make it to the salon, or would you rather return to the cabin and lie down for a bit?

22

We could dine in there if you don't feel up to sitting at the table."

"No, really, I'll be all right as soon as I get something to eat." She must not ever allow herself to be so affected again, to let her emotions dominate her will. Fortunately, there would soon be nothing more to remind her of Baptiste; and if there were no externals to make her think of him, then she must also erase internal memories as well. At least until she could think about them without succumbing to their power.

The table to which they were led was spread with a fine, monogrammed damask cloth and set with exquisite crystal and engraved sterling. Fresh flowers centered the table. A string trio in one corner of the room played soft chamber music and lilting waltzes. With thick floral carpet on the floor and rich red velour draperies at the windows, the salon was as elegant as any restaurant in New Orleans. Immediately they were seated, the maître d' handed each of them the *carte du jour*.

Amazed as Leah had been at the opulence of the stateroom and the dining salon, she was absolutely overwhelmed by the variety of selections on the menu. She read down each of the two columns slowly.

SOUP
Calf's Head
FISH
Red, baked
Trout, boiled   Sheepshead, boiled
BROILED
Turkey   Tongue   Ham
Mutton, caper sauce
Chicken, egg sauce
Corned Beef
COLD DISHES
Spiced Beef   Roast Turkey
Tongue
SIDE DISHES
Loin of Lamb with Peas
Stewed Kidneys, with Sauce
Duck with Olives
Teal Duck with Sauce

Tenderloin of Trout
Timbly of Macaroni
Leg o' Mutton with Vegetables
Chicken, Larded
Veal Fillet
Chicken Pie
Oysters Scalloped

ROAST

Beef   Mutton   Veal
Chicken   Turkey   Duck

VEGETABLES OF THE SEASON

CAKE

Pound   Fruit   Jelly
Almond and Sponge

NUTS AND FRUIT

Bananas   Raisins   Almonds
Oranges   Figs   Peanuts
Apples   Prunes   Pecans

PASTRY AND DESSERT

Pies: Coconut, Blackberry, Orange
Apple, Cranberry
Tarts: Plum and Cranberry
Puggs: Jelly and Quince
Fruit Pudding   Lemon Custard
Italian Crème   Blancmange
Peach Meringue
Calf's-Foot Jelly   Cooper's Jelly
Apricot or Quince

CLARET AND WHITE WINE

Coffee

MADEIRA

Gordon's Old; Howard, March & Co.'s Pure Juice;
Old Bual, Very Delicate; L.P., Old

SHERRY

Gordon's Old Pale; Gordon's Brown, Very Old

PORT

Smith & Co's; London Dock, White

HOCK

Sparkling and Hockheimer

SAUTERNE

Haut Sauterne; Châteaux Cotet Brasac

24

CHAMPAGNE
Schrider's; Heidsick
CLARET
St. Julien Modoc; Château Lafite;
Giscour Modoc; Châteaux Belair;
Château Margaux; La Rose
FRENCH LIQUORS AND CORDIALS
Maraschino; Anisette; Curaçao; Kirsch
MALT LIQUORS
London Brown Stout; Bass' London Ale;
Metcalf's Ale

A waiter came over to fill their water goblets. "Shall I bring the soup, M'sieu, while you are deciding on an entrée?"

"Yes, please," James said.

Not until it arrived and she began eating did Leah realize how really hungry she was. She didn't look up until she finished her soup.

"Has it helped?" James asked after the waiter removed their bowls.

"It was exactly what I needed. I feel much better."

"Good. Then what would you like?"

"I can't decide. You order tonight, and I'll do it tomorrow night."

"All right." James studied the list intently, as if dedicated to selecting the most tantalizing dish in each category. Actually he was trying to keep from watching Leah, whose eyes still betrayed the ordeal she'd suffered while standing at the rail. He knew very well why she'd almost fainted. He'd been out to Belle Fontaine once with Baptiste, and he, too, recognized the gazebo. He knew Leah's nerves were still close to the surface from making the decision to leave Baptiste and come with him. He yearned to tell her how much he loved her and how he would do all in his power to ease her hurt. But not yet. Not even his love was an opiate equal to the task of numbing her senses. Only time could do that; and he'd give her all the time she needed. He wanted her as his wife, and to force himself on her before she was ready would be to destroy what he wanted most of all: a mutuality of spirit, a oneness in all ways. He had her respect; what he sought now was her love.

James saw Leah waiting quizzically for him to make a selection, and he concentrated on the wine list until he saw what he wanted.

"We'll have the Châteaux Cotet Brasac with the broiled trout and scalloped oysters and then Château Lafite with the roast beef."

"Very well, M'sieu. I will bring the pastry cart around when you are ready for dessert."

"Now," James smiled at Leah, "that's taken care of. Do you approve?"

"Very much so. It's just what I would have chosen."

"I'm no connoisseur of wine," James laughed. "Did my ignorance show?"

"No," she smiled back, "you looked very knowledgeable the way you studied that list."

"Not knowledgeable, just confused," he laughed.

Good, she thought, *let's keep the evening light. No serious conversation; not yet.* "Shall I tell you," she smiled, "about my introduction to wine?" She saw the relief spread across his face and crease his cheeks as if he, too, was feeling a little unsure about their relationship. "It was my tenth birthday, and Papa wanted to celebrate. With champagne, no less." She clapped her hands as she had when she saw the bottle in her father's hand. "Mama shook her head and said I was too young, but Papa insisted. Believe me, I was no connoisseur of wines, either. Papa poured me a small glass; and when they toasted me, I felt quite the grown-up young lady. I sipped it slowly, as I'd been instructed."

"I've had champagne once—no twice—but both times just one glass, so no one had to tell me to sip it. I wanted to make it last all evening."

"So did I. Or rather I wanted more. Mama and Papa were deep in one of their discussions. Probably about whether he could stay the night. Often he did, but just as often he had to return home. Those seem to be the nights I remember best—Mama rushing me off to bed so I wouldn't hear her crying. Well, enough of that. Those times are past. Anyway, I went back into the kitchen, and would you believe I finished off the bottle?"

"I would," he said, "because I've never known you to do anything halfway. With you, it's the whole distance or you don't start at all."

"How can you know me so well in such a short time?" Leah asked. "Maybe too well."

He deftly avoided that question. "I can also surmise what happened after you drank all that champagne."

"And you'd be right. I was miserably sick. I can still hear Papa saying, 'At least, Clotilde, she won't have a hangover in the morning.' She scolded and Papa sympathized. That was always their way. Suffice it to say, that was the last champagne for several years."

"If you like it," James said, "we'll have it at home, though I'm a sherry or beer man myself. Of course Hickory Falls is too small for a wine shop." He laughed again. Leah was beginning to love his deep, hearty laugh. Up until now he'd always been so—not stern, but serious. "I can't imagine Zeke's General Store carrying imported champagne, but we'll buy it in Indianapolis or Louisville."

"No, I love sherry, and maybe I'll even learn to drink beer. Now—tell me about Hickory Falls, this so very small town I'm moving to."

"When we get off the train, you'll be able to see it at one glance."

"All of it?" she gasped.

"Well, most of it." He reached into his pocket for a pencil and then searched for a piece of paper. He finally found a wrinkled envelope, smoothed it out, turned it over, and began drawing a large square.

Leah looked at the man who was going to be her husband. He had the ruddy complexion of a man who spent a good deal of time in the out-of-doors and the rough-textured hands of one familiar with hard, manual labor. His clear, honest blue eyes were set deep within his rugged-featured face: high, prominent cheekbones, a nose that had obviously been broken at some point, a strong but not massive chin, and broad forehead. His was a square but not symmetrical face, set off by rust-colored, slightly wavy hair that always looked as if he'd combed it with his fingers, and a thick mustache that needed trimming. Never looking completely at ease in his tailored suits, James was much easier for Leah to visualize in rumpled work clothes

27

or a buckskin jacket. The complete antithesis of Baptiste, who looked as if he'd been born in his snug-fitting evening wear, James seemed to fit the part of a frontiersman or even a hard-working farmer better than he did the role of successful lawyer.

"James, while you're making that very artistic sketch of Hickory Falls, tell me something. Why did you become a lawyer?"

"That, my love, is a long story, but I can give you the gist of it at least. My father was a lawyer in the East. But never successful. Unfortunately, he was a failure at most of the things he tried. I think he was too honest. Someone has said there are no honest lawyers. If that's true, then my father was the exception that proves the rule. He came west to Indiana with just enough money to buy land near Hickory Falls, and he farmed. Or I should say, we all farmed—my mother, my three brothers, and I. I know now that my father was a wonderful but impractical dreamer. And he loved his books. Among his dreams was the one that all his sons should return East for an education."

"And did you? All of your brothers, too, I mean."

"No, we couldn't. There wasn't the money, and we had to work the farm. Two of my brothers—William and John—went West, first to work the gold fields and then to stay in California on ranches. I did a bit of that myself. By this time we were all tired of the farm and Father had been offered enough for several acres to be able by investing the money to live modestly but comfortably. He wanted me to take some of the money and go East to get a law degree. It was his hope that one of his sons would be the successful lawyer he hadn't been. But I had other ideas, and I knew my folks would need every bit of what he got from the land. So I, too, headed West. Did some exploring, some mining, cut timber. It was hard, physical work, but I loved every minute of it."

That accounts for his rugged appearance, Leah thought. "And you had your nose broken. I don't assume that came from a falling tree."

"Indeed it did not. Some evening when we're sitting around the fire, I'll tell you about the wild life of young James Andrews. Anyway, I finally got my fill of being

28

completely independent, and I returned home. My youngest brother, Steven, was still at home and working what land we had left. Then Father became ill. I knew he was still deeply disappointed that none of us had followed him into law. I'd saved a good bit of money, and so before he died I promised him I'd go East for my education. Mother died soon after. She and Father had been inseparable. I guess she couldn't imagine life without him. Steven became a wanderer, eventually joined the army and was killed at Shiloh."

"I'm—I'm sorry. I don't see how you could have come South after that. And been so understanding, I mean."

"Well, Steve and I were never very close, and he was away all those years. My sorrow is not so much over his death, but that we didn't know each other very well. So that's it. I earned my degree and returned to the old homestead to set up practice. That, my love, is how I became a lawyer."

"I was right," Leah said emphatically. "I knew you weren't always one. You just don't look like a lawyer."

"And how is a lawyer supposed to look?" James grinned.

"Oh, I don't know, all sleek and sophisticated. One eye on his client and the other on the client's purse," she teased.

"Lincoln was a rail-splitter and could hardly be called sophisticated."

"He doesn't count." Beginning to feel confused, Leah decided the subject needed to be changed. "I think I'd rather hear about Hickory Falls."

James moved his pencil and paper so the waiter could remove the dinner plates and set down the peach meringue.

"Coffee now, M'sieu, or later with a liqueur?"

"Leah?"

"I'd like mine later, please, with an anisette."

"Later for me, too," James said, "and a glass of port."

While Leah started on the delicate dessert, James pushed his aside and concentrated on his small map.

"James, your meringue. It's delicious. You can tell me about the town when you've finished."

"You can have mine. I'm not much for these frothy desserts."

"If you're sure you don't want it. I'm certainly not going to let anything as good as this go to waste." It would add pounds, all that sugar in the meringue and the whipped cream on top, but if she couldn't splurge once in a while— Anyway, in a very short while it wouldn't matter if she put on weight.

"Now," James said, pointing to the large rectangle, "here is the park."

"Where cows sometimes graze. You see, I remembered."

"Used to, not much anymore. But it is a beautiful park. At this end, the south end, is the town hall. It's a favorite meeting place for farmers who come in and sit on benches under the elm and hickory trees. And on the steps, too, on court and market days. Once a month during the season the square becomes a huge country market."

"That sounds nice. Something like the French Market in the Vieux Carré?"

"Something like that, yes. Booths and tables with homemade items as well as produce."

"Well, maybe it will be a little bit like home. Now," she said, "what's that peculiar shape at the other end of the square—surrounded by those little dots?"

"That peculiar shape, as you call it, is supposed to be a church—the community church—with the cemetery around it."

"Your church?"

"When I attend, yes. It's the oldest one in town; was the only one for a long time. Now there's a smaller one farther out."

"And around the park, all those odd-sized squares?"

"Shops, bank, café, and the doctors' and lawyers' offices. No point in trying to identify them now. You'll know them all in one day. You can walk around the square and window-shop at every one of them in less than an hour. Sound too small for you?"

"No, not a bit." Leah smiled. "I think I'm going to like it, and—and like being there with you."

"I think the stores you'll be most interested in are these." He pointed to two of the squares, and Leah would have laughed if he hadn't been taking it all so seriously.

"Mr. Simpson's Milady's Emporium and Aunt Tabby's Tea Shoppie."

"Shoppie?" She imitated his pronunciation.

"Well, she spells it with two *p*'s and an *e* on the end so people like to tease her and call it that. Elizabeth Jackson spent two months in England once, came back with a new name, and claims everything in the shop—including the pastries—is identical to one she frequented in London. The food is good, and the ladies love it. They meet their friends there in the afternoons."

"And the men? Do they have a favorite place to congregate?"

"The Corner Café, part restaurant, part saloon."

"So everyone has a place for gossip sessions," she laughed.

"Oh, no. The women gossip, but the men talk business." He said it without smiling, and Leah thought he actually believed what he said. Then he started laughing again.

The coffee and after-dinner liqueurs arrived, and they sipped them quietly. Leah looked at James and then at the rough map he'd drawn. She tried to imagine the buildings planted 'round with grass, trees, and shrubs; the streets, which wandered off along the original, meandering cow-paths that once led from the farm to town. The homes near town, James said, were surrounded by small, picket-fenced yards. Farther out were small farms and beyond them larger ones. As the magical panorama unfolded before her, she began to be more and more apprehensive. Hickory Falls sounded idyllic: calm and peaceful. But try as hard as she would, she could not put herself into the scene. It was not the quiet she worried about; after the hectic years in New Orleans, that would be welcome. It was the strangeness of it all.

Then she forced herself to reconsider. The park was probably not so much different from Jackson Square, and she could walk there with the baby. And shops were shops, selling the same things, whether in the South or in the North. The tea shop sounded nice; maybe it was similar to the Café du Monde in the Market where friends met each day. What was the real difference between the two cities that worried her? The fact she would be accepted by everyone and not ostracized by one segment of the popula-

31

tion? Could she leave behind the natural inclination to stand back and wait for someone else to be served first or accept friendly overtures without feeling she had to explain who she was? Those were the things that had her trembling inside, but they all melded into one gigantic concern: she would be living a lie.

While adding cream to her coffee, Leah thought about Baptiste, really thought about him for the first time since she'd boarded the steamer. He took his coffee black, no cream. The strong, rich Louisiana coffee reputed to be almost as thick as Mississippi mud and with the power to corrode metal. She always teased him, said it was ruining his stomach. But he only laughed and said nothing could destroy a Fontaine who'd been nursed on bourbon and weaned on absinthe.

Was he drinking his coffee now? While she was enjoying dinner with James, had Baptiste eaten alone the special dinner he'd planned for the two of them to celebrate the beginning of their new life on the plantation? The picture that thought conjured up made her chest hurt with the excruciating pain of a heart attack. But it was not a failing heart she was suffering from; it was a broken heart. She remembered his face as she last saw him—trying to hide his feeling of loss behind a devil-may-care smile while the fine lines in his forehead deepened into fissures. Sitting here across from James, she forced herself to continue laughing and talking in a lighthearted manner in order to hold back the tears that threatened to flood her eyes.

Chapter Two

BAPTISTE STARED AT the door that Leah slowly but unhesitatingly closed behind her. He listened to her footsteps following the slow, plodding cabdriver across the wooden
gallery, down the four steps, along the stone path, and
through the gate. The rusty iron latch rasped as she
opened it quickly, then again as she closed it securely.
Then there was silence.

For a moment Baptiste sat motionless, not even breathing, as if turned to stone. Suddenly he reached for the object nearest to hand and hurled it violently at the door, as
if to break through the wall of pain her leaving had
created. It crashed through the stained-glass window. Not
until he heard the clatter of glass and saw the jagged
pieces glinting red, blue, and green in a fantastic new
design on the floor, did he realize it was his crutch he had
thrown.

"Damn!" Now he had to admit his helplessness. Not
only to himself but to another. "Benji!" He pounded the
floor with his other crutch. "Benji!" Where the hell was
that worthless bastard?

"Yes, suh?" Benji appeared almost immediately from

33

the kitchen. His gait was the soundless, loping one mastered by servants who over the years became as omnipresent but as unobtrusive as the furniture. Born a slave on the Fontaine plantation, he had at one time been Baptiste's boyhood companion and was now his personal servant, but the "sir" was said with love, not subservience.

"Dammit, Benji, don't *sir* me. We've known each other too long. Hand me my crutch and push me into the bedroom."

Benji took a minute to look around the parlor. "Where's Mam'selle Leah? Supper's ready."

"Leah's gone. Eat it yourself or give it away," Baptiste stormed. "Throw it away for all I care. I don't want any. All but the wine. Bring that here. No glass. The whole bottle."

Benji turned his deep, sensitive brown eyes on Baptiste, and his bronze hands shook as he pushed the chair slowly through the parlor. Almost the same age, the two men had been inseparable until Baptiste left the plantation to come to New Orleans and establish his cotton brokerage. Benji stayed at Belle Fontaine to manage the stables. When war broke out and the elder Fontaines fled to Virginia, Benji remained behind. There were no longer any horses to care for; all of them had gone to provide mounts for Baptiste's men when he formed his own cavalry unit, the Crescent Cavaliers. Benji, along with the few slaves who did not run away, took on the responsibility of trying to maintain Belle Fontaine as it was before the war. Like Benji, they considered the plantation as much their home and their land as it was the Fontaines'. Their labor had made it produce and love for it ran deep in their blood.

Until the Northern troops came. The slaves were freed and then immediately pressed into labor gangs to continue working the cane fields for the benefit of the Federal troops now occupying New Orleans or to work on the fortifications around the city. Benji had no way of knowing that Baptiste had been severely wounded just prior to the attack on New Orleans and was only slowly recovering from the amputation of both legs that had brought him perilously close to death for several weeks. If he had, nothing could have kept him from his master's side.

Instead Benji went west, helping other refugees, both

Negro and white, who were fleeing by wagon, by boat, and on foot before the Yankee scourge burning and looting their homes along the river. Young and strong, he carried bundles for women to whom he had served tea at Belle Fontaine; for elderly men for whom he had saddled horses when they attended hunting parties at the plantation; and he carried children he had once bounced on the joggling board beneath the oak trees. He had made his way first into Arkansas and then west into Texas, where temporary refugee camps were set up. Then farther west when Federal sympathizers harassed them.

After the war, Benji planned to remain in Texas or continue on to California, where he'd heard fortunes were being made every day in the gold fields, on ranches, and in lumber camps. Because of his love for horses, he found work on a ranch and spent over a year there, branding cattle and working around the stables. Then, in charge of the ramuda, he went north to Kansas City with a cattle drive. There, he was suddenly struck by an acute case of homesickness, a longing to see once again the plantation, to hunt the swamps, and to feel the soft mud of Louisiana between his toes. Having saved only enough money for deck passage on a steamboat to New Orleans, he walked the distance between Kansas City and St. Louis, occasionally catching short rides on wagons but going most of the way by shanks' mare. He worked three weeks for a farmer outside St. Louis for the food he had to provide for himself on the boat and for a single blanket, but once in sight of the Mississippi, he knew he could have lain on a bare deck and gone the whole four days without meals just to be sailing south on the river.

On one of his trips to the plantation while Leah was in prison, Baptiste had found Benji in the stables. He was raking the dirt floor and cleaning out the stalls just as if he'd been doing it every day for the past six years.

"What the hell you doing here, Benji?" Baptiste said.

"Dammit, what da ya think I'm doing. I'm cleaning up this mess. Since no one's seen fitten to do it."

Then they threw their arms around each other, laughing and crying as they had not done since they birthed a colt, all alone, in the dark hours of a morning when they were still boys.

Now Benji was deeply worried. He'd seen such intense sorrow on Baptiste's face only once before, when his adored younger sister died. Having been on the plantation before the war and then away during it, Benji had not met Leah until after she was freed from prison. For the short time since then, his own personal feelings about her were reserved. She was beautiful and she seemed deeply attentive to Baptiste. For Benji, the important consideration was that Baptiste loved her. What mattered to Baptiste, mattered to Benji. If he held Leah dear, then Benji would accept her.

But that was in the past. Now Leah had hurt Baptiste, and for that Benji hated her. He could never know the depth of his master's pain, but if Baptiste were as distraught as he looked, then Benji must do everything in his power to ease that pain. Right now that meant silence, complete obedience, and no questions asked. He pushed the wheelchair partway into the bedroom and then went to the kitchen for the wine. Since Baptiste was in no condition to struggle with the cork, Benji pulled it out and set it aside. He'd never known Baptiste to finish a whole bottle. One thought kept going through his head: if Leah had left a man as fine as Baptiste, then good riddance. That was what he had to convince his master. When the right time came.

With one hand clutching the bottle and his other on a wheel, Baptiste whirled furiously around the bedroom, crashing into a crate, swearing violently, backing off, and running into another one. "Smash them all, that's what I should do." The chair careened into the rolled-up carpet, and Baptiste lurched forward. Just as he felt himself falling forward, he grabbed the footrail of the bed and finally managed to steady himself in the chair. "Damn! Be damned if I'll call Benji again."

He looked at the bed, now stripped of all covering and looking naked. Denuded not only of its sheets and pillowcases, but of any meaning it had in his life. It was now no more than a piece of furniture. Yet it was not bereft of the power to stir Baptiste's memory of the tender, joyful, passionate, and even hilarious moments he and Leah had shared on it. Like the time he'd been brushing her hair and then impulsively pulled her down on the bed beside him. He'd forgotten to drop the brush to the floor, and he rolled over on it while she was still locked in his arms. He'd screamed as if stabbed and jumped up so fast in his frenzy to get off the stiff bristles, he nearly threw her off the bed. How they'd laughed over it every time she handed him the brush, her signal she wanted to make love. He could not laugh now.

There were many moments he might forget, but one memory would never fade. The night she proved to him he was still a man even though his legs had been amputated, the night she made love to him in spite of his fear and conviction that he was impotent because of the surgery. The word *impotent* had never been mentioned, and he kept pretending he had not yet recovered. Then she had dared to threaten the fragile, tenuous thread of his sanity. If she'd been wrong in her assumption that it was only fear that was keeping him sexually inactive, if she had failed to arouse him physically, he would not have been able to go on living. Her courage and her love had saved his life as well as his sanity. Now he had to find the strength to go on without her.

In wheeling away from the bed, he passed Leah's dressing table. All her perfumes and toilette articles had been removed from the top and packed carefully away. He could still smell the fragrances she wore. They were never anything heavy or overpoweringly erotic, but light, floral fragrances that he found more seductive and sensual than any of the exotic ones. Her favorites, tea olive and valley lily, had a faint odor that suggested she exuded a pleasantly aromatic aura. She'd been proud of her silver toilette articles—the mirror, brush, comb, and small boxes—and she kept them so highly polished she could see her face in either side of the mirror. Now there were just faint outlines of dust where they'd lain.

Only one item remained on the dressing table. Its surface was faintly tinged with dust stirred up during the packing, and the hazy motes gave the deep-blue velvet a slightly muted, smoky cast. Baptiste reached out for it and then drew back, as if in awed reluctance to touch something sacred. He passed his hand over his eyes. That was a foolish notion. It was a valuable object but not a holy relic. On the memories it conjured up he could put no price. He reached again and grasped the flat, oblong box in both hands and held it a long time before opening it. Inside, nestled in folds of white satin, was a triple-length strand of perfectly matched pearls. He knew Leah had not meant to leave it. She had saved the box from being packed in either the crates or her suitcases so that she might carry it in her hands. When they were not around her throat or sitting on her dressing table, she never let the pearls out of her sight.

At first Baptiste thought she might have left them as a reminder of her. But no, as heartrending as her decision had been to leave him, she would never hurt him that way. In her distress—and he knew she had been genuinely distressed at her decision—she had simply forgotten them.

While he ran the pearls through his fingers, Baptiste thought of the night he'd given them to her, six months after she became his *placée*. To celebrate, they were going to see Edwin and John Wilkes Booth in *Julius Caesar*. Leah had just emerged from the bath and was wrapped in one of the big towels she so loved. The pearls had been just a long double strand then, and he put them over her head and wrapped them around her warm, fragrant, and still damp breasts. They had glowed as if alive against her tawny skin. With her long black hair she was like an ancient love goddess, dressed in jewels and nothing else. When he pulled her down on the bed, she had protested, saying they would never make it to the theater on time and he had promised she could see the Booths. But the protests had stopped when he began kissing her mouth, her shoulders, and her breasts, and she surrendered with the intense passion he could always arouse in her. They had gone to the theater; and when they returned, it was to a night of lovemaking such as he'd never experienced before.

Leah had not loved him then. She had never lied to him about that, as easy as it might have been for her to mouth the words he longed to hear, but he never felt he was buying her embraces. She always came to him willingly and ardently, and what he gave her he gave because it afforded him pleasure to see how delighted she was with his gifts. When their son, René, was born, he

38

added the third length to the strand, and they were always her pride. During the three years of the Federal occupation, she'd had to sell many of the beautiful jewels he'd given her—the amethyst set that matched her eyes, the diamond-and-sapphire earrings, among them—to keep food on the table, but never would she part with the pearls. She'd gone to work scrubbing floors in a Federal office instead.

Baptiste had argued against her working for the enemy because the job was so very demeaning. Now he knew he must have had a premonition of danger. It was there she met Major Charles Anderson, the man she was later accused of murdering. True, she'd been found innocent, but it had brought James Andrews into their lives, and now he had taken Leah out of Baptiste's life.

Baptiste could stand the room no longer. He closed the box and started to put it under his coat. Then he changed his mind and returned it to the dressing table. If—if Leah ever did come back, she'd find the pearls waiting for her.

Having drunk more than a third of the bottle of wine, he wove the wheelchair erratically toward the nursery on his way to the kitchen where he trusted Benji was disposing of the supper. The nursery. René had been his pride and joy, the delight of his life. In spite of censorious glances from aristocratic Creole families, he had proudly pushed his son's carriage through Jackson Square every afternoon. He knew what was being whispered beneath the colorful parasols as he strode past: *plaçage* might be an accepted custom in the Vieux Carré, but a man was expected to be circumspect about his side-street liaison, not ask everyone to admire the issue of it.

Then, barely more than a year old, René had died during the yellow fever plague that also took Leah's mother. Baptiste had been in Europe on business, and Leah had borne all the horror, all the sorrow, all the savage loneliness of the great tragedy. He'd been deprived of a son, the seed of his body, but he'd not had to nurse him through the pathetic, heartrending days or see to having him buried without the final rites of the church. Leah had done all that. Whatever else, he could never fault her courage.

He looked at the crib which she had refused to move

from the room. Her one sorrow was that she never had another child, even though the years of the war and the occupation were no time to bring one into the world. Maybe she and James would have the child she so desperately longed for. He hoped so.

He thought of Leah on the boat. He'd always promised her a trip up the Mississippi, and now she was taking it, but without him. He'd been stunned at her decision yet not completely surprised. From the night she became his *placée*, she made it clear that at the first opportunity she would go North. In spite of the war that intervened, in spite of her finally admitting she loved him, he knew she had not changed her mind about that. It was time to accept the fact she was gone, but he would always wonder: At what moment had her decision become irrevocable?

"Benji!"

"I'm right here." He looked at Baptiste and at the bottle. Getting drunk was not the answer, but it was no time to try to persuade Baptiste of that. He'd have to find that out for himself.

"Get the carriage. We're going to the plantation."

"Right away." Benji knew there were no words to ease the pain; but he could humor Baptiste and do everything he wanted without argument.

Baptiste wheeled himself to the front door and waited for the carriage to come around. He looked through the shattered stained-glass window. He'd been idiotic to break it, but he had to admit he felt better afterward.

At times he was stubborn enough to insist he could maneuver himself down the steps and make it to the carriage himself, but tonight he was too tired. Without a word, he let Benji lift him up, carry him the distance, and place him on the cushioned leather seat. He'd gotten accustomed to his wooden legs, but now the leather cups and straps irritated his stumps, and he was looking forward to taking them off. He rested his hands on his thighs, and he could feel the swollen and puffy flesh under his smooth broadcloth trousers. They hadn't swollen like that for a long time. It must be because he was tense and on edge. His nerves were raw, and he needed a drink. Well, Benji could fix one for him as soon as they arrived at the plantation.

Once Benji had him carefully settled in the carriage, Baptiste handed him a key. "Now lock the door and give me back the key."

"Ain't no use since you done smash the window."

"Don't argue, damn you. Do as I say." Then Baptiste was furious with himself for speaking so brusquely to Benji, who patiently put up with his moods and his temper. Well, he'd make it up to him later. . . .

"Yes, suh." This time Baptiste didn't correct him, but Benji knew it was only because he hadn't heard.

Slowly they drove along Royale to Canal and then toward the river road.

"Benji, turn around. I want to go back into town."

"You forget something? I'll run in and get it."

"No, I didn't forget anything," Baptiste said. "Drive to Le Coq d'Or."

Without a word, Benji turned the carriage around, retraced their route, and pulled up in front of one of the Vieux Carré's most popular bars. He lifted Baptiste down from the seat and then looked inquiringly at him.

"No, I don't intend to be carried in," Baptiste scowled. "Hand me my crutches. And wait here."

Benji lounged his long, lean physique against the side of the carriage. He'd come here often enough to be familiar with the routine. Baptiste might be in the bar for twenty minutes or for several hours. Soon more carriages would be driven up, and then he and other drivers would stand under the lamp and talk, or they'd start a crap game in the angle formed between the bar and the shop next door. They'd always be on call but could keep themselves entertained at the same time. Tonight he had no heart for a game. He was too worried about Baptiste.

Balanced on his crutches, Baptiste entered the bar and looked around the dimly lit room with its small, round tables and long, highly polished mahogany bar.

"Where's DeLisle?" he asked while making his ungainly way toward one of the rear tables.

"He hasn't come in yet, M'sieu Fontaine. It's still a bit early for him."

"Well, not for me." He sat down and braced his crutches against the corner wall. "Bring me the usual, Angus. Not a single glass, a whole bottle."

"A whole bottle?"

"A full bottle. And several glasses. I want to see exactly how many it will take."

"To pass out or just get drunk?" Angus LeBrun, half Scots and half French, was friend as well as bartender to his patrons; and his personable, easygoing, chiding manner was familiar to all of them. None objected when he said they'd had enough or suggested it was time they went home for dinner. He knew everyone's dinner hour.

"To make me forget," Baptiste said. "Now bring it and leave me alone."

Angus disappeared behind the bar. He also knew when to keep quiet and make himself invisible. Reaching under the bar for a fresh bottle of absinthe, he opened it and placed it on a tray with half a dozen glasses. Then he paused and looked at Baptiste Fontaine sitting at the table, his whole body as taut as a man's finger on a trigger and his manicured nails drumming the table. Angus reached for six more glasses and put them on the tray.

Baptiste poured the first glass, passed it slowly before his face to inhale the bouquet, and then sipped it leisurely, a drop at a time. He was beginning to relax, but that was not enough. The second and third glasses warmed and aroused him to an aching pitch of desire. But there was no Leah to welcome him home and assuage that hunger. Quickly he drank two more, but they only made him maudlin and brought him to the verge of tears. They were not enough to befog the memory of Leah in his arms, pleading with him to let her go.

The bar was getting more and more crowded, and Baptiste nodded to several who spoke to him. But he was waiting for one particular friend. Finally he saw Pierre DeLisle come in and walk toward the bar. Baptiste watched as Angus spoke to him and then nodded toward the rear table. Pierre hurried over.

"What the hell you doing, Baptiste? Getting drunk has never been your style." He looked at the oft-tipped bottle and the meticulously placed row of soiled glasses. The spaces between each were exactly uniform. Baptiste might be drunk but his hands were as steady as ever.

"I'm starting a new style." He spoke clearly and concisely, without a hint of a stammer or thickened tongue. "As of today I'm a new man—no longer the old Baptiste."

"And what the devil does that mean?" Pierre had seen Benji lounging outside with the other drivers. He should have spoken to him. Benji would have offered Pierre a clue. But seeing him there was so commonplace an experience, it never dawned on Pierre to question him.

"She left me."

"What?" Pierre was confused rather than enlightened by that terse statement.

"Leah's left me—"

"The devil you say!" Now Pierre was completely stunned. In his mind the two of them were inseparable.

"That's right, Pierre. Gone North with Andrews. Gone North to be white. If she can change her color, Baptiste can change, too." The liquor was beginning to take effect. "Yes, sir, gonna be reborn a new man."

"Or dead at the rate you're going through that bottle of absinthe."

"Then I'll—I'll switch to bourbon."

"Oh, no," Pierre insisted, "black coffee. And I'm taking you home."

"Here." With an exaggerated effort, Baptiste reached into his pocket and pulled out a key. He looked at it a long time, smoothed it between his fingers, and then slid it across the table. "I'm never setting foot in that house again." He slapped his leg and laughed hysterically at the ironic jest. "Why aren't you laughing, too? Don't you think it's funny?"

"No, I don't."

"Well, keep the damn key anyway. Until—she may need it someday."

"You should sell the house, Baptiste," Pierre said in an even tone. "Get completely away from everything that reminds you of her." He was still finding it impossible to believe that Leah was gone. He'd met and worked with James Andrews on Leah's case, and he'd found the Northerner a ruggedly interesting but completely uncultured man. No two more disparate men could have been found than James Andrews and Baptiste Fontaine. He would never know how Leah could go with the one after having loved the other. But then, in spite of having three sisters and a wife, he'd never been able to fathom the way of women.

"No! The house will never be sold." Baptiste's eyes glared at him, and Pierre knew better than to argue with him when his temper was aroused. Then Baptiste's eyes glazed over, and Pierre knew his friend was deeply absorbed in his misery. While waiting for Baptiste to return to the present, Pierre thought about the many times he'd seen Baptiste lose his temper and about one occasion in particular when he was almost killed for his rash inability to control it.

A number of years before Baptiste met Leah, he and Pierre had attended a stag dinner during which Baptiste made an unfortunate slip of the tongue. He incurred the wrath of another guest, who immediately demanded an apology for the tarnished honor of his family. Baptiste's temper flared, and he said he'd be damned if he'd apologize for anything he said. The next thing Pierre knew, he was being asked by Baptiste to be his second at a duel the following morning.

The young lady who was the subject of the words which Baptiste would not have spoken if he'd been sober was the daughter of an old and wealthy Creole family. In addition, Patrice Morceaux was very beautiful, extremely talented musically, and envied by other unmarried belles for her reputed dowry of several thousand dollars. Unfortunately, she was also a nymphomaniac. Unlike other Creole girls who'd perfected the act of flirting with their fans into a fine art, but who would have been appalled at any suggestive overtures by their escorts, Patrice's glances were direct invitations. She could not be with a man for more than a few minutes before she began touching him, running her fingers lightly across the palm of his hand, and flicking her slender red tongue around her open lips. No place was too bizarre for her assignations: the seat of a closed hansom cab, a dark hallway, or a stone bench secluded among the azaleas at the rear of a garden.

Pierre, himself, had known the pleasure of her favors more than once, the first time braced against an oak when she had suggested they take a turn around the garden between dances at a private ball. Before he knew what was happening, she had slipped her bodice down over her breasts, raised her skirts above pantaloons that went no higher than her knees, and pulled Pierre toward her.

"Hurry, Pierre, please hurry," she gasped.

Stunned as he was, Pierre had no intention of resisting such a delightful invitation. With the first sight of her rosy-tipped breasts, he was ready; and less than a minute later, she gave a small sigh of relief and relaxed in his arms. With a single deft movement, she readjusted her bodice, brushed a piece of bark from her skirt, and smiled at Pierre.

"My, that was lovely," was all she said.

At the stag dinner, Baptiste had unfortunately referred to Patrice as "Mademoiselle Round Heels" just as her brother, Henri, entered the room. Every man there had been a willing victim of her seductive wiles, and each knew why her dowry increased in value as the months passed. Nevertheless, there had been up to that time a tacit agreement among the young men of the Vieux Carré not to bandy her name about like that of a common whore. She was a member of the élite, and as such she was to be protected. They might slyly wink at one another as she passed from partner to partner at a ball, and they were not above angling for invitations to her home, but no one ever solicited her favors directly. She was always allowed to make the first move.

For these reasons, each of the men at the dinner was almost as shocked by Baptiste's words as Henri Morceaux. Henri carefully removed his cape and placed it casually over a chair. Pierre winced at the sting Baptiste felt when Henri flicked the white gloves across his cheek and demanded that the family honor be redressed. He cringed at the thought of Baptiste having to face Henri's sabre, which had already scarred or mortally wounded a number of their friends. As the one challenged, Baptiste had the choice of weapon. Pierre breathed a little easier when he chose pistols. Neither Henri nor Baptiste was a particularly good shot, and thus his friend stood a better chance of coming out of the encounter alive.

Baptiste sobered up in a hurry after Henri challenged him, but he was pale and shaking when Pierre accompanied him to his apartment and insisted they try to get some sleep.

Baptiste's apartment was above a haberdashery, a bootery, and a *porte-cochère* wide enough for a landau to ride through but which usually saw only the passage of finely shod pedestrians. A corridor of cobblestone pavement and plastered walls led from the banquette to a large, square courtyard filled with aromatic orange and lemon trees.

Silently Pierre followed Baptiste up the broad wrought-iron stairs leading from the courtyard to the apartment.

"I'm sober now and well able to take care of myself," Baptiste said. "You can go home."

"And leave you alone? No, indeed. Anyway, you invited me to stay the night. Remember?"

"Sorry, there's been a change of plan," Baptiste had insisted. "But I won't be alone. I'm expecting company in less than an hour. Some condemned men like a hearty meal. I favor catering to other appetites, and the dish coming tonight offers a whole menu of Epicurean delights."

"You need a good night's sleep!" Pierre hit the table with his fist. "Not to spend hours wearing yourself out with a piece of tail."

"Oh, I'll get my rest. Sophie is a terrific aphrodisiac, but after two hours with her, I sleep like a baby. You come by here at five, and I'll be ready for Henri Morceaux. Damn his sorry hide: he'll feel more than the sting of white kid gloves."

That was when Pierre learned not to argue with Baptiste when he was angry or aroused. As Baptiste's second, he had a number of responsibilities. He had to meet with Henri's second, select the matched weapons to be used, and choose the spot for the duel.

It was still dark when they drove the several miles to the clearing in a vast forest of oaks that was traditionally reserved for such encounters. Henri and his second were there when they arrived, as were the referee and a young doctor of their acquaintance who had a reputation for taking care of wounds on the spot and for keeping his mouth shut about the illegal combats.

Pierre took the matched pair of guns to check them for

alignment and accuracy. One at a time he loaded them, took aim at a distant oak, and shot. He was satisfied that both of them were well balanced and would shoot true.

The dueling ground was paced off by the doctor and the referee. Pierre, helping Baptiste remove his cape and jacket, saw his friend shiver in the early-morning chill. A pale ground fog swirled in from the nearby bayou and enveloped the whole area in a cloud of mist that obscured all but the closest trees. There was something eerie and malevolent about the whole scene. Pierre had never before seen a man die, and he swallowed hard to keep back the fear that clogged his throat with bitter gall. If *his* gut felt like jelly, he wondered what Baptiste's insides were like? He had to excuse himself three times during the preliminaries to go behind a tree.

Baptiste and Henri stood back to back, arms stiff, elbows bent, and pistols cocked. In slow, even cadence the referee counted out the ten paces. The two men turned and aimed, and the two shots sounded like a single volley with almost no echo. Henri remained standing and clutching his arm, but Baptiste fell forward to the ground. Immediately Pierre ran across the field to where Baptiste lay, still conscious but biting his lips in pain while pointing to his leg.

With the drawing of blood, the referee declared the combat a draw and ordered an end to the duel. Honor had been satisfied. Fortunately, Baptiste had merely nicked Henri just below the shoulder, and once the blood was stanched, the skin washed, and a gauze pad put over the wound, Henri was able to walk to his carriage and be driven back to town.

Baptiste's wound was deeper and more serious, but since the bullet had gone straight through the leg, there was no need to probe. The doctor did what he could to cleanse the wound, and he suggested Baptiste stay off his leg for several days.

"It's going to bleed for a while," he said, "but that should wash out all infection." He turned to Pierre. "Can you stay with him and keep the bandages changed?"

Pierre nodded.

"I'll check around late this afternoon," the doctor

added, "and you know where to reach me if he gets feverish."

"Okay, sport," Pierre said to Baptiste, "think you can ride in the carriage?"

"I'm alive, aren't I? God damn, Pierre, do you see where that bullet went through? Three inches higher and he would have shot off my balls." He began roaring with laughter. "That would have been real justice for what I said. I bet if he'd thought about it, he'd have aimed better. I may be out of action for a little while; then, Madame Broulé watch out, 'cause here I come." He began laughing so hard he started the blood flowing faster, and Pierre told him to shut up while he pressed clean gauze against the wound.

Pierre signaled to Angus for another drink, leaned back in his chair, and stared intently at Baptiste to see if he'd returned to the present, too. From the time Baptiste came to the city to start his cotton brokerage, the two had been inseparable hunting, whoring, and drinking buddies. Then Leah became a part of Baptiste's life. No other woman had ever held his interest for more than a few weeks at a time, and Pierre understood how deeply hurt Baptiste was by her leaving. Now the one thing he could do for his friend was try to understand and help.

Suddenly Baptiste put aside a half-finished glass of absinthe and looked quizzically at Pierre. He'd momentarily forgotten his friend and their conversation about the house. Then he remembered.

"Pierre, how about calling Benji for me."

"I will, but I think you should come home with me if you won't go to your house."

"Thank you, but no. I have other plans. Just call Benji." He stood up, adjusted his crutches, and walked unsteadily to the door. Pierre made no effort to help him. What Baptiste was going through, he would have to go through alone. He wouldn't want it any other way. In a few days, Pierre thought as his sad eyes watched his friend disappear through the door of the bar, he would drive out to the plantation to see how Baptiste was getting along.

Baptiste gave one simple direction and then lay back against the seat while Benji drove. Both were silent until they pulled up before the door of a large, stately house on a street of three- and four-story residences that had once belonged to wealthy Creole families and were the first to be commandeered by Federal officers. From the outside, no one would have thought this particular house anything but a private home. Its formal façade and intricate wrought-iron balconies bespoke conservative wealth. Few would recognize it as the most famous bordello in New Orleans.

Baptiste had decided that a night with one of Madame Broulé's girls was the only way to get Leah out of his system. Beautiful and hotly passionate, they knew all the ways to soothe a man's frustrations. Madame Broulé picked her girls with meticulous care; and when they became jaded or temperamental or careless, she shipped them off to Baton Rouge and Natchez. Baptiste was ready to deliver himself into the hands of any one of them and let her take over completely.

An elderly, liveried Negro opened the double doors; and with Benji's help, Baptiste made it up the broad carpeted stairway to the parlor where Madame Broulé presided by the front window. Her mammoth body filled the enormous chair from which she watched everything that happened in the street below. At the same time, she could appraise each of the customers who passed by the portièred arch between the hall and parlor. She selected her clientele with the same care she did her girls. Men might think they had chosen her establishment, but two or three quiet regrets from her tall Negro butler that the girls were all occupied, and the prospective customer knew he was being politely refused admission to the sought-after inner sanctum.

The remainder of the room was in startling contrast to Madame Broulé's elephantine body and outsized chair. A delicately carved Empire couch and two chairs were upholstered in hand-worked petit point. Gilt side chairs with cut-velvet seats and backs flanked a pink marble fireplace. A magnificent Aubusson rug covered most of the parquet floor. Watteau and Fragonard prints and Sèvres accessories carried out the fragile pastel motif of the room.

Across the wide hall was a drawing room that served as a hospitality suite. Unlike Madame Broulé's personal suite, it was a profusion of red velvet hangings, huge gilt mirrors, plush couches—no single-occupant chairs—and crystal chandeliers. In one corner was a carved rosewood bar and, all around, there were bouquets of fresh flowers.

It was Madame Broulé's avid curiosity and alert eyes that helped Leah prove her innocence of Major Anderson's murder. Madame Broulé's testimony finally forced Mrs. Anderson to admit she'd killed her husband. Baptiste shook his head. No matter where he went, he could not rid himself of Leah.

"Baptiste, you're drunk!" Madame Broulé greeted him. It was one of her rules that no man who'd had too much to drink laid a hand on one of her girls. She was not going to have them pawed by an inebriate, or be put in danger of physical abuse.

"I know it," he mumbled.

"Well, you can sleep it off here." She took pity on him as an old customer and friend whose story she knew well. She was curious about the reason for his visit. He'd not been inside her doors since he'd taken Leah for his *placée*. Something was wrong. She turned to Benji. "Come back in the morning. He'll be all right then."

Benji looked at Baptiste and then at Madame Broulé. Baptiste was more than drunk; he was in a highly agitated state. Somehow Benji had to let her know what had happened without alerting Baptiste, who was leaning unsteadily against an ornately carved sideboard and trying to light one of his long cigars. So far he'd only succeeded in burning his fingers, and he was swearing softly to himself.

Since Madame Broulé never left her chair, Benji walked over to her as if to verify the exact time he could come for Baptiste. Then he spoke in as audible a voice as he dared without arousing suspicion. "M'sieu Baptiste, he powerful upset."

"I know, Benji, I saw that right away. What's wrong?"

"Mam'selle Leah done left him."

"Not—not for good, I trust. Just for a visit?"

"No, ma'am, for good. She done gone up North with that lawyer fellow what helped her during the trial."

Baptiste looked toward them, and Madame Broulé noted his glassy but not oblivious stare. "Ten o'clock, Benji. He'll be feeling better by then." She lowered her voice. "I'll find a girl who understands. Don't worry about him tonight."

"Joshua," Madame Broulé called to her butler. "Please ask Lorene to come in here."

In another minute a slender young woman entered from the entertainment parlor across the hall. Baptiste neither looked up nor acknowledged her appearance. Preliminaries were unimportant to him at this moment. He didn't want polite introductions or casual conversation. He wanted only to go to one of the back rooms, get on the bed, and do something—anything—to get rid of the oppressive misery that made him feel as if he would explode at any minute.

He heard a name, Lorene, and he looked at the smiling young woman. She wore a simple, green off-the-shoulder gown, nothing especially seductive, and yet there was something disturbing about her. She held out her hand to lead him down the hall while Benji took his other arm. Baptiste looked closer at her black hair and sparkling eyes. Her skin had the creamy softness of a camellia petal, with a faint blush of pink on her cheeks.

Suddenly Baptiste felt overpowered by something that threatened to suffocate him, and he saw on her face the features of Leah, her skin that always reminded him of precious old ivory, and her deep amethyst eyes. He inhaled the girl's perfume; it was Leah's favorite: tea olive. As if haunted by a merciless specter, Baptiste grabbed Benji's shoulders and screamed, "Oh God, no!"

"It's all right, Baptiste," Madame Broulé tried to calm him. She'd had plenty of experience with men who suffered from uncontrollable guilt feelings or liked to play out strange fantasies. For that very reason, she had chosen Lorene, who could remain calm in the most disturbing situations and yet not insult the patron. "It's all right. You'll feel better in the morning. Go with Lorene. She'll take care of you."

Baptiste was suddenly starkly, nakedly sober. "Thank you, but—" He turned to Benji. "Drive me to the plantation. Damned if I'll stay here and see her face everywhere I turn."

Benji was wise enough to know that Baptiste did not want to talk about either Leah's leaving or his experience

51

at Madame Broulé's. Silently he helped Baptiste back down the long flight of stairs and into the carriage, then retraced the route through the city and along the river road. The moon was bright on the water, and in the space of ten minutes he counted three luxury steamers headed upriver toward St. Louis and Louisville. He wondered if Mam'selle Leah were on one of the boats, and he hoped Baptiste had not seen them. Turning around on the box, he looked into the rear seat. Baptiste was slumped down in one corner, but Benji didn't think he was asleep, just completely fatigued from all he'd been through.

To keep himself company, Benji began singing a favorite spiritual in a low, mournful, crooning voice.

"Shut up, Benji, you sound worse than a bleating goat. I don't need your wailing to make me feel any worse."

"Sorry. Thought you were asleep."

"Asleep! Who can sleep with this head of mine. Oh God, how many glasses did I drink? Last count it was an even dozen. I should have followed Pierre's advice and gone home with him."

"Or back to the house. There's still some coffee there."

"No!" Baptiste screamed at him and then held his head in his hands. It felt as if it had been caught between two clanging cymbals. "And don't ever mention it to me again. I've given the key to Pierre DeLisle. He'll take care of it from now on."

"Food and coffee," Benji said. "That's what you need, and what I'll get you soon as we arrive. We's 'most there now. I see the drive just ahead and Jessie lit the oil lamps on the gate like I told her."

Baptiste lay back again. At least the headache drove away any other pain he'd been feeling. Benji was right. Some coffee and food and then a good night's sleep. In the morning, he'd begin overseeing the work in the fields and forget all about Leah. No, that was wishful thinking. He'd never forget, but he'd drive her out of his mind by working until he was so exhausted he was no longer able to think about anything. Hard work, that was what he needed. Damn his legs! If only he could ride around the fields and be his own overseer. He'd think of some way to ride again. Damned if he wouldn't.

The carriage moved easily along the smooth, hard-packed dirt drive. His men had done a good job of filling in the ruts and smoothing it over. He must be sure to tell them he was pleased.

Benji brought the carriage to a halt and then helped Baptiste up the steps to the front-porch entrance. Jessie opened the door for them, listened to Benji's suggestion of food and coffee, and hurried off to the kitchen. A former house slave, Jessie had taken command of the kitchen without a by-your-leave when she found there was no cook. Baptiste had known better than to argue with her; one never argued with servants who considered themselves part of the family. So Jessie was installed as the cook/house-keeper/ruler of Belle Fontaine.

Once Baptiste was settled in a comfortable chair, he stretched out his legs.

"Benji, how about taking them off for me." He didn't have to say anything more. Benji knew exactly what he meant. Without saying a word, he unlaced the straps and carried the artificial limbs into the bedroom and placed them under a sheet in the bedside cabinet. For Baptiste they were dead things, and they might as well be treated as such. He wore them because he couldn't walk without them, but he didn't have to look at them. Returning with a creamy salve, Benji began massaging Baptiste's stumps.

Regina, Jessie's daughter, brought in a tray of sandwiches and hot coffee. "Welcome home, M'sieu Fontaine. I lives in the third cabin anytime you needs or wants me for anything." She lowered her lids and smiled seductively. When she leaned over to set the tray down, he saw her breasts swelling against her dress.

"Thank you, Regina, I'll remember."

Having finished the sandwiches and two cups of thick, strong coffee, Baptiste found his head beginning to clear, and his stomach felt less like revolting. He sat back and lit a cigar.

Benji came into the room from the kitchen. "You want me to help you get ready for bed?"

"No, thanks, Benji. I'm not sleepy. I think I'll sit up a while, and I can manage. Oh, by the way, will you go into town tomorrow and order a fresh supply of cigars. I'm almost out."

Bidding Baptiste goodnight, Benji returned to his rooms

on the lower level, in easy calling distance if he were needed.

Baptiste relaxed in the chair. In the morning he'd explore the fields as extensively as he could in the small buggy. Then he'd talk to Benji about designing a special saddle that would allow him to sit a horse. Damned if he'd let his disability prevent him from riding any longer. It had kept him a prisoner far too long. And Benji was clever with his hands. A few straps, a higher pommel and backrest. Yes, Benji could do it. It would take a while to strengthen his thighs enough to grip the horse, but that was what he needed: something to use his energies and keep him occupied. Yes, tomorrow wouldn't be a bad day at all. He thought about Regina and her less-than-subtle invitation. There were a lot of things to look forward to.

Chapter Three

LEAH FINISHED HER liqueur and was sipping her coffee.

"You want another?" James asked.

"No, I think not."

"You've been a long ways away for the last few minutes." He smiled and put his hand over hers on the table.

"Have I? I'm sorry. I didn't mean to leave you alone." She returned the pressure of his hand.

"That's all right. I understand. You've had a long, trying day. It's enough that you're here with me now."

"James, I want you to believe one thing. I'm here because I want to be. Please don't ever forget that."

"Thank you, Leah. I won't."

"For me the future is more important than the past. There are certain things I could never have endured if it were not that way. Now it's more important than ever that I put the past completely behind me. If, at times, it seems to intrude, it won't be for long. Can you be patient and bear with me during those times?"

"I waited for you, didn't I?" he asked.

"You did, and I'm grateful." Yes, she would be happy

with James. There might be moments when she had to create her own happiness, not depend on others to do it for her; but she knew the dream that she had pursued all her life and was now within her grasp was worth it.

So far, it's only gratitude, James thought, but he could live with that and with her respect until she learned to love him. And he never doubted that she would.

"If I've been a long ways away," Leah said, "you've been staring pretty intently at something yourself."

"Two of the passengers."

"You know them?"

"Slightly. Look to your left and slightly behind you. They won't notice; they're too engrossed in conversation. The two men in evening wear with flowered satin vests. They should make for an interesting boat ride."

Leah looked to her left and began flicking her fingers across her bare shoulder as if brushing back a strand of hair. Raising only her eyes, she looked at the men James had indicated.

"So, what's so interesting about them?" she asked.

"They're professional gamblers."

"Really!" Leah was immediately alert. Before the war she'd heard plenty of stories about riverboat gamblers, and a kind of legendary or magical aura had grown up around them.

"Don't they look like the type, with their beady eyes and smooth, sleek mustaches?" With a menacing leer, James fingered his own.

"Not at all," Leah laughed. "They could be respectable businessmen."

"They could be, but they aren't. They were on the boat with me when I came downriver."

"Did you gamble with them?"

"A game or two, but I decided I had better ways to spend my money."

"You lost? Did they cheat?"

"I don't know. The way I play they didn't have to. But I enjoyed watching some of their techniques."

So James wasn't a gambler. If she were keeping a ledger of virtues and failings, that would be one checkmark for the plus side.

The main salon was as large as the dining room. Heavy, fringed velvet draperies matched the dark-green leaves in the elaborately patterned Brussels carpet. More deeply piled velvet in greens, golds, and blues upholstered chairs arranged in informal conversational groups and placed near the windows for those who wished to watch activities on the river and along the shore. Behind a white marble bar that extended the width of the room were shelves of silver goblets and sparkling crystal glasses in various shapes and sizes. Three bartenders stayed busy filling the orders from red-jacketed waiters. Near the bar were a number of card tables, and three were occupied by passengers playing picquet and whist. The two professional gamblers and four other players were seated at another, and all were deeply engrossed in their cards.

At the opposite end of the room, stained-glass skylights set into the ceiling were beautiful in themselves, but Leah couldn't help imagining what the salon would be like during the day when the sun shone through them and cast jeweled lights on everything its rays touched. Tonight, three crystal, oil-lamp chandeliers lighted the entire room and were reflected in massive mirrors on the end walls. Between the floor-to-ceiling windows were large oil paintings of famous steamboats and scenes along the river. Beside an ebony piano, a string quartet was tuning up, and part of the floor had been cleared for dancing.

"Care to dance, Leah?" James asked, after they'd made their way to two chairs by a window. "I'm not too graceful, but I think I can glide you through a waltz."

"Thank you, James, another night. I think I'd rather sit here and talk." Glancing around the room at the women in their beautiful evening gowns and the men in their black evening suits and crisp white linen, she felt drab in her simple dinner dress. She hoped the boat would dock long enough in Natchez for her to shop.

"Are you a people-watcher, Leah?"

"Oh, I am definitely a people-watcher. It's a fascinating occupation. And you?"

"Always, wherever I go," he said. "And what do you see tonight?"

"Several families with children, some going home, others to visit relatives, maybe for the first time."

"And how do you tell the difference between them?" James asked.

"Easy. The ones going home have rather dusty, wrinkled clothes. They've already made their visit, so it no longer matters how they look. Those over there," she nodded toward a couple with three children, "are on their way for a visit. Notice how new and spotless everything is. See, the mother is worried because the boy has spilled something on his shirt. And the two girls sit very straight and uncomfortably in their chairs."

"You're very observant, Leah," he laughed.

"People-watchers have to be. That's one of the rules."

"All right," he asked, "what about those two women sitting by the window?"

"They are spinster ladies taking their first trip."

"And just how do you reach that conclusion?"

"They are very particular about the way they sit. And they are not used to leisure because one is knitting and the other is crocheting instead of sitting back and enjoying the trip."

"You seem very positive."

"I am." Then she laughed. "No, I saw them in the dining salon. Neither wears a wedding ring, and they were obviously confused about which silver to use and how to order from the menu."

While James took out his pipe, filled it, and then brushed stray shreds of tobacco from his shirtfront, Leah looked out the window. "I do believe we've stopped," she said, pulling the curtain back and peering into the dark beyond the mirrored reflection of the room.

"Probably to take on passengers and cargo as well as wood. These boats burn a hundred cords a day. We'll be stopping briefly at many small towns along the way."

So engrossed was she in the activity on shore, Leah scarcely heard him. In the light of numerous flares and lanterns she saw people running toward the wharf from all directions. There must be somebody very special embarking or debarking. To her surprise, just crates and bundles were being loaded onto the lower deck: squawking chickens, bushels of fresh vegetables and fruit, some barrels, several bales of cotton, and wagonloads of firewood.

"Why all the people?" she asked, more to herself than to James.

"Happens anytime a boat stops. Not all do at these smaller hamlets. So whenever one does—day or night—it's quite an occasion. These boats are almost their only link with the larger towns, and they provide all the necessities of life the farmers can't produce. Also steamboats are like traveling newspapers, bringing all the news from up and down the river. If a small town has goods to sell or people waiting to board, the flares are lighted in the hope a boat will stop. Sometimes it's only a few hours, but sometimes it's days before one comes along looking for wood or cargo or passengers."

"So we won't stop at all of them?"

"Not likely. We'd never get to Louisville if we did. I doubt we'll stop again until we get to Natchez sometime around noon tomorrow."

"And I can go shopping!" Her eyes lit up at the prospect.

James nodded knowingly. "You've been looking forward to that, haven't you?"

"What woman doesn't?" She stifled a yawn.

"You're tired. Why don't you go to bed. I'll walk you to the stateroom and then come back here and read a while."

"I think I will." Leah got up, smoothed her skirt, and started for the door. When they reached the deck, James took her arm and they walked slowly along the rail. Above them the whistle blew three long blasts, and the boat began to move away from the small, crowded wharf. Unlocking the door, James preceded her into the cabin and lit an oil lamp. A steward had already turned down her bed and laid out gown, robe, and slippers. On the table by the bed was a crystal goblet and a carafe of fresh, cool water.

"Looks like everything is ready for you," he said. "Think you'll be all right?"

"I'll be fine, James. You go back and read or join that poker game I saw you eying."

"Maybe I'll watch, but I won't play. I have some purchases to make tomorrow, too, and I need all the change in my pockets." During the days Leah had been making up her mind to come with him, he had sailed to Natchez and selected something very special for her. He hoped she would be pleased with his choice. Standing in the warm, pale light of the oil lamp, she looked more beautiful than he'd ever seen her before. He wanted nothing more than to take her in his arms and hold her forever. Instead he turned and started toward the door. "Good night, Leah, sleep well."

Before he could leave, she glided across the carpet and into his arms. "Good night, James." Her warm, moist lips opened beneath his, and this time there was no tensing of her body. As he tightened his arms around her, he felt the pressure of her thighs, her stomach, and her breasts. Her natural, yielding response aroused an urgent yet tender desire to possess her.

He's strong, Leah thought; *he is strength itself. If nothing else, I'll always find comfort being held in his arms and against his broad chest.* She was not ready to give herself to him completely; but she would welcome his embraces by the time they were married. She took one of his hands from around her waist, moved it gently up her side, and rested it for just a moment on her breast. The pressure of his fingers stirred her, sent sharp pinpricks of desire through her entire body, and came to rest as a throbbing ache in her loins. Yes, she would welcome him after the wedding.

"Good night, James," she said again softly and moved out of his arms.

Lying in the large brass bed, Leah wondered how well she would sleep. Suddenly one long and two short blasts of the ship's whistle startled her and she sat up. Close by, like an echo, she heard an identical signal. Sitting on the edge of the bed, she pulled the curtain aside and saw they were passing a southbound steamboat. She lay back down. The river was a busy place. She listened to other sounds: voices hallooing from the shore, scavenging night birds shrieking overhead, the moaning of the huge paddle wheel, the rushing of water at the stern, and the lapping of a gentler wake along the hull. The boat moved steadily and surely upstream, veering to port or starboard as it followed the bends in the river. The rhythmic swish-swish beneath her was like a melodic lullaby. Tomorrow in Natchez would be a lovely day. She closed her eyes and was immediately asleep.

In her dream, Leah heard the woodpecker drilling for breakfast in an old dead tree in the side yard. She turned over and smothered her face in the pillow. Maybe he'd find the bugs he was looking for and go away. No, there he was again—tap, tap, tapping more noisily. She flopped over on her back and opened her eyes. She wasn't at home; she was in a strange bed in a strange room. And the room was moving. Then she remembered. She was on a boat going North with James. But what was a woodpecker doing in the middle of the Mississippi River? Now the sound became more distinct. Someone was knocking on her door.

"Leah, are you awake?"

Oh, good heavens, it was James. She'd promised she'd be up and dressed in time to breakfast with him at eight. She looked at the small traveling clock by her bed. Ten o'clock!

"Wait, James, wait just a minute. I'll be right there." She reached for her robe and fastened it around her as she walked to the door.

"Morning, love." He kissed her on the forehead.

"Morning! It's nearly noon. I *am* sorry. You must be starved."

"No, I ate at seven. But I'll wait for you on deck and have coffee with you while you eat." He turned to go. "Oh, and dress for town. We've made good time and will be arriving in Natchez earlier than scheduled."

"I won't be fifteen minutes."

Hurriedly she bathed her face, then chose a pale-green linen suit with smoked pearl buttons. There was no time to do more than brush her hair into a soft bun and cover it with a fine mesh snood. On top of this she perched a jaunty Empress Eugénie green straw hat trimmed with a long pheasant feather that swirled around the crown. She felt chic enough to shop in Natchez's most fashionable store.

James was waiting by the rail, and she took his arm. "You look beautiful, Leah."

"Thank you, James."

"I went ahead and ordered for you," he said, "so you won't have to rush to finish breakfast before we land."

"Rush! How soon will we be there?" She looked up-river, expecting to see Natchez around the next bend.

"About an hour, I think."

"An hour? Goodness, that's enough time for a second cup of coffee."

James led her to the table they'd had the night before, and she gasped at what she saw at her place: fruit juice, hotcakes, sausage, eggs, and hot breads. "What is all this?"

"Your breakfast. Something wrong with it?"

"It's—there's so much. I never have more than a crois-sant and coffee." She saw James's face fall, and she realized he had ordered everything he thought she might like. "I know," she said, "this is what you have in Indiana, isn't it?"

"If it's more than you want, hand it over and I'll order the croissants." He spoke to the waiter and then shook his head. "But I don't see how you survive on such meager fare."

"We make up for it at dinner," she laughed. "Didn't you see how much I ate last night?"

Leah drank the juice but handed the well-filled plate over to James after the waiter brought the rolls.

An hour later, they stood by the rail and watched the ship dock at Natchez. As they walked through the famous Mississippi city, Leah thought about her flight from New Orleans years earlier. At that time she was alone; and she was finally forced to return home. This time she was not alone, but she would need all of James's strength to make this journey successful.

"There are several fine shops on this street, Leah. You want me to go with you?"

"No, you'd be bored while I selected all the things I need. And you said you had plans of your own." She real-ly wanted to shop by herself, yet she didn't want to disap-point him if he thought to tag along. She looked forward to choosing lingerie, gowns, shoes, hats, and one very special, very important ensemble.

"There's a good restaurant, the Candelabra, right around the corner." He reached for his pocket watch. "Would you be ready to meet me there in, say, three hours? Will that give you enough time?"

"Yes, plenty of time."

"It won't be too far for you to carry all the boxes I expect you'll have with you." He smiled. "Then I'll help you get them to the boat."

"How much money do you think I have, James?" she asked in mock horror.

"Well, if you don't have enough for all you need, I can give you more."

"No, indeed. After we're married, yes, but I'll take care of my trousseau."

"Well, have fun, and I'll see you in three hours." James bent down and brushed her cheek with a gentle, familiar kiss, as if they were already married.

But they weren't married yet, and as she watched him walk away, she suddenly felt she was looking at a stranger. Here she was getting ready to shop for a trousseau in an unfamiliar town, and she didn't really know the man she was going to marry. She hoped that buying her trousseau and spending two more days on the boat with James would close the distance between them. She sensed that James was still feeling somewhat ill at ease with her, too.

It had been different with Baptiste. Because her life was threatened, he had hidden her in his apartment for two weeks, but as a friend, not a lover. By the time she became his *placée*, she'd learned all his moods and habits. Her knowledge of him, as much as the physical intimacy, was what helped to forge a secure, satisfying relationship. And these facets of James she had yet to learn. Then she smiled to herself. James was a kind and gentle man; there was nothing to be apprehensive about. Together they would learn to know each other, and perhaps that was the way it was meant to be.

In the first shop she stopped at, Leah selected underclothes of fine, lace-trimmed cambric. She bought two petticoats that were not nearly so wide or boned as they had been before the war. Then she lingered a long time over a beautiful nightgown and peignoir of pale daffodil-yellow chiffon with wide bands of ecru lace shirred around the off-shoulder neckline of the gown and falling over her hands from the cuffs of the peignoir. They cost more than she wanted to spend, and she recounted the money in her reticule.

Throughout and after the war, she had carefully hoarded the gold coins her father gave her before he fled New Orleans. Some of them had gone to clear the title of the plantation, but Baptiste insisted she spend the rest on herself. Although she had more than enough for a splurge today, she wanted to take some money with her to Indiana so she could afford small personal luxuries and gifts for James. She didn't want to be completely dependent on him.

She looked again at the pale-yellow gown and peignoir. If she bought one dress fewer than she'd planned, she could stay within her budget. She closed her eyes and counted to ten. When she opened them, she told the salesgirl to put the nightgown and peignoir in a box. And the yellow satin slippers to match.

"Will you keep the boxes here for an hour or two?" she asked the shop owner. "I have more shopping to do, and I'd rather not carry them around."

"Certainly, madame. They will be here when you return."

Leah took a few minutes to walk along the streets and gaze in the shop windows. She was looking for a very special ensemble. She had no particular design or color in mind, but she would know the outfit when she saw it. If there had been time to go to a dressmaker in New Orleans—but there hadn't been, so she had to find something ready-made. Then, in the window of a very small shop tucked between a bank and a meat market, she saw it. On the solid wooden door was a single word: *Cecile's*.

When she opened the door, a bell rang in the back room, and a young woman came through the dividing curtain. Much to Leah's surprise, the proprietor greeted her in French, and then, flushing with embarrassment, spoke hesitantly in English.

"Please," Leah assured her, "I'm from New Orleans and would prefer to speak French."

"Oh, madame, from New Orleans! It is my dream to go there."

"But it's only a few miles downriver."

"A few miles, but much money. I make a living here,

but down there—" Although voiced as a statement, her lilting tone turned it into a question.

"And you would make a living there, too." Leah looked around the small shop. "These are your own designs, aren't they?"

"*Oui.* In France I was a modiste. With my own shop. Then I met— Well, my friend brought me over here and set me up in this shop. It was just a frivolous hobby at first, to keep me occupied when he was—"

"With his family?" Leah asked.

"*Oui.* Then he died, and now it is not a hobby; it is a living."

"Go to New Orleans," Leah said. "You'll be very successful. I'll give you the name of a well-known lawyer, and he'll help you find a place in the Vieux Carré. Before you know it, you'll have all the patrons you want."

"Thank you, madame," Cecile said. "I will think about it."

"Now," Leah said, "will that suit in the window fit me?"

Cecile stepped back and with her eyes took careful measurement of Leah's figure. "*Oui.* Maybe a tuck here or there."

"But my boat leaves in about three hours," Leah sighed.

"I can alter it in an hour. Come, we'll go in the back, and try it on."

She led Leah to the small room in the rear that was sewing room, parlor, kitchen, and bedroom for the young seamstress. After slipping into the skirt and jacket, Leah looked in the long mirror. She was delighted with what she saw.

The powder-blue faille suit was fashioned with the bell-shaped skirt just coming into fashion. The short jacket was nipped in tightly at the waist over a slightly flared, stiffened peplum. An ivory lace fichu filled the low, V-shaped, collarless neckline, and additional lace edged the wide cuffs. It was just what she wanted for the wedding. When the boat stopped at Cairo, they were going to be married in a small, informal ceremony, but she longed to wear something bridelike, and the blue suit was perfect.

"See," Cecile was saying, "just a nip here and another there. It will be ready in less than an hour."

"It's—it's for my wedding," Leah said.

"Oh, *oui*, that is wonderful." Cecile sat back on her heels and surveyed Leah. "Then you must have a chapeau, and I shall make it for you."

"But there's not time," Leah insisted.

"Not time! Faugh, I'll make it for you right now."

Cecile scurried around the room, took some material off the shelf, more out of a drawer, and returned with a mouth full of pins. "I'll make it right on your head. Sit—sit," she ordered.

She refused to let Leah watch her progress as she worked at something on her head. In less than fifteen minutes, she said, "There, all *fini*, and *très chic*, *très magnifique*. You see?"

Leah turned around and looked in the mirror. A slim toque was skewed jauntily to the right side of her head. Made of the blue velvet that trimmed her suit, it was swathed with yards of veiling in the same shade. It was simple, yet stylish.

"Oh, Cecile, it is perfect, and you say you could not be a success in New Orleans. You will have every woman in the Vieux Carré rushing to your door."

"If you like it, I am pleased. Right now, it is just pinned, but I will have it and the dress ready when you return in an hour."

"Wait," Leah said, "I need two more ensembles. A simple walking suit and an evening gown. Something very—"

"Provocative?"

"Yes, exactly. Not too daring, but alluring."

"I have just the one," Cecile said. "I made it for one of my patrons here, but she will be away for a few weeks, and I can easily make her another. You will not be living in Natchez?"

"No, no, we're on our way to Indiana. No fear. She won't know someone else is wearing a duplicate."

Leah gasped when she saw the gown. Of shimmering aurora silk, its off-the-shoulder décolletage dipped to a point between her breasts. The skirt was embroidered with scattered pearls and brilliants that reflected the subtle rainbow lights in the silk. She'd wear it tonight and surprise James. He'd be pleased. From among the array of suits she selected one in rust-colored linen. The color was not the best for her, but it would be practical in a small town.

Cecile put the dresses over her arm. "They will be ready when you return, madame."

"Please have them all boxed. I'll be returning with my fiancé, and I don't want him to see them."

"*Mais oui*," Cecile nodded. "Especially the wedding suit."

"Now," Leah said, writing a name on the paper Cecile gave her, "when you get to New Orleans, go to the office of Pierre DeLisle. Here is his address. Tell him I sent you. He is a good friend, and he will take care of everything for you. You cannot help but be a success."

"And will I see you when you return?"

"I—I won't be returning. I'm going to live in Indiana."

"Oh, I am so sorry," Cecile said. "But—*merci, merci*. I will do just what you say."

Leah looked at her pendant watch. She'd spent far longer shopping than she'd meant to, and there was no time to see about new shoes. But she had enough, and plenty of gloves, too. She hurried to the restaurant, and she saw James sitting at a table near the window. Oh, why was she always late! He had to be a very patient man to put up with her tardiness.

"You look mighty pleased with yourself," he said, smiling as he took her hand and held out a seat for her. "Where are all the mountains of boxes! I was sure you'd come in here laden with them after all this time."

"Then I am late. I'm so sorry."

"No, indeed, early in fact. I just finished sooner than you did."

"The boxes are at the shops because I shall need your strong arms to carry them for me. A lady does not walk the streets laden with packages." She felt the waiter hovering near her shoulder. "Tea, sugar, no cream, and an éclair—no, two éclairs." She looked up at James who was grinning at her. "I'm starved."

"I'm not surprised after that huge breakfast you ate."

"It's not that. Shopping takes so much out of you. Don't laugh, it does. Deciding between this and that, making sure everything fits. You've no idea what we women go through to please you men. And you must say you're pleased, or it will all be for naught."

"I would be pleased if you wore—"

"Nothing?" This banter between them was fun. It was what she'd hoped life would be like with James.

"That is not exactly what I was going to say, though I don't deny I might have had it in mind. No, I was going to say a burlap sack."

"Never that. Unless trimmed with lace. Much too unfeminine." She liked the tiny laugh wrinkles fanning out from his mouth. "You're grinning like a 'gator from ear to ear. Did you have a successful day, too?"

"I did." He patted his coat pocket.

Moving forward in her chair, Leah leaned over the table and tried to see. "Something for me?"

"Not yet," he said, "later. And how do you know it's something for you?"

"Because of the way you smiled when you patted your pocket. I'm curious, but I'll try to be patient. Did you buy anything for yourself?"

"I did. Want to see?"

She'd noticed the large, flat box on the chair beside him. Bless his heart, he'd also bought a new suit for their wedding.

"Look, isn't it handsome?" he asked proudly.

Leah put her hand to her mouth and nearly choked on her tea. What she saw was anything but a neat, conservative business suit. James held up for her inspection a suede hunting jacket with deep pockets and leather patches at the elbows. The pockets at the hips were roomy enough to hold small game, and the two breast pockets had expansion pleats to carry ammunition. Well, James was no Beau Brummel, but he did have excellent if expensive taste in hunting clothes.

"It's—it's very handsome." That she could say with all honesty.

"I've always wanted one like this. I'll wear it forever; that's the beauty of it."

She could see it hanging on a peg in their back hall—if the house had a back hall—and getting older and grimier and smellier through the years. Also softer and more comfortable. Somehow she knew it would never be thrown out. Already it seemed to be a talisman for their marriage—something that would become more comfortable and more familiar through the years.

That night Leah dressed more carefully for dinner. She had the steward bring in a brass tub and she took a long, leisurely bath. She luxuriated in the lavender-scented suds and then rubbed herself down with a thick warm towel. While she sprayed herself from head to foot with her favorite tea-olive cologne, she looked in the long mirror. Her pregnancy was beginning to show in a slight thickening around the waist. Her breasts were fuller, too. So far her arms and legs were still slim, and there was no puffiness in her face.

She put on her new undergarments, still fragrant with the sachets the salesgirl had tucked among them. Next her fine silk hose and satin slippers with the new, slim French heels. She had to suck in her breath when she fastened the dress. Her breasts swelled in round, seductive curves above the tightly fitted bodice, and the low neckline came no more than an inch above her nipples. She'd wanted something especially provocative, and this dress was certainly that.

Now for the *pièce de résistance*. She looked in the drawers where she put her personal items from the small bag she'd carried onboard. First she moved the long glove boxes to one side. Next, she anxiously pulled out a whole pile of handkerchiefs and another of scarves. It wasn't there. But it had to be! She would never have left the house without it. When she bought the dress, she thought how perfect they'd be together. She pulled out all the boxes and piled them on the floor. Finally, she did the same with all the drawers. But it wasn't there. There was no flat, velvet-covered box.

She sat on the bed, weeping and remembering. She'd left the pearls on her dressing table. In her hurry to get out of the house after the confrontation with Baptiste, she'd forgotten them. How could she forget the one gift from Baptiste that she loved above all else? She felt utterly disconsolate. Although she knew they were almost priceless, their real value lay in the sentimental meaning they had for her, the precious moments she and Baptiste had shared together.

Even worse than that was how Baptiste must have felt when he saw them. He must surely think she had purposely left them behind, that she was discarding them as she had discarded him. He would be deeply hurt, and she had never intended to do that.

When she heard the first bell for supper, she realized James must not see that she'd been crying. She wiped her eyes and dampened her flaming cheeks with cologne. In Natchez she'd bought a box of rice powder, and with the rabbit-fur puff she carefully dusted enough on to cover the shine. With a moistened fingertip she smoothed her brows, and she felt better. She took time to arrange her hair in large, soft poufs, quite unlike the severe style she usually wore. Since she didn't have the pearls, she hung a gold locket around her neck and it nestled enticingly just above the cleft between her breasts.

"Leah, you look positively radiant," James greeted her in the main salon. "Shopping must agree with you."

She smiled into his eyes. "Not just shopping, James." Although not quite ready to voice her growing feelings for him, she hoped he would infer them from her words. Before leaving the stateroom, she'd reconciled herself to the loss of the pearls and had decided that perhaps it was best she'd left them behind. As she'd told James, she preferred looking to the future to being haunted by the past. Except for her worry about what Baptiste would think, she was relieved she did not have them to keep reminding her of the night he gave them to her as well as all the other times she'd worn them. It was James she was marrying and James she would live with as a loving and faithful wife. She needed only to recall her feelings when their hands had touched in the prison to realize that she'd been attracted to him by more than his legal abilities. Handsome in a distinctive, rough-hewn way, he was masculine and authoritative yet strangely compassionate and ingenuous. Now as she looked at him across the table, she knew she was succumbing again to the magnetic charm he had first captivated her with.

After a supper as sumptuous as the last evening's, they

went into the main salon. Leah began people-watching again, but James would not take his eyes off her. Over and over he repeated to himself her words: "Not just shopping." He saw a new brilliance in her eyes and a less strained, more natural curve to her smile. He had carried all her boxes from the shops and laughed with her all the way to the boat about how much she had bought. He knew she was wearing a new gown tonight, and it pleased him to think she had chosen that very seductive dress for him. Once again he patted the small, square box in his coat pocket. He was impatient to give it to her. But not here. He'd waited until now; he could wait a little longer.

"Leah," he leaned toward her, "you want to see a mouse skin two cats?"

"What in the world are you talking about?"

"That table over there," he said, "where they're playing poker."

"Yes, the gamblers. But who are the cats and who is the mouse?"

"When I came back here last night," he said, "I wasn't the only one watching. See that young man sitting between them?"

"The one with the foolish grin?" She shook her head. "He's going to lose everything he has."

"No, he's not. He was pretending to read last night, but he was observing the action as closely as I was. You see the fourth man?"

"The one frowning? He looks miserable."

"Well, he should. Last night he won everything. Tonight he is losing every time. From the beginning I was suspicious, and so was our young friend."

"Then they *are* cheating."

"More like a razor's edge between cheating and playing a very sharp game. I'll bet you everything I have in my pockets the young man will be the big winner tonight."

"And lose it all tomorrow night," she said, feeling very smug.

"No! He won't be on the ship tomorrow morning."

"But why would they let him win tonight if they know he's getting off?"

"They don't know. He was originally traveling farther upriver, but when he saw a way to make a killing he

71

changed his plans. We make a brief stop sometime around two in the morning, and he'll be off the boat."

"How did you figure all this out?" Leah asked.

"I didn't. We got to talking and he told me himself. He'd been suckered into a similar game on a gambling boat anchored just below New Orleans. While he watched the game last night, he realized what was going on. Then when I saw him sitting in tonight, I knew he was betting he'd figured out their scheme. He's headed west to join up with a wagon train. After this night is over, he'll be able to afford the best horses there are. I can't wait to see those gamblers' faces in the morning."

"Well," Leah said, "I hope you're right. He looks like a nice young man, and I'd like to see those professionals get their comeuppance." She reached over and squeezed James's hand. "I'm glad, though, you didn't decide to cash in on that trick. I'd hate to find myself abandoned in the middle of the Mississippi."

"At the risk of sounding too sentimental, you are worth all the gold on that table."

"Thank you, James, and don't—don't ever be afraid to be sentimental. I like it."

"Would you like to see what I have in my pocket?"

"You know I would. Curiosity has been nibbling at me all evening."

"It's such a nice night, let's go up on the promenade deck," he suggested.

With James's arm around her, they climbed the marble stairs. "Too many people," he mumbled. "We'll try the hurricane deck."

The roof of the topmost cabins, the hurricane deck was completely unsheltered from the wind. At the forward end was the pilothouse. Open to the sky, the rest was surrounded by an elaborate rail. The moon was almost as full as the night before, and the waves from the boat's wash caught and held the stars. The thousand sparkling lights were like the thousand lights of New Orleans she'd seen as the boat pulled away from the levee.

Encircled by James's arms, Leah responded eagerly to his ardent kisses, and when he caressed her silk-covered breasts, she yielded to his touch. She waited for him to suggest they go to her stateroom, but she hoped he wouldn't. This much she could give of herself tonight, but no more. She wanted his kisses and his caresses, but not yet the final, total intimacy.

When James felt her willing response, he longed to touch more than the silk of her bodice. He wanted to unfasten her dress and bury his face in the fragrant cleft so temptingly exposed. He didn't think she would stop him, but that was exactly what kept him from doing it. In her yielding to him, she had made herself completely vulnerable, and he could not take advantage of that vulnerability. He wanted her, but at the perfect moment, and this was not it.

He withdrew his arms from around her, reached into his pocket, took out the small white box, and opened it. As he slipped the ring on Leah's finger, the diamonds glistened brilliantly in the moonlight.

"Oh, James." She buried her face against his chest and began crying.

"What is it, Leah? I thought you'd be pleased."

"I am. Oh, I really am," she assured him. "Haven't you ever seen a woman cry because she's happy."

He reached for her hand. "Let me look at it on your finger."

Leah looked, too, at her engagement ring, a square-cut emerald surrounded by diamonds.

"Oh, James, it's beautiful."

"Then you like it?" She noted the hesitancy in his voice, and she knew she was marrying a man who would devote his whole life to pleasing her.

"Like it? I love it because it means I belong to you."

James was satisfied. He knew she did not love him yet, but to hear her say she loved belonging to him was more than he'd hoped for.

They returned to the main salon and danced until after midnight. Held in James's strong arms, his face smiling down on her, Leah glided in rhythm with the music as if there were no floor beneath her feet. There was no past to haunt and no future to worry about. There was only tonight.

When they returned to her stateroom, she was once more in his arms, responding to him as passionately as she had on the upper deck. She made no protest when he unfastened the top of her bodice, and the gown dropped to her waist. She herself undid the ribbons of her chemise, and her mouth passionately sought his when he caressed her breasts.

"Oh God, Leah, I love you. Only two more nights." He kissed her again and then pulled away. "I'd better leave now. If I don't, I won't be able to leave at all."

"I know. Kiss me goodnight, and then I'll let you go."

Lying alone in her bed, Leah could not sleep. She longed for James to make love to her, to release the tension building in her since she fled the house. Not until she belonged completely to him would she be free from the bondage of memory. James would be a strong, powerful lover, equal to her own passionate nature. She had long ago learned that she did not have to love a man to need his love. Until she became Baptiste's *placée*, she had thought herself cold and in complete control of her emotions. With Baptiste she discovered her sensuous nature and her need for love. Now she knew that James could satisfy that need.

In the adjoining stateroom, James also lay awake. He thought about Leah's rich beauty and warm body, and he could not forget how she responded to his touch. Their marriage would be completely different from his first.

He'd met Zadah when he returned to Hickory Falls from the East, and he was immediately attracted by her petite, almost childish charm. She was totally unlike the women he'd associated with before: the pleasant, easygoing farmgirl who had introduced him to the rough, animal-like delights of love in the hayloft when he was only thirteen; the quick, satisfying, ego-building Eastern affairs that had left him exhausted but highly pleased with himself; the lusty women out West who traveled to the small mining towns to fill their stockings with money.

He had fallen in love with Zadah's innocent naïveté immediately. She was to be adored and cherished, not just serve as an outlet for lust. Yet he had expected that eventually she would respond to him. In spite of his tender and patient approach, however, she froze each time he came near her. He had expected her to be afraid at the beginning. After all, she came to him untutored in the facts of marriage, but she never changed. To her, physical intimacies were hideous and insufferable.

James thought about Leah's response when he touched her breasts. He had touched Zadah's only once in all the years they were married. While they were on their honeymoon, she lay reluctantly beside him and shook each time he touched her. When his hands traveled up from her waist and his fingers caressed her, she was so upset by the sensation she leaped crying from the bed and sat in a chair. There seemed to be no way he could convince her that what she had felt was normal, nor did she allow him near her again for three weeks. After she let him return to the bed, she always wore long, full gowns carefully buttoned clear to her throat.

For Zadah, it was God's will and therefore her duty to bear children. It was the only reason she tolerated an occasional intimacy. Rather than an expression of love, it was a conjugal necessity, and she never raised her gown above her hips. Although James found these cold encounters less satisfying than those in the hayloft or the crowded tents out West, they relieved some of the pressure. Never more than once a month would Zadah allow him to approach her. Lying stiff and motionless, she held her breath until the hated deed was completed. Then she got up, scrubbed herself thoroughly to rid her body of his contaminating touch, opened a small diary, and put a checkmark by the date.

As soon as Zadah knew she was pregnant, she closed the small, black book and locked it in a drawer. She had conceived. She had done her duty to James and to God, and there was no longer any reason for him to come near her. From then on he slept in the spare bedroom.

Their child, a little boy, was stillborn, and Zadah remained an invalid until she died. James never touched her again. Nor was he ever unfaithful to her. Strangely, he still loved her deeply and immutably. Because he never looked at another woman, people praised him for being a good husband. He knew he conformed to the ancient meaning of the word *husband*, "to care for." They were the same thing. It was as simple as that. Until she died, he never kissed her anywhere except on the cheek. When he kissed her in the coffin, her skin was no colder than when she was alive.

Lying awake in the cabin, James could still feel the warmth of Leah's body, the tautness of her nipples, and the beating of her heart beneath her breast. In two more days they would be married, and he would be able to love her as he was never allowed to love Zadah. Through the years of his first marriage, he had become phlegmatic and not easily aroused. Now the vision of Leah and the recollection of the faint perfume that always surrounded her stirred up desires he thought destroyed by the cold, sterile years. He ached with the longing to make love to her. He wanted to get out of bed, go to her room, and crush her beneath him right then. Until tonight he had not considered sleeping with her before the wedding. Though his Puritan, Presbyterian morals did not condone premarital coitus, he could so easily succumb to temptation now by arguing that she was not a virgin; she had been Baptiste's mistress. But he knew why he didn't. She had been almost but not quite ready to yield to him. If he went to her cabin now and she was the least bit reluctant, their tenuous relationship would be destroyed, and he knew why.

Leah had never told him all she had suffered in the prison. However, he knew enough about some of the tortures she'd endured—the shackles on her wrists, the putrid conditions of her cell—to surmise what else had taken place. Too well he knew what rough, uncouth jailors were like and what they demanded of women prisoners. He had no doubt she'd been raped more than once. He would never know how she had remained sane through it all and could still tolerate the touch of a man. But then, it was a long time before he'd realized just how strong a person she was. She had not broken under the force of her jailors, but she might under the pressurings of someone she thought loved her.

It was this, more than his own natural morality, that persuaded him to be patient. Because Leah was passing as white, they could have been married at any of the towns along the way; they did not have to wait until they arrived in a Northern state with no miscegenation laws. But he wanted to give her the time she needed to welcome him

76

with no hesitancy or reservations. After her response tonight, he thought she was ready to become his wife.

Sometime around two in the morning, the boat made a brief stop at a hamlet on the river's western bank. Each unknown to the other, Leah and James simultaneously pulled aside their window curtains and watched the activity on the wharf. Leah crawled back into bed smiling. In his stateroom, James was laughing. By the light of a single flare, they'd seen a young man emerge from the cargo deck, crawl between two rows of crates, and run like crazy into the woods beyond.

In the morning, Leah was awake and out of bed before eight o'clock. She met James in the dining salon, and they shook hands across the table in a victory salute. At a nearby table, the two gamblers stared into their coffee. Every so often, one would shake his head or hold it in his hands. There was no sound from them, but Leah could well imagine how they were silently moaning and berating themselves.

"Well, he did it," James said, "just like he said he would."

"Yes, he did. I wonder how much he won from them."

"Plenty, if the pile I saw in front of him when we left at midnight was any indication."

"Good for him." Leah clapped her hands.

James looked up from stirring his coffee. "How would you like to do something completely different today?"

"No stops to make?"

"None that I think would be of any interest to you. We make a pretty long run this morning before we pull into shore."

"What did you have in mind?" Unconsciously she ran her right hand across her left and touched the ring to assure herself it was still there, that she hadn't just imagined receiving it.

"I talked with Captain Henderson, the pilot, yesterday before you were awake, and he's invited us to come up to the pilothouse and learn how he navigates the river. It's trickier than you'd think. Want to go up?"

"I'd love to." She started to push her plate aside.

"Finish your coffee. There's no rush. He said anytime this morning."

Leah looked over at the remains of sausage, eggs, and hotcakes on James's plate and then down at the crumbs from her own roll. Breakfast to her was merely something to aid the waking-up process rather than a complete meal. She scarcely had her eyes open before the second cup of coffee. How in the world would she get used to being awake and industrious enough to cook so much food every morning? She'd have to bestir herself and try to get her brain unscrambled at least half an hour earlier than James.

The pilothouse was a small, compact structure a few feet aft of the curved bow. From this vantage point, the pilot looked directly between twin smokestacks that rose an additional fifty feet into the air. The four glazed sides of the pilothouse offered an unobstructed view in all directions.

Henderson, a huge, powerfully built man with a shaggy mane of red hair and an unkempt beard, wore a traditional flat, leather-billed pilot's cap low over his eyes. In his rough, serviceable clothes, he looked more like a deckhand than a river pilot, many of whom dressed like dandies and were reputed to sport genuine diamond stickpins. Henderson, however, was proud of having served a long apprenticeship as a deckhand, until the river was more familiar to him than the streets of Baton Rouge, his home town.

"Good morning," Henderson called; "come in." Scarcely glancing out the window, he spun the huge solid-oak wheel a full turn, and the boat veered enough to port to avoid an obstruction in the river that was invisible to Leah but which Henderson knew was there. "Hope you slept well."

"Best night's sleep I've had in a long time," James said.

"The river'll do that for ya. No better life than steamboatin'."

He turned back to the wheel, changed course slightly again, and called to the engine room for more steam.

"The current's running pretty fast today," he said. "Could mean more trash to look out for."

James and Leah stood quietly on either side of the pilot,

who stared intently, eyes squinted against the sun, from under the bill of his cap. They saw nothing ahead but clear water until he veered to starboard, and a submerged sandbar came into view. Henderson steered the boat around it with only inches to spare and then swung back toward the center of the channel. James was duly impressed, and Leah found herself expelling breath she didn't even realize she'd been holding.

"Son of a bitch wasn't there on the trip down," Henderson swore. "Sorry, ma'am, that just slipped out."

"Think nothing of it," Leah said. "I heard much worse when I nursed soldiers during the war."

"A nurse now? In New Orleans?"

"Yes."

"And a mighty rough time of it you had, I imagine. Now I was lucky. Went through it all without a scratch. Manned a blockade runner out of New Orleans. Some near-misses, but made it through every time."

"Then you're one of the men we wanted to thank for bringing in the medicines we needed," she said.

"As long as we could, ma'am, as long as we could. Too often we had to hole up at one of the islands."

James was staring intently into the water and trying to see what Henderson watched for. Even while talking, the pilot never relaxed his vigilance.

"You know all the sandbars on the river?" James asked.

"If I didn't, I'd soon be sitting on 'em."

"Is that why you keep going back and forth across the river? To avoid them? I'd think it would be faster to go directly up the middle."

"Downriver, yes," Henderson nodded, "to get speed from the current. When we go upriver, we fight the same current all the way unless we find deep water on either side of it." He pointed toward one shore. "See how the river twists and turns? As fast as it flows, the water keeps changing the shape of the banks, washing them out on one side and building them up on the other. The current is less strong on the concave side, so we make better time by crossing over from point to point."

"If the river keeps changing," James asked, "how do you know where the water is deep enough?"

Leah leaned back against one of the windows. She vacillated between listening to the men and watching the changing vistas on shore. As interested as she was in what the pilot said, she was more intrigued by James's fascination with it. A man not satisfied with superficial knowledge, he wanted to know the *hows* and *whys* of everything. Yes, she was indeed learning more about him every day. Life with James might be placid, but it would never be dull.

Henderson was explaining, "We watch the banks themselves, for one thing, and keep sounding the river. See that bank up ahead?"

"Yes." James stared as intently as the pilot.

"Is the river rising or falling?"

James laughed. "I'm too much of a novice to try answering that question."

"Well, see if you can tell me this," Henderson said. "Is the river higher or lower than normal? Look carefully. Let's see how observant you are."

James looked for a long time before answering. Henderson said the banks themselves could give a clue. If the river were lower than normal, there would probably be some indication of a waterline. But how would he know if it were higher? His eyes moved first along the bank and then from the top of it to the edge of the water.

"Those scrub trees," James said. "If they don't normally grow in the water, I'd say the river has been rising."

"Right you are, Andrews. That could mean floods on the Ohio or Missouri rivers have raised the water level. Now if there'd been a narrow shelf of sand, the river would be falling. If the river is high all the way up, we're in luck. I'll show you why in a few minutes."

Henderson guided the boat from one concave side across to another and then began to steer it between an island and the shore.

"This is called a chute," he said, "this space between an island and the bank. You'll notice the water is calmer here, with no current. If the river is high enough, we can go up quicker by traveling from chute to chute."

As the boat entered the narrow passage, the engines went from full to half to quarter speed. A gauge indicated the steam pressure had dropped as low as it could go and still keep the *Louisiana Belle* moving, and the great rear paddle wheel seemed barely to be turning. Great boughs of forest giants arched over the top deck. Leah felt as if she could reach out the pilothouse window and pluck a leaf from one of them.

From below, the leadsman continually called out the depth of the river as he plumbed the murky waters: "Mark three, mark three; half twain . . . quarter twain . . . mark twain!" Now the very banks themselves were pressing against the boat. There was no sign of human habitation on shore and no sound except an occasional redbird's chirp.

James was familiar enough with the depth calls from the leadsman to know the hull would soon be scraping bottom.

"No danger," Henderson assured him. "Just wait."

"Mark four!" the leadsman called out.

"We're all right now," the pilot said. "Just a shallow spot. Saw it coming."

He also saw the submerged tree trunk, an underwater bridge from island to shore. He could reverse engines, back down the chute, and go around the island, or he could maneuver over the obstruction. His eyes squinting almost shut beneath his wrinkled forehead, he took the measure of the log and continued moving forward.

With one mighty heave of her bow, the boat rode up over the tree trunk and crossed it with a din like the continuous roll of a hundred drums. When the big rear wheel reached the log, its mighty paddles flailed the air. Leah held her breath, sure that in spite of his confident air, the pilot was taking a dangerous chance with the lives of over two hundred passengers. She also wished they hadn't come up to the pilothouse if this were Henderson's idea of showing off for them. Finally one blade on the paddlewheel shuddered, but the next one pushed the tree behind it as easily as if it were rolling it down a hill.

"Well, we made it through that one," Henderson said as they came out of the chute and headed for deep water on the far side of the channel.

Having said good-bye to the pilot, James and Leah went out onto the deck. The boat now seemed to be gliding as swiftly and easily upstream as the driftwood and other debris were carried downstream by the current. Also traveling down the Mississippi were flatboats propelled by nothing more than the river's current and an occasional sweep of a long oar to keep them on course. Most of them were large square rafts topped by a match-box shelter or a canvas lean-to at one end. Barrels, crates, and gunnysacks were piled and balanced precariously on every square inch of deck space.

"Look at that one, Leah." James pointed to a flatboat just pulling out from shore. Crates of squawking chickens formed a two-layer wall around the edge of the raft, and corraled in the middle were a half-dozen cows that added their lowing to the raucous symphony that also included the boatmen's shouts, the steamboat's whistle, the waved hellos from a small dock, and the cries of barefoot children running along the muddy shore.

"It's like a floating meat market," Leah said.

"If their luck holds, they'll make it all the way to New Orleans, sell both produce and flatboat, and then return home as deck passengers on a riverboat."

"And if it doesn't? Their luck, I mean."

"Many of them don't make it around the bends," James said. "These points bed the skeletons of wrecks that've washed ashore. Some are destroyed by the river, some rammed by a steamboat. Anyway you look at it, it's a dangerous and tricky way to make a living."

They passed slowly by a landing at the end of a narrow dirt road that wound between a few ramshackle wooden buildings. A flatboat was tied to one of the uprights, and the time-warped boards of the landing were thronged with women in loose cotton dresses and calico bonnets, men in baggy cotton trousers whose suspenders crisscrossed bare chests, and more barefoot children.

"It's a floating general store," James said.

The *Louisiana Belle* was close enough for Leah to see the women examining bolts of cloth while men hefted a plow blade or checked the sight on a rifle. Children were trading pennies for peppermint and horehound sticks. Clutching the sweets in their grubby hands, they ran dangerously near the edge of the planks.

"These people are miles from any town and completely isolated," James added. "Since few of the large boats stop at hamlets like this, they're completely dependent on the flatboats."

To Leah, the Mississippi had meant steamboats, huge, busy levees, and magnificent natural beauty. Now she realized that to many it was a vital lifeline.

The morning had been enlightening, and Leah was ready to spend the afternoon resting and reading on a chaise longue on the promenade deck. James sat in a chair beside her and studied the briefs of upcoming cases that his law partner had sent down to New Orleans. The day was warm with a pleasant breeze, and Leah felt more and more a loosening of the tension that had kept her on edge since they'd come on board.

"I'm becoming very lazy on this trip," she said.

"It's easy enough when there's nothing you have to do."

"But you're at least occupied with those briefs. I feel I should be doing something."

"No, you needed this rest. How long since you've done nothing but indulge yourself?"

Leah reached for his hand and smiled, but she was thinking about all the hard years since the beginning of the war. "You're right. I can scarcely remember that far back."

"Then relax and stop feeling guilty. Remember, you've a second reason for regaining your strength."

Leah put her hand over her stomach. Yes, she needed to eat well and rest. It was a wonder she still carried the baby after the brutal treatment in the prison. Day after day, she'd waited apprehensively for signs she'd miscarried, but they never appeared. As much as for herself, she'd chosen to go North for the child; she hoped they'd both have the life she'd been previously denied.

That night after supper, she told James she thought she'd go to bed early. "I really am getting lazy or else this boat is making me sleepy."

"It'll do that. You go along. I'll stay here and join some of the men at the bar. One is an Illinois lawyer who's been telling me about a particularly interesting case he's working on. I'll see you in the morning." He bent down to kiss her goodnight.

"No, I'm just going to read a while. Come by and tell me goodnight again."

Before going to her stateroom, Leah found a steward and asked him to bring a number of things to her cabin. While she waited, she took off her earrings, bracelet, and locket, put them carefully inside a box, and replaced them in the drawer. In a few minutes the steward and two maids arrived with a large brass tub and pitchers of hot water.

"Would you like me to bring the other things, madame, when I return for the tub?"

"Yes, thank you, that will be fine."

Leah carefully removed her clothes, hung her gown in the armoire, and put her folded undergarments into a drawer of the large chest.

She knew James would stay in the salon discussing the legal case for at least another two hours. That gave her plenty of time. After lathering herself all over with the fragrant soap, she lay back in the warm, soothing water and let it flow around her for several minutes.

While she dried off with the soft towel, she looked around the cabin. Tomorrow she would be Mrs. James Andrews. James's suits would hang in the armoire and his shaving mug would sit next to her toilette articles on the washstand. Did he put his clothes away carefully or did he leave them thrown over chairs and lying on the rug? These were the things she wouldn't know until after they were married. There were many of his habits she had yet to learn, and these, not just the physical intimacies of the bedroom, were what made marriage such a close relationship. But he would also lie beside her in the bed. Was he a snuggler or would he prefer to sleep apart from her on his own side of the mattress? She'd soon know, and she was ready to adjust to his preferences. Time and experience had taught her it was better not to have any of her own.

While waiting for the steward, she put on her cashmere robe. In another few minutes he returned, carried out the brass tub, and brought in a tray with the other items she had requested.

It was almost midnight when James and the Illinois lawyer finished their discussion with snifters of brandy and a promise to keep in touch. It was late to disturb Leah, but she had especially asked him to stop by. Nor would he sleep well if he didn't kiss her goodnight.

He rapped lightly on the door in case she was already asleep.

"James? Come in."

He opened the door, closed it quietly behind him, and then stood transfixed. The only light in the room came from the lamp on her bedside table. Silhouetted against it, every curve, every indentation, and every ripple of flesh on Leah's body were revealed as she walked toward him. In the brief second before she closed her robe, he saw through the yellow gown the deeper amber of her skin, the rise and fall of her rounded breasts, the rose-tan areolae around her nipples, and the darker shadow between her thighs. He released the breath caught in his throat. The pain of wanting her was so intense, he tightened his grip on the door handle. As much as he'd loved Zadah, she had never inspired such a deep-seated, primeval desire to possess. Nor was it just an urge to sate a physical hunger. This was more. It was a need to have Leah belong to him completely, body and spirit.

"I'm—I'm sorry," he said. "I thought you'd be in bed reading. I should have given you more time after I knocked."

Slowly, purposefully, Leah tied the yellow satin ribbon around her peignoir. Her body was hidden now, but when he closed his eyes, the after-image lingered, tantalizing and drawing him closer.

"No, I was waiting for you." Her long, glistening black hair fell loosely around her shoulders, and her perfume filled his nostrils. Into his mind came a vision of Astarte, pagan goddess of love, and he knew why men worshipped her and went wild at the very mention of her name. "I had the steward bring champagne and a light supper for us," she said.

James forced his eyes away from her and to the table. Champagne was cooling in a silver cooler. Beside it were plates of cold chicken, fresh fruit, and thin slices of bread.

Laughing, Leah pulled him farther into the room. "I

thought we should celebrate the eve of our wedding." She helped him off with his jacket.

"It was a lovely thought, Leah." He willed himself to concentrate on the food and the two places set at the table.

"Then how about opening the champagne. I'd begun to think you weren't coming and I'd have to drink it all myself."

He pulled the bottle from the ice and dried it off with a linen napkin. His hands shook so he could hardly open it or pour it into the glasses she held out for him.

"To us, James, and our future together." She looked invitingly into his eyes.

"To—to a new life." God knew how much he wanted her then, but he was restrained by one desperate fear. Leah had been mistress to a Creole, and James knew the reputation the French had as lovers. Could he satisfy her? With Zadah he'd always had to be cautious, gentle, and restrained while pleading for permission to touch her. If his advances had always left her repulsed and frigid, then somehow he must have failed as a lover. He'd been left not only frustrated but unsure of himself.

Before they had taken more than a few sips, Leah took the glass out of his hand and moved into his arms. Without a word between them, he picked her up and carried her to the bed. There were no preliminary caresses or prolonged kisses. They reached for each other and clung fervently together, surrendering to a passion that obliterated the past.

For a long time James lay silently beside her. Then he leaned up on one elbow, looked into her eyes, and saw himself reflected there. He was searching for something but was afraid of what he might find. "Why, Leah? Why tonight?"

"Tomorrow I will be your wife. Whenever we make love, you might wonder if I want you or if I am being a dutiful wife. I needed you to know it will always be because I want you."

He turned on his side, put one arm across her breasts, and buried his face in her hair. "Oh, God, Leah, I do love you. I know you don't love me yet, but I'll be good to you and do all I know how to make you happy."

"You have already, James," she said, running her hand over his cheek. "You'll never know what having your name means to me. It is a most precious gift."

Leah meant what she said about having James know she really wanted him. But she was also surrendering to him in order to exorcise a demon that haunted her. By going with James, she betrayed Baptiste; worse, she betrayed her love for him. Marriage to James was an honorable act. Only by doing something dishonorable, by allowing James to make love to her before they were married, could she feel no longer worthy of Baptiste.

James got up and began to put on his coat.

"Do you want to go to your stateroom?" Leah asked. "Or—or would you rather stay here?"

James looked at her on the bed. Her gown and peignoir were now pulled modestly down around her ankles, but her face was flushed and her long hair lay in tangles around her shoulders. He felt a new stirring of desire, not to take her immediately as before, but to discover what pleased her and to linger over each caress.

"We won't get much sleep if I stay." He smiled at the beauty that was now his.

"Does it matter? We don't dock until noon."

James removed the rest of his clothes and laid them carefully across a chair. Leah slipped out of her peignoir, but she waited to let him remove her gown. Once more they were in each other's arms, the first frantic passion now gentled to a more leisurely, satisfying embrace. He caressed her breasts, ran his tongue around the nipples, and felt her quiver in his arms. He moved his fingers along her thighs and across her slightly swollen but all the more sensual stomach. Both reveled in the exquisite pain of prolonging the moment when they would seek each other and cling together in the ultimate rapture. Just as Leah tensed for the moment of her release, she felt his love flooding her, and she collapsed in his arms.

"I never knew, Leah," he whispered. "It was never like this before."

"It's meant to be something beautiful, James." He'd said his wife was an invalid. And he was faithful all those years. How he must have yearned for someone to really love him. She might not love him, but she would be a more responsive wife.

"With you, Leah, it is. That and so much more." He'd been a man thirsting for something he did not even know existed, and Leah was the well wherein he drank long and deep each time they came together that night.

By the time the boat slowed down for its stop at Cairo, both James and Leah were up and dressed. James had laughingly kissed her good-bye just before he left for his cabin. "What is the steward going to think when he sees those untouched plates of food?" During the night, they had finished the champagne, but the chicken and fruit lay forgotten.

"I'll wrap the meat in some of this tissue paper, and we can feed it to the fish later. The fruit." Giggling like a schoolgirl who might be caught with a contraband bottle of whiskey, she looked around the room. "I know, I'll put it in one of the drawers. We might enjoy it tonight."

While she dressed, she ate a peach and a pear, all the breakfast she wanted, and left the pit on one plate, the core on another. Having slipped into fresh underclothes, including the new slimmer styled petticoat, she carefully donned the blue silk suit. She gathered her hair into a large, soft bun high on the back of her head and set the jaunty little matching hat over one eye. She brushed a hint of rice powder over her face and sprayed on just a whiff of cologne. James said he could knock at the door when it was time for them to go ashore; but too restless to wait in her cabin, she walked out on deck and stood by the rail. Cairo, at the juncture of the Mississippi and Ohio rivers, was one of the busiest ports along the waterways. She watched the stevedores offloading the massive bales, the huge barrels, and the awkward crates. She smiled at a number of joyous reunions on the wharf. All the while she wondered where James was. They had been in port at least half an hour. Was he taking as much time with his toilette as she had with hers? She laughed to herself at the thought he might wear his new hunting jacket for the wedding. If not exactly the most appropriate attire, it suited him perfectly.

She thought about the night before, and she knew she

had been right to seduce James. There was certainly no other word to describe what she'd done. Her fears he might think her wanton had been laid to rest with his tender and endearing assurances of his love for her. After he confided he'd never before known how wonderful and deeply satisfying lovemaking could be, she knew she'd not been wrong in making the first overtures. She did not doubt their marriage would have been consummated tonight; his desire for her was too evident. But it was right that the first time they came together was with a wild abandon that banished all fears and triggered no memories or comparisons.

Leah had been keeping one eye on the door to James's stateroom, and so she was surprised to see him coming up the gangplank from the wharf. With his hands behind him, he walked up the marble staircase and along the deck to her.

"You look—you look—well, I can't think of the right word," he said haltingly.

"Ravishing?"

"It's certainly appropriate after last night. Are you ready to go? The church is just a short walk from here."

Instead of answering, Leah took his arm, because her mouth was inexplicably dry and she was unable to speak.

He brought his other hand around from behind his back. "Here, for the bride." He handed her a miniature bouquet of sweetheart roses.

"They're beautiful, James." Feeling tears welling in her eyes, she began searching for a handkerchief and then remembered she had no pockets. "Do you have a handkerchief?"

He pulled one from his breast pocket. "Here, let me."

"No, I'd better. I need to blow, too." She was sobbing and laughing at the same time. "That's one thing you'll have to learn. I seldom have one with me when I need it."

Leah watched him tuck it back in his pocket. He looked ruggedly handsome in a dark-brown coat and fawn-colored trousers. He might not be a dandy, but he knew what to wear with his rust-colored hair and massive build.

The church was an easy walk, and the minister was waiting for them. With its austere interior, the small, simple, wooden church was as unlike the magnificent St.

Louis Cathedral as anything she could imagine. The clear windows opened onto the river on one side and onto a garden on the other. The minister's wife and the pianist, who played softly throughout the brief service, were the only witnesses. Yet it was a holy sacrament as binding and as meaningful as if there had been a thousand people in attendance. James spoke in a loud, positive voice, but Leah found she could do no more than whisper the responses. When James slipped the gold band on her finger, she heard Baptiste's voice: "Is it what you really want, Leah?" Yes, yes, it was what she wanted! But she could find no answer to another question: *Then why do I feel like crying?*

Since the boat would be leaving in half an hour, they accepted the good wishes of the minister, his wife, and the pianist and returned to the wharf.

While they were gone, the steward had moved all of James's things into Leah's stateroom and had left another bottle of champagne on the table. A gold-embossed ribbon around the neck of the bottle read: "Congratulations!"

"How do you suppose he knew?" Leah asked.

"Did you want him to think we were starting an illicit affair," James laughed, "when I asked him to transfer my clothes?"

"Well, no, I guess not. But it might have been more fun. Just think how he would have enjoyed gossiping with other stewards and waiters."

"Not on these boats. Promenade flirtations frequently end in brief shipboard affairs, but I would never allow anyone, not even a steward, to think that of you."

"Thank you, James."

While Leah helped him arrange his things for the one more night they'd be on board, they drank the champagne and ate some of the fruit she'd squirreled away. It was their first domestic scene, and it made her feel more married than either their impassioned embraces the night before or the wedding service.

The boat docked at Louisville, and they took the ferry across the Ohio to Indiana. When Leah stepped on the Northern soil that was to be her home, she was filled with trepidation. If only there were some way to shed her past like a snake sheds its skin. She was white now, and she must think like a white. The real test would come when she met James's friends. Like someone perfecting a new language, she knew the words, but she wouldn't really feel at ease until she no longer had to translate in her mind before speaking. She must no longer think or respond as a woman of color, but must think white at all times. Could she, for example, defend Southern traditions as a Louisiana white woman would be expected to do? She must always be on guard yet not let her shield show. Overcome now by real fears, not just apprehension, she reached for James's arm.

They were approaching the railway platform where the train that would take them to Hickory Falls waited. Only a few more hours and she would be riding in a buggy to her new home.

She clutched his arm more tightly. "I can't do it, James. I can't go any farther."

"Yes, you can, darling. There's nothing to fear, and I'll always be close by. People are going to love you as much as I do."

"Your wife's friends?"

"Zadah's been gone a long time, and they—they knew she was an invalid."

"It's not just being a second wife among your old friends." Leah was on the verge of tears.

James reached for his handkerchief. "Here, you look as if you're about to need this."

"Thank you. I must look as miserable as I feel." She sniffed and wiped her eyes. "It's the dual role I have to play. I'm not just a new wife—I've got to be a whole new person."

"In your mind maybe." He reached for the damp linen square. "Here, let me do it. You're smearing soot from the engine all over your cheeks." He moistened one corner of the handkerchief in his mouth, and she raised her face so he could wipe it off. In his eyes she saw tenderness and love and a yearning to protect her. Maybe—maybe everything would be all right.

"To the people you meet now," he said, "you will be the person I introduce, and that's the only person you have to think about." He could not know the depth of her fears, but he was not insensitive to the past that engendered them. Nothing, he swore, nothing must ever bring those fears to fruition or turn nightmares into reality.

"At least," she suggested, "let me pretend to be a widow. Then I'll not have to watch myself about the house or René or—or Baptiste." It was hard to say the name, but she knew there would be times that would evoke it, and she'd best be prepared. "I'll feel better if I can talk naturally about—about things a widow would. Then there'll be no slips and no wondering on their part whether I was married before."

"You're right," he agreed. "It will be natural after the war for you to be a widow."

Yes, it would have been more natural for Baptiste to be killed than to live on as he had. So she must learn to speak in the past tense. She shivered, but it would be easier to mourn one who was dead.

Leah moved forward a few steps. The ground felt no different under her feet. The grass was just as green and the sky just as blue as in Louisiana. She had been looking for something tangible to distinguish Indiana from the South. With so much around her that was familiar, maybe she need not worry about being a different person.

"You are what you think you are." She had to keep those words uppermost in her mind. She was Leah Andrews, wife of a prominent and respected lawyer. "Never look down, Leah," Baptiste had told her in one of her most desperate moments. She lifted her head, rested her hand in the crook of James's arm, and walked beside him to the train.

Chapter Four

AT TWILIGHT SITTING on the gallery at Belle Fontaine, Baptiste gazed across the lawn to the river. Leah had been gone little more than a month, and he wondered how much longer it would be before he stopped missing her so desperately. He wasn't just lonely, though God knew he'd give anything for the sound of her voice. It was worse than that. He felt completely lost, as if he'd been savagely jerked up from all that was familiar and set down in a strange, uncharted land. There were no guideposts to say, "This way to peace and tranquility" or "Watch out, swamp ahead" to steer him around the waters of despair in which he might get bogged down.

As well as feeling lost, he felt as if he'd lost a part of himself. As in the hospital after he lost his legs. Flesh and bones had been sawn off, but with the strange quirks of the human nervous system, there was still pain in them. He felt that way now. Leah was gone, but memory was shot through with pain.

Day after day he'd wheeled himself through all the rooms of Belle Fontaine, as if looking for her even though there was little in any of them to remind him of her.

They'd been stripped by marauding Yankees or fugitive slaves, and the furniture in them now had been selected by Catherine Fouché so that all might be ready for Leah when she was freed from prison. No, nothing bore her touch. Even the floors, roughened by heavy boots and iron horseshoes, had been sanded and refinished. In no way was the house like it was the day he and Leah drove out to it when they finally learned the plantation was to belong to him again.

Yes, there was one room, his sister's small bedroom on the first floor and overlooking the garden, that was not changed. Somehow her narrow wooden bed with its carved tester rails had been overlooked by those pillaging during the war. Even her coverlet and patchwork quilt remained. It was the one room Baptiste never entered now. On that bed, on that afternoon many months earlier, he and Leah had lain and made love. He would never forget her remark as they dressed: "I feel as if I've come home, too."

During the day, Baptiste managed to keep busy supervising the work in the cane fields, adjudicating arguments among the workers, and studying the account books.

In twos and threes many of Belle Fontaine's former slaves had returned when he sent out word he needed field hands again. The men were free now, but more free to starve than to find work, so they listened avidly to his plan. He had the land, and he had enough money to plant the fields and provide for them and their families until the first cane crop came in. There were some cabins still standing that could be repaired, and more could be built. Houses and land for gardens, that's all he'd been able to promise them. When the crop was harvested and sold, they would all share in the profits. Would they agree to that? He had the land and needed laborers; they could provide the labor, but had no land to work. Each would be supplying what the other needed.

Most of them agreed. They knew how to work the fields, and they had families who were hungry.

"It be 'nuf for us, M'sieu Fontaine, suh," most of them said. "We sho' nuf knows de land, and it be better than what we been doin' in town."

"It's share and share alike," Baptiste had told them. "A good crop and we all benefit. A poor one, and—well, it'll be a long winter. But I can promise you this. You will have a house, food, and plenty of fuel."

The workers had not disappointed him. They returned to the fields as if it had been only a few months rather than years since they'd plowed and planted and harvested the acres of sugarcane around Belle Fontaine.

Within two months, the fields had been planted and all of the cabins finished or in final stages of construction, with a small vegetable garden by each. Then Baptiste made a suggestion that would have been unheard of before the war. They were to elect their own overseer from among themselves. A man they could trust and who could also work with Baptiste. He would get a larger share because of the responsibility, so they must be sure to choose wisely. Baptiste nodded his approval at the man they selected. Septimus, a former field hand, had been one of the best workers. The gardens were already beginning to produce, and the cane crop looked to be a bountiful one.

The money Baptiste received from his former father-in-law for a section of land adjoining the older man's plantation would last through the next year if all went well. The families in the snugly built cabins could live from their own gardens. In the fall they would butcher the hogs that grew fat in the swampy fenced-in area, and the chickens were producing enough eggs to eat and keep the poultry yards full. They might even be able to sell several crates of chicks as well as four or five hogs and add to the cash the cane crop brought in. Baptiste didn't think any of the returned ex-slaves would complain about the bargain they'd entered into.

Yes, daytimes were not bad. Mornings he was usually in his library office, and afternoons he drove around as much of the plantation as he could in the buggy. Benji was still trying to engineer a saddle that would allow him to ride horseback again.

"M'sieu Fontaine, suh."

"Benji! What have I told you?"

"Baptiste then, but only iffen nobody's around." Benji was upset. This informality between them wasn't right; it wasn't the way he'd been brought up and trained. A master was a master whether one was a slave or a servant.

"And no *iffen* either. Damn! You can speak as well as I do, and you know it."

"I've almost forgotten how," Benji acknowledged. "It wasn't wise to speak correctly when the Yankees were around. They thought I was being uppity."

"So jog your memory. What is it you wanted?"

Benji knew why Baptiste spoke crossly. He'd been thinking about Leah. If only he'd fall in love and get married. Not likely he would though, if they stayed out here in the country. In New Orleans were the places where folks his age went for socializing. M'sieu DeLisle, now, he could have found someone for him. But no, they had to come out here with nothing for company but moccasins and crickets. Benji shook his head.

"You've been here since late afternoon," Benji said. "I thought you might like a cool drink and something to eat. Bourbon?"

"Thank you, Benji, I would." If it weren't for Benji, he'd probably never eat or go to bed when he should.

Benji. How many years did they go back? Since they were ten? Eight? Almost as long as he could remember. Benji was the grandson of Marcus, their old butler. His mother was Marcus's daughter, but his paternity had never been determined. Most certainly it was white or at least quadroon. For a time, Baptiste had suspected his own father, which would make Benji his half-brother, until he realized that the elderly Fontaine was rigidly moral. He was not one of those slave owners who procured new slaves free by begetting them on the young women in Cabin Row.

Benji might not be his brother, but they had been as close as two sired by the same father. Only a few months younger than Baptiste, Benji had been part of the plantation scene since both were toddlers, but Baptiste's first memory of their friendship was the day they watched the breeding of a favorite stallion and mare. Baptiste looked out over the river. He could recall that day and the resultant events as if it were yesterday, yet he had been only ten years old.

When Baptiste had arrived at the stable yard, Benji, a stable hand training under the strong, swift hand of Big

Jim, was already there. This was to be Benji's first lesson in the art of controlled breeding, and he was expected to watch closely. Baptiste had come because his father had promised him the foal from this mating.

The two boys nodded to each other, climbed on the fence, perched on the top rail, and tucked their feet behind the middle one. The mare was already in the yard, neighing an urgent mating call. Louis Fontaine, Baptiste's father, and Big Jim were trying to calm her while waiting for a stable boy to lead out the stallion. Knowing he'd be expected to remember everything and be prepared to answer Big Jim's catechism afterward, Benji was so tense he had to scramble down from the fence and relieve himself behind the stable. Almost tripping over his own feet, he rushed back and sat with his legs dangling. So far the two boys had merely glanced surreptitiously at each other but didn't say anything. For each of them this was a far too important, momentous occasion to be diluted with boyish nonsense.

When Job, the stable boy, brought Beau Geste to the breeding pasture, he made the mistake of leading the horse out of the stable upwind from Fancy Lady, instead of taking him around the length of the building to the far gate and downwind from the mare. The stallion immediately caught the scent; his nostrils flared and his ears pricked up as he began snorting and pawing the ground. Trying to release Job's hold on the bridle, he shook his head wildly. When that didn't work, the horse reared up, jerked the skinny boy off the ground, and tossed him back down. Poor Job was half crazy between trying to stay on his feet while keeping out from under the forelegs of Beau and preventing the horse from injuring himself. The horse's safety was his greatest concern. He didn't fear a broken leg as much as he did a whipping from Big Jim.

Louis Fontaine continued to hold the mare, now even more aroused by the sight and scent of the stallion, while Big Jim raced over and grabbed the bridle from Job. Digging into the hard ground with his calloused feet and using both hands on the bridle, Big Jim managed to keep Beau from rearing up again. The stallion hit out with his forelegs and threatened to strike the trainer. If that happened,

97

Big Jim would fall directly between the front legs, an easy target for Beau's deadly hoofs.

As the trainer spoke to him, Beau gradually calmed down enough to be led to the mare. The men could easily have fled the pasture and allowed nature to take its course, but with a nervous mare and an impatient stud, there was danger Fancy Lady would be injured by the flailing hoofs or a too-hasty mounting. She was too valuable a brood mare to let that happen.

Both boys sat far forward on the fence rail. Baptiste thought about the promised foal and hoped his father wouldn't decide to halt the breeding. Benji began to think about whether he really wanted to become a stable hand—a definite step up from working the cane fields—or return to the rigorous labor of a field hand. At least the only danger there was being bitten by a moccasin, and that he could avoid if he were careful. Ain't no way, he thought, to keep from handling a wild horse if he stayed at the stables.

Louis got the mare into position, and Big Jim led the stallion up to her. But now Fancy Lady was skittish. Each time Beau started to mount her, she bucked, forcing him off her and increasing his frustration. Louis called Big Jim over and suggested they both hold the mare steady, release the stallion's bridle, and let him approach her in his own way. At last Beau completed a successful mount, and Baptiste prayed Fancy Lady was impregnated. The stables on the plantation were filled with horses, but this foal would be his very own.

However, just as the stallion dismounted, Fancy Lady bucked one more time and kicked him between his hind legs. Roaring with pain, Beau raced around the pasture.

Tense from watching the horses, Benji began to slide back and forth on the top rail, until suddenly he tumbled off and landed on the thick grass inside the fence. Stunned by the fall, he lay a minute before shaking himself and moving to get up. Prepared to jump down and make sure Benji was all right, Baptiste was unaware of what was happening in the far end of the pasture where his father and Big Jim were leading the mare to a gate.

Not until he heard the pounding of hoofs and saw a flash of color did Baptiste realize that Beau was racing toward Benji. He jumped down but not in time to move Benji out of the way before Beau reared and came down with both feet on the arm Benji was using to brace himself. As the stallion retreated before attacking again, Baptiste rolled Benji under the lower rail and out of further danger. Baptiste climbed to the top rail and dropped to the other side where Benji was moaning in anguish from a broken arm.

For a moment all was confusion. Then Louis waved Baptiste into the pasture to help him and Job capture the stallion while Big Jim first led the mare to the stables and then ran to attend to Benji. It was a good half-hour before the stallion was cornered, gentled down, and led back to his stall. To Baptiste it was more like an eternity. He'd never been so exhausted in his life. Big Jim was in the stable to rub Beau down.

"How's Benji?" Baptiste asked him.

"He be all right. Only his arm is broke. I done set that. He had the liver scared outta him, das all."

"And Fancy Lady?"

"She all right, too. Don't know iffen she'll foal. Might. Might not. Jus' have to wait and see."

Benji lay on a pile of hay, his arm splinted between two narrow boards and bound with ragged strips of cloth. His white teeth showed in a broad grin, but drops of sweat glistened on his brown face. Baptiste collapsed beside him.

"Hurt much?" he asked.

"Like hell!" Benji said. "But I'd rather be hurt than daid. Ya coulda bin gentler when ya shoved me under the rail. Think I cracked a rib or two. But at least," he motioned Baptiste down close to him, "at least I won't have to do no work 'round here for a few weeks. Ooooh!" He let out a deep moan for Big Jim's ears.

Baptiste pulled a sliver of straw through the gap between his front teeth. "Boy, Benji, that Beau is some horse. Races across the pasture as smooth as the wind."

Benji snorted. "Mebbe so, but he don' kick like no wind. Guess I'd be daid iffen it warn't for you." Then he gulped twice and said, "Thank ya." The words came hard for him.

"Just did what came natural." Baptiste spat out the piece of straw and picked up a fresh one.

That was an important day in their lives. Later, there was a foal, but more important, it was the beginning of real companionship between the two boys.

When Benji's arm was healed, they sneaked off to the deep swamp to fish for bream, check out 'possum and 'coon dens, and catch baby 'gators in the mud-bank nests while Mama 'Gator was off feeding. Benji found a leaky flatbottom someone had abandoned at the edge of the swamp, and as long as one baled while the other poled, it took them wherever they wanted to go.

"What in hell you got there, Benji?" Baptiste asked one morning when they met at their usual secret rendezvous, a huge live oak at the end of Cabin Row.

"Who? Him? That Unc' Willie." Slouching along behind Benji was the most bedraggled-looking mongrel Baptiste had ever seen. Lop-eared and long-tailed, the small white dog was spattered with various-sized black spots and had one large, almost perfectly shaped, solid-black circle on his rump at the base of his tail.

"What's the matter with him?" Baptiste asked. "He can't hardly move."

"Ain' nuttin' the matter wid him. He jus' tired. He been courtin' all night. He keep all de she-dogs happy."

When Baptiste knelt down to inspect this Casanova of the cabin dogs, he looked into the biggest, most soulful brown eyes he'd ever seen. At that moment he lost his heart completely to the mutt, in whose blood flowed all the strains of international dogdom. Like any good Southern aristocrat, he probably had relatives in all parishes of Louisiana.

"I done brung him to you," Benji said with a twinkle. "For savin' my life."

"Thank you, Benji. He's the finest gift I've ever received. Does he hunt?"

"Do he hunt! Jus' wait. C'mon, Unc' Willie, let's go after 'possum."

As if he knew exactly what Benji was saying, Unc' Willie pricked up his ears and began sniffing the narrow path to the swamp.

"Ain' but two things gonna make him ack like that," Benji said. "The sight of a she-dog or the scent of the swamp. Elsewise he kinda lazy and no 'count. But he a good dog. Do whatsomever you tell him."

The boys and Unc' Willie followed the narrow, winding, vine-tangled path to the mud bank where the boat was tied up. Baptiste stopped, pulled out his pocketknife, and bent down to cut a short black sapling growing straight up from the ground. Knobby but barren of twigs and leaves, it would make a good stick for whacking at things.

"Dear Jesus, Baptiste! Oh, Lordy," Benji screamed, "don' do that!"

"Don't do what?" Baptiste asked, cutting through the last quarter-inch of wood and trying out his new weapon on a limp spiderweb.

"You done it! You done done it now," Benji wailed.

"Damn it, Benji, done what?"

"Gawd, Baptiste, ain' you know better than to cut de devil's walkin' stick? Now he send all his haints after us."

"That's a bunch of bullshit, Benji. Just superstition."

"No, it ain't. Look there at his horns," and Benji pointed to the pair of elongated terminal buds at the tip. "Iffen you throws it as far as you can, turn around three times, and spit till your mouf's dry, mebbe you rid yo'self of his curse."

"And if I don't?"

"I ain' goin' no farther."

"Oh, all right, if it'll make you happy." Baptiste threw the stick away but refused to go through the incantations.

Mumbling about dumb white folks who didn't believe what haints could do to them, Benji reluctantly followed Baptiste toward the swamp.

Dank and gloomy to the uninitiated with its twilight darkness brightened only in the rare open spaces among the cypress, dogwood, water oak, gum, and pine, the swamp was a place of unequaled beauty to the boys. They poled their way easily around bulbous cypress knees, half-submerged stumps, and small islands with great clumps of fern, holly, and bay. They floated among gigantic water lily pads with their fragrant white and yellow flowers whose aroma mingled with that of decaying wood and muddy water. Long tendrils of Spanish moss—the age-old gray beards of ancient cypress—brushed their faces; and brittle fingers of leafless twigs plucked at their shirts as they glided close to an island of dogwood.

A fallen log, decorated like an old soldier with sparkling, medal-shaped fungus, was surrounded by an honor guard of golden violets and wild pink azaleas. Among the dead branches resting on the water were three small turtles, lazily enjoying the rare pleasure of the warm sun on their backs as they watched the boat glide by.

"Shall we catch one?" Benji asked.

"Naw, leave 'em be," Baptiste said. "They look too comfortable to disturb."

They passed a tree from which a small, gray, bright-eyed 'possum as surprised as the boys to find himself awake at mid-day, grinned down at them. In another second he twitched his pointy nose, wrapped his rat tail around the branch, and fell asleep.

"Down, boy," Benji said, patting Unc' Willie, who'd begun panting at the scent of his favorite prey. "We ain' huntin' 'possums today."

Farther along they disturbed a family of silver-blue skink feeding on insects along the branch of an old water oak. The tiny lizards turned and slithered back to their nest under the bark of the dying tree.

"You bring the fishing poles?" Baptiste asked.

"I forgot 'em," Benji said apologetically. "I was tryin' to round up Unc' Willie for you, and I jus' forgot 'em."

"Damn, Benji. How're we gonna fish without no poles?"

"We can hunt," he said, shamefaced.

"You bring a gun?"

"You know I ain't 'lowed to have no gun."

"So what do we hunt with?" Baptiste asked disgustedly.

"We can look for a 'gator nest."

"Yeah, like last time when Mama 'Gator chased us all the way to the boat and hissed at us while her jaws opened and closed like one of Big Jim's steel traps."

"Well, I done tol' you to drop her youngun while you ran. That's all she wanted."

"I couldn't slow down long enough. I was too scared."

Baptiste started laughing so hard, Benji was afraid he'd turn the boat over.

"What you laughin' 'bout?"

"The day I brought that baby 'gator home. Oh, lordy,

Benji, you shoulda been there. I didn't know where to keep it out of sight of Mama, so I put it in the washbowl in my room." Baptiste was now laughing so hard he couldn't talk.

"So," Benji said, "what so funny?"

"Aunt Sookie sent Lucybelle up with hot water just before supper. You could hear her scream all over the house when she went to pour water into the bowl for me. She dropped the pitcher and made it back down two flights to the kitchen in three seconds flat."

"Hot damn!" Benji exclaimed. "Sho wisht I been there. What happened next?"

"Well, that ain't so funny. My mother came in from her room and told me in no uncertain terms to 'get that varmint out of my house.' It's the only time in my life I heard her raise her voice. Then my father came in carrying his razor strop. And you know what he did? He actually made me pull down my pants. He some more blistered my behind so's I was sore for a week."

"No more 'gator hunts?" Benji asked.

"Yah, let's go see. Nothing else to do."

They found one nest with baby 'gators so young some weren't all the way out of their shells. Knowing Mama 'Gator wouldn't be very far away, they kept a wary eye out for her while they watched the little ones wiggling and squirming in a convoluted mass of tiny heads and tails.

"They no bigger'n a minute," Benji said.

"No, but I'll bet they can already bite."

"Where's Unc' Willie?" Benji sat up suddenly.

"He's right around here someplace."

"We gotta find him quick. Ain' nothin' a 'gator likes to eat better'n a dog."

Praying Unc' Willie hadn't taken a notion to go for a swim, the two boys scrambled along the mud bank and through the underbrush. On land the dog could outdistance a 'gator without becoming winded; but in the water, the 'gator was a sure winner every time. Baptiste climbed the trunk of an oak bent low out over the water. He hoped that from there he could spot the dog, but no luck. As he turned around, he came face to face with a water moccasin. Baptiste couldn't move ahead, but he didn't want to drop into the water for fear he'd fall among some of the snake's friends. Why had he forgotten his gun? He never went into the swamp without it.

So far the moccasin hadn't moved any closer, but Baptiste knew that, unlike other snakes which wouldn't attack unless provoked, a moccasin was always looking for a fight. His safety lay in not antagonizing the snake by even the slightest move, but he wondered how long he could remain on the tree in a standoff. He didn't like snakes, and he especially didn't like being within breathing distance of one. What he wouldn't give for a stout stick or a fish jumping in the water to divert the snake's attention. Hell! If he just hadn't listened to dumb Benji and his dumb superstitions, he'd have a good, strong weapon right now. On second thought, maybe he should have turned around three times and spit. He sure was cursed by something.

The moccasin moved slightly and raised its heavy, triangular head. It could be getting ready to strike, and Baptiste wondered just how fast he could move to avoid its deadly bite.

So intently was Baptiste watching the viper, he didn't see another head rising up behind it. Not finding Unc' Willie, Benji came back to check with Baptiste, but he didn't see him either. For a minute he panicked. Then he looked along the trunk of the water oak and really got scared. Baptiste was his friend; no, he was more like a brother, and he had to do what he could to help him. Cottonmouths were deadly mean, and had to be snuck up on. Benji began crawling along the sloping tree trunk and doing his best to keep it from swaying. He carried a heavy stick, and he prayed he'd be able to hit before the snake struck.

Just before he got close enough to raise the stick and whack it down on the moccasin's head, Benji saw the snake rise up. The boy froze. He was not afraid of the snake turning on him but of causing it to spring toward Baptiste. If he could inch along just a little closer, he might have a chance to save his friend. When he saw Baptiste's sickly grin, Benji took that chance. With one quick movement he slid just the distance he needed and brought the stick down at the same time. It worked. Benji and Baptiste collapsed on the trunk and sweat poured off their bodies. They didn't know whether the snake was dead or had just been knocked off the tree, but they didn't wait to find out. Scrambling down, they got as far away as they could while still looking for Unc' Willie.

"Lordy, but that was a mighty fine cottonmouf," Benji said.

"Fine! Whatta ya mean, fine?"

"I mean it sho' was a big 'um."

"Well, you saved my life, so now we're even. Maybe I'll give Unc' Willie back to you. If we ever find him. Damn, where's that mutt gotten to?"

"I jus' hope he ain' headed back toward that 'possum we seed. He gonna get lost sure'n my name Benji."

"Think we oughta pole back up that way?" Baptiste suggested.

"Well, we ain' seen him, and I don' hear him."

The boys walked solemnly back to the skiff, neither one wanting to voice the fear that Unc' Willie had become a victim of Mama 'Gator.

When Benji stepped into the boat, Baptiste heard him whooping and hollering.

"What's the matter, Benji?"

"That no-'count dog is laying right here sound asleep. Where you been, boy? Why you make us run all 'round lookin' for you?"

"Watch how you talk to my dog, Benji. He's got more sense than us. Knows better than to fool around with 'gators."

Baptiste shifted position in his chair on the gallery and lit another cigar. Benji should be coming with that promised bourbon and food. Focusing on the past again, Baptiste remembered that whenever Unc' Willie didn't respond to his whistle in the morning, he headed down the dirt road to the cabins where he knew he'd find the mutt doggin' around with his mongrel cronies. They might be chasing squirrels, sashaying after rabbits, or just leaving their calling cards at every tree and fence post. Unc' Willie liked to assert his independence now and then, but he always came loping up when Baptiste appeared. His big brown eyes begged his master's forgiveness for having run away and his tail curved between his legs in abject humility. Then he'd roll over on his back, his legs up with paws folded over, so Baptiste could scratch his stomach.

"I know, boy," Baptiste always soothed him, "you need to see your friends now and then. Let's go get Benji and see what we can find for breakfast."

At regular intervals Unc' Willie would disappear for three or four days; but after the first time, Baptiste didn't worry.

"He just off on a courtin' spree," Benji said. "Probably smelled somethin' interestin' on the next plantation. He be back."

"You sure?"

"Sure I'm sure. Jus' wait and quit frettin'."

Four days had gone by with no sign of the dog. On the morning of the fifth day, Baptiste and Benji saw Unc' Willie drag himself up the driveway and collapse at the foot of the steps. He'd lost so much weight his skin hung slack around his ribs, and his fur was matted with blood and dirt. Briars clung to his tail, and his ears were chewed up as if they'd been caught in a cotton gin. When Baptiste spoke to him, he painfully opened one eye, but he couldn't lift his head.

"He's hurt, Benji. He's dying."

"He been in a fight, that's for sure. But that ain't all his blood. Some other dog's worsen off than him. He ain' cut up enough to lose all that blood. Jus' wash him off, you'll see."

"But look at him," Baptiste said. "He can't move. He ain't hardly breathing. Are you sure he ain't dying? Maybe he's sick."

"He ain' sick. He jus' plumb exhausted. Hee-hee," Benji snickered. "Ain' I done tol' you he a gen-u-wine pussy hound?"

Unc' Willie continued to go on courting sprees, but he always returned. Baptiste thought about the many fine 'possum hunts they'd shared. The dog was also good at alerting them to the danger of rattlesnakes. Whenever he caught the scent of one, he began to tiptoe stiff-legged, his warning to step carefully and keep eyes open.

Good old Unc' Willie, Baptiste thought. After he'd begun to suffer from heart trouble, he was allowed to stay in a basket near the parlor fireplace. Baptiste laughed to himself, remembering the dog's last days. Undaunted by pain or weak legs, he'd crawled out of the wicker basket and gone off on his last romantic adventure. He'd come home two days later and died a happy dog.

Just then Benji's footsteps sounded on the front stairs and through the hall.

"Where's my bourbon? It was your idea, and now you've forgotten all about it."

"No time for bourbon. There's trouble, boss." Benji had finally reached a compromise satisfactory to his pride and his position. Forbidden to address Baptiste as *sir,* he couldn't bring himself to call him by his first name. *Boss* had a friendly but proper ring to it.

"What kind of trouble?" Baptiste was immediately alert. Things had been going smoothly, maybe too smoothly.

"At the cabins. That no-'count Jeremiah who refused to come back and work for you is down there. He's riling everybody up. Telling them they should demand wages, not work on shares."

"Did you tell him he was trespassing?"

"You think he's gonna listen to me? Called me a white man's nigger."

"What do you suggest?" Baptiste asked. Trouble like this could ruin everything they'd been working for. With no one to work the crops and cut the cane, the plantation couldn't continue operating.

"You gotta go down there yourself."

"How? In my wheelchair? That would make quite an impression on him, wouldn't it?" God damn, whenever he was just about reconciled to his handicap, something always cropped up to frustrate him.

"I been working on the saddle today," Benji said. "You want to try it?"

"Think I can stay on?" Baptiste had been both excited and apprehensive about the prospect of riding again.

"Well, the straps might not be adjusted just right. That's gonna take some time and work, but ain't no way that Jeremiah's gonna leave 'less you go down there with a gun."

"Not a gun, Benji. I don't want any killing."

"He's worse'n any moccasin you done tussled with. He ain't gonna give you no warning."

In spite of the dire situation, Baptiste smiled to himself. Had Benji also been remembering that day in the swamp? The old incident gave Baptiste an idea.

"I won't carry a gun, but you're going to back me up with one."

"Me? A gun?"

"Don't look so innocent, Benji. You're not a slave now, and I know you had one out West. Go get my rifle. And remember, if you have to shoot it, aim to kill. We won't give him a second chance. But only," he stressed the point, "only if he draws on me. You stay in the shadows with the gun cocked so he can't see you."

It took several minutes for Baptiste to get mounted safely and comfortably in the saddle. An ingenious combination of straps kept his artificial legs attached to the stirrups, and he pressed his thighs tightly against the horse's body. The muscles were still too weak to be depended on, but daily practice would soon correct that. God, but it was good to feel a horse under him again. He'd have to walk the horse. It would be a good while before he dared try even a slow trot, but at least he was no longer dependent on that damned buggy to get around the plantation.

The dirt road to the cabins was no more than two hundred yards long. Baptiste walked the horse slowly so Benji could follow him easily on foot. Once they reached Cabin Row, there were plenty of places where Benji could conceal himself and still see everything that transpired.

Jeremiah, more white than Negro, stood on a chair in a small open plot fronting on the cabins. In the light from a bonfire, his yellow skin glistened with sweat and his small black eyes shone with fury. He was ranting like a madman, extolling the virtues of a regular wage and berating his listeners for allowing themselves to be forced back into slavery. Dressed like a dandy in plum-colored coat, flowered satin waistcoat, and dark-green trousers, he was a startling contrast to those wearing homespun and denim.

Baptiste stopped a few yards short of the gathering and listened in the darkness to what the rabble-rouser was saying.

"What you live in? Cabins! Just like before. And who lives in the big house with servants to wait on him? *Mon-*

sieur Fontaine." He spat out the words. "And what do you eat? What you grub yourselves from these pitiful gardens. Do you work when you want to? No! When he orders it. And you think you're going to get your share when the crop is sold? Fools! That's what you are. Fools! He gonna deduct for the cabins, for the food you eat, and for the clothes you wear. And he gonna get it all. All of it, I say! You better listen to me or you're gonna find chains around your ankles and brands on your faces again."

"Yes, suh!"

"Dat's right."

"He speak the truf."

"You, Maryanne." Jeremiah pointed an accusing finger at an older woman who crouched nearby. "Why you got that bandana on your head?"

"It—it comfortable."

"No, it ain't. It's habit! And the mark of a slave. Tear it off your head!"

Baptiste chose that moment to ride in among them. Maryanne's hand stopped in midair. She cowered as fearfully as if she'd seen a haunt. On the rest of the faces Baptiste saw startled bewilderment at the sight of him on horseback. It was truly as if he'd returned from the dead. With his thumb, he slowly and deliberately pushed his flat-crowned, wide-brimmed hat back on his head. He twirled his cigar with the other hand and spat out a shred of tobacco at Jeremiah's feet.

In a deep, low, controlled voice—cooler than the temper flaring up inside him—he spoke to Jeremiah. "You're trespassing. Get off my land and don't come back."

"You can't make me," Jeremiah sneered. "These are my friends. Or are they being held against their will and not allowed to have visitors?"

"Any one of them is free to go anytime he wishes."

"I don't believe it." Now Jeremiah spat and hit Baptiste's horse on the rump, startling him so, he nearly threw his rider. Baptiste had to clutch the pommel without appearing to do so.

"I am not here to argue with you," Baptiste said, "but to tell you to get going." He turned to those sitting on the ground and standing under the trees. "Any of you want to leave with him?"

109

"No, suh."

"No, we stay."

They were swayed too easily by words, Baptiste thought. They were ready to say whatever they thought someone more powerful wanted to hear. But he knew why. Throughout their lives, during slavery and Federal occupation, they'd never dared to raise their voices in protest.

"All right now," Baptiste told Jeremiah. "I said to leave and I meant it. And I don't want you back here again. Next time I'll say it with a shotgun. Anyone else want to follow, let them go now." He finally raised his voice. "Right now!"

Jeremiah walked toward his horse and buggy. "You'll be sorry, *Monsieur* Fontaine. You've won this round, but there are other ways to persuade these people. You haven't seen the last of me yet." He cracked his whip over the horse's flanks and drove off.

Most of the workers hurried back to their cabins; a few moved more slowly, but none followed Jeremiah. Baptiste was surprised. More than that, he was worried. Jeremiah might have gone, but he left his voice behind, and that could mean trouble in the fields. He heard Benji uncock the rifle, and Baptiste waited for him to catch up. At least he hadn't needed the gun.

"I'll take that bourbon now, Benji," he said once they were back at the house and he was settled in the library. "Bring the bottle and that food you promised me. You might as well stay and share it with me."

Benji brought the tray, but he shook his head when Baptiste offered him a glass.

"Sit down," Baptiste ordered, "and take this. I think we've got a long night ahead of us, and we might as well wait it out together."

"If you say so, boss. I got a bit edgy handling that rifle. Jeremiah had a gun in his belt under his jacket."

"I know. I saw it. But he's a coward, cunning as a snake but a coward. He wouldn't do anything overt that could land him in trouble, but I'm sure he's going to try something sneaky. Do you trust Septimus?"

"Best man on the place," Benji said. "I was glad when he was elected overseer."

"I felt the same way," Baptiste said. "I told him to keep

an eye on things tonight and let me know if he spotted even a hint of trouble. That's why I want to stay up a while. And want you to keep me company. I may need to ride again."

"Glad to do it. Want me to get Jessie to make some more sandwiches?"

"Good idea. We may be sitting here a long time."

Benji went to the kitchen and was back in a few minutes.

"You know, Benji," Baptiste said, settling back in his chair, "I was sitting out on the gallery earlier, and remembering some of the things we did together when we were younger. The time you broke your arm, catching 'gators in the swamp, and the fun we had with Unc' Willie."

"God a'mighty, I'd forgotten all about him. He sure loved to hunt." With a drink in one hand and a sandwich in the other, Benji began to relax. With the recollections of their boyhood pranks together, he once again felt more like a companion than a servant to Baptiste. "He loved them girl dogs, too."

"He sure did. Got off his death bed to go courting."

"But I bet he came back smiling," Benji laughed. "Bet you don't remember the hayloft above the stable."

"I bet I do. You were a precocious son of a gun, but it didn't take me long to catch up."

"Don't know what *precocious* means, but if it's got anything to do with having a piece now and then, you are so right."

The two of them looked at each other, began to laugh, and then reminisced over the night that Benji introduced Baptiste to the delights of the fair sex.

Baptiste and Benji had been slumped lazily against the rough wall of the stable, chewing on hard, skinny cigars hand-rolled by Benji from a few dried leaves snitched from one of the field hands.

"You like these?" Baptiste asked.

"Sho'," Benji said. "Let 'em soften up in yo' mouf."

"Ever light them?"

"Naw. Chawin's better."

Baptiste kept working his around in his mouth, but he became irritated at having to spit every minute or two.

"That's it," Benji said. "Chaw and spit. Don' your daddy chaw?"

"Naw, he smokes a pipe."

Still chewing hard, the boys relaxed in the warm spring sun.

"Hey, Baptiste, you dipped your wick yet?"

"Huh?"

"You dipped your wick yet?"

Baptiste sat up. "What are you talking about?"

"Ah, come on, you know." Benji stood up, opened his pants, and proudly showed off his manly accomplishment. "Can you do that?"

"Of course I can," Baptiste frowned. "So what?"

"It's for more than peein' through, you know," Benji said with a wink. "Iffen you ain't had a gal yet, come to the stables tonight, and I'll show you sumpin' mighty fine."

Baptiste thought all afternoon about Benji's suggestion and became more excited with each passing hour. Once he knew his parents were asleep, he tiptoed shoeless down to the kitchen and out the pantry door. When he reached the stables he looked all through the stalls, the tack room, and the storage room, but saw no one. Furious at Benji for fooling him, he turned to leave when he heard scuffling sounds from the hayloft above. He climbed the ladder to where the bales of hay were piled and moved toward the corner from which muffled giggles and heavy panting came. There was almost no light, but he could make out a sort of wall made from piled-up bales. Peering around them, he saw Benji and a girl on a rough croaker sack.

"Hey, boy," Benji said, standing up, "you made it."

"Hello, white boy," the girl greeted him. "Benji says this yo' first go-round. Come on over. I'll show you a good time."

She lay on the sacks with her arms behind her head. In the hazy darkness, Baptiste couldn't see her face, but judging from her arms and legs sticking out from under a faded calico dress, he thought she was about his age.

Baptiste started to open his trousers, when the girl said, "Take 'em off."

Nervous, Baptiste did as she directed. When he entered her soft, warm flesh for the first time, he experienced an ecstasy unlike anything he'd ever imagined, and he let out a low, exultant cry. Long, firm fingers massaged his buttocks in a frantic but soothing rhythm. Then they moved up under his shirt, and broken nails raked his back and shoulder blades. Suddenly, when he thought he couldn't stand it any longer—it was like trying to hold back a scream—he experienced a pulsating release of emotion and energy. With a low moan, he collapsed and rolled over next to the girl. His legs were as weak as when he'd had the fever, but he felt wonderful.

"Hey, boy," Benji said, "you done all right."

Baptiste didn't answer him, just lay on his back. Looking up at and beyond the low ceiling, he concentrated on a single star that glowed through the crack between two boards.

The girl got up and brushed off her skirt.

"Whatcha doin'?" Benji asked, hitching at his pants. "I ain't ready to go yet. How 'bout one more time."

"Well," the girl said, "once more. Then I gotta go. Mammy gonna whip me if I be late."

Not so much from shame as out of respect for another's privacy, Baptiste kept his eyes shut while Benji was occupied.

"Okay, white boy," the girl said, "you want some more?"

Although completely exhausted a few minutes before, Baptiste felt fresh blood surging through his veins, hardening and firming him up again. He knew now he wouldn't sleep unless he experienced another satisfaction of this newfound urge. This time he took over and led the action, and once the movements became familiar, he took masculine pride in knowing he was increasing the girl's pleasure. Even though he again collapsed momentarily, he imitated Benji in standing right up, and he felt more like an experienced man than an ignorant boy.

"See you here tomorrow night," the girl whispered, as she skittered down the ladder.

From then on Baptiste slipped out and hurried to the stables every night. One morning several weeks later, Marcus, the butler, called him into the pantry. "Come here, Baptiste. I know what you been doin' every night. If you're not careful, your daddy will, too."

"How did you know?" Baptiste looked startled.

113

"Benji's my daughter's boy, and I know he slips out at night. Seeing you together so much, I been watchin' you. Don't rush so hard at being a man."

"Yes, sir," Baptiste said. Although he didn't usually say *sir* to a black servant, he'd been taught to respect the older man.

"Just take it easy, Baptiste; don't wear yourself out."

"You started something that night, you know," Baptiste said to Benji.

"It didn't seem to disagree with you none. You was a pretty steady visitor to the cabins till your daddy found out, and then you shifted to Madame Broulé's in town."

"Did I ever tell you about my first visit to her place?"

"No, but I thinks you're going to." The third glass of bourbon made Benji feel like Baptiste's equal.

"I think I was seventeen. And you were right. My father laid down the law about fooling around here on the plantation. Anyway, a group of us dared one another to go to her house as a lark. I was some more overwhelmed with the gaudy opulence of the place. It was filled with ornate furniture and masses of black lace and red satin. Well, you've seen it; you know. And the mirrors! My God, you saw three of yourself every way you turned."

"In the bedrooms?" Benji asked wide-eyed.

"Everywhere, on the ceilings as well as the walls. And that's quite an experience. Anyway, I was feeling pretty daring and was flush with money. I spent the night drinking champagne and sporting with two of the girls."

"Two?"

"Two."

"You was flushed with more than money," Benji said with a grin.

"Until about four in the morning. Then I got sick as a dog. My friends had to half-lead, half-carry me to the carriage. It was a very weak, pasty-faced young man who finally managed to crawl into this house."

"We did have us some good times, Baptiste." Now the name came easily to him. "I'd forgotten a lot of those things."

"Any special one you recall?" Baptiste filled his glass. If

they had to wait together through the night, these recollections were a good way to pass the time.

Benji thought for a minute. "I guess maybe that time we birthed the foal."

"When both my father and Big Jim were away?"

"Yeah. I remember how scared we were."

"I know," Baptiste laughed. "I think you turned a pale gray."

"You can laugh now, but I mean I was scared. She was a valuable mare. There I was, holding her head in my lap while you reached inside her belly."

"I had to turn the foal, didn't I? I'd seen Big Jim do it, but I had no idea what the birth canal would feel like or how I'd know when everything was finally in the right position."

He'd been covered with sweat as well as urine, feces, and bloody fluid from the ruptured birth sack. By swallowing hard, he was able to keep from throwing up. Only Benji's presence enabled him to remain calm and hold his arm steady.

"Dear Jesus," Benji said, "look at that mess of stuff."

"Shut up, Benji. Move around here and keep her legs still."

"Oh, God," Benji moaned, "what we gonna do if she die?"

"She ain't gonna die," Baptiste said, more to reassure himself than Benji. "Didn't I tell you to shut up." *But keep talking,* Baptiste thought, *keep saying something so I won't have to think about what I'm doing.*

"Feel the head yet?" Benji asked.

"I don't know, dammit. How the hell do you tell the difference between the head and rump when it's all just a wet mass."

"Hee, hee, hee," Benji snickered, "you don' usually have that trouble."

"Damn you, Benji. If my hands were free, I'd knock you across the Mississippi."

The mare roared in pain. Benji jumped up, and Baptiste almost lost his hold on the unborn foal.

"Sit down, you fool!" Baptiste yelled. "Hold those legs.

Rump or head, this baby's gotta come out now. Get up and gimme a hand."

With Benji's brown hands next to Baptiste's white ones, they clutched at the first portion of the foal to emerge. It was the rump, but together they eased out a beautiful, perfectly formed colt. They watched almost tearfully as the mare licked her baby clean and thanked them with her eyes.

"Boy, you sure did stink that night," Benji said, looking across at Baptiste, who'd taken off his legs and was trying to find a comfortable position in the chair.

"Well, you weren't no orange blossom yourself," Baptiste snorted.

"But we done a good job. Even Big Jim admitted that."

They were brought harshly back to the present by a loud pounding at the door.

"Go see what that is, Benji." Without waiting for him to return, Baptiste began strapping his legs back on. He knew it was trouble, but what kind he had yet to learn.

"God a'mighty," Benji said, running back to the room. "Most of the cabins is on fire."

"Jeremiah! The bastard! Damn his no-good hide. Even if he ain't here, his hand is. He's behind this. Get me downstairs and back on my horse."

"No, boss." Benji was startled at his own daring, but he went on. "This ain't no time for talking. You're good at that, but we gotta move and move fast." He didn't tell Baptiste that the flames were already threatening the stables and barns. "And that you cannot do."

"Damn you, Benji, are you telling me what I can and cannot do on my own place? We're friends, but don't forget who's still master here. Now get my horse saddled, and I'll be down by the time she's ready."

"You can't. It's too dangerous for you. Any quick turns, any sudden jolt and you'd be off the saddle but caught by the straps." Then he saw the fury in Baptiste's eyes and watched him reach for his riding crop. Baptiste had never hit any of his servants, but Benji knew he was aroused enough now to lash out unthinkingly. "All right. I'm going. But take it easy on the steps. The saddle will take a few minutes."

"Not that much time to waste. Get it on, and I'll be there."

Benji hurried off and Baptiste made his way laboriously across the floor with his crutches. When he reached the top of the stairway that wound down past the lower level to the driveway, he looked down. Time and many feet had eroded hollows into the steps that could send feet flying out from under if one were not careful. He had to place his crutches on the smooth outer edges if he were not to take a nasty spill. Unable to work the crutches and grip the railing at the same time, he had to take time to place each rubber tip exactly right.

He was tired and he was angry; he was worried about the fire and he was furious with Benji for suggesting he shouldn't go. With the second step he almost lost his balance, and he let out a string of oaths. His stumps hurt like hell, the way they always did when he felt frustrated and helpless.

"To hell with these things," he shouted and threw the crutches ahead of him. He heard them clattering a step at a time to the ground. He didn't give a damn if they broke or not. He was sick of being dependent on them and sick to his stomach over the way his body had been mutilated. He gagged every time he thought of the ugly stumps, and he could bear to look at them only when forced to. Now everything he'd put into the plantation was being threatened by that bastard Jeremiah.

Well, none of those things was going to destroy him. He grabbed one rail and lowered himself to the step. By half-sitting, half-sliding he made his way to the bottom like a child just learning to navigate a stairway. And he made it faster than when he was helped by Benji.

"Benji! Is the horse ready?"

"Oh my God!" Benji came running. "Did you fall the whole way? Are you hurt?"

"No, dammit, I'm fine. I didn't fall. Now get me on the horse."

In less than a minute he was mounted, and they were riding toward the cabins. Baptiste saw in an instant that more than one torch had been used to set the fires. The grass, tinder dried to pale-yellow from the hot summer sun, was blazing in several places around the cabins. A number of them already engulfed in flames were past saving. Thank God he had insisted on their planting gardens between the homes or all of them would be gone. What was important now was saving those not yet ignited. The grass near them was already in flames, which had to be put out immediately.

Women stood around screaming and children were crying. A couple of men had a little water in buckets, but they were wasting time by throwing it on the flaming cabins. The rest stood around wringing their hands, or they ran in and out of their homes with articles not worth saving.

"Jessie," Baptiste yelled, "go man that pump. You and you and you," he pointed at three men, "get those buckets over there. Septimus," he called to the overseer, "keep the buckets filled so the men can just pick them up when they bring empty ones back. Let those three cabins go. But get that grass fire out. Now! Don't stand there gaping, move!"

All this time Baptiste was riding around among them, scattering the children toward the main house so they wouldn't get burned, giving orders to the men and women, checking on the spread of the fire, and sending people where they could do the most good.

It wasn't until he felt he had things somewhat under control that he slowed down and then stopped beneath a tree to catch his breath. Only then did he realize his hands had been off the pommel and he'd been gripping the horse's flanks with his thighs the whole time. Now he was no longer just sitting a horse; he was riding it. He began to relax. The cabins would have to be replaced, but there was plenty of time before cold weather set in. Meanwhile, they'd just have to double up. A few of the gardens had been badly burned over. All of this meant he'd have to spend the money he'd been hoarding against a poor cane crop and the need to carry the plantation through another winter. Well, it couldn't be helped.

A red glow caught his eyes. The storehouses! He'd seen no fire near there earlier. He saw Benji waving frantically and Septimus running, followed by two other men. While concentrating on the cabins, they were unaware of the small rivulet of fire that had wound through the dry grass toward the barns and stables. Baptiste wheeled around and headed over that way. There was a good pump outside the stables and another near the barns.

"The stables!" he yelled to Benji. "Check the stables." With all the hay stored in them they'd go up in a blazing explosion if the fire were not stopped in time. "Daniel," he called to a Negro running in answer to Benji's calls, "check the stalls. Should be plenty of water in the troughs and the supply barrels. Douse everything and get the horses out!"

Other men concentrated on the storehouses filled with supplies. Several of the buildings, awaiting the cane harvest, were still empty, and they would be no great loss. The same with the cutting sheds. Once more it looked as if the men might have the fire under control.

He smelled the acrid smoke and felt his eyes stinging before he noticed the flames inside a stable. Even as he put the mare into a trot, he saw that Benji and the others had spotted them and were running toward the stable. Maybe only one stall had caught, maybe Daniel had gotten enough water on the floors to keep the fire from spreading. He saw the horses, prodded from behind, coming out one by one through the dense smoke.

The last one out, a mare in foal, was neighing loudly. Suddenly the neighs became screams of pain, and she began dashing wildly around in circles. Her mane and tail had caught fire. As she ran, the wind spread the flames over her whole body. Trying to escape the searing agony that engulfed her, she went tearing across the open yard.

Baptiste grabbed the pommel, slapped his horse's neck, and raced after her. His legs hurt like hell as he gripped the flanks, but he had to put her out of her misery. He forced his mount into a canter, not daring to wonder if he would be able to stay on. His stumps were rubbed raw by the leather cups. His artificial legs were strapped immobile to the stirrups, but his thighs moved constantly back and forth as he sped along. He'd have to remember to loosen the straps or secure the cups more snugly. He'd been in too much of a hurry to check them carefully.

Now blazing from ears to tail, the mare was still several yards ahead of him. Her speed had so far kept the flames from her muzzle, but Baptiste knew she was running blindly. His sweat-soaked shirt and trousers stuck to his skin, and the salty irritation intensified the jarring pain that speared up his spine with every move. His stomach churned at the sight of the tortured horse and the smell of its burning flesh, and twice he had to pause long enough to throw up. After each stop he urged his mount to move on faster.

Finally he caught up with the mare. She had fallen beside a stream that ran into the river. Even in her agony, she had instinctively headed for water. Still alive and moaning in pain, she looked up gratefully when Baptiste pulled the trigger of his pistol. He'd have her buried in the morning.

Baptiste rode slowly over to a giant oak, leaned forward in the saddle, and threw up the rest of the bourbon and supper.

More slowly still, he walked his mount to where Benji and the others waited. As far as they could tell, the fires were all out, and there were no more hot spots to flare up. The crowd gathered around Baptiste as he rode up. Some of the women were crying, and many of the men were covered with burns. They looked up at Baptiste and waited for him to tell them what to do.

"Thank you," he said, panting for breath, "you did a good job. What you all need now is sleep. Tomorrow we'll start rebuilding, but for tonight— Don't think about that. Those of you who lost homes, go to the house. Benji will find blankets and mattresses." He turned to the cook. "Jessie, check the food supplies. You'll be in charge of getting food to those who lost their gardens."

He looked at each of his people. Not one had hesitated to follow his orders, not one had complained about what was lost or about having to work to save the buildings that were not their homes. He had tried to tell them that as long as they were on shares, the whole plantation belonged to them, not just to him. Until tonight he hadn't thought they understood what he meant.

From the moment he saw the buildings on fire, Baptiste had been consumed with hatred for the man who had done this. One thought alone had dominated all his actions, a thought challenged only momentarily by a flicker of doubt as to whether he could succeed. Now, having put

120

the mare out of her misery, that doubt had been extinguished by the pain in the horse's eyes.

Benji walked up, his face blackened almost beyond recognition, most of his clothes burned away. In spite of that, he spoke in an optimistic tone. "It ain't gonna take long to rebuild. We didn't lose that much."

"But we could have," Baptiste grimaced.

"Yes, if you hadn't been down here. I was wrong," Benji shook his head, "but I still don't see how you did it."

"By gritting my teeth and cussing every minute. God damn, but I hurt."

"You think it was Jeremiah?" Benji asked. "I do."

"I know it was."

"You think he'll try again?"

"No." Baptiste said nothing more for the moment.

"If he thinks he's won these people over, he's dead wrong. They're madder'n hell at what happened tonight. Ain't nothing he could have done to get them all behind you more than setting those fires. And then the way you rode down here. Hell, you got 'em all with you. You can sleep easy."

"Not yet." Baptiste pulled out his watch. It was nearly four in the morning. "Help me down and put this saddle on a fresh horse, one least exposed to the smoke."

"What you aimin' to do now?" Under the soot Benji's face was wrinkled with concern.

"I'm going hunting."

"This time of night? You crazy or something? What you gonna hunt in black dark?"

"Very special game—a two-legged, yellow-bellied son of a bitch."

"No, Baptiste! You're dead on your feet. You'll never find him now, and if you do—"

"I want a horse, Benji. And I want a canteen of wine, some biscuits, and my deer gun. Now!"

The fury in Baptiste's eyes put speed into Benji's tired legs. "Should know better than to argue with him," he muttered to himself as he ran. "But he's gonna get killed, and I can't stop him."

"Oh, Lordy, what we gonna do?" Jessie moaned when Benji asked for wine and biscuits. "Do Jesus, who gonna take care of us iffen Mistuh Ba'tiste get killed?"

"We ain't studyin' on that." Benji's calm voice belied the dread in his heart. "He be back by sunup. Just wait. At sunup he be here."

Morning dawned and still no Baptiste. Throughout the long dreary day, the men and women labored to clear up the remains of the fire and set things to right as best they could. While they worked they sang spirituals and stopped occasionally to look toward the long avenue of trees. For the first time in her life, Jessie remained in the kitchen and cooked without singing or issuing orders. Save for the sounds of lap babies suckling at their mothers' breasts and the knee babies shuffling on the brick floor of the kitchen, all was silent. Everyone knew the danger Baptiste faced in hunting down Jeremiah. Only Jessie and Benji, however, were aware of the greater danger for Baptiste if he met and killed his quarry. Before the war, if a Negro killed a white man—whatever the reason—he was hunted down and hanged. Now, under the Federal laws, no white man dared kill a Negro—whatever the reason—without fear of immediate reprisal. If Baptiste were successful, word of how Jeremiah died must never get beyond the plantation.

Finally, as dusk became dark, Baptiste rode silently into the yard where Benji and Septimus had been keeping a mournful vigil. In another minute, Baptiste was surrounded by all of his people, their faces alert with the unasked question.

Still sitting erect in the saddle, Baptiste threw down a gaudy, plum-colored jacket. "The rat is skinned. There is his hide. No one—no one!—takes what belongs to Baptiste Fontaine."

With that he let Benji help him off the horse, and he collapsed on the ground, bereft of the final modicum of willpower that had kept him going the last few miles.

Once settled in the library with a bite to eat and a snifter of brandy, Baptiste found his strength returning.

"How did you do it?" Benji asked.

"I don't know, Benji. As God is my witness, I don't know. It was a job that had to be done, and I did it. But that's all I'm going to say about it, so don't ask any questions."

Benji nodded. The less anyone knew, the safer they'd all be. "Need any help getting to bed?"

"No, but I'll tell you what I do need. Go get Regina. I'm master of the house now, with no father to shake his finger at me."

"Yes, suh!" Benji shouted. They'd had a rough night, he thought, as he walked to the cabins, but at least it had allowed Baptiste to forget Leah for a few hours. Maybe Regina would continue to help ease that loss.

Baptiste wheeled himself into his room and prepared for bed. He ached so intensely he could hardly get out of his clothes. It hurt just to raise his arms or pull off his trousers. The raw and swollen stumps were almost too painful to touch, but he smoothed on some salve and bound them loosely in linen cloths. Then he slid naked between the cool sheets, fragrant with the spicy sachets Jessie kept in the linen closet. He remembered when Leah first came to his apartment and teased him about being a dandy because of his scented soaps and sweet-smelling linens. But he told her in no uncertain terms that he preferred pleasant odors to the stink of sweat.

He waited in the dark for Regina. The memory of her swaying hips and her full breasts straining against her tight blouse stirred him up. It was time for him to stop playing monk and resume a normal life. Leah was gone, but there were others to take her place. All he wanted was a warm body to ease the ache her going had created.

He heard Regina's footsteps brushing across the floor and then she was in bed beside him. Her skin was hot, and there was still the smell of the fire about her. As soon as he touched her, all the pain was gone, and there were only her moist lips opening under his and her soft flesh cushioning the weight of his body.

Exhausted from grappling with the problems Jeremiah had caused and the hours spent with Regina, Baptiste slept until after ten in the morning. Just the antidote he'd needed, Regina was gone before he woke up. That was good, too. With her there'd be no emotional entanglements, and that was the way he wanted it. He required nothing but her physical presence.

When he wheeled into the kitchen and saw Benji waiting for him, he knew he had a hard day ahead. For a brief time he'd been able to forget the fire; now he must face the destruction it had caused.

He pushed up to the table, took the coffee Jessie handed him, and motioned for Benji to sit down.

"Well," he said, "what do we do first?"

"The cabins," Benji said.

"I thought so, too. The workers need their homes. They showed their loyalty, and they need to be rewarded. Have the horses returned?"

"Back in the yard this morning, pawing the dirt and wondering why they were locked out of the stable."

"Can they go back in?" Baptiste asked. The crop was his livelihood, but his real love was the horses. After the workers, he worried most about them.

"It's already cleaned out," Benji said, "and they're back in their stalls." Neither mentioned the mare who'd died. The only one in foal, she'd been the beginning of a new generation, but there were other mares to help them get started again.

"How about asking Septimus to come in here. We need to do some planning."

While Benji was gone, Baptiste cleaned the plate of sausages and hotcakes Jessie set before him.

"Delicious, Jessie. How about another pile. Any more sausage?"

"All you wants, suh." She refilled his plate. "Ain't seen you eat like this in a mighty long time."

"Hard work makes a man hungry," he said, spearing a hefty chunk of hotcakes and dripping sorghum all the way to his mouth.

"Uh-huh, that and other things." She turned her back and tested the sausage on the stove with a fork.

Did she approve or disapprove of Regina's being with him last night? The girl was free to do as she pleased; he hadn't forced her to come. Nor was he the first. Well, he'd be damned if he'd let Jessie be his conscience. He concentrated on the food.

Benji returned with Septimus, and they went out onto the gallery that overlooked the driveway and the fields in the distance.

"How many men do you think we can spare from the

fields, Septimus," Baptiste asked, "in order to build the cabins. Benji says the stables are in pretty good condition and can wait for repairs and shoring up. Nor should it take long to throw up sheds for the cane."

"Cane's in good shape," Septimus said. "Several weeks 'afore harvest. Don' need too many men in the field. Should be able to spare enough to get started on the cabins right away."

"And get them finished?"

"Oughta." Miserly with words, Septimus was a hard worker and extremely effective in dealing with the workers. Of all the men who'd returned, he was the one Baptiste had been most thankful to see.

"Then you take the wagon and go with Benji to the lumber mill. You know how much you'll need? Nails and everything?"

"Measured yesterday, while you was gone."

"Good. Benji, go to the top drawer of the desk in the library and look in the lockbox. It's open. Take what you think will cover everything."

Benji looked startled. "You want me—" He'd often bought things for Baptiste with money given him, but never before had he been given free access to the lockbox. He lifted his head with pride at this new trust.

"Yes, and don't waste time. As it is, it'll be tomorrow before the building can start. Let's just hope there's enough lumber already cut so you won't have to make a return trip."

Within a few weeks, the cabins were rebuilt, the stables repaired, and open sheds constructed. Sitting on the gallery overlooking the river, Baptiste was enjoying a bourbon after an exhilarating ride along the New Orleans road and through the fields to check on the first cane cutting. After the bone-wearying night of the fire, he began a more leisurely regimen of increasing his riding time each day. Slowly his thigh muscles tightened until they were strong enough for him to walk the horse without his artificial legs strapped to the stirrups; three days earlier he had put his horse into a canter, and today he had galloped at full speed along the Natchez Trace. Feeling very satisfied with himself, he sipped the bourbon.

He'd also enjoyed several nights with Regina, and he was laughing to himself over Benji's disapproval after the first time.

"It ain't right, Baptiste," he'd argued the day before. "Once or twice, yes, but it gone on too long."

"You're a fine one to talk. Hasn't Evalina moved all her things into your rooms?"

"That's different. For you, it ain't right."

"Don't start talking like your grandfather. I'm not a twelve-year-old sneaking off to the stable. I mean to take my pleasure where and when I can get it, and I don't need your moralizing."

"It ain't that, Baptiste." He'd discarded *boss* after their long reminiscing the night of the fire. "What I mean is, you need a wife. This place needs livening up with parties like in the old days. Jessie's fussin' 'cause she don't get to cook anything fancy, and nobody see the silver I keep polished. That's it, you need a wife."

A wife. That was the same thing Leah had said. Well, he'd think about it. He was pouring a second bourbon when Benji came out to the gallery.

"Mam'selle Catherine DeLisle Fouché is here to see you."

Baptiste raised one eyebrow quizzically and frowned.

"No, suh, I didn't tell her to come over. Though if I'd a thought about it, I would have."

"Where is she now?" Baptiste asked.

"She stop to chat with Jessie, but she be here in a minute."

"Thank you, Benji. Ask Jessie to fix something—tea and cakes, if she has any."

"Yes, suh, boss!"

Damn that Benji, sirring him again. Just to make an impression on Catherine probably.

Baptiste looked up as she walked through the double doors. With her wheat-colored hair, green eyes, and pale, fragile skin, Catherine had an exquisite, flawless beauty. Yet there was a synthetic quality about it that disturbed him. There was never a hair out of place, and her delicate features reminded him of a china doll. At the same time, when she was pleased about something, her thin lips curved into the beguiling smile she gave Baptiste now, and her

126

green eyes sparkled with inner delight. She had the knack of making whomever she was talking to feel as if he were the one person in the world she wanted to be with.

Today she was dressed in a white dotted-swiss gown embroidered with yellow daisies, and Baptiste noted that they matched perfectly the daisies on her hat. In spite of having driven several miles along a dusty road from the DeLisle plantation, her white gloves were spotless and her dress was unwrinkled.

"Sit down, Catherine, it's good to see you. Jessie will bring something out in a few minutes."

"Thank you, Baptiste. Since you didn't deign to invite me over during all the months you've been out here, I decided it was time I came to call."

"I'm glad you did." He smiled at her and found he was genuinely pleased to see her.

"I see everything in the house is still just as I arranged it."

"Not a chair has been moved," he said.

"Then you must be pleased with me as a decorator." The house had been her opening gambit. She'd planned for the next move to be his; but when he hadn't made it, she'd decided to do so herself.

"To be perfectly honest," he laughed, "I've been too busy to think about it." Just the slightest change in her expression indicated he'd hurt her feelings. "But it's very comfortable. If it hadn't been, I'd have changed things around."

"Thank you. It was always my intention to please you." A bit daring, but Baptiste could infer that she spoke as either an old friend or one who wanted to be more than a friend. She hoped it would be the latter. Catherine's delicate features belied a steel will and an I-always-get-what-I-want attitude. Seeing Baptiste after the war, she made up her mind she wanted to marry him, and she had not wavered in her determination. When she learned that Leah had left him, she waited for Baptiste to call on her or at least ask her to the plantation to help him in some way. To that end, she left her small apartment in the Vieux Carré and moved in with her brother's family, an arrangement which was proving to be most unsatisfactory. She had to speed up her campaign, and so she was here this afternoon.

Benji brought in the tray and smiled so obsequiously at Catherine, Baptiste could have whipped him on the spot.

"It sho is a pleasure to see you, Mam'selle Catherine. It been a long time. I jus' telling M'sieu Fontaine here, we needs more life around dis place."

God damn, Baptiste thought, *listen to him. Sounds like he's serving the Queen of England.* Then he looked at Catherine. She was beautiful. Maybe Benji was right. He did need to entertain now that the plantation was settling into a regular routine. And she would make a gracious hostess for him. His thoughts went no further than that.

"I'm glad you came today, Catherine, and I hope we'll see more of each other now that we're almost neighbors."

Chapter Five

LEAH AND JAMES had arrived at Hickory Falls late in the evening. They drove through the east end of town and past the now-quiet square and darkened town hall. There were a few lights in the store windows but not enough for Leah to get more than a glimpse of her new town. She looked forward to driving back and familiarizing herself with it, but at that moment, she was more eager to see the home James was taking her to.

A mile out on the dirt road they turned into the driveway. She was amazed and pleased by what she saw. James had called it an old farmhouse, but it was much more attractive than what she'd imagined. The one-story, white clapboard house sat back from a green lawn bordered with flower beds. Flowers also edged the walk. A pillared porch along the entire front of the house shaded tall, green-shuttered windows. A slatted wood swing hung at one end of it. Around the other three sides of the house, small patches of farmland spread to the horizon of wooded hills.

"It's a lovely house," she said. "Looking at the garden, one would never think you'd been away for several months."

"I have a good man—Ambrose—who works for me part-time. He said he'd keep the yard up." James helped Leah down from the buggy. "Go on up to the porch. I'll take the buggy 'round back. If the front door's open, go on in. I won't be a minute."

Leah walked across the porch and tried the door. She opened it partway, saw there was a light on in the hall, and started to go in. Then she smiled to herself and closed the door again. She'd wait on the porch for James. Peering through the sheer-curtained oval window in the door, she saw one gas jet lighting the broad center hall that seemed to extend the depth of the house, but the rooms leading off it were dark, and she could not distinguish parlor from bedrooms. She saw another light at the far end of the hall, which she assumed gave onto a rear porch.

In another minute James appeared at the side steps to the long porch.

"Door locked, Leah? I thought John or Mary Howard might have left it open."

"It's open. I waited for you."

"No light inside? Yes, there's one in the hall. I'll carry this small bag in and then get the others off the back porch."

He set the bag down, opened the door, and motioned Leah to precede him.

"Haven't you something else to carry in first?" Suddenly Leah felt foolish for sounding so coy.

James looked quizzical at first and then broke into a smile. "You really mean it, don't you?"

"Certainly. I want to follow all the bridal traditions."

Returning from a call in the country, Dr. Judson Simmons noticed the light on James Andrews's porch. It would be good to have James back home. He'd missed him and their stimulating discussions about everything from the proper way to skin a rabbit to the existence of Heaven and Hell. Dr. Simmons would have scoffed if anyone called either him or James an intellectual. Both were more country-wise than book-learnèd, but they shared an innate intellectual curiosity and a skepticism that refused to accept surface appearances as truth. There were few others in town to whom Dr. Simmons could pose an absurd question and be assured of a serious willingness to debate the issue. Yes, it was good to have James home. And in plenty of time for hunting, too.

Dr. Simmons looked at his watch. It wasn't late. Martha wasn't expecting him home for another hour. He'd stop for a minute and then go on home for a late supper. He pulled gently on the reins, all the signal needed for Hippy, short for Hippocrates, to begin slowing down. But he didn't turn in the drive. Instead he paused long enough to watch James lift a young woman into his arms and carry her through the front door. Dr. Simmons smiled to himself. He'd forgotten that James was bringing a bride home from New Orleans.

It was right for James to marry again, and he hoped he'd find real happiness this time. Remembering all the sad years with Zadah, Dr. Simmons shook his head. A real pity she'd lost the baby. It had done something to her. Only he and James knew that Zadah hadn't been physically invalided and both had borne the secret in silence. James was not a man to indulge in self-pity or to confide his conjugal problems to even his physician and best friend, but from a word dropped now and then, Dr. Simmons surmised they had stopped living as man and wife. Zadah's move to the back bedroom merely helped to confirm his suspicions.

Dr. Simmons shook his head again. A pity. She'd been such a sweet, pretty woman, and loved by all who knew her, but not even with all his medical knowledge could he fathom the depths of the female psyche in its relation to the marriage bed. He smiled and thought of Martha waiting at home. Married thirty years and still as loving as the day he carried her across the threshold.

Dr. Simmons clicked his tongue to start Hippy moving again. James's front door was shut and the porch light put out. Well, he hoped this marriage would be a happier one. Lord knows, James deserved it.

Just inside the door, James set Leah on her feet but continued to hold her in his arms. "Welcome home, darling."

She pulled his head down to hers and kissed him long and tenderly. "Thank you, James."

"Now," he said more matter-of-factly, "let's go see what's in the kitchen. If I know Mary, she'll have left something for us."

Between the big cast-iron wood stove and the sink, with its indoor pump and drain hose to the garden outside, was a square wooden table. While she removed the linen napkins from plates of bread, cake, sliced tomatoes, and fruit, Leah watched James explore the well-stocked icebox. Mary Howard, his partner's wife, had indeed seen to the provisioning of the kitchen for their homecoming. James handed over plate after plate of ham, chicken, and salad.

"Now for some coffee," James said, lighting the stove and pumping a kettle of water. "And we'll sit down to the first meal in our own home. Already this kitchen seems brighter and more alive now that you're here."

"Ah, yes, the kitchen, in which I must prepare those gargantuan breakfasts you like so well. What does the icebox hold for tomorrow morning?"

"Don't worry about me. You can sleep and I'll fix my own. I'm used to doing it."

Leah did not miss the resigned tone in his voice. Nor, she was sure, had it been just since Zadah's death that he'd prepared his own meals.

"Indeed not," she said. "You shall have a proper wife-cooked meal before you leave for the office. So—what will it be?"

"How about frying up some of this ham with a couple of eggs and coffee? And toast?"

"Are you quite sure that will be enough?" Leah asked in mock horror.

"If not, I'll whip up some hotcakes," he said, just to see the expression of alarm on her face.

"Speaking of ham, I'd better put the rest of this food away. I look forward to meeting Mary and thanking her for this welcome. I assume she knows you were bringing me with you."

"She and the whole town. I sent John a wire from Baton Rouge."

"The whole town! It's frightening to think of meeting them."

"You won't meet them all at once," James assured her.

"Just one at a time. What were you picturing? A horde of them descending on you?"

"Something like that, yes." She tried to laugh, but James would never know the fear gnawing at her stomach. "It's trying to remember all the names! I've never been good at names anyway, and now to have to keep more than two or three in mind at one time . . . Impossible!" The last word exploded from her mouth in French rather than in English, and James laughed at the ferocity of it.

"Oh dear," she sighed, "I must also remember to speak English all the time. With you, a lapse now and then is not fatal, but here—" She threw up her hands in dismay.

"Nor will it be fatal with others. It will be charming."

"No, no. Of that I am sure. It must be English all the time. I am in 'ickory—no, *H*ickory—Falls now, not New Orleans."

"Would you like to see the rest of the house," he asked, "or are you too tired?"

"I think I'm ready for bed. I can explore the other rooms tomorrow. It will help me feel more at home if I can take my time and become accustomed to them."

In the immense double bed, Leah lay on her side and stared through the window James had opened. She was looking at but not seeing the trees, listening to but not hearing the soughing of the wind through their leaves. A branch scraped the upper pane, and she shuddered with an uncontrollable spasm that was like the tremor that follows the first violent shock wave of an earthquake. She sensed James reaching toward her and then drawing back. Now she lay absolutely motionless. It was as if her body lay next to him but she herself had fled from something she found intolerable or beyond her ability to cope with.

She lay as if in a coma. She was cold to the bone yet the covers were stifling. Her chest filled with the tears she could not shed. Like the tears, her thoughts flowed inward, and she was afraid of what she saw. In submitting to the alchemy of color change, would she also lose her own identity? If the blackness penetrated to her soul, might she eventually destroy herself?

She remembered the time she had tried to remove a stain from a favorite dress. She had watched in dismay as

the cleaning fluid, after first fading the spot to a pale gray,
had gone on to eat away at the threads and finally burn
away the part of the fabric it had touched. In a fit of
pique, she'd thrown the dress to the ground, poured fluid
all over it, and watched as it shriveled to a small pile of
accusing shreds. Now she seemed to be watching herself
being shriveled in the same way. Her taint—if taint it
be—was like the blemish in Hawthorne's "The Birth-
mark." Obliteration of it meant death. Its roots were desiccated fingers of people long dead clutching and piercing
her heart. They left their touch on more than the pigment
of her skin. They were in her blood and bones, in her flesh
and muscles. She could deny her heritage to others, but
never to herself, and that was where the pain lay. For
years she had sought to discover who she was. She thought
being Mrs. James Andrews would provide an identity. It
had, but with it had come a shocking, bewildering, horrify-
ing truth. She knew who she was, but she could no longer
be herself.

She came to that realization the moment she walked
into the bedroom and looked at the towering headboard
and solid footboard of the sleigh bed, the symbol and
heart of marriage. From now on she would be walking in
the footsteps of another, trying to fit the mold James had
consciously or unconsciously created, and living the role
others expected of her.

Leah felt the weight of James's body as he turned in the
bed, and with his movement came a consoling reassurance.
She'd been in thrall to foolish fears, and she needed his
strength even if she shrank from having him make love to
her. She knew now what was disturbing her, and what had
created the fear, but how could she explain it to him?
Would he understand or would he scoff and call it a
woman's foolish whim?

James sensed a change in Leah from the moment they
entered the bedroom. She undressed hurriedly but quietly
and merely nodded her head when he opened the doors to
the wardrobe. She'd stood stiffly by the bed and allowed
him to turn back the covers. If this had been their
wedding night and she a frightened virgin, James might
have understood. But after the last two nights on the boat,

he was puzzled and concerned. Had he said or done something to offend her? In an all-concealing pink silk nightdress, she was more desirable than in her seductive gowns. She needed to be tenderly cherished as well as passionately loved. In some way, he had unknowingly hurt her. He couldn't for the life of him think of how. Something he had said? Done? Not done?

He turned on his back, stretched, and touched the headboard of the bed. His fingers traced the design carved in the solid walnut. He'd always been fascinated by the rudely carved border of vines and leaves and flowers. Suddenly he sensed what was disturbing Leah. He should have known. He shied away from coming right out and asking her, but he could approach the subject obliquely.

"Tired, Leah?"

"A little." Her voice had lost some of the tension he'd sensed when they first lay down.

"It's been a long day. I hope you'll sleep well. You know, this is the most comfortable bed I've ever slept in, but maybe that's imagination or memory. My father built it just before he and my mother were married. It was his first gift to her. When they came west, she insisted on bringing it along. She loved to tell the story—with constant interruptions from him—about how she helped him take it apart so they could get it into the wagon. And it was the first thing set up in this house.

"My three brothers and I were born in this bed. Anytime we felt sick or we woke up from a nightmare, we knew we could always crawl in here and be comforted. This bed knew a lot of love of all kinds. When—before I married Zadah, I knew she'd been admiring a brass bed she'd seen in Louisville. So I ordered it and had it put in here before the wedding. Later she said she preferred to have the back room overlooking the garden, and I moved the brass bed in there, and brought this one back where it belonged. My mother and father slept together in it for over thirty years, never in another as far as I know, and I always thought—"

James got no further. Leah was in his arms and he was kissing away the tears. Gradually her sobs subsided, her body relaxed, and he felt her hand guiding his up under her gown. He smiled at the foolish but delightful vagaries of women. Who'd have thought that the idea of sleeping in another woman's bed would upset Leah enough to have her lying stiffly beside him as if he were a stranger.

Leah had known it was foolish to be so affected by the thought of sleeping in the bed that James had shared with his first wife. Strangely, if the first marriage had been a happy one, she might not have minded so much, though she still would have wished for a new bed. Now in that dreamlike euphoria that always enveloped her once passion was spent and her body released its hold on James, she realized her elation had come not so much from learning that this had not been Zadah's bed but from knowing that James had sensed what was troubling her. He hadn't thought her foolish, nor had he embarrassed her by coming right to the point. Instead, he'd told her about his parents and his own childhood, and in doing so had shared with her his own unspoken wish that their marriage would be as happy as his mother and father's. Leah knew she'd married a wise and considerate man. She might yet come to love him as she knew he loved her.

In the morning, as soon as she felt James stirring beside her, Leah slipped out of bed and put on her robe. The night before, they'd done no more after supper than put a few things in the icebox, covered others on the table, and left the soiled dishes to be washed this morning. Now she had to learn where everything was kept in the kitchen as well as get breakfast started. Coffee first; that was a must. Thank heaven for the pump by the sink; she wouldn't have to go outside. She filled the kettle, lit the paper and kindling James had put in the stove, and measured out enough beans in the coffee grinder to make a full pot. She could enjoy a second and third cup after he'd gone and she was finding her way around the house.

The ham was sizzling, the coffee hot, the buttered toast keeping warm, and the eggs ready to break into the pan when James came in, shaved and dressed.

"Something smells awfully good in here." He kissed her on the cheek. "You found everything all right?"

"Everything but some jelly or jam. I even looked in this funny little cupboard in the window, but it's completely empty." She pointed to the partially raised window and the attached, snugly fitting box that jutted outside. Its open

136

side faced into the kitchen and its only door was the window itself, which could be pulled down in front of it. Having never seen anything like it before, Leah couldn't begin to think what its purpose was.

"Oh, no," James laughed. "That's not a cupboard. That's our winter icebox. As soon as it gets cold enough, we use that and don't have to buy ice."

"Well, how was I to know," Leah sputtered. "I've never lived where it gets cold enough to keep things outside."

"You'll find it handy, and if we need more room, we'll use the icebox, too." He looked around. "Now for the jelly you were hunting. Probably in the fruit cellar with some other food I had put up last year."

"The what?" Leah had heard of cellars, but there were none in New Orleans where the water table was so close to the surface, most houses were built high off the ground.

"Come," James said, "I'll show you." He led her out the back door, across the porch, and to an almost horizontal door just a few inches above ground. "Be careful, it'll be dark farther along, but the shelves we want are right inside."

Leah followed him down the few steps, and saw rows of shelves lined with glass jars of fruits, vegetables, and preserves.

"They stay cool down here," James said, "as well as out of the way. These steps are a bit treacherous, so you'd probably better let me know what you need, and I'll get it for you."

"There are so many jars," she gasped. "We'll never use them all."

"You'd be surprised. That's just one winter's supply. Remember, we can't get fresh vegetables most of the months the way you could in the South. Now, here's what we're looking for. How about strawberry jam with our toast?"

"Sounds perfect, and that I know how to do. Make preserves, that is. Maybe not many fruits and vegetables, but preserves, yes."

More and more for me to learn, she thought. *But by next summer, I'll know how to put up everything in his garden.*

Once Leah saw James off to work, she collapsed with a second cup of coffee and another piece of the toast that had to substitute for her favorite croissants. There was so much to get used to. Iceboxes in the window, storage rooms underground, a big breakfast to cook every morning. She'd thought about asking James for money to go shopping in the afternoon and buy something special for his supper. But she changed her mind. Today she would devote to the house.

"It's a good thing you're not going to be here," she'd said while telling him of her plans, "because you'd probably laugh at me. I shall spend a long time getting familiar with each room and sitting in each chair until I feel comfortable in it. I know I sound like a ninny, but it's the only way I know to make something feel like my own."

"You're not a ninny," he said, kissing her fondly. "You are to do exactly what you want today. Then tomorrow, I'll leave the buggy for you and you can do the same with the shops. Or would you rather wait until I can go with you?"

"You're sweet, but I think I'd like to explore them myself. And I wouldn't mind walking. It's not that far, and I probably need more exercise. I shouldn't get too lazy."

So now she sat contemplating the toast. In his diagrammed tour of the town, James hadn't mentioned a bakery, and it dawned on her with a kind of horror that probably the women of Hickory Falls baked all their own breads and pastries. How uncivilized! How primitive! She supposed she would have to get receipts for all the baked goods she was accustomed to buying at the Market. Would anyone in Indiana know how to make light, fluffy croissants or éclairs or cream puffs? She enjoyed cooking, but she hadn't planned to spend all her time in the kitchen.

She cleared the table, piled the breakfast dishes in the sink along with the ones from the night before. She'd take care of them after she dressed and saw the rest of the house. Probably after she had a bit of lunch and was fixing supper.

In the bedroom, Leah arranged a few toilette articles on the dresser and then selected a simple cotton gown. With the house closed up for so many months, she knew the rooms would need a good dusting and airing. She picked up her brush, thinking to twist her hair into a bun, but she changed her mind and tied it back with a ribbon. She was still making up the bed when she heard the front-door knocker strike twice. It couldn't be James back so soon, and anyway he'd come around to the back if the front door were locked. Surely there wouldn't be a caller at this time of the morning. Moving to the bedroom door, she looked through the sheer curtains of the front door and onto the porch. Oh bother! There was someone standing there. She hurried to open the door.

"Good morning, Mrs. Andrews. Welcome to Hickory Falls. I'm Mrs. Judson Simmons—Martha Simmons."

Leah looked at the short, plump, pleasant-faced woman who was handing her a large plate covered with a linen napkin.

"Won't—won't you come in?" She took the plate and then stood there wondering what she should do with it and where to invite her guest to sit down. She knew the formal parlor was across from their bedroom and the family sitting room behind that. But maybe she ought to put the plate in the dining room. Oh, she did hope it wasn't something that had to be put on ice and the woman—Mrs. Simmons—would follow her to the kitchen where all those unwashed dishes still lay in the sink.

"Come," Mrs. Simmons said, "let's go into the sitting room. It's more comfortable than the parlor, don't you think?" She led the way as if this were her house and Leah her guest.

"Yes, yes, you're right. Much more comfortable." Leah followed her into the room, and she saw for the first time the flowered cretonne curtains and slipcovered chairs. Separate from the rest on one side of the smoke-bedarkened brick fireplace was an oversized chair with seat cushions and back hollowed out from long use. A large stand with several pipes and a tobacco humidor stood beside it. *That must be where James sits,* Leah thought automatically. Over the mantel was a gun rack with three guns.

"Why don't you take the plate through that door to the dining room," Mrs. Simmons suggested. "You can just leave it on the table. It's a raisin spice cake. I baked two yesterday and thought you might like one."

"Yes, I will. Thank you." Leah fled through the indicated door, glad for a moment to breathe and get her bearings. She also took time to close the swinging door into the kitchen.

"Now, dear, sit down and relax," Mrs. Simmons said. She was already seated on the flower-covered sofa. "I know I'm early, but I wanted to be the first. To prepare you, so to speak."

"The first?" Leah's dismay increased.

"It's an old Hickory Falls custom. Not one of my favorites, I might add. To call on the new brides *just* as soon as they arrive. I suppose some do it out of kindness—at least I'm sure it started that way. To bring food, don't you know, before you've had time to get in supplies. But I think many of the women do it just to get the poor girls flustered. Though you don't look like a girl. Oh, dearie me," she fluttered her hands, "I didn't mean that to sound ugly, but you're not a child. And you don't look as if you fluster easily."

"I don't know, Mrs. Simmons. You gave me quite a shock." Leah managed a weak smile.

"I'm sorry, but as I said, I wanted to be first, because I understand how upsetting it can be. Oh my, wasn't I a nervous one right after the doctor and I were married. My husband is Dr. Simmons. Has taken care of James for years. Good friends, too. Saw you arrive last night while he was driving in from the country."

If he saw us on the porch, Leah thought, *he saw James carry me in. And I thought we were alone.*

"Don't blush, my dear. Judson carried me across the threshold, too, though thank goodness, I wasn't nearly so plump as I am now." She laughed a cheerful, warm-hearted laugh. "I'm afraid he'd never make it today." She reached over and patted Leah on the knee. Although Leah usually found such demonstrations of familiarity from strangers unpleasant, she sensed the sincerity behind the act. "Judson and I are very pleased you are here. We hope you and James will be very happy. And we want you over for dinner soon."

"Thank you, Mrs. Simmons, and for the cake, too."

Her soft, full bosom rising and falling, Mrs. Simmons chuckled again. "You may think differently by the end of the day. But I will say this for my cake. Wrap it in a cloth

140

soaked in wine or brandy, put it in a tight container, and
it will keep for weeks."

"I'll do that right away," Leah assured her.

"Or as soon as you can. Now, I must be hurrying along.
Judson's surgery is attached to our house, and it's time for
his morning coffee." She slid forward on the sofa to allow
her small feet to reach the floor and then bustled into the
hall. Her tiny straw hat bounced precariously atop her
bun. She pointed to the front door. "See, I told you.
There's Mrs. Jacobs—he owns the lumberyard—and Mrs.
Simpson—he has Milady's Emporium. I'll just introduce
you and then run along."

Leah could only gasp at the thought of meeting two
more of the town's wives so soon. Was it going to be like
this all morning? From what Mrs. Simmons said, she was
afraid so.

Once Mrs. Simmons had introduced them, Leah found
her head in a whirl while she tried to keep up with the
dual conversation, answer questons, and balance two
plates—a peach pie and a coconut cake—at the same
time.

"How do you do, Mrs. Jacobs. Mrs. Simpson. Yes, my
name's Leah. No, Leah—L-E-A-H. No, not Mississippi,
Louisiana. Yes, that's right, New Orleans. The Vieux
Carré, I mean the French Quarter. Is it a Southern ac-
cent? No, more a French one. I grew up speaking
French."

"You spoke French? In the United States?" That was
Mrs. Jacobs, the one who asked most of the questions. Although obviously curious, Mrs. Simpson seemed more reluctant to quiz her. Leah tried to distinguish some
individual characteristics of each so she would remember
them. She knew how important that was. In their early
forties, she guessed, both were about the same height and
had brown hair and blue eyes. Mrs. Jacobs had a large
mouth and was slightly buck toothed, whereas Mrs. Simpson's slim lips were drawn into a tight bow, but she had a
softness in her wide-open eyes.

"Yes," Leah answered the surprising and somewhat disapproving question about language. "Southern Louisiana
was settled by French and Spanish, or Creoles. There are

not many Spanish-speaking Creoles left, but those in some of the parishes—or counties—still speak French."

"Really!" Mrs. Jacobs exclaimed. "French and Spanish Creoles? I thought all Creoles were partly darkies, of mixed blood that is."

Leah cringed and then tensed. *This is it*, she thought. *This is the beginning. How I handle it today will determine whether I can succeed in living the lie well enough to convince myself as well as everyone else.* She swallowed hard. Her hands holding the plates were beginning to shake. She could avoid the question by saying she had to take the food to the dining room or she could stand there and speak naturally. The first time would be the hardest, so she'd best get it over with.

"No, indeed, Creoles are pure French or Spanish, though you're not the only one who has thought differently. I assure you, they—we do not like to be considered as having tainted blood." *Bon Dieu!* She hoped no one had noticed the slip of her tongue. "And we value our French language and customs very highly."

"Maybe so," Mrs. Jacobs said, "but it seems mighty peculiar that you haven't become more Americanized in all these years. Pure French, eh? Didn't know they were so dark-complexioned."

She hates me, Leah thought. *She must have been one of Zadah's close friends, and she could become my enemy. I have to tread carefully.* "Some are, but many are blond. I suppose it depends on what part of France one's ancestors came from."

"Well, we'd best be going. Come, Cora."

"Thank you for coming," Leah said, grateful they were not staying any longer. "And thank you for the cake and pie. I know James and I will enjoy them." Her arms were beginning to ache, and she prayed she would not drop the plates before the women got out the door.

"Such a pleasure, my dear." Mrs. Simpson spoke for almost the first time. "Do come to see me. I live just a block from town."

"Yes, do come to call," Mrs. Jacobs said. "My, it does seem strange to come in here and not see dear Zadah. I find it hard to keep from crying."

Still clutching the plates, Leah closed the door behind

them. She started toward the dining room and then stopped when she heard Mrs. Jacobs's voice coming loud and clear from the porch.

"Pure French, indeed! Never saw one yet with skin and hair that color. And wearing it long like that instead of put up in a decent bun. I've heard about those Creoles and the way they behave. Shameful! John told me about some kind of special dance or ball where they actually—"

Her voice trailed off and Leah could hear no more. Nor did she want to. She managed to set the plates on the table before she dropped them, but now her whole body was shaking as violently as her hands. She'd thought she knew what she was going to have to endure, but she never imagined it would be as hard as this. The woman was positively rude. And that parting remark about Zadah.

Leah walked into the kitchen and put the coffeepot back on the stove. She needed something to calm her down. She had to make a decision right now. She could get angry at Mrs. Jacobs and be rude to her in return, or she could recognize that the woman was uncouth and ignorant and learn to tolerate such outbursts. She knew what the choice had to be if she were to live in the town as James's wife. Her acceptance by the town was more important to him than it was to her. Nor did she have to associate with Mrs. Jacobs more than absolutely necessary. Instead she would cultivate friends like Mrs. Simmons. She had learned to tolerate much worse while living in New Orleans, especially during the four years of occupation and while working in the Federal offices. She could do it again for James's sake.

Three more women came within the next half-hour, the wives of two other businessmen—whose names she couldn't remember, but she could learn them from James—and Mrs. Peters, the minister's wife. None of them stayed for long and all seemed sincere in welcoming her to Hickory Falls. Mrs. Peters was especially gracious and said she would be in touch with Leah about the next meeting of the church's afternoon sewing guild and the morning missionary circle. Missionary circle? Sewing guild? Leah wanted to throw up her hands in despair. She had no idea what either of them involved or how sewing, in particular, was connected with church. Two apple pies and a chocolate cake joined the other baked goods on the dining-room table.

Leah was headed once more for the kitchen and the longed-for cup of coffee when Mrs. Benson, wife of the town's other doctor, and Mrs. Shelby, the mayor's wife, arrived. With Mrs. Benson was Carrie, her six-year-old daughter.

"Welcome to Hickory Falls," Mrs. Benson said, "and please call me Elizabeth." She handed Leah a second coconut cake. "Oh, my, you have had a lot of callers, haven't you," she said, following Leah into the dining room.

"And this, my dear," twittered Mrs. Shelby, "is my very own rice pudding and custard sauce. I'm very famous for it. Everyone begs for the receipt, but it's my prized possession and I never reveal it."

"Thank you so much," Leah said. "I feel very honored that you would bring it to us." Rice in a pudding? Whoever heard of cooking it for dessert? Northerners had strange tastes.

"It must go right in the icebox," Mrs. Shelby said, heading for the kitchen door. "Let me help you with it."

"No, no," Leah put her off, thinking of the unwashed dishes in the sink. "I can manage very nicely. I'll get it on ice and be right back."

When she returned, Mrs. Shelby had disappeared, but Elizabeth Benson stood by the table.

"I'm sorry," she said, "you've been so plagued with us today. I would have waited until another day, but—well, to be perfectly frank, I know what you're going through and I thought I could lend a little moral support. Mrs. Rhinehardt, the banker's wife—and the self-proclaimed leader of Hickory Falls society—will be here soon, and—to put it bluntly—she can sometimes be a little hard to take. But don't let her get you down. I'll do my best to keep things going smoothly. Most of us are delighted for James and hope you'll be happy here, so don't let any of the old bats intimidate you."

"Thank you, Elizabeth." Leah was grateful for her words. She judged Mrs. Benson to be about the same age as herself. She was a pretty, open-faced woman whose eyes sparkled when she talked and whose smile came as

144

naturally and pleasantly as a child's. "I could have used some of that help a little while ago."

"Mrs. Jacobs?" Leah nodded. "Don't let her upset you. She was a close friend of Zadah's."

"I thought so."

"But more than that, she just likes to badger people, to make them feel she has some kind of hold over them. If she weren't married, I'd say she was a frustrated spinster." Then she laughed, "Or maybe she is—frustrated, that is."

"Tell me something," Leah said in hushed tones, "should I serve any of—of these things to the people who are here? I haven't so far, but then I didn't know."

"No, that's not expected. No, not even Eloise Rhinehardt will stay that long. By the way, Mrs. Shelby's pudding and custard sauce are very good if you want them for supper. It's her one claim to fame—and doesn't she play it for all it's worth?—but it is delicious."

Leah and Elizabeth were about to join Mrs. Shelby, who had made her way to the front parlor and looked stiffly but properly uncomfortable on the tufted sofa. Leah glanced quickly around the room, shaded by heavy wine velour draperies edged with gold fringe, seeing it, too, for the first time. Formal walnut chairs upholstered in green velvet flanked the white fireplace, its interior scrubbed so clean it was obvious a fire seldom burned in it. In one corner stood a lovely spinet piano. The flowered rug repeated the dark green and wine of the sofa, chairs, and draperies.

There was another, more commanding knock at the front door.

"It's Mrs. Rhinehardt," Elizabeth whispered. "I'll go with you and introduce you." She settled Carrie on the floor with a picture book she'd thoughtfully brought with her.

From Elizabeth Benson's description, Leah would have recognized Mrs. Rhinehardt without an introduction. She was not a tall woman, but her imperious, domineering mien and ramrod stance gave an immediate impression of redoubtable superiority.

Leah took the plate she was offered, mumbled a polite thank you, and trailed the banker's wife into the parlor. Her eyes followed her guest's to the badly tarnished silver candlesticks, the dirt-spattered windowpanes, and the dust that rose from the chair when Mrs. Rhinehardt sat down. Sitting severely erect, she looked as if she were encased in steel. *Well-corseted,* Leah thought, *but I'll bet she sits that way even without whalebone.* Leah had met that unbending, indomitable type before: the woman who never gave an inch, for whom everything was either black or white, and who considered compromise an unforgivable sin.

Leah sat up just as straight and smiled. She must try to remember she was now the wife of a successful, well-loved lawyer. She was no longer a non-person.

"Do I smell something burning?" Mrs. Rhinehardt seemed to speak without opening her mouth, but she flared her thin nostrils.

"Oh, dear!" Leah gasped. "It's the coffee. Would anyone care— No, I suppose not. Excuse me." She fled to the kitchen. Black smoke curled up around the tin pot and she almost burned her hand trying to get it off the stove. Bother! If she could she would have sat right down and cried. She was hot and flustered and furious at these women who came calling at such an indecent hour before she'd even gotten settled in the house. It wasn't fair! And she had hoped to make a good impression on everyone. Well, there was no help for it now. She'd have to suffer it out until they left.

Leah had barely returned to the parlor when the catechism began again.

"And where did you meet James, my dear?"

"In New Orleans, Mrs. Rhinehardt."

"Oh, yes, he went there *right* after Zadah died." Leah noted the emphasized word, but she also knew it had really been some three or four months later.

"And when were you married?"

Leah's heart sank. What date should she give? Oh, if only she could remember what date James said he'd arrived in New Orleans. And the baby. It had to be a date that would cover when the baby was due. If she figured wrong on either count, it could be fatal. "March, we were married in March, around the middle of the month."

"The middle of the month. What an odd way to put it."

"The sixteenth. Yes, it was the sixteenth."

"My, so soon after he arrived." Mrs. Rhinehardt al-

146

lowed a sardonic smile to form on her lips. "It must have been truly love at first sight."

"Yes, it was." It would be best not to elaborate. A simple lie was enough; anything more involved could only get her deeper into trouble.

"You were a widow, I understand." Leah felt trapped. Why had Mrs. Rhinehardt said that? She and James had decided only the day before that she would pass herself off as a widow. But it was a good way to get that word spread throughout the town. She had no doubt Mrs. Rhinehardt would pass along everything she heard or saw.

"Yes. I was married to Baptiste Fontaine. He was killed in the war." There, she had said it. Baptiste was dead now, for good and always. Nor could she ever resurrect him again. She felt like a murderer, and she hoped God would forgive her for both sins, lying and killing.

"And such a useless death, too," Mrs. Rhinehardt said. "Such stupidity on the part of the South to think they could defeat the Union."

"Please, Mrs. Rhinehardt," Elizabeth Benson interposed. "I'm sure it's hard enough for Leah to remember without having to talk about it. The South did feel they were right in what they were doing. And I'm certain they have suffered enough."

"Perhaps." She rose from the chair gracelessly but completely sure of herself, as if pulled by taut, invisible wires. As she headed toward the parlor door, she ran her fingers along a table, leaving a smooth, straight line in the dust. "It seems strange not to see Zadah here. She was such a meticulous housekeeper. Poor dear, even in all her pain, she always kept the house absolutely immaculate. She was an angel, an uncomplaining angel in all her adversity."

Leah bit her lip. She mustn't say anything. They would be gone soon, and she'd have the house all to herself again. Maybe by the time James came home for supper, she would have regained her composure and some semblance of sanity.

"And who were you before you married Mr. Fontaine?" Mrs. Rhinehardt caught Leah off guard, and she said "Bonvivier" without thinking. Not that it mattered. Neither name meant anything to people in Hickory Falls.

"Oh, yes." Mrs. Rhinehardt turned from the door and

added, "I do hope we will see you in church on Sunday. I'm afraid James became something of a backslider, but with you to prod him, perhaps he will begin coming again. You will be there on Sunday?" It was posed as a question, but Leah knew only too well it was meant to be an irrefutable statement of fact.

"Yes, yes, I'm sure we'll be there."

Leah knew she should go straight to the kitchen or to the sitting room and pull herself together, but paralyzed by the voices coming from the porch, she found it impossible to move away from the door.

"Did you see her waistline, Elizabeth?"

"Yes, and I'm so happy for them. James will make a wonderful father."

"If you ask me, they had to get married. Did you hear how she hesitated over the date? And so soon after he got down there."

"Oh, no, Eloise," Elizabeth said. "That's not fair. You shouldn't say things like that."

"Well, then she got him on the rebound," Mrs. Rhineband. If he fell in love and married right away, it is no

"Zadah was ill for many years. James was a fine husband. If he fell in love and married right away, it is no business of ours."

Leah wished she could rush right out and thank Elizabeth for those words. But her relief was short-lived.

"Mama," she heard Carrie speak up, "why does Mrs. Andrews talk funny?"

"Not funny, sweetheart; she has an accent."

"Well," Mrs. Rhinehardt continued, "I have a second cousin by marriage in Baton Rouge, and I intend to write and have her find out just who this Leah Bonvivier Fontaine is or was. We haven't been in touch since before the war, of course. After all, we had to cut them off when they became hostiles, but I'm quite certain she will be only too glad to do this favor for me. Then we will see just who it is James married."

Leah collapsed against the door jamb. So that was why she wanted to know her maiden name. She'd already planned to ferret out Leah's past. *Dear God*, she thought, *please don't let there be any more callers.* Feeling a sudden wrenching in her stomach, she rushed to the kitchen and leaned against the sink, but it was only dry heaves that shook her body. She couldn't bear the thought of going into the dining room and looking at all those cakes and pies and puddings. James could throw them out. She'd become really ill if she put even one bite into her mouth.

Only one thing calmed her down when she was this upset—hard work. She picked up the smoke-blackened coffeepot, set to with scouring powder and a brush, and worked out all her frustration on the stubborn black crust inside and the sooty residue outside. She'd get it clean if it killed her! After tearing one of her fingernails, she started crying; but she kept right on scrubbing with the powder and polishing with her tears. She didn't hear the buggy pull into the yard.

"Leah, what in the world is wrong with you?" James bent over to kiss her.

"James! What are you doing here now?" She hadn't meant for him to find her like this. She thought she'd have all afternoon to straighten the house, start supper, and pretty herself up.

"I came home to eat. But it seems you've got more on your mind than my dinner."

"There's cake, pie, or pudding. Take your choice," she choked and then began crying without restraint.

"Forget about that." He lifted her out of the chair and held her close. "What's wrong?"

In between sobs, she tried to tell him. "Oh, James, it was awful. All these women came and handed me plates. And they asked all kinds of questions. And I couldn't remember when we were married. Someone said I talked funny. Another said all Creoles were darkies. And one said she has a cousin in Baton Rouge who will tell her all about me. I said all the wrong things. And the tables were dusty. I've ruined everything for you."

"Now, just sit down and take it slowly. Nothing could have been as bad as you think."

"Yes, it was. Except maybe for Mrs. Simmons and Mrs. Benson. They were very kind. And the minister's wife."

"All three came to see you?" At the moment he was puzzled over this premature influx of callers.

"And more. Lots more."

"Oh, yes," he remembered, "the Hickory Falls tradition

for a new bride. I'd forgotten all about it." He brushed her hair back from her face and wiped her eyes with his handkerchief. Then he reached into the cupboard for a bottle of wine, poured a full glass, and handed it to her. "Now what was this about forgetting our wedding date? That was just two days ago. How could you forget so soon," he laughed.

"No, not that one. The one for the baby. We never decided on a date."

"My fault," he said more seriously, noting how really upset she was. "I didn't think people would be that nosy."

"Well, they are. And I didn't even know when you arrived in New Orleans."

"Near the end of February."

"We're all right then. I said March sixteenth. Of course, now we're being accused of marrying rather quickly—or because we had to. Either way, I caught you on the rebound."

"There, there, darling. Don't worry. It will all be forgotten within a week. Something else will set the gossips' tongues rattling."

"It's not that simple. Mrs. Rhinehardt has a second cousin by marriage in Baton Rouge. She's going to ask her to find out all she can about the Bonviviers and the Fontaines. You know what that means. The trial was in the papers for days, headlines even. And a Mrs. Jacobs looked skeptical when I tried to explain that Creoles were not people of mixed blood. So you see, I'm under suspicion on all sides. And I've been here only one day."

"Well, we're not going to worry about it now. I love you, and I'm not going to let you be hurt." He poured himself a glass of wine and looked thoughtfully out the window. "Hickory Falls isn't the only town in the world. There are plenty of places out West that could use a good lawyer. I doubt Eloise Rhinehardt will learn anything damaging, though. If they've been out of touch since before the war, that second cousin might not even answer her letter. Meanwhile, keep your chin up, and I'll see what I can find for lunch."

Leah began to feel better and could even joke about the dessert-laden table and some of the women who came to call.

"James, what is a missionary circle?"

"Oh, no," he hollered, "not that already."

"Yes, the minister's wife said she would be in touch. All I could think of was a group of missionaries sitting around in chairs talking about their work, but ours are all priests and nuns. And how can they do their work if they come here every month to talk?"

"No, my love," and he started laughing again. "I'm sorry, but that picture you created of missionaries sitting in a circle, hands folded piously, was too much for me. It's the women in the church who do things to earn money for the missions. And I think they study the Bible and discuss conditions in foreign lands. I'm sure they do some very good things, but it's also a social get-together."

"Oh, and Mrs. Rhinehardt said I was to prod you into going to church every Sunday. She said you had become a back—a backslider, I think she called it."

"Dammit, no!" James struck his fist against the table and then had to shake it to ease the pain. "It's bad enough they come here and try to intimidate you, but they're not telling me when and how to worship. Unless," he looked at her, "you want to go."

"It might be a good idea if it means being accepted here."

"But it's not even your church, Leah."

"Does that really matter, James? Religion is not a building or a particular set of formal creeds. It is a personal belief. Let me try to explain how I feel. When I was a child, my mother and I went to the St. Louis Cathedral. There was no segregation there nor in any of the Roman Catholic churches. Then one day I saw my father sitting with his wife and children. It was the first time I really knew I was different. I seldom went back.

"Later my religion became embodied in two very wonderful people. Sister Angelique at the convent, who taught me how to value myself, and a young priest who buried my mother and son during the yellow fever plague. He had buried well over a hundred people in twelve hours, but he took time to say a few prayers and assure me that my loved ones were saved even though they'd not had the final rites. They were the most truly religious people I've ever known, and they helped me to find my own faith. But it is a faith within myself, not within a church. I can go with you because I take my faith and my beliefs with me. I don't need to go looking for them."

James shook his head slowly. "Leah, you never cease to amaze me. And you're right. We'll go on Sunday because it is part of life here, and I don't want you to be left out of any of it. It probably wouldn't hurt me, either. Now, what do you plan to do this afternoon?"

"What I'd hoped to do this morning, get to know the house better. It was something of a shock to have other people lead me into my own dining room and parlor. And I shall get out the dust cloths and silver polish."

"Then don't worry about supper. We've plenty left over from last night."

"If I just knew what to do with all those cakes and pies."

"I have an idea. If you don't mind having more company tonight, I'd like you to meet John and Mary Howard."

"By all means. I want to meet them and thank her for all she's done."

"There they are, Mary," Leah said, pointing to all the plates on the dining-room table. "What do I do with them? I can't just throw everything out, and we can't possibly eat it all."

"No," Mary Howard said, "someone would know if you did, and anyway, that would be a waste. Let me think."

Mary said nothing for a moment or two, but Leah knew she was considering something. Near Leah's age, Mary was a slim-faced woman who, having kept some of the pounds gained with each of her three children, now had a figure with a soft, generous roundness. She was seldom serious about anything, and when she was really pleased, she broke into infectious laughter.

"I know," she said. "There's a small settlement of Irish immigrants about a mile beyond the railroad tracks. Martha Simmons—you met Martha?"

"Yes, she seems very nice."

"She is. You'll like her. Anyway, a number of the immigrant women have brought their children to Dr. Simmons, and Martha became interested in them. She asked me to help. It's a terrible situation. Poor housing, just shacks really, and very large families. The church sewing guild has as one of its projects making layettes for the poor, and even though the Irish are Catholic, we've supplied the new mothers. Oh!" Mary stopped and put her hand to her mouth. "I'm sorry. You're Catholic, aren't you?"

"I was. I suppose I still am, but don't worry about that. What did you have in mind?"

"If you'd go with me, I thought we could take these things out there. Either Martha or I usually visit them at least once a week. She takes medicines and I see what else they need."

"I'd be delighted," Leah said, "and I think it's a splendid idea."

A few days later, when they returned from distributing the desserts and some clothing Mary had gathered, they washed the plates and then surveyed them again.

"Now to return these," Mary said.

"But to whom?" Leah asked. "How do I know who owns which? Do I ask them all in for tea and let them find their own?"

"No," Mary said. "That's just what they expect you to do. We're going to surprise them. There have been enough church socials and teas that I should be able to identify them for you. Then you'll return their calls. They'll be dumfounded," Mary laughed, "and it will serve them right. Get some small slips of paper."

While Leah stood by ready to write down names and place the slips on each plate, Mary surveyed them carefully. "This one is Mrs. Jacobs's. I'd know that florid design anywhere. And this is Cora Simpson's. She prides herself on using nothing but hand-painted china. Hideous, isn't it?"

Leah couldn't help but laugh with her. What had threatened to be an unsolvable conundrum had turned into a game.

"This dish and jar have to be Mrs. Shelby's. She always brings her rice pudding and custard sauce."

In a few minutes, names were attached to all but two. Mary stood drumming her thumbnail against her teeth. "I can't decide between them. One of them is bound to be

Mrs. Rhinehardt, but which one. And as you say, she is the one person we don't want to make a mistake with. Who have we forgotten?"

"I think," Leah said, "it must be Elizabeth Benson. She came in with Mrs. Custard—I mean Mrs. Shelby."

"Mrs. Custard! Oh no, that's priceless." Mary doubled over laughing. "And perfect. Her face looks like a custard. So one of these is Elizabeth's. We're safe then. Just call on her with both plates and let her pick hers out. She'll understand right away. Now, how about some coffee."

Leah spent two mornings making courtesy calls and returning the plates with her own homemade yeast rolls on each. But she was still tormented by the fear that Mrs. Rhinehardt would learn about her past. She tried to put it out of her mind by keeping busy around the house, accompanying Mary Howard and Martha Simmons on visits to the Irish settlement, and—to her own surprise—getting involved with the church sewing guild.

Her first visit to the church had been a miserable experience. The trouble started while she was dressing. She wanted to wear the very conservative rust suit, but James insisted she wear the blue she'd been married in.

"I'm proud of my wife," he said, "and I want to show her off."

The blue suit would have been all right if she hadn't made herself conspicuous in other ways. It seemed as if the whole town was gathered outside when they arrived, and James was welcomed home with handshakes and slaps on the back while the women greeted her with sedate smiles. When they entered the church, speculative eyes were watching the newcomer in their midst, appraising her gown, and looking for the slightest hint of uneasiness. Others were merely curious about James Andrews's new bride. Because the act came naturally to her, Leah genuflected just before she entered the pew. Simultaneously every eyebrow went up and she felt the cold, disapproving stares clear to her bones. Flushed with embarrassment, Leah slid onto the hard bench and watched as others merely walked in and sat down. *But surely*, she thought, *showing respect to the cross on the altar is not a serious faux pas*. Then she looked up. At the head of the aisle was a lectern which she supposed did double duty as a pulpit. Behind it were two straight-back chairs with a simple wooden table between. There were also two rows of chairs to the right and a piano to the left. No cross and nothing that looked like an altar.

She moved forward on the seat and down on her knees to pray, even though there was no kneeling pad or bench. She supposed that, as in many European churches, the people simply knelt on the floor. She felt James's hand on her shoulder and then under her arm as he lifted her off the floor and back onto the bench.

"Not here, Leah," he whispered. "People don't kneel here."

Again she had done absolutely the wrong thing, but worse, she had embarrassed James. He wanted to be proud of her, to show her off, and she was only humiliating him. When the choir walked in, women as well as men, she was surprised, but she was grateful for the chance to sit back and compose herself while listening to them. To her amazement, the congregation stood up and began singing with them. Oh dear, nothing was the way it ought to be or the way she was used to. James handed her the left side of the hymnal to hold while he held the right, but all she could do was mouth the words. Her throat was so dry and her chest so constricted, she found it impossible to utter a note.

She had known the service would be in English rather than Latin; and although it seemed somewhat informal to her after the sonorous rubrics of the mass, she enjoyed listening to the selections from the Bible. Only when Reverend Henry Peters began praying did she feel discomfited again. No one went down on their knees; they merely bowed their heads. For that she was grateful, because no one saw her when she unconsciously crossed herself after each prayer. Only James looked at her out of the corner of his eye and smiled. When the service was over, it took all her willpower to keep from genuflecting again as they left the pew, but since there was no cross on the table, she found it less difficult just to walk into the aisle. Now all she wanted to do was leave the church as quickly as possible, get in the buggy, and drive home.

Most of the men lifted their hats and a few of the

women nodded their heads, but all seemed most anxious to go about their business. Something other than her *faux pas* during the service was wrong. Some of the women who'd called on her must already be spreading rumors about her. James walked jauntily along, smiling and greeting but not stopping to chat. Surely that was not his usual custom, nor could he possibly be unaware of the tension in the atmosphere. Leah remembered the night she'd attended a private Mardi Gras masquerade ball with Baptiste and overheard two of the women commenting on her appearance. She'd wondered then what it would be like to go North and try to pass. Feeling smothered by a simple black domino and yet fearing to have it removed, she'd also wondered what it would be like to hide behind a mask of lies and live in dread of being stripped naked by whispers and innuendo. Her fevered brain now thought the disrobing had already begun.

Seated in the buggy beside James, Leah looked straight ahead, past the stores she'd looked forward to shopping in, and toward the fields beyond. "James, it's not going to work. I don't belong here. I'll never fit in, I know it."

"Nonsense. Accept the fact you're a stranger and they're bound to be curious and a bit aloof at first. Give yourself and the others time. You've been here less than a week."

"It doesn't matter. You noticed the strain too. You're not a stranger. Why should they treat you like a pariah? No, everything is all wrong. The threat that Mrs. Rhinehardt will learn about my past. My behavior in the church. The way people look at me as if I were a freak because I'm from the South and speak with a French accent. I wasn't prepared for all this. Some, yes, but not all of it."

"Darling, I've never seen you this disheartened. Not even in the prison when everything seemed so hopeless." He put one hand under her chin and turned her face toward his. "What's happened to my little fighter?"

"Maybe I can't fight any longer, James. After years of it, I wanted peace and a life free from having to consider every word I said, watch every step I took to make certain I stayed in my place. It's not the attitudes that have me distraught; it's the disillusionment at finding them here.

Not because I'm a woman of color. I'll concede that no
one suspects. Now, it's because I'm Southern and French.
It's all wrong, but I can't fight it anymore."

"Or maybe being here is not worth it?" He did not say
being married to him, but she knew that's what he meant.

"No, James, never that. I'm sorry. I just had to blow off
a little steam." She reached over and took the hand not
holding the reins and put it between her own. "I'll be all
right, I promise."

"You need to meet another friend of mine. No," he answered her questioning look, "no one I've mentioned before. We'll drive out there this afternoon."

"Who is it?" And why must she meet and be scrutinized
by still another person?

"I'm not going to tell you. I want you to see for yourself."

"Man? Woman?"

"Not going to tell you that either. No prejudgments."

"My, you are being inscrutable and mysterious." But at
least she was able to smile, almost laugh.

"There, that's better," James said. "I thought if I tickled
your curiosity you'd stop worrying about all those other
minor matters."

"Minor? That Mrs. Rhinehardt might learn about who
and what I was in New Orleans?"

"Forget it, Leah," James said with a surprising
sternness. For a brief moment she was stunned at his
seeming cruelty and lack of understanding. Then she realized he was like a parent who chastises because he loves.

Hickory Falls sat in a hollow among wooded hills in Indiana's Uplands. From the town, the valley narrowed like
a sleeve toward a cuff as it continued through the hills,
widened for a space, and then divided into two fingers between three hills. The Andrews farm had originally included all of this valley, but was now only a few acres a
mile from town. The valley was split by a dirt road, and
there were small patches of farmland nestled among low
hills on either side. After following the road almost to
where it forked, James turned into a corrugated mud drive
and stopped before a sagging, weather-beaten, unpainted
pioneer house covered with vines.

Leah was surprised by the woman who opened the door at James's knock. She was in her late sixties or early seventies. She had once been tall, but now her gaunt, spare figure was bent slightly at the waist, as if in a stiff, formal bow. However, her shoulders were squared, not hunched as with so many of her age. She had a long, square face that never, even in her youth, would have been considered pretty, but now, in spite of its lines and creases, radiated the beauty of strength and endurance. Her eyes were illuminated with an inner faith and contentment.

The woman's hands embodied an amazing contrast: large and practical yet with slim, artistic fingers that had just a suggestion of knobby swellings at the joints. Her face was haloed by a great mass of luxurious hair in all shades of gray and white, like clouds on the horizon before a storm. She wore a simple dress of homespun in a nondescript color, but it was covered by a voluminous apron of colorful patchwork—squares and triangles of stripes, polka dots, floral designs, and solids in every conceivable color from pale pastels to brilliant blues and reds. The remnants from many quilts that had gone to friends and relatives as gifts.

"James, what a wonderful surprise. Come in, come in. I've just put the pot on for tea, and I've a sour apple pie in the oven."

"Sarah," James said, urging Leah forward, "I want you to meet Leah, my wife. Leah, this is my very good friend Sarah Toffer."

"What a pleasure it is to meet thee. A real pleasure, Leah."

"Thank you. It's a pleasure to be here." She wondered at Sarah's strange way of speaking.

"You were expecting company?" James said, thinking of her remark about the apple pie.

"No. I simply had to have another pie from the last of the sour apples. I'm glad thee is here. I would probably have eaten it all myself and been sorry tomorrow."

"There are those who say you have the gift of foresight," James said, following Leah into the large room that did duty as parlor, sitting room, and kitchen. He sat down in one of the rockers pillowed with more quilted patchwork.

"There are those who say many things about me, but I listen to none of it." She laughed as one laughs at childish taunts and superstitions, giving to them no more credence than to a fairy tale.

"Leah," James said, "Sarah is a Quaker. She and her family moved here a number of years ago and bought a part of my father's farm."

"And do you still farm it?" Leah asked, wishing instead she dared satisfy her curiosity about Quakers, whom she'd often heard about but never seen.

"No," Sarah said, "only a garden large enough to keep me supplied with vegetables during the summer and to can for winter."

"Have you thought about leasing the land, Sarah?" James asked. "It's good land. A pity to waste it."

"If thee knows of anyone, James. I don't go to town and don't know who might want it."

"Let me think on it. You could use the money, too."

"I could, though I've no urgent need for it. I manage quite well now that I'm alone."

James finished the last of his pie, put the plate aside, and concentrated on his tea. "Any more harassment, Sarah?"

"Not since the war ended. Having the boys gone is the worst part."

Leah listened intently to the conversation. She'd suspected from the first that James had brought her out here for more than just to meet a friend. Now she was getting further clues that she was right.

"Have you heard from them?" James asked.

"Yes, they've settled in the Oklahoma Territory. They want me to join them."

"Are you going?"

"Thee knows I cannot leave here. This is the home Richard and I built. I have everything I need right here, and with friends like thee, James, I'm very happy."

"You still have your horse and buggy, so if you need us, come by the house. Leah and I will ride out often."

After another few minutes, they left, James carrying a huge sack of sour apples and Leah folding the receipt for the pie.

"She seems like a most remarkable woman," Leah said as they drove away.

"She is. Someday she'll tell you her whole story. Being Quakers, she and her family have suffered harassment of one kind or another wherever they've lived. During the war here was perhaps the worst because they were conscientious objectors and the boys didn't join the army. Their crops were destroyed more than once and their barns burned down. One son burned to death trying to save the barns. There were tragedies of other kinds as well. That's why she never goes to town now. Richard, her husband, was killed by a falling tree about a year after the war started. Then her other two sons left. They waited until the war was over, said they wouldn't desert her during that time, but they saw no point in staying where the people were so intolerant of others' beliefs and customs. Sarah probably should join them, but I'm glad—selfish as it is—that she's staying."

Leah was quiet while the horse trotted along for almost a mile. "I should be ashamed of myself, shouldn't I, James?"

"No, just a little more patient. You saw Sarah's quiet fortitude. She's learned to put the past behind her, and she doesn't worry about what hasn't happened yet."

"Quiet fortitude," Leah said. "I like that. And I have worried about things that might not happen. Do you think Sarah would talk to me about her beliefs?"

"I'm sure she would, but you can learn more about them just by seeing how she lives."

Leah knew James was right, but she also knew that when Mrs. Rhinehardt heard from her cousin in Baton Rouge, it would take more than quiet fortitude and patience for her to remain in Hickory Falls.

Chapter Six

BAPTISTE WAS DISTURBED the first time Catherine came to call. He didn't want anyone intruding on his private misery. Before the afternoon was over, however, he found himself captivated by her fragile beauty and was agreeing they should see more of each other. She came back for a second and a third visit, excusing her aggressiveness by saying it was easier for her to travel between the plantations than for him.

One afternoon she was chiding him for remaining so much alone. "You should entertain here, Baptiste. Belle Fontaine was always so famous for its parties and galas."

"I don't know, Catherine. I'm not sure I'm ready for that."

"Nonsense, you don't have to do a thing but invite a few friends. Why, with Jessie and Benji everything else will be taken care of for you."

Baptiste saw Benji nodding and grinning behind Catherine's back.

"And," she continued, "I'd be delighted to play hostess for you. After all, there's not much else for a young widow living in her brother's home to do." She sighed, as

161

if life were completely passing her by. "He has Helene and the children and—well, I just feel in the way. They always have to find a partner for me, though since David's death, I'd just as lief remain in my room or not have a partner." She gracefully wiped away an imaginary tear with a spotless, lace-edged bit of linen. "There are so few young men around. I feel it's really an imposition asking them to escort me."

Baptiste was not fooled. He'd known Catherine since pulling her long curls on her sixth birthday. She was very much aware of her own beauty, and she felt any man should consider himself honored to be seen with her. Nor was she as young as she liked to pretend. She was nearly the same age as Baptiste, and he would be thirty-three on his next birthday. He knew she was waiting for a flattering, reassuring response, but he changed the subject instead.

"I've been far too busy getting the plantation going again to think about entertaining. It's considerate of you to offer to be my hostess, but I wouldn't think of imposing on you. I'm sure you've more to keep you occupied than you say, and of course I'm not certain how proper it would be."

"Pooh on propriety. Anyway, we're old friends and people would understand." Catherine was not going to be put off by such feeble excuses as Baptiste was proffering. If he were still mourning the flight of that octoroon mistress of his, there was one good cure for that. He needed someone else to occupy his thoughts. She got up and slowly walked to the small table beside Baptiste's chair where Benji had placed a tray of cakes. She bent over a little farther than necessary to pick one up and remained in that pose a little longer than required as she selected one.

Baptiste looked at the full, white breasts now more than half exposed by the low-cut gown. He felt his body grow warm and the veins at his temples throb. Tonight he'd send for Regina right after supper. He sensed the game Catherine was playing. There were far too many young widows in New Orleans; and in spite of his handicap, he was an eligible bachelor. More eligible than many since the plantation began doing so well. *No, Catherine,* he thought, *don't play the huntress with me. Save your bait for more easily snared game.* Looking at her, he ached to seduce her. As chaste and pure as she appeared, he sensed she could be a real hoyden in bed. He'd love to muss that immaculate hairdo, rub his hands over her white skin, and feel her body trembling beneath him. But she was too cool and calculating to submit without a wedding ring. And that he was not going to offer her.

"So what do you think, Baptiste? A small dinner party?"

"What are you talking about, Catherine?" He forced himself to concentrate on her words.

"You haven't listened to a word I've been saying." Catherine was not used to being ignored, and she tried to cover her ruffled feelings by smoothing her already perfectly arranged skirt.

"Sorry. I have a lot on my mind."

"I was saying I thought you should start with a small dinner party. Perhaps just the two of us with Pierre and Helene."

No, Baptiste thought. That would be too much like announcing I'm part of the family. "No point in going to all that trouble for just four of us. Better to have six or eight."

"Then you agree. You should give a party."

"A dinner, Catherine, not a party."

"Good." She sat back and smiled to herself. Things were beginning to go much more as she'd planned them. She must not be too possessive at first, but she could certainly make it look as if she were Baptiste's choice. A few parties given by their friends to which Baptiste would escort her, and they would soon be an acknowledged couple. It was only a step from there to marriage. Some people would call her conniving, but she thought of herself as one who made plans that covered every contingency. From the moment she suggested to Baptiste that she could help with the decoration of Belle Fontaine while Leah was in prison, Catherine had been determined to become mistress of the plantation. Leah's release had been a setback, but not one she hadn't foreseen. About the time she was ready to put her substitute strategy into effect, Leah had gone North, leaving the path free and clear for Catherine.

"Set a date," Baptiste said, "and I'll confer with Jessie."

"No indeed, you're not to trouble yourself one bit with it. Jessie and I will put our heads together, and you will be delighted with the results."

"If you don't mind, Catherine, I prefer to make my own plans."

Two steps forward and one step back, Catherine thought. *Well, so be it. It's far too early to challenge him.* "Of course, Baptiste, I only thought— Well, you did say you had a lot on your mind."

"And this will relieve some of it." He was beginning to get irritated with her presence. "Benji, how about finding something besides this tea. Care for a drink, Catherine?"

His offhand manner was not an invitation, and Catherine was wise enough to know when she was in danger of overstaying her welcome. She was also aware that some of her suggestions had aroused Baptiste's ire. Any other man would have been falling all over himself to be amiable to her, and she would have been the one holding off. Well, Baptiste wasn't any other man, and that was what made him such a challenge. Her usual feminine tactics would have to be put aside. In fact, she'd have to reverse herself completely. Well, she could do that, too. *Just wait, Monsieur Fontaine,* she thought; *I'll have you snared before you even know you're being hunted.*

"Yes, suh," Jessie said when Baptiste conferred with her in the kitchen. "Just as easy to cook for ten as for six or eight. You tells me what you want and I fixes it."

Baptiste wrote out the invitations and Benji carried them around by hand. "I would say, boss, that this is going to be quite a proper affair."

"Indeed it is, Benji. When did you ever know me to do anything except first class?"

"Never, and that's a fact."

"Then go into the city and get yourself a proper uniform. If you're going to be a butler, learn to look like one."

"Yes, sir."

"Oh, and you may call me *sir* that night. I know that will please you."

"Mam'selle Catherine's done got to you, hasn't she?"

"No, dammit, she has not. Now then, just because I said

164

you could say *sir* doesn't mean I want to hear any more *done gots* from you. Hear?"

"I hear."

"And while you're in the city, have them make up a new set of dinner clothes for me. They have my measurements."

"And the liquor? I may need to buy more."

"A variety for before dinner—including wine for some of the ladies. Check with Jessie for the meat course and get the appropriate wine for that. Champagne with the dessert, and liqueurs for the men afterward—brandy, absinthe, crème de menthe, and so on. Oh, yes, and cigars. I need a new supply anyway, so get several boxes."

"You paying for my suit of clothes?" Benji asked after mentally totaling up all that Baptiste ordered.

"Certainly, but not if you get pugnacious about it. Look in the cash box. You know where it is."

Baptiste's gruffness never disturbed Benji because it concealed a genuine fondness and respect.

Baptiste looked over the guest list one more time. Everyone had accepted, and he was surprisingly pleased at that. Maybe others, too, were beginning to feel the need of more socializing after so many years of deprivation. In addition to Catherine and Pierre and his wife, there would be the Beauchamps, an older couple and friends of his father's he had not seen in several years; Seth Perrier, his former partner in the cotton brokerage, and Lucy, his bride; and George and Coralee Dulange, life-long friends who, like Baptiste, were trying to restore the family plantation. Baptiste had first chosen these particular guests because he thought ten was a congenial number for general conversation around the table and then when they separated after dinner—the women leaving the men to their cigars and liqueurs—five in each group assured there would be no lack of subjects to talk about. When he looked again at the names of the men he'd invited, he realized it would be more than a pleasant evening. From each of them he could garner good advice about prospects for the future of the plantation. Yes, he was pleased with his selection and doubly pleased that they were all coming.

From Baptiste's point of view, the dinner was an unqualified success. From Catherine's, it was not. She had dressed with special care in a gown not too revealing but not dowdy either. The new, slimmer modes complimented her figure better than even the low-bodiced, hoop-skirted style had done. The modest, almost demure neckline curved just below her throat, where it was outlined by a single strand of pearls. The silk bodice, however, was fashioned so ingeniously that it clung to her figure in such a way as to reveal every curve of her breasts. The skirt, highlighted by a slight bustle in the back, hung almost straight to the floor in front, accentuating her slim waist and flat stomach.

She styled her hair into a soft, full bun and let a single long curl fall in front of each ear. When she looked in the long mirror, she smiled with satisfaction. No man, not even Baptiste Fontaine, would find her resistible tonight. She had fully expected him to send a small bouquet—after all, she was his partner and hostess—but when he didn't, she plucked a few white camellias and tucked them into her ribbon belt.

If only she'd suggested that Baptiste send Benji over in a carriage for her. She could be there by his side when the others arrived and join him in greeting their guests. Well, maybe that would have been a bit too much for the first dinner. How she hated going with Pierre and Helene. Her sister-in-law was such a dawdler, always late for everything. And Catherine had to sit in the carriage with her back to the horses, like a servant or barely tolerated maiden aunt. It always put a damper on everything right from the beginning. And of course Helene had to precede her into the house. Well, once that was over, she would come into her own. Baptiste would see just how pleasant and charming she could be.

As Catherine had predicted, they were the last to arrive; as a result, the only chair available to her—after Helene had been seated—was in a far corner. Not given to pouting, she sat there as regal as a queen, as if to show everyone that where she sat was the center of the room. She looked around the formal parlor she had decorated with such care and meticulous attention to detail. There was no predominant color, no dark greens and maroons, as in so many formal parlors. Here a mélange of pale, delicate colors blended as perfectly as in a flower garden. She had envisioned herself as the butterfly, flitting among her guests and making each one feel as if he were the one the party was given for. She did not think of her dream as shattered, merely postponed.

Immediately Catherine had approvingly taken in Benji's correct attire for serving a formal dinner and Baptiste's elegant, smooth-fitting evening clothes. She smiled. Baptiste would not have gone to all that expense unless he intended to entertain frequently and accept invitations to social functions hosted by others. She sipped the wine Benji offered her from a silver tray, and her eyes sparkled with a new intensity at the sight of all the gleaming silver and crystal Baptiste must have acquired since the days she helped him choose furnishings for the house. She'd no idea Baptiste was doing so well, and her acquisitive heart pounded at the thought of possessing all these riches. She had coveted the house and its master; now the wealth it contained inflamed her luxury-loving nature.

If Catherine had been discomfited at being the last to arrive and having to take the one chair left, she became even more upset at the attention Baptiste was paying to Coralee Dulange, a simpering little nobody. Like Baptiste, her dull, phlegmatic husband was trying to restore his family's plantation. Catherine had been to call on them; and when it came to redecorating, Coralee had absolutely no taste at all. Now, in her *passé* hoopskirt and frizzed hair, she was batting her eyelashes like a bird flapping its wings for takeoff. And Baptiste looked enthralled by whatever Coralee was saying and captivated by her moronic giggles at his answer.

No, Catherine thought, *I will not get upset. This is but a prelude to the main part of the evening.* Nor was she disturbed when it was suggested that Monsieur Beauchamp take her in to dinner. After all, the host and hostess never entered together. Thanking Monsieur Beauchamp for his arm, she walked to the foot of the table.

It took all the willpower Catherine could muster not to appear nonplussed when she saw the place card at the foot of the table, the position of hostess, carried Madame Beauchamp's name.

"How thoughtful you are, Baptiste," Catherine said

above the voices of the others, "to have place cards. It does help to avoid confusion and—and keep the wrong people from sitting next to each other."

With the poise of one who knew exactly where her place would be, she walked around the table toward the chair to the right of Baptiste. This time it was harder to keep the fury, which was stronger than her shock, from showing. Lucy Perrier, the bride of Baptiste's former partner, was standing behind that chair.

"I believe you'll find your card over there, Catherine," Baptiste said, pointing to the most ignominious position of all, the left side, near the foot, between the elderly Monsieur Beauchamp and George Dulange. To add to her irritation, Helene was seated on Baptiste's left. Well, at least Coralee was across from her, well away from Baptiste, and seated between her husband and Pierre, neither of whom was likely to be beguiled by her flirtatious ways.

It was a miserable dinner. George seldom spoke, and when he did, it was to Madame Beauchamp. Like an idiot savant, he could talk about only one thing, his cane crop. So she had only old Monsieur Beauchamp, with his loose false teeth, bad breath, and a penchant for repeating everything he said at least three times when none of it was interesting at first hearing.

The food was delicious, but Catherine tasted none of it. She was fuming, and her stomach was churning as it always did when she was frustrated. She had let Marie lace her corset too tightly—no, she'd insisted on it herself—and she felt trapped in a tightening vise. The tips of the whalebone were piercing the undersides of her breasts, and she wanted to scream from the pain. When the dessert came, she admired the fluffy, perfectly baked meringue, but she was more interested in the champagne Benji poured into the gold-rimmed, hollow-stemmed crystal. She let him refill hers three times. Anything to dispel the gloom that had taken possession of her. Instead, it only made her giddy and sick.

Catherine felt both relief and desperation when Baptiste stood up, suggested the women might like to retire to the parlor, and then motioned for Benji to bring in the liqueurs and pass the cigars. It was a relief to get away from the formal strictures of the dinner table, but she was also desperately aware that once the men were finished, it would be time to leave. She would have no chance to talk to Baptiste. He had put her down, tactfully but assuredly, by seating her where he did. Nor had he spoken more than the polite words of a host to his guest.

While she suffered through the inane female chatter, the gossip and the discussion of new styles, Catherine planned her revenge. Baptiste might think he had shown her the place she held in his life, but she was playing a game where the winnings went for the best two out of three, not for a single encounter. She was not a flirt like Coralee. Anyway, flirtations were like the meringue, sweet and delicious for a moment, but insubstantial. Nor could she play the helpless female, Baptiste knew her too well. But tonight had shown her one thing. Baptiste was his own man who wanted to run his own life. Suggestions, yes; interference, no. So she must work on what was most important to him—the fact that he was the complete master of the house and the plantation in spite of his handicap. She must never, in any way, belittle him or let him think she considered him less than a man because of it.

When the men came in from the dining room, Helene immediately indicated it was time to leave. *Always the last to arrive and the first to go,* Catherine mumbled to herself. A pity her sister-in-law looked on social functions as a duty rather than a pleasure. All hope for an intimate farewell with Baptiste was aborted when Benji brought her cape. She had thought that surely everyone would leave at once; then she could drop something like her gloves or mesh bag behind, discover the loss when they were in the carriage, and insist she had to go back for it. But, no, the others had reseated themselves in the parlor, ready to enjoy the coffee Baptiste ordered, and engage in stimulating, informal chatter. It was just the sort of witty conversation she relished and at which she shone.

Once in the carriage, she became furious with herself. She hadn't had to leave with Pierre and Helene. The Beauchamps would have been more than happy to take her home on the way to their house farther up the river. But belaboring the point would only make her more miserable. In the morning she could put her new strategy into play.

Baptiste lay back in the deep leather chair. The late-September evening had turned surprisingly cool, and he was enjoying the last of the fire he'd had Benji build in the library. The Beauchamps had left soon after Pierre and the two women, and it was then Baptiste had suggested the other four go with him into the library. These were friends he'd known all his life, and he'd forgotten how pleasant it was to sit around and reminisce over old times.

In a way he was sorry Catherine had left so soon. He looked into the dying coals, the same iridescent red as her dress, and he saw the silk of the bodice clinging to her figure, the rise and fall of her breasts as she sought to control her emotions when he'd pointed out where she was to sit. Perhaps he had been unnecessarily cruel to her, so pointedly ignoring her and flaunting his independence of her. Even if she had brought it on by trying to insinuate herself into his life and assume the supervision of the dinner party, he needn't have been so blatantly unkind. After all, the dinner was her idea, and now he was pleased she'd suggested it. No, he would have to find some way to make it up to her. She was a beautiful woman, with a sensuality just waiting for someone to break through her cool exterior and release it. Her husband, killed at Shiloh, had been dead for several years; and Baptiste sensed that after the long, enforced abstinence, she was close to the breaking point.

Try as hard as he would, he could not refuse to acknowledge why he'd avoided her all evening, why he had hastily asked Benji to switch Lucy's place card with Catherine's when he saw her walk in. He could not have sat beside her throughout dinner, breathing her perfume and feeling the warmth from her body, without aching to touch her. Nor did he think, after seeing her in that dress, she would be averse to an affair. The clinging red silk was as much an invitation to a seduction as any spoken word. Yes, an affair with her would be delightful and far less restrictive than marriage. Baptiste never for a moment let himself doubt that Leah would someday tire of life with James in Indiana and return to him. When that day came there must be no obstacles.

Baptiste threw the end of the cigar into the fire and called for Benji to help him undress. As pleasant as the evening had been, he was brutally tired and his legs hurt intensely. It was too late to send for Regina, though his body ached to find release from the tension produced by the vision of Catherine in his bed and the memory of Leah. He lay awake a long time, mentally undressing Catherine, seeing her white body emerge vibrant and voluptuous from the red dress, and then feeling her respond wildly and convulsively to his lovemaking. When he finally fell asleep, he dreamed of Leah.

In the morning, Baptiste slept late and breakfasted on the back gallery, overlooking the garden and the river. He'd had little time to think about the flower beds and shrubs. While he was considering the amount of work needed to make the garden flourish again, he heard horse's hoofs on the drive. In another minute they were coming along the path by the side of the house and around to the back.

"Good morning, Baptiste."

"Well, you're up early, Catherine." Her blond hair, pulled severely back under a pert riding hat and snood, gave her face an especially fresh and appealing look. The dark-blue riding habit was set off by an immaculate white scarf at her throat.

"Not so early. It's nearly noon. I rode over to tell you how much I enjoyed the dinner last night. It was delicious. In fact everything was perfect."

"If you say so, Catherine, then I know it was." What was she up to now? She'd had a miserable time, and he knew it. Yet she seemed sincere, and there was nothing of the coquette about her.

"How about joining me in a ride along the river?" She'd first planned to have him invite her in for a cup of coffee. Then a few words with Benji and she learned that Baptiste was now able to ride. That fitted her new plan—to play up to his masculinity—even better. She was not so foolish as to indulge in any ploy like a runaway horse or a fall from her mount. Those things he could not handle and would only be embarrassed by. No, they would just go for a long ride, as they did when they were younger. That would suffice for the present. Ask him for a bit of advice maybe. She'd see.

"I'd love to. Give me a few minutes."

"I'll meet you at the stable," she said. No, that wouldn't do. "Or better yet, by the river. I want to look at those early camellias down on the bank." She'd seen that Baptiste did not have his artificial legs attached, nor would he want her to see him being helped down the steps and onto the horse by Benji. She shuddered. It was not just to keep from embarrassing him. The sight of those mangled legs, even covered by a shawl, horrified and sickened her. Disfigurement or imperfection of any kind was anathema to her. From the beginning she'd known she would have to swallow her revulsion and conceal her abhorrence from him. But that, too, was well worked out in her plans.

Baptiste raised one eyebrow as she headed toward the stable to get her stirrups checked before she rode through the garden. She was either genuinely very tactful or wanting to appear so. The real reason for her actions eluded him. Catherine was a fascinating enigma; her deeds so often belied her words and her appearance belied both. Perhaps that was why Baptiste continued to play her game. He'd known it was a game from the beginning. And although she'd begun it and appeared to be making the rules, that did not necessarily mean she would be the winner. Playing it added spice to his life, an ingredient sorely lacking since he'd come out to the plantation.

Calling for Benji to saddle his horse and bring him to the front steps, Baptiste wheeled himself into his room and dressed. No formal riding habit for him, just a pair of work pants, a comfortable shirt, and a casual jacket. He let Benji help him down the steps and get settled into the saddle. Now that he was riding every day and able to grip the horse's flanks with his thighs, he could use the stirrups much as any rider by pressing down on them for balance or greater security. Most of the time, however, they were simply a place to put his boots. He walked his horse around to the back and along one of the paths to the river where Catherine waited for him.

"Do you think I can restore the garden to what it was before the war?" he asked.

Involuntarily she raised her eyebrows. She'd been planning to seek his advice, to let him feel masterful and superior. Now he'd turned the tables on her. Yet, maybe it was better this way. He must still have confidence in her opinions.

"No reason why not. The original design of the beds and paths hasn't been destroyed, and most of the plants seem to be healthy enough. You just need someone to prune the shrubs and clear away the rubbish and weeds. The lawn needs the most work."

"You think any of the hands—excuse me, the field employees—could do it?" he asked.

"Under your supervision, yes." She was not going to make the mistake she had with the dinner party. If he wanted her help, he was going to have to ask for it. She would volunteer nothing.

"But I don't have that kind of time or talent. I'd probably have them pull up an azalea and leave the weeds." He'd opened the door for her, but she hadn't walked through. With her coming here this morning, his suspicions that she wanted him as much as he wanted her were verified. He had slapped her down—hard—but she had returned in a most conciliatory mood. That meant just one thing: she was ready to give herself to him on his terms. Not at either house, that would be compromising her and playing right into her hand, on which she wanted a ring. No, he'd have to find an appropriate place for their trysts.

"Oh, I doubt that," she laughed. "Once you take a real look at them and remember how the garden was before, you can differentiate between them with no trouble."

"But remember, I can't walk along the paths the way you can." He had to know if she were willing to face that truth or if she shied away from the subject. There could be no seduction if she did. "I'd have to supervise from the gallery."

"Or from your chair or from horseback. You seem to manage that very well." Amazing how normal he looked when fully dressed with trousers and boots. It was the thought of seeing him naked that repulsed her. Or the patch removed from his shattered eye. The patch itself gave him a bold, dashing look. But without it? She shuddered inside.

They left the formal grounds of the plantation and rode along a path that edged the river. "Will you come over once or twice a week to advise me?" he asked. "You speak of pruning as if it were as simple as picking the flowers. I don't want to kill any of the plants."

"I'd be happy to, Baptiste."

Both thought the arrangement ideal for their individual plans. Baptiste sensed that Catherine was willing—but not yet ready—to enter into an affair, and by seeing her often he could make time work to his advantage. Catherine knew that if she helped him with the garden, she would find other ways to make herself indispensable. If her opening gambit had been a foolish one, she had made a satisfactory recovery with her second. Baptiste was a shrewd opponent, but she doubted he thought more than one move ahead. To win, one must plan for several contingencies, and for that she had time on her side.

Baptiste looked up suddenly, startled by a sound that always stirred his blood and sharpened his eyesight. Three teal—two drakes and a hen—flew overhead.

"First sign of fall," he said. "They're early. Must be a cold winter ahead in the North."

"You sound like Pierre. Let him hear a duck quack and he forgets about everything else."

"Naturally. Hunting's in a man's blood. Ducks won't be any good for shooting, though, for another two or three months, when the snow drives them down. Those are just some that got their time clocks confused."

"Must be something ready to hunt," Catherine said. "Pierre has had his guns out, oiling and checking them, for over a week."

"Dove. The men were talking last night about scattering grain in their fields now that the cane has been cut."

"Have you? Scattered grain, I mean."

"Can't afford to. We need every bit for seed. I wish I could; I'd like to be able to invite friends over to shoot my fields."

The horses were ambling along in a slow walk. The path was wide enough now for them to ride side by side, and for the first time, Catherine felt as if she and Baptiste had reached an easy stage of camaraderie, a better prelude to the long-term relationship she desired than the game of wits they'd been playing.

"I remember," she said, "the hunt breakfasts my father had every fall."

"I do, too. They were a tradition in your house. The table and sideboard were covered with enough food for a banquet. But you know what I remember best? The popovers. Filled with butter and jam. Our cook never made them, but they were the best things I ever put in my mouth."

Catherine thought a while and wondered if she dared suggest what was in her mind. Earlier, her approach had been less than subtle. This time she would be more careful. And Baptiste had brought up the subject of hunting and wanting his friends over.

"If you can't have the men over to shoot the fields," she said, "you could have a hunt breakfast after they've been somewhere else."

"I'll think about it," Baptiste said. "But there wouldn't be any popovers."

"I can show Jessie how to make them. It was my mother's receipt, and I know exactly how they're made."

"The first shoot is tomorrow," Baptiste said. "That's too soon. But there'll be another in about two weeks. And you can show Jessie how to make the popovers?"

"I promise you. They will be perfect."

During those next two weeks, Catherine came five times to help with the garden. She worked for hours with the young man Baptiste selected to be trained as a gardener. She supervised the cleaning of the walks, showed him how to prune and thin out the bushes, and designated which should be transplanted. While he sat on the gallery watching, Baptiste couldn't help but admire her stamina. She was putting a real effort into restoring the garden. Always she came in the morning while it was still cool, and she stopped just before the sun was hot enough to make her perspire. When she joined Baptiste for a midmorning cup of coffee, she looked as cool and fresh as if she'd just stepped from her bath. Not a hair was out of place under her large-brimmed hat, and her gown was still clean and wrinkle-free.

"You amaze me," Baptiste said, wondering whether he was really thinking about the way she looked or what she was doing with the garden. "You've done wonders with it already."

175

"Thank you. It's coming along. The real work on the lawn, of course, will have to wait until spring. And we'll—you'll want to plant some annuals then, too."

Baptiste had caught her use of the first-person pronoun, but then it would be natural for her to take a proprietary interest in the garden after all the work she was putting into it.

Catherine was relieved and pleased that Baptiste approved of what she was doing. But if he thought she was working this hard for him, he was sorely mistaken. This was going to be her home, and she meant for it to be not just *a* beautiful plantation, but *the* showplace along the river. He'd never know the hours she spent redesigning the garden in her mind and planning for the most breathtaking vistas from the house to the river. Paths winding among the shrubs and trees would lead one to a half-hidden statue or bench. There would be other surprises, too; a small shrine to St. Francis amidst a cluster of dogwood trees and a miniature waterwheel where the narrow stream tumbled down an incline on its way to the river.

Baptiste's small dinner party seemed to provide the impetus for a new, more active social life on the plantations in the district. The Beauchamps had an informal dinner to which Baptiste escorted Catherine; then Pierre and Helene, at Catherine's suggestion, hosted a supper dance and turned their long, wide hall into a ballroom while serving the buffet on the gallery. Pierre had raised a questioning eyebrow when Catherine mentioned dancing.

"Nonsense," she said, "Baptiste won't mind. He can visit with all his friends and keep the older widows happy. There's scarcely room for fifty people to dance at the same time, so there'll always be more than enough to share his company. It's not as if he'd be sitting all alone."

Catherine failed to mention that she wanted Baptiste to see her in her real glory on a dance floor. She was a beautiful dancer, and in the gown she'd ordered from her dressmaker in New Orleans, she would be the cynosure of all eyes. There would be no better way to make Baptiste jealous than to see her smiling as she was held close in another man's arms.

It was not the elderly widows who clustered around

Baptiste at the supper dance or his cronies who kept him company. Catherine, trapped in the arms of one partner after another, glared at the belles and young matrons who hovered around him like bees around a honeysuckle vine. She longed to go over and gouge their eyes out. But there was nothing she could do about it. She'd accepted every man who asked her to dance until she realized with a start that her card was filled and she hadn't saved a single number to sit out with Baptiste. Only supper was reserved for him, and she'd written his name in herself before he arrived. Worst of all, he didn't even look at her while she was gliding around the floor but laughed and chatted as if he were thoroughly enjoying himself. Nor did it seem to bother anyone that Baptiste never stood up, that it was Benji, positioned behind his chair, who filled the requests for more punch and escorted the women to meet their next partner.

Catherine realized too late she'd forgotten to consider two things about Baptiste: he was still an entertaining person to be with and he was a handsome, wounded war hero. More than that, he had lost his legs while trying to strengthen the fortifications at the mouth of the river and prevent New Orleans from being attacked. So he was their own hero, even more than the beloved Beauregard, who'd been ordered away from Louisiana to lead the fighting in South Carolina. Many others here this night had also been wounded, but he carried his scars like a badge of honor.

Finally it was time for supper, and Catherine allowed her partner to escort her to the chair next to Baptiste's. Benji filled their plates from the buffet table and remained nearby should they need him.

"Here, Benji," Baptiste said, handing him his coffee cup, "hold this for me. I never could manage the damn thing and a plate at the same time. If I get invited to many more of these affairs, I think I'll have you invent a tray that can be screwed into my legs. I might as well make them good for something."

Catherine ignored the reference to his handicap. "You seem to be having a very good time."

"I am. I've enjoyed it more than I thought I would. So many people I hadn't seen in a long time. And some I hadn't met before."

Catherine didn't like the twinkle in his eyes at the reference to some of the younger, unmarried women. He might find it more fun to play the field for a while. She remembered that his marriage before the war to Marie Louise had not prevented him from finding pleasure in the arms of a number of compliant young women. His reputation as a roué and gallant had made him a fascinating, albeit brief, conquest for several of her friends. She'd not been one of them then, nor did she intend to be now.

"Yes," she said, returning to the subject of his older friends, "I can see where you'd enjoy talking over old times with the men."

"Not all of it enjoyable, except that it was good to see them alive. Three of them were prisoners of war, caught in a plot we were working out to attack Federal forces from within New Orleans whenever our troops were ready to march down the Mississippi and lay siege to the city."

"But they never came."

"No, the siege didn't materialize, and the men I was working with—civilians as well as officers recovering from wounds—were taken prisoner. I was allowed to remain a prisoner in my own home as long as I never went out and never received visitors. That lasted for two years. But still, I was better off than they."

"Well, it's over now," she said, wanting desperately to turn the conversation to something more cheerful or, better yet, herself. "Such reminiscences always seem so maudlin to me." She smoothed her skirt. "You haven't said a word about my dress."

"It's beautiful. In fact, you're looking especially lovely tonight. I've watched you dancing, and there's no question about your having a good time."

So he had been looking at her. Then she hadn't wasted all those precious minutes when she might have been sitting next to him in place of those fawning juveniles and silly matrons, who looked at him as if they were ready to commit adultery that very minute.

"By the way," he said, "when are you coming over to help me plan the hunt breakfast?"

"Tomorrow. Tomorrow morning in time for coffee. If Jessie will promise to make some of her cinnamon rolls."

"You hear that, Benji? Be sure to tell Jessie we want cinnamon rolls at ten o'clock."

Baptiste surveyed the long dining-room table. It had been set for twelve, with his place at the head, Catherine's at the foot, and five on each side. This time there was no reason not to acknowledge her as his hostess. She would be the only woman there. It was she who'd suggested modestly that a hunt breakfast was traditionally a stag affair and perhaps the guests would prefer that she not join them in the dining room. She could greet them and then remain in the background to make certain all went smoothly. But Baptiste knew perfectly well she did not intend for him to agree with her. Nor was he averse to letting her preside. With her beauty, charm, and scintillating wit, not a man among the hunters would object to having her with them. Baptiste owed it to her to make up for the earlier dinner party and because of the real help she'd been in preparing for this breakfast.

In the center of the table was an arrangement of camellias and magnolia leaves. On the side tables and buffet board were bowls of autumn leaves and pyracantha berries. All of these Catherine had picked fresh this morning and arranged herself. On another morning she'd spent hours showing Jessie exactly how to mix and bake the popovers that Baptiste insisted must be part of the menu. Yes, Catherine most definitely deserved to join them at the table.

In the brick-floored, smoky-raftered kitchen on the lower level, Jessie oversaw the preparations for the hunt breakfast. Children and grandchildren were making coffee, beating eggs for omelettes, mixing ingredients for the popovers, and readying the ham and sausage for frying. One small girl had the sole responsibility of checking the temperature of the plates in the warming oven. Jessie kept a stern eye over them, all the while smiling broadly and singing. There was something to sing about now that M'sieu Baptiste was entertaining again. No more simple suppers carried on a tray to the library, and most of them only half-eaten. Mam'selle Catherine had brought more than her beauty to the house when she came to call that first day. She brought life and sparkle back into it. And such a lady. Coming into the kitchen to show Jessie just how to make M'sieu Baptiste's favorite popovers. Belle Fontaine needed a mistress like her, and M'sieu Baptiste needed a wife. If only he'd realize what a treasure was his for the asking.

Benji had helped Baptiste dress and now he was on the gallery waiting for the men, out in the fields since sunup, to return from the dove shoot. When he saw them coming, he'd fix the drinks and have them all ready to hand out by the time the guests came up the steps. Only after downing a few drinks and relating a few of their wilder experiences, would they be ready to eat.

Baptiste moved slowly out of the dining room and into the library. Sitting down, he reached for the cup of coffee Benji had left him. He had more on his mind than the midmorning brunch, although he looked forward to being with his friends and hearing about the shoot. It didn't bother him that he couldn't join them. It was enough to have them come back to his house and let him share in their exploits or, more likely, their friendly exaggerations. He'd loved to hunt when he was younger, and at first it hurt that he could no longer walk the fields for dove or seek out the best potholes for ducks. Since he was able to ride again, he accepted what could and could not be.

No, right now his thoughts were on Catherine. The afternoon before, she'd made a daring suggestion, and he'd almost succumbed to her wiles. Just in time he'd recognized it for what it was—a snare from which the only escape was a proposal of marriage.

"Since I need to be here very early, Baptiste, to pick and arrange the flowers, why don't I just stay the night. I could sleep in the small bedroom and be right here to help with all the preparations."

The small bedroom, Baptiste thought. His sister's room. The room kept as a shrine to her memory. Perhaps that was foolish, and it should be used as a guest room instead. Certainly it would be easier for Catherine than having to drive over very early. Then something pricked his conscience and alerted him to the attractive danger.

"Somehow I don't think that's such a good idea," he said. "The two of us under one roof? That would really set tongues wagging."

180

"Nonsense, Baptiste, I'm an old married woman. No one would think anything about it. Besides, who would know?"

"Pierre and Helene, to begin with. And then everyone. Don't forget, Pierre's your brother and bound to uphold the honor of the family. No, Catherine, you are not an old married woman. You are an eminently desirable young widow."

"Times are changing, Baptiste, and there are no more duels fought over family honor, as you call it. You and I are certainly old enough to live our lives as we please. But if you insist, I'll get up at the crack of dawn and drive over."

Baptiste was sorely tempted to relent and let her stay. One of Jessie's granddaughters could sleep on a pallet outside Catherine's door to vouch for the fact that neither he went in nor she out during the night. And before that there might be the opportunity— No, best not even consider it. He would be the one compromised, not she.

"Sorry, Catherine, much as I'd like to have you stay. Why don't you pick the flowers this afternoon, and then you won't have to come over so early."

"No, they have to be gathered while the dew is still on them. So I'll be here very early, probably even before you're awake. Then I'll see you at the breakfast."

Catherine was never one to admit defeat, and Baptiste felt again that he'd been put on the defensive, a position he was not used to. He would be appreciative and considerate for all she'd done, but he was not going to let her get the upper hand. He'd been right not to let her stay the night, and he was determined to remain master in his own home—and of his own future. Even now Catherine was changing and freshening up in his sister's room, which she'd appropriated for herself without a by-your-leave.

"Naturally I can't use your room," she said when she had finished with the flowers and given a final approval to the preparations in the kitchen and the arrangements in the dining room. Normally both Jessie and Benji would be fuming at the thought of having someone overseeing their work with a critical eye. If Baptiste had done it, they would not have hesitated to let him know he was trespassing in their domains and asked him to please remove himself. Not with Catherine. They were being sickeningly servile and obsequious. He knew what they were thinking —he should marry Catherine—and he wanted to tell them it was none of their damn business, but at times Baptiste was as intimidated by them as he had been by his family's butler and cook when he was a child. They ruled the house, and everyone knew it.

"So," Catherine had said, "I know you won't mind if I use the small room. Benji has already put my things in there for me."

Baptiste couldn't very well tell her to remove them when there was no place else for her to go. But this was the last time. No more dinner parties, no more hunt breakfasts. Even if it meant no opportunities to entice her into an affair. Catherine was not the only desirable woman around eager for masculine attention. The bevy of attractive, unwed females surrounding him at the supper dances had delighted him; and, in spite of his handicap, more than one had dropped hints that they desired very much to see him again. Baptiste had never lacked for female companionship; and now with the dearth of available escorts after the war, he began to feel that his was an enviable position.

Catherine stood before the pier glass and tried to tame a single strand of hair that would not stay in place. When for the third time it slid down ever so slightly from where it belonged in her sleek coiffure, she plucked it out furiously but with no more thought than if it had been a speck of dust on her skirt. Nothing in Catherine's life must ever be out of place; nothing must ever defy her will.

Smoothing the skirt of her dark-green gown, she admired what she saw in the mirror; the slim waist, the perfectly formed breasts, and the womanly but not too generous hips. The forest green was a perfect compliment to her blond hair and pale skin. She thought of herself as Diana, the chaste goddess of the hunt, desired and sought after but never captured. No man would ever possess her any more than she wished to be possessed. She belonged, unconditionally, to herself alone.

At the hunt breakfast, Catherine charmed the men with her grace and poise and by listening avidly to all the old and new hunting stories they regaled her with. The food and liquor were praised lavishly, and all agreed it was an auspicious opening of the winter social season.

As the guests began to leave, Catherine walked over and put her arm casually but therefore all the more possessively through Baptiste's. When the men cheered him for reviving some of the spirit of the good old days before the war, it was Catherine who answered.

"Yes, Baptiste and I thought it time to get out of the doldrums and put a little vitality back into life." She noticed eyebrows go up, and she was pleased. She seldom cared what other people thought, but there were times when public opinion could be turned into an asset. It was amazing how often the assumption by peers that something was an accepted fact would make it so. "Now—you must all give parties so we can attend. And if I have my way," she who shunned coyness like others shunned rattlesnakes looked coyly up at Baptiste, "Belle Fontaine will have a Christmas gala that will outshine any put on here before."

"We'll be here for that, Catherine," said one of the men.

"Keep this up, Baptiste, and you'll be as famous a host as your father," a second guest predicted.

"Belle Fontaine always was noted for its hospitality. It's good to see it returning," another agreed.

"Touché," Baptiste said under his breath so only Catherine could hear him. What had been a tacit combat of wills was now manifestly declared, and Catherine had scored another point, but that did not preclude victory for Baptiste. He knew he could make the ultimate move right now and win, but it would embarrass Catherine and bring the match to an end. No, it was rather fun to watch her plot each move and exult in her winnings. While he waited for the propitious moment to score the final point, one thing was certain: with Catherine and himself as adversaries, the game would not end in a draw.

Chapter Seven

ALTHOUGH SHE WAITED like Damocles for the sword of her past to fall after Mrs. Rhinehardt heard from the cousin in Baton Rouge, Leah had gradually begun to feel less and less like a stranger in Hickory Falls. She enjoyed walking to town, getting to know the stores and shopkeepers. Occasionally she joined Elizabeth Benson or Mary Howard for tea at Aunt Tabby's Tea Shoppe. So far they and Mrs. Peters and Mrs. Simmons were the only ones she felt really comfortable with. They talked about homely things like receipts and children and seldom referred to Leah's being Southern or French. Nor were they curious about her past. They accepted her as James's wife. If at times their conversation seemed superficial, it was better than getting into discussions of politics or race.

Leah always ended her shopping sprees at the small candy store owned by Alex Siokos, a tall, aristocratic Greek whose mouth was almost completely hidden by a huge white mustache until he welcomed each customer with a beaming smile. He and Amelia, his wife, made all their own candy in the tiny rear kitchen, and they lived in the one small room above the shop. As soon as Leah opened the door, she inhaled air redolent with peppermint, chocolate, vanilla, cinnamon, horehound, wintergreen, and other spices.

The Siokoses had come to New York from the old country in the thirties, and then in the fifties had been caught up in the national craze for gold. On their way West, their wagon broke down in Hickory Falls, and so they decided to stay right there and open a shop. Now it was a mecca for all the children and most of the adults in town. One rarely saw Amelia Siokos, who remained upstairs or in the kitchen overseeing the pots of boiling sugar, but Alex greeted everyone in his still heavily accented voice and gave away as much candy as he sold. No one ever left his shop feeling cheated.

Sucking on a peppermint stick while she walked home one afternoon, Leah thought about the barn-raising she'd attended two Saturdays earlier. The idea of everyone in town helping a man build his barn was such a novelty to her, she'd looked forward to it with real anticipation. The men had gone out early in the morning to get the work started. James went by to pick up John Howard, and Mary came just before noon to take Leah with her.

"Need any help?" Mary called down from the buggy seat.

"Yes, if you'll take this basket of fried chicken, then I think I can manage this other one."

"Ooh, what's in there that smells so good?" Mary lifted the linen napkin.

"Raised doughnuts like the ones I used to buy in the Café du Monde. Don't laugh," Leah said, "but I just had to have something to remind me of New Orleans."

"I'm not laughing if they taste as good as they look."

"They will this time. I wrote a friend of mine—Sister Angelique in the convent—and begged her to get the receipt and send it to me. You'll never know how many batches I made before one finally turned out right. Some James struggled politely to eat; some he didn't see went right out for the birds. But these should be perfect."

"They make them in the convent, too?" Mary asked.

"No, but Sister Angelique can go out in public. She's not cloistered. She probably had to bribe the chef and promise to say special masses for him, but she managed to send it to me."

When they arrived at the farm, the men had already framed in the sides of the barn and raised the rafters on the roof. With luck, they would finish before dark. Now they were opening fresh kegs of beer, having demolished several during the morning's work, and gathering around the long wooden planks laid over sawhorses where the women were spreading out the food. Children ran around with drumsticks in one hand and chunks of cake in the other. There was lemonade for those who wanted something milder than beer, and whiskey for those feeling the need for something stronger.

Filling plates for herself and James, Leah joined him under one of the trees.

"Beer or whiskey?" he asked.

"Lemonade, I think. As hot as it's turned off, I'd love a cold beer, but," she patted her stomach, "I don't think I'd better."

"It's hot all right." He wiped his face with his already sweat-soaked bandana and sat down. "Real Indian summer."

"You seem to have gotten a lot done this morning."

"It's going fast. No trouble at all. We'll be through before dark."

"I'm amazed," Leah said. "I've never seen people work together like this."

"An old Midwestern custom, ma'am. Remnant of the frontier days when everyone had to pitch in and help everyone else. We get the work done and have fun at the same time."

During the afternoon, after the plates were washed in tubs of soapy and then clear water, and the remaining food was covered, the women brought out sewing or knitting and sat around talking. A few were nursing babies; others took the opportunity to rest with their backs against the trees while small children slept in their laps. Leah embroidered a baby gown and found herself listening with interest to local gossip and chatting easily about receipts and child-rearing. Her doughnuts had been an immediate success, and every woman there wanted to know exactly how to make them. With no Mrs. Rhinehardt or Mrs.

Jacobs in attendance—barn-raisings were beneath their dignity—there seemed no way the day could be spoiled.

Finally the last piece of siding was nailed up and the last cedar shingle tacked to the roof. Supper finished off the remains of the food, another barrel of whiskey was opened, and two of the men brought out their fiddles. With the planks taken down and the sawhorses moved into the new barn, there was a wide-open space for square dancing.

"Now you'll see some real fun," James said.

"Can we just watch?" Leah asked apprehensively when she saw the first couples take their places in the strangely patterned figures.

"If you like. I'm not sure I've the energy anyway. After today I've decided I'm not as young as I thought I was."

Fascinated, Leah listened to the unfamiliar music and the almost indistinguishable words of the caller. She decided everyone must already know what was coming next. They couldn't possibly follow the caller and move through the figures that fast unless they did. She tapped her foot in time to the squealing fiddles and thought what fun it would be to join them if only she knew the steps. She'd watch closely, and after the baby came, she'd be ready for the next time. James might think he was getting old, but she'd have him romping right along with her while her skirts twirled as gaily as those she was watching now.

There were others not dancing, and gradually they clustered in a group near the whiskey barrels. When James and Leah joined them, the talk was centered on local politics. Leah had already noticed that one of the men dancing had lost an arm, and now she saw that one in their group had a trouser leg pinned above his knee. Strange, she'd never thought of Northerners being wounded. These had been her enemies, yet now she found herself joining them as casually as if there'd been no bloody, fiery conflict just a few short years ago.

"Come sit down, James. Here, Mrs. Andrews, take my seat."

"James," said one man sloshing whiskey down his throat, "I'm getting tired of debating the merits of Grant for president once we get rid of that Rebel-lovin', Carolina-born Johnson. Come tell us how you handled Morgan and his men when they dared cross the Ohio and invade Indiana. Never did give us all the details."

"I'd rather not," James said, looking at an older woman sitting across from him. "You forget that Mrs. Hutchinson lost a son in that raid." He avoided looking at Leah.

"That's all right, James," Mrs. Hutchinson said. "Walter died for the cause, and he maybe helped prevent all of us from being killed in our beds."

Leah looked at James, but he continued to stare straight ahead. So he had fought and killed Southerners in spite of his saying he hadn't gone to war. She'd known about Morgan's Raiders and remembered praying that the Copperheads, or Southern sympathizers, would join them and harass the Northern border states enough to draw large numbers of Federal troops away from the Southern siege. If they had—if they had, Southern troops might have been able to regain control of the Mississippi River and lay siege to Union-occupied New Orleans. That's when Baptiste and his friends would have led the disabling attack from within. Now she learned that James was one of those who put Morgan to rout and prevented the joining of the two forces. Would she have married him if she'd known? Her stomach tightened sickeningly as she listened to him.

"There isn't much to tell," James said. "We heard that Morgan's men were fighting at Shepherdsville. Unless they crossed the Ohio, we didn't have to worry, but the local militia here and at several other towns were alerted. So when we learned they were threatening to cross at Cummings' Ferry, the men from here headed south in the direction of the ferry at Brandenburg. We met up with Morgan at Corydon. He'd already skirmished with a number of home-guard forces along the way, but none of his troops seemed any the worse for it."

"No wonder," one man interposed. "Heard they plundered homes and farms all along the way."

"Dreadful, absolutely dreadful!" one woman said. "Daring to enter private homes like that. Stole food, too."

"That's what plundering means, Lessie," her husband said.

"Means other things, too," she argued, puffing up like a maddened toad; "things you can't talk about in mixed company."

Wonder what they would say, Leah thought, *if I told them how we were treated in New Orleans. Homes plundered, owners forced to move so Yankee officers could use the houses for offices or to move their families into. And the plundering or rape Lessie referred to. None of the women in New Orleans was safe from that, especially after General "Beast" Butler issued his infamous order that labeled as prostitutes all women who ignored Yankee soldiers.*

"They had plenty of supplies, that's for sure," James said. "We gave them a good fight, there and all the way to Salem. Never could defeat them, though. They fought like Indians, darting from one ambush to the next. But we did send them hightailing it toward Ohio."

"Scared us half to death," another woman said. "Left a light on all night just so's we'd be ready if they came."

"Went across old Mrs. Hiram's farm, you know. Took three pigs and several laying hens."

"How many men did you lose, James?"

"Seventeen men, six horses, and a supply wagon. Stole that damned wagon right out from under my nose."

"Well, James," Will Henderson said, "we took care of plenty of their wagons for you. The one I remember best was somewhere around Chattanooga. Can't recollect the exact spot, but I do remember all those Rebels shooting at us from Lookout Mountain. Anyways, we heard this rumbling coming toward us from some distance away. Scared the bloody piss out of us. 'Scuse me, ladies, but that's just what it was. Didn't know whether it was their cannon or our reinforcements. Since we'd been told not to expect any for two days, we was pretty sure it was cannon. Then an old lop-eared mule came into sight. Danged if he wasn't the prettiest sight I ever seen. Pulling a rickety, broke-down wagon. But, man, what that wagon held! Fresh-churned butter, sides of beef, stacks of bread with none of them mealy worms in 'em.

"Old man driving it just come from some of the farms where the womenfolk wanted to make sure the sweet Rebel boys got something to eat. Poor old soul lost his way and wandered right into our camp. Boy, we some more ate that night."

"And I suppose the man just handed it over to you," Leon Jeffords chortled.

"Danged if he didn't. Just pulled off our caps and told him we were a forward Rebel outpost. Our clothes were so damned muddy, he wouldn't have knowed the difference even if he could've seen. We thanked him kindly, helped him turn the mule around, and sent him back to the farms.

" 'Bless ya, bless ya,' he says. 'Them women'll be mighty proud to know they helped in some way.' 'Sure thing, Pop,' we said, 'and you tell 'em we're mighty grateful.' And since that was no lie, we set to and ate with a relish."

"Yeah, but it wasn't all fun and games, Will," Leon said. "You were at Bull Run. You helped count the dead and bury what we could."

"It wasn't the dead that got to me so much as the wounded. God, the screams. The blood and guts everywhere. Men with faces shot off or legs dangling. I fought till I got it at Dalton, Georgia, but damned if I ever saw anything worse than that. Maybe 'cause it was my first battle. But I don't think so. Never did get used to it. Got worse 'stead of easier. Seeing someone I'd just been talking to fall down right beside me. Wondered why in hell the bullet hit him 'stead of me. Or keeping a man alive when he should've been dead, dragging him under gunfire to the hospital tent, and then seeing him die when you think he's finally got it made."

I know, Leah thought, remembering how she'd seen the same thing over and over in the New Orleans hospital. *I know just what you mean.* But she didn't say anything. This was their war they were talking about, not hers.

"It's the unexpected that gets to you," an older man named Bob Lunsford said quietly. "It was winter in the Shenandoah. All quiet and peaceful, it seemed for a while. I remember thinking it looked like a Christmas picture, snow on the ground, stars all bright in the sky. Right after midnight we went up to relieve the men on watch. Ten of us, I think, maybe twelve. Anyways, we crunched through the snow. Each step on that frozen surface sounded like the booming of cannon through the valley. Thought sure'n hell we'd be shot at. But not another sound.

"Saw the outpost on duty. Some standing, a couple

resting against the trees. Waited for the challenge, but
none came. You talk about being scared. That just wasn't
right. So we got down on our bellies and crawled. Not a
man on the watch had moved. It was spooky, like we
wasn't really alive. How can nobody know you're there
when you know you are?"

"All right, Bob," Will said, "so what happened? We
ain't interested in your feelings or the description of the
night. Get on with it."

"I am, I am. Don't get a burr under your tail. Just
wanted to set the scene for you. We finally got up and
walked the last few yards. And then one of our men began
screaming. They was all dead. Frozen to death. Frozen
solid, right where they stood or laid. God, what a sight!
Still gives me the chills when I think of it. Never did thaw
'em out. Had to bury 'em just as they were, straight or
curled up. But not a one of 'em had deserted. That's what
got to me. Freezing to death and they stayed at their post.
Worst thing, worst thing I saw."

"I don't know, I think the worst thing I seen was those
two brothers strung up for spies," Leon said. "You remember, Will, across the river. Just kids, they was. Maybe ten
and thirteen. They'd wandered across the river while hunting. But they had guns. And they'd picked up some army
caps somewheres."

"Should have made them prisoners, not spies," James
said.

"I know that and you know it, but did those Rebels
care? No, dammit! Me and my men had to sit on the opposite banks—just six of us, helpless as kittens—and
watch. Not a danged thing we could do. Had no trial. Just
strung a coupla ropes around a branch. That was Bragg's
doing. Understand even the Rebels thought he was a
bastard. Was that true, Mrs. Andrews?"

"I—I don't know," Leah stuttered. "We were under
Federal occupation for four years, so we didn't know
much of what was going on in other areas except when a
battle was won or lost."

"Is that so? Four years, huh? Didn't know we held anything for four years. Anyways, Bragg was a bastard.
Wouldn't listen to what the boys tried to tell 'em. Damn
but those kids were scared. The older one trying to be so

brave. We was close enough we could see he didn't shed a tear. Stood straight and tall, just like a real soldier. But the younger one, crying something pitiful. Wrung our hearts, I tell you. That son of a bitch Bragg! Even some of his men was weeping, standing around watching and crying. Terrible thing, terrible."

"We got our revenge, though," Hank Crowe said. "Not too long afterward. Just down the river apiece. It was hot, hotter'n I remember in a long time, and none of us'd had a bath in Lord knows when. We snuck down to the river, shucked off our clothes, and dove in. Just then the captain rode up on his fine horse. We knew we'd catch hell for being out of uniform. Instead, danged if he didn't tell us to enjoy ourselves, swim up and down the river a ways. 'Can't swim, Captain,' Tommy Woodbine said, 'but I sure can splash around.' 'How about seeing how far you can wade then,' the captain said. 'See if you can make it to the opposite bank.' Well, we all started making bets as to how far Tommy'd get before he had to turn around and come back. Danged if that river wasn't no more than chest deep the whole way. Without saying a word, the captain just turned around and rode off.

" 'Now what did he want me to do that for,' Tommy asked.

" 'Don't know,' we laughed. 'Maybe he just thought you needed a good bath.' But we found out the next morning. We got orders to hitch up the cannon and move across. That captain had been looking for two days for a good place to cross the river and surprise the Rebels who figured we'd have to march till we found the bridge where they was just waiting for us. Came right up behind 'em instead, and you never saw such a shocked bunch in your life."

"I guess I'll never forget the Battle of Missionary Ridge, when our own captain got his," Hoby Whitcomb said. "Took him two days to die from a hole in the belly. And everybody else dying around him."

"That wasn't the battle where he died," Will said. "It was at Chickamauga."

"What the hell difference does it make?" Hoby said. "They were all the same: death, stinking bodies, horses howling, men screaming, blood running everywhere. Either freezing cold or burning up. I don't remember being comfortable the whole time."

"War ain't meant to be comfortable, Hoby. I don't know what it is good for, but it sure as hell ain't ever like being home in your own bed."

At first Leah wondered why James had stayed and forced her to listen to all these disturbing tales. Then it dawned on her. He wanted her to know, firsthand, that those in the North had suffered, too. If she'd thought some of the people were prejudiced against her for being Southern, he was forcing her to recognize her own intolerance.

"Guess we'd better be going," James said, looking over at Leah. "This has been a long day for Mrs. Andrews."

"Early yet," Josiah Walker mumbled. He'd been drinking steadily throughout the evening and now his hands were shaking and his speech was slurred. "Whatsa matter? Can't Mrs. Andrews take all this Yankee talk?" He tried to get up but fell back into his chair. He pointed an accusing finger at her. "You high-and-mighty Southern women, treat slaves like scum. Don't know what it means to soil your lily-white hands. I heerd them stories 'bout spittin' on our fine, courageous Northern boys."

"Why, you—" Livid with rage, James started toward Josiah. "If you knew what my wife had to endure—"

"Please, James," Leah begged, "don't say anything. You were right. It's time we went home."

"I can't let him get away with saying things like that."

"He's drunk, and you've had more than enough. A fight isn't going to change his mind or make my position any better." She deliberately walked toward the buggy.

While James hitched the horses, Leah gathered up her empty baskets and folded the linen napkins.

"I'm sorry the day ended this way," James said after they were settled in the buggy.

"I am, too, but the rest of it was fun, a wonderful new experience. I got to know many women a lot better."

They rode in silence for a few minutes.

"Did the war stories bother you?" James asked.

"Yes, but as any stories of death and bloodshed would. I was surprised at first at my own feelings of pity for those who were killed or wounded and for the travail of those at home. Then I realized how really tragic and needless a

civil war is. Which side was right? I don't know. You
didn't tell me you'd fought against Southerners."

"Didn't seem any reason to. Especially since I was just
defending my own land, not invading yours."

"Maybe there's a difference there," Leah said, "but I
don't see it. We were defending ours, too, but the trouble
is, we lost."

"Does it bother you, Leah, that I fought against the
South?"

"Not really. As Hoby Whitcomb said, what the hell difference does it make—which battle or which side. It was
all horrible." She changed the subject abruptly. "I think
I'll go out and see Sarah on Monday. Oh, but you'll need
the buggy."

"No, John and I will be riding the circuit together. I
didn't tell you for fear of worrying you, but I'll have to be
gone for three days of court. Why don't you stay with
Sarah. She'd like that, and I'd feel better about you."

Leah had forgotten that once the fall and winter court
sessions started, James would be away for at least three
days each week. On Monday morning, once James had
left, Leah packed a few things. He'd hitched up the buggy
before he kissed her good-bye, so all she had to do was
climb in and ride the mile and a half down the road. Most
of the leaves had begun to turn. It was colder than the day
before, and she was glad she'd done some winter shopping
during the past weeks. The horse trotted eagerly along,
seemingly as glad as she to be out in the bright, crisp air.

In spite of missing James more than she'd any idea she
would, those three days with Sarah were some of the hap-
piest she'd spent since coming to Indiana. Sarah welcomed
her with open arms and led her to a chair before the
cheery apple-wood fire.

"Hated to see it cut down last year. Last thing the boys
did for me before they left. But listen to it sizzle. Almost
sounds like the apples themselves when I roast them on
the hearth."

"And smells like them too," Leah said, removing her
shawl and bonnet.

"No," Sarah laughed. "That's the dumplings in the

oven. Planned to bring some to thee and James this afternoon. But I'm mighty pleased thee came here instead."

"Not just to call, Sarah." Leah hesitated. Now she was here, she felt uncomfortable about suggesting that she stay. It had seemed so easy when James mentioned it; now she felt like an interloper. "James is out on the circuit for three days."

"Then thee must stay with me. I'll accept no arguments."

"Nor will there be any." Leah smiled. "I have my bag in the buggy."

"Good, good! Thee can get it after some coffee and one of the dumplings. They're about ready to come out, and I've a fresh brewed pot on the stove."

"More of your foresight, Sarah?"

"No, an inordinate love for coffee. It's my one luxury. And one of the few reasons I hope James can rent out some of the farmland. My monetary needs are few and I'm not desperate, but if James thought I was lacking at all, he'd be handing it to me out of his own pocket. Thee has a very kindly and generous husband."

"I know that, Sarah. But if you need anything before he rents the land in the spring—"

"I've more than enough to tide me over until then."

Sarah poured the steaming coffee into earthenware mugs and gingerly pulled the dumplings out of the oven. "Here, try a bit of cream on them. Fresh from Old Bossy this morning."

"Oh, Sarah, you're going to make me fatter than I am already."

"Good for thee. A fat, healthy baby is what thee wants."

When Leah returned from unhitching the buggy, carrying in baskets of food, and getting Dobbin settled in a stall, Sarah was sitting before a large wooden loom Leah hadn't remembered seeing before.

"You weave your own cloth?" She was amazed.

"And spin the thread, too. I've three fine sheep in the barn, and they produce as much as I can work up each year."

"I didn't know people still did that anymore," Leah said.

"Many do. For either pleasure or necessity. With me it's both." Sarah changed the threads and shot the long shuttle through with expert hands. "Does thee mind if I go on? I find it tedious to be idle."

"Please. Don't let my being here stop you." Leah walked over to the large spinning wheel, its smooth wood polished by years of use. She touched the spindle, about half-filled with new thread, and looked at the basket of carded wool ready to be spun. Her fingers itched to feel what it was like to turn raw wool into thread ready to be woven.

"Sarah, would you—would you consider teaching me how to spin and weave?"

"If thee really wants to learn, thee must start from the beginning. The wool has already been washed, but there is still much to be carded before it can be spun."

"From the beginning it is," Leah agreed.

During the next three days, while Sarah patiently taught and Leah slowly learned, there developed a very special closeness between the two. Each had endured periods of trial and stress; each knew what it meant to be ostracized or looked upon with a mixture of curiosity and suspicion. Several times Leah started to tell Sarah the truth about herself and then stopped. She did not doubt that the older woman would accept the information as no more important than any other Leah had confided; but the fewer people who knew, the more easily would the facts recede into the past and be obliterated.

"I, too, came from the South," Sarah said.

"But I thought all Quakers came from Pennsylvania," Leah said.

"Another of the myths surrounding us. Many have settled in other states. My husband and I went to North Carolina in 1842 and worked a small farm with three other families. We left ten years later and came to Indiana. We had no slaves, of course. Slavery is an abomination. I'm sorry if my plain-spoken words offend thee, but that is our belief."

"No, Sarah, they do not offend me. I—I was too familiar with many of its evils."

"Nor could we live among people who owned them. Quakers believe that God makes Himself known through the Light of Christ in the heart of every human being. All are equal, all are children of God; therefore, no man can own another."

"This light you speak of," Leah asked, "do you consider it as direct communication from, or with, God?"

"More than that. It is our primary source of religious authority. We read and study the Bible, but it is secondary to the Spirit that is in all of us. The Light was also in the heart of those who lived before the coming of Christ and is in the heart of those not yet acquainted with Him."

"You speak as though you believe in salvation for everyone; even those who are not Christians."

"For those who have not had the opportunity to know Christ, yes."

"Your belief does not condemn them to Hell?" Leah was amazed.

"Oh, no, because the choice was not theirs."

"How about the unbaptized or those not receiving the last rites?"

"We do not celebrate baptism or Holy Communion or other sacraments. Those are merely external rituals for what are really spiritual experiences which need no outward manifestation. Every day is the Lord's Day, not just Sunday, and thus every meal should be a communion with God and a reminder of the Last Supper. In the same way, the Spirit should be baptized on reawakening every morning."

"It sounds so simple, Sarah, and so right. I've long felt that one's real faith is found within oneself, not in outward expressions of it."

"We speak of our feelings in prayer, but only when moved to do so in our meeting houses, which often are homes. We have no formal ministry because all are ministers of God."

"Men and women?"

"Men and women. We are equal in every way and make equal promises in marriage."

"Why are you pacifists?" Leah asked. "Why didn't your sons fight if you were so violently opposed to slavery? I should think you would have been strongly moved to take up arms."

"Friends—the real name for Quakers—believe in following the Christian way of life in all circumstances, and part of the Christian way is 'Thou shalt not kill.' It is as simple as that."

"And so you were harassed and brutally treated for that belief. James said you lost a son in a fire."

"He died trying to save some of the animals."

"And yet you stay on here, why?"

"I've found a certain peace and contentment. 'Twould do me no good to leave. One carries one's burdens in the heart, not on the shoulders. And," she laughed, "I might pick some more up if I left here."

Leah returned home to a joyous reunion with James. She had feared that with her increasingly enlarged stomach he would no longer find her attractive, but there was no denying the desire that lit up his eyes when he swept her off the floor or the ardor of his caresses when they retired. Whether because of a new contentment after being with Sarah or the real surge of joy she felt at seeing James again, Leah realized that respect and physical compatibility could make for a happy marriage.

Leah looked at the bright blue October sky through the window she was washing. Near the house the poplars shimmered in the sun like beaten gold; and along the drive, the maples fluttered dark, burnished-red leaves. In the front borders and along the walk, the last of the chrysanthemums and asters echoed the gold, red, and blue of the trees and sky. It was the kind of day that enriched the spirit and imbued muscles with new energy.

She finished polishing one pane and moved on to the next. James would do the upper halves tonight. He'd strictly forbidden her to touch those. She'd have to stand on a chair and she might fall. With the baby due in about two months, James insisted she take every precaution. So far she'd managed to dissuade him from hiring even a part-time servant, but she didn't know how long he would agree.

Tomorrow she was to be hostess to the church sewing guild. The chairs were already arranged in the formal parlor, and she'd baked and iced enough small cakes to feed an army. In the morning she'd make the chicken salad sandwiches. She stepped back and scrutinized the window. It sparkled. Only one more and she'd be finished. This time when the women walked in, she and the house would be ready for them. No more nightmares like the first day. Remembering her arrival in Hickory Falls, she knew that everything had to be just right for the critical eyes of her guests. She sighed as she moved to the last window and worked on a speck of soot that refused to budge under the most strenuous rubbing.

Having finished the last of the windows, and nodding with satisfaction at the way the October sun shone through them, Leah walked outside to see if there would be enough chrysanthemums and asters for more than one bouquet. Satisfied there would be plenty for both the dining room and the parlor, she decided to wait until morning to pick them. Then she lay down for a short nap before preparing supper.

The baby was becoming more and more active, especially when she wanted to rest, but she didn't mind. It was their private time together, just she and her child. Was she carrying a boy or a girl? Funny how you could share so intimately with something you'd created and not know its sex. She caressed the spot she thought was the head and then felt a little foot or hand thumping vigorously against her ribs. Whichever, it was certainly energetic.

By noon the next day, everything was ready for the meeting of the sewing guild. James came in and said a couple of the chicken sandwiches and a glass of milk would suffice for lunch.

"Everything looks bright and shiny," he said, settling himself at the kitchen table. "And there certainly seems to be plenty of food."

"I hope it's enough. And there's both tea and coffee. I've asked Mrs. Rhinehardt and Mrs. Peters to pour. They agreed, so I assume it was the right thing to do."

"Oh, speaking of Eloise Rhinehardt. When I was getting the mail today, the postmaster said she'd had a letter from Louisiana. He noticed it because a letter from the South is rare. He thought I'd be interested since it was from Louisiana."

Leah collapsed inside, but she continued holding onto the edge of the table. Would Mrs. Rhinehardt make known her findings to all the women or would she call

Leah aside and simply tell her she knew all about her past? Either way, her sojourn in Hickory Falls was coming to an end. Her first tea, which she'd looked forward to, planned so carefully for, and hoped to be a gracious hostess at, was now going to be a disaster no matter how Mrs. Rhinehardt handled the news. Mentally Leah stiffened her spine and threw back her shoulders. No one, not even Eloise Rhinehardt, was going to destroy her. By two o'clock she would be bathed, dressed, and ready to meet the old dragon. Whatever the outcome, Leah was determined to cope with it on her own terms. "Quiet fortitude" had become her watchword.

James's words had stunned, but even more unbelievable was his attitude.

"I don't understand you, James. You say, 'By the way, Mrs. Rhinehardt got a letter from Louisiana.' How can you be so casual about something that could destroy me?"

"Don't you know by now, darling, I'd never let anything destroy you?"

"Not just me, James—us. The end of everything here for you. I admire Sarah, but I'm not her. I can't live in a vacuum, shut out from life. It would be the end of your practice; there'd never be another client."

"And you really think that would happen? You think everyone would ostracize us?"

"I've lived through it, remember?"

"And you had no friends?" James asked. "How about Madame LeConte who gave you her husband's uniform for Baptiste to wear?"

"It was for Baptiste, not for me."

"But she welcomed you into her home, and you said she gave you all those dresses you later remade. Or Madame Seignious, for whom you sewed. She saved you from being taken prisoner by the patrols because you didn't have a pass."

Leah smiled, remembering how Madame Seignious had threatened the patrol leader with a stout cane and then given her a pass belonging to one of her runaway slaves.

"And the women who rescued you from the soldier who called you a prostitute even though their own safety was in jeopardy and they lost their places in the coffee line. None of Baptiste's friends refused invitations to your home. Don't you think I've friends just as loyal? Are you being fair now to prejudge them before the evidence is in?"

Leah felt ashamed and dismayed. "I'm sorry, James. I was doing the very thing I abhor."

"So—let's wait, shall we?"

It was easy for him to say, Leah thought. Hoping to catch a short nap, she lay down after he left. Instead she stayed awake and weighed the alternatives if Mrs. Rhinehardt had learned the truth. James had said something earlier about leaving Hickory Falls and setting up his practice out West. Yet, that wouldn't be fair to him. This was his home, and he had a successful practice and all his friends here. It might be better if she returned to New Orleans and allowed him to divorce her. This was the question that tormented her. Which would hurt him the least? Staying and facing up to the truth? Leaving for a new life? Or getting out of his life completely?

In spite of her emotional turmoil, Leah was outwardly poised when the women arrived. They were profuse in their compliments about the house and the food she served. Even Eloise Rhinehardt smiled, albeit condescendingly, when she sat down to pour from the now highly polished silver coffeepot. When they settled down to the serious business of sewing warm flannel layettes for winter babies, they made themselves quite at home in the family sitting room as well as the front parlor, and Leah felt a gratifying sense of acceptance. Also, she was glad she'd taken as much care with that room as with the others, including arranging a large bouquet of fall flowers on the mantelpiece. As hostess, she was kept busy carrying coffee to those who wanted more, passing plates, and distributing needles, scissors, and materials from the two large boxes of goods and findings on a table in the hall.

With tongues and fingers racing to outdo each other, the women sewed and chatted. Leah, delighted to be a part of the town's social life at last, paid little heed to what was said, only catching a name now and then or pausing when someone called her over to listen to a bit of news. Reaching into a small box for more needles, she heard her name mentioned from the front parlor. If she went in, the conversation might stop. She knew eavesdropping was a dangerous practice; people seldom liked what they heard, but she had to know what they were saying about her. She continued looking for the needles, but all her attention was focused on the voices.

"But you've never heard from your cousin in Baton Rouge?" That was Mrs. Jacobs.

"Oh, yes, several days ago," said Mrs. Rhinehardt.

James hadn't mentioned that the letter arrived some time ago. She assumed it was this very morning. Several days. If the word from the cousin were detrimental, surely Mrs. Rhinehardt had told people by now. Leah's heart rose. That must mean the woman was not interested in snooping into someone's past or she simply had not bothered doing so. Mrs. Rhinehardt said before that they'd not corresponded for many years. Even as these thoughts flew through Leah's brain, she continued to concentrate on what was being said.

"It was rather a huffy letter, to be sure," Mrs. Rhinehardt was saying. "Hurt that we'd ignored them during their time of privation and so on. Actually, she should never have married the man in the first place. We all told her so at the time. Anyway, to get back to the question. She's written to someone in New Orleans, a friend or professional associate of her husband's. Said she'd write if she learned anything."

Leah's heart pounded and her hands shook so badly she spilled the box of needles and had to go searching for them among the piles of flannel already cut for the layettes. Pricking her finger, she dropped blood on several pieces of fabric. Even as she sorted them out from the spotless ones, she looked at the blood, the cause of all her despair. It marked her as surely as it now stained the material. The letter was only a reprieve, nothing more. The hanging had merely been postponed.

Somehow Leah managed to get through the rest of the afternoon, smiling and chatting until she could bid her guests good-bye at the door. By then she'd decided to make the most of the reprieve and to enjoy whatever time she had left with James. If her decision to come North with him proved to be the wrong one, she would leave Indiana and return to Baptiste.

With the deepening of autumn came colder evenings, and Leah was content to sit before the fire and listen to James's tales of his younger days while she sewed on her own layette or embroidered flannel receiving blankets. The subject of the dreaded letter was dismissed after Leah told him Mrs. Rhinehardt had heard nothing from the cousin. She let James believe, as she had at first, that the cousin either would not or could not supply any information.

"You see, love," James said, cradling her in a bear hug, "I told you there was nothing to worry about. There are some people who have more to do than spread gossip."

Through those long evenings, Leah learned to love the warm cheerfulness of the family parlor, as comfortable and familiar as an old dressing gown. The braided rug was scuffed and worn, and its once-bright colors had been muted by time. The old sofa, on which James loved to stretch out and nap, sagged in places, but its chintz cover was as clean as hard scrubbing and drying in the sun could make it. As were the white cotton curtains at the windows.

Her favorite place was a large, overstuffed chair in front of the smoke-grimed red-brick fireplace. Unless lying on the couch after a long day in court, James sat by the fire, too, in a chair similar to hers. The seat of his contained a broken spring and the cushion a permanent depression from long use, but he said it fit him so perfectly in all the right places, he refused to have it mended. Next to Leah's chair was her sewing cabinet and above the long, solid-oak mantel was James's gun rack; the well-oiled barrels of the three guns gleamed in the firelight. This was their room, as intimate and personal as their bed, in which they shared highlights of their days and of their lives before they knew each other.

Leah looked over at James; the fingers of his right hand curled around the pipe always in his mouth, and his unruly, dark-red hair rested against the white linen antimacassar. Even in repose, the muscles of his arms and chest bulged against his rumpled tweed jacket. The fingers that held the pipe in one hand and a legal journal in the other were strong and powerful. If one word could be used to describe James it would be *strength*, strength of will, strength of purpose, strength of honor. Everything he said, everything he did exuded that word.

Leah knew that, given time, respect and admiration would engender love for him. She'd attended several court sessions and felt a new warmth of pride when he out-maneuvered his opponents with carefully constructed lines of argument. Against those who were more flamboyant or clever, he seemed almost stodgy and slow, but always he moved deliberately and surely toward the verdict he wanted, and most of the time he won for his clients. He was the same way with the land he was clearing for a larger garden. He attacked one tree at a time, cut it, and cleared all the debris before moving on to another or uprooting the underbrush. Strength and steadfastness, the two qualities Leah most needed in him now to keep her from falling apart at the thought of the letter that would someday arrive from Baton Rouge.

James laid aside the journal, began refilling his pipe, and smiled across at her. "What are you thinking about so hard?"

"Not thinking at all, really, just looking at you and the way you caress that pipe as if it were a magic lamp or a precious treasure."

"Don't laugh at my pipe. I'd sooner go without eating than lose it."

"I know. I sometimes think you were born with it."

"Not quite. But in one sense, it saved my life or at least my sanity. In fact, that's when I started smoking. When I was out West."

Leah put down the infant sacque she was embroidering and sat back prepared to listen. The stories James told about his earlier exploits were always entertaining, but more than that they gave her a deeper insight into him as a person.

"There were three of us traveling together at the time," James said. "I'd put in several months at a lumber camp in the north woods and decided to try something different. I didn't know whether I'd make it as far as California, but the time was my own, and I figured I'd see what lay beyond the prairies. I'd met up with John and Clay—can't even remember their last names—in St. Louis while I was buying a horse and pack mule. We decided to throw in together, figuring it was safer that way.

"We'd been several days on the trail when we saw huge billows of smoke some miles in the distance. Now a fire like that can mean several things: a wagon train, a woods fire, or an Indian campsite. Most Indians in the early fifties were pretty friendly, but it was still a good idea to approach with caution. After what we did come upon, we all wished it'd been Indians instead." He stopped, refilled his pipe, tamped down the tobacco to his satisfaction, lit it with a squill from the fire, and continued.

"As we neared the top of one rise, we dismounted and led the horses to keep them as quiet as possible. A few scrubby bushes gave us a vantage point from which we could look down on a small valley below without being seen. We tied up the horses and bellied along the ground for the last hundred feet or so to where the hill began its downward slope."

He paused, poked the fire, and added a log. "God, Leah, I really don't know how to describe what we saw. At first it seemed all peaceful. A small house of weathered boards sat near a small stream. There were roofed enclosures for animals and a well-tended garden. The house had a narrow sagging porch, but it was surrounded by a garden filled with flowers. I'll never forget those flowers."

"But the bonfire," Leah said. "I was sure you were going to say the house was on fire."

"No, the fire was several yards away. A huge campfire. When we saw it, we all went rigid, all three of us unable to move. A woman and two children were gagged and tied to three trees. They were still alive—but barely. Several Indians were taunting them, and one Indian was pulling the woman's long hair and forcing her head back."

Leah nodded. "An Indian attack while the man was away. I've read about such."

"No, the man was there. That's what the Indian wanted the woman to see. Her husband being tortured. Two strong saplings had been bent over toward each other, and their tips were tied to short stakes driven in the ground. A tall, rawboned man stood between them, helpless to move while Indians tied his left arm and leg to one tree, his right arm and leg to another."

"And you could do nothing," Leah sighed.

"We tried. We were three guns against at least ten of them, and we had to consider how to save the family as well as ourselves. We waited, conferring in whispers, each word sounding like a shout to our ears. But the yelling and whooping from below masked our voices. We could easily kill three of them at that distance, maybe even six, before they reacted, but what would they do then? We watched, fearful, afraid even to breathe. We wanted a moment when none of the Indians was close to the family. Then one of them cut the woman from the tree, threw her on the ground, and began raping her. We couldn't wait any longer. We shot simultaneously and killed three of the savages instantly. Before we could reload, we witnessed a horror no man in his right mind could envision. If only we'd known what was going to happen, we'd have chosen our targets more carefully and shot the two standing near the man instead of three others. They cut the ropes holding the saplings to the stakes. For a brief second there was no sound but the man's screams before the trees sprang apart, ripping him in two."

"Oh, dear God, no!" Leah shuddered.

"It was horrible. The man was well muscled and strong, so his own strength provided the ultimate in torture. A weaker man would have been dismembered instantly. But, as if in slowed-down motion, I could see his muscles stretching to their utmost, extending his agony by a fraction of eternity. I pray I never see anything like it again."

"And the others? The woman and children?"

"We killed three more of the Indians from where we stood and started to run down the hill. Almost immediately the wife and children were split open with hatchets. With that, John, Clay, and I collapsed on the ground."

"And you just left them?"

"No. We lay there a long time, or at least it seemed long to me. Clay kept mumbling they were not Indians while John was insisting we should bury the family. Over and over Clay kept using the word *renegades* and John was saying how he couldn't bear the thought of touching the mutilated bodies. It was like I wasn't even there. Or I was alone in my fear. Leah, I don't know how to describe the feeling I had. My stomach was a block of ice but I was vomiting up something hot and bitter. When I tried to move, my legs were no longer part of me. Like they lay behind me, separate and apart. I finally lifted myself up by my arms. Then there was a new, ugly sensation. My bowels had turned to water, and the excrement stuck my long johns to my legs. I was disgusted by the stink of my own body."

"I know, James. I know what you were suffering."

"No, Leah, you couldn't. You've never been through anything like that."

Leah thought of her experiences in the prison, of being raped and tortured by the guard. Having her own body betray her in the same way as James described. She'd never told him all that. Those were shameful secrets for her to live with, but she could tell him something else.

"Believe me, James. I do know. I've never told you about assisting at Baptiste's surgery."

"I knew you were in the hospital, but that's all."

"I was asked to assist at an amputation. The man's face was covered, so I didn't know who it was. Both legs had to come off. I was all right as long as the doctor was cutting through the flesh; I'd already seen enough bullets removed and mortified flesh cut away to stand that. But when he reached for the saw and I heard the steel cutting through bone, the room started spinning, and it was all I could do to keep from fainting. I had to hold the lower leg, grasping the mangled flesh securely, to keep it from jarring when he made the final cut. When, moments later and after the second leg was removed, I learned it was Baptiste, I had to flee from the room. That same block of ice in the stomach and hot gall in the throat attacked me. Then for two weeks I kept him alive, staying day and night by his bed, fighting fever and blood poisoning. Do you see now why—why the choice was so hard for me to make?"

"I do." He reached over and took her hands in his. "And I'm glad you told me. I accused you of making him too dependent on you, and all the while it was your need for him."

"I'd lost my son. Keeping Baptiste alive was like giving birth again, and this time I would not give him up. But then, I finally realized you were right. By staying with

207

Baptiste I would be depriving him of the life he was entitled to even more than I would deprive myself."

"Whatever the reasons, darling, you'll never know how happy you've made me by making the choice you did."

"Now, tell me, did you bury the family?" She'd not meant to bring Baptiste's name up again, and the only way to keep James from knowing the pain it caused her was to keep him talking.

"We did. At first I was afraid, really afraid of the dead bodies. I'd looked on the torture and killing with horror, but not fear. Then suddenly I recoiled at the thought of touching those dead bodies. But the buzzards were already circling, and we had to move quickly. First I hurried to the small stream, stripped off my filthy clothes—God, how they'd begun to stink. I rinsed off my trousers as best I could and put them back on, shivering all the while. I offered to dig the graves while John and Clay wrapped the bodies in blankets from the house. I couldn't even watch while they gathered up the remains of the father, picking up an arm here, a leg there. I started gagging again when they had to use a shovel to scrape up the entrails. We worked for at least three hours in complete silence. I don't know whether we were honoring the dead or keeping our mouths shut to keep from being sick."

"But the Indians? The rest of them?"

"They fled as soon as they killed the woman and children. We left the dead ones lying on the ground. But, you know, Clay had been right. They weren't Indians. They were white men—renegades, we learned later, who'd been attacking wagon trains and settlers while disguised as Indians. Anyway, we filled in the graves and then put up some markers. Found what we thought must be their names in a family Bible. Then we sat for a long time by the stream. Clay noticed how wet my clothes were and asked if I'd wet my pants. When I admitted I'd gotten sick, John said he'd thrown up like crazy the first time he saw an ambush, so I felt better about my weak insides. It was then Clay handed me a pipe. 'Here, try this,' he said, 'it'll help settle your stomach.' It did, and I haven't been without one since."

"Well, you'd better refill it, because I think it's gone out. Is that when you decided to come back East?"

"No, the three of us stayed together a few more months, doing a little trapping and hunting, shooting game for a wagon train we joined up with, fought off a few real Indians. Then I'd had enough. I'd proved a point, and I was ready to settle down with the books."

James got up to go out back and get another log. Leah watched him as he moved slowly yet purposefully toward the kitchen door, and she was once more amazed at the many men contained in the one man. He was at times a shrewd, competent lawyer; at others, a rugged frontiersman and hunter. She'd gone out in the fields with him as well as sat in the courtroom, and she marveled at the way he could bring down a wild turkey on the wing as easily as he destroyed an opponent in court. Yet at the same time he was sensitive and gentle.

He would be a good father. He was looking forward as eagerly as she to the birth of their child. Never did he refer to the coming baby as "her" child, but always as "theirs." She had known a certain kind of contentment as Baptiste's *placée*. Now she was experiencing a calmer, more placid life as James's wife, and she would feel perfectly secure if it were not for the constant threat of a letter from Louisiana that could destroy that happiness.

Chapter Eight

BAPTISTE LAY BACK against the cushions of the landau. He was pleasurably exhausted after three exhilarating days in the city. Miraculously his apartment had been spared the worst ravages of Federal occupation. Maybe it was because the Union officers thought only the grandest houses worthy of their attention. After he moved into the small house he bought for Leah, Baptiste had visited his apartment a few times, but only to make sure everything was in good shape. Since the beginning of the war, he'd not entered the rooms until he decided to make this trip to New Orleans to check on the sale of his sugarcane. The apartment was filthy, but that was easily remedied by Benji and a Negro woman Benji met and hired at the Market. Within hours he settled in as comfortably as when he lived there before Leah came into his life.

In a better humor than on the night he fled the city some months earlier, he shared drinks with Pierre at Le Coq d'Or, spent a riotously gay night at Madame Broulé's, partied with friends, talked business with many of his old cronies, and checked with his broker. Cane was selling for a good price at the sugar mills, and there would be twice as much money as he'd hoped for for both himself and his workers. Before leaving the plantation, he'd met with Septimus and the workers. They agreed to his proposition that one-third of the harvest money should go to Baptiste as owner of the land. Out of this sum would come the cash for next year's planting as well as general costs of the plantation; one-third would be divided among the workers, with two shares going to Septimus; and one-third would be saved against future crop failure. The last provision hadn't provoked any argument; all of them had known what it was to starve and be deprived of their homes, and they saw it made sense to save against future privation.

The talking really began when Baptiste tried to persuade them to keep their own shares in the bank and let him pay them a monthly salary. They only shook their heads in disbelief when he started explaining the interest they could earn on their savings, and he soon gave up. As Baptiste had feared, they were ready to splurge with the money their back-breaking work would bring them. The next spring and summer they'd expect him to carry them, as he had this year. Finally it was Septimus who saw reason in doling out their shares a bit at a time each month, and he convinced them of the wisdom of letting the master keep the money for them. They agreed, but only if he put it in his lockbox so they would know exactly where it was and look at it from time to time. Inwardly Baptiste laughed at their fear of having their earnings lost in the depths of a big building in New Orleans, but he said he'd keep the cash in the house, and yes, they could look at it whenever they wanted to.

So two-thirds of the income was in the bank, and one-third in a strongbox at his feet. Baptiste patted his left leg. The money was not the only thing making him feel jubilant. He'd also visited the hospital, where extensive work was being done to aid amputees. Dr. Honoré, the surgeon who'd operated on him, had been experimenting with various devices to improve artificial legs and arms. For three days Baptiste had conferred with him and been measured for new prostheses that were much more natural-looking than his old ones. Strapped to his hips so that the stumps of his own legs didn't have to bear all the weight, they were more comfortable and could be worn longer without hurting or tiring him. He'd never be able to move without his crutches; no real miracles had been performed that would allow him to dance or walk unaided, but his endurance would be greater and there would be no more nights of lying awake because of tender flesh and throbbing, aching muscles.

In an almost manic state of elation after all his successes, Baptiste was strangely moved to see Catherine waiting for him on the gallery when Benji swept the buggy around the curve in front of the house. She *was* beautiful, standing there in a blue velvet cloak with the cold December sunset frosting her blond hair.

"Welcome home, Baptiste." She ran down the curved flight of steps, her cape billowing out behind her like wings.

"Thank you. It's good to be back." He remained in the carriage and waited for Benji to descend from his perch and come around to assist him.

"You look like the hound that caught the fox," she smiled. "Things must have gone well in the city." It was very important for her plans that they had. This was the day she would make a decision, and what it would be depended on whether there had been a good sale for the cane harvest.

"They did indeed," Baptiste said. "The plantation is on secure ground at least for another year."

The plantation! That's all he ever considered. But she'd give him something else to think about. "Jessie has a fine dinner waiting, and she's invited me to stay." She noted that Benji was grinning from ear to ear; nor did Baptiste seem displeased.

"Good. I'm starved. Just let me get out of here and up the steps."

If he noted that Catherine turned her head away while Benji assisted him to alight and then to maneuver the long stairs, he thought little of it. She busied herself rearranging her cape that the chill, blustery wind off the river had whipped about her legs, and then she followed the men up the steps and into the main hall. She'd ordered one of the boys to light a fire in the library and now she turned to Benji.

"We'll eat in here. It's much more cheerful than the dining room."

"But trays are so awkward," Baptiste said, "and I can't manage a full dinner plate on my lap."

"We won't use trays. Benji, pull over that side table. M'sieu Fontaine can stay on the couch, and I'll sit on one of these side chairs. You can serve dinner and then close the door so we won't be disturbed." She wouldn't have him hovering around when she was trying to create an intimate, beguiling atmosphere.

Benji winced at the peremptory orders and began to have second thoughts about the woman he'd thought would make an ideal wife for Baptiste. Maybe he'd been wrong in encouraging her to come around as often as she did, and encourage her he had. But Baptiste didn't seem to object to her taking the upper hand, and his master's happiness was all that mattered to Benji.

"So, tell me all about the city," Catherine said, once they were seated before the fire and Benji had served the baked chicken, herb-seasoned rice, hot fruit compote in wine, and thick coffee. "It's ages since I've been there."

"Things are going well, considering the Union troops still occupy it. Most people ignore them now. I was glad to find my apartment still the same, with everything just as I left it. I think I'll spend more time there during the next few months, at least until spring planting. Had a good time with old friends."

The money, the money! Catherine wanted to shout. *How much did you get for the crop?* "That's all you saw? Just friends, I mean?"

"I saw my broker of course, to make certain all the cane had been sold." He reached over to pour a second cup of coffee. "And what have you been doing?"

Catherine fidgeted in her chair. How could he be so casual about it? Or was he being deliberately irritating? No, he'd have no idea how much the sale meant to her.

"Nothing," she answered, forcing herself to keep from being petulant. "This sudden cold snap ruined all my plans for working in the garden; and since it's Advent, no one's having any parties, not even a tea or small supper. I'll be glad when Christmas arrives so people will begin entertaining again." Which brought to mind the Christmas gala she wanted Baptiste to have and at which—but all that depended on what he'd learned from his broker. Why didn't he say something!

"I should think you'd be glad of the rest," Baptiste laughed. "I never saw anybody who gadded about as much as you do."

"Isn't that what life's supposed to be, having fun all the time, not sit cooped up in the house in front of a fire with no one to talk to except Helene, and you know how dull she is. No wonder Pierre spends most of his time in the city. I would too, if I were married to her. I wish I could, but he insists his apartment is too small, and he wants me to stay in the country to keep Helene company. I sometimes think there's another reason why he won't even let me visit him and go to all those splendid parties and balls they're having again."

Baptiste raised his eyebrows but said nothing. Catherine might not be shocked that Pierre had acquired a mistress, but she would be sure to tell Helene and then all hell would break loose. Helene was not the typical complacent French wife who accepted her husband's side-street liaisons as natural while hating the tradition that had been brought to the Vieux Carré from France.

"Well, you've only two more weeks to wait," Baptiste said, "and I saw at least five invitations on the hall table for open houses and galas, so I'm sure you've received twice as many."

"And accepted every one of them!" she said. "You—you will escort me, won't you? I mean, it would hardly be seemly for me to attend alone."

"And deny all those other men who hover around the pleasure of taking you? I couldn't be that selfish. No, I'm afraid I'm not up to more than a few of them."

That wasn't part of her plan. He had to be her constant escort. She'd thought to suggest he have his Christmas party near the end of the holiday season. Maybe it should be earlier. If only she knew what he'd learned in the city.

"You said things went well," she said. "Does that mean you sold all of the cane? And for a good price?" There, she'd asked it, and she'd know.

"More than I'd hoped for," he said casually. Now that

he no longer had to worry about a poor market, he could be unconcerned about it.

He wasn't as explicit as Catherine wanted. She wanted figures; she wanted to know whether he was now wealthy or of just moderate means. But evidently, "more than I'd hoped for" would have to suffice. She knew he was conservative where money was concerned, so that could mean the crop had sold very well. On that she'd have to bank.

"Well then, you must feel like celebrating," she said, smiling most bewitchingly and reaching for his hand. "So maybe we ought to talk about the Christmas gala you agreed to host."

"I did?" All the way home, Baptiste had been thinking that now, with no crop to worry about, he could relax, enjoy the house, share drinks with Benji before the fire, and get in some duck hunting. While he looked forward to the Christmas and New Year's open houses, they were all the social life he desired. What in hell did Catherine have in mind now?

"Don't you remember?" He was really being exasperating. "When we planned that first supper. We said it would be only the first, and you'd have a really splendid affair at Christmas. Don't disappoint me, Baptiste. It's the one party I've really been looking forward to."

"All right, Catherine, for you I'll do it." Her pale hair was a rosy nimbus in the firelight, and her long, white fingers lay gently on his hand. He felt a powerful urge to crush those fingers with his and to pull her down onto the couch. He watched her breasts rise and fall beneath the pale-blue gown and he wondered if they were as white as her fingers or as delicately pink as her cheeks. Instead, he forced himself to listen to her and make plans for the party he'd give.

"And so," she was saying, "I think it should be the day after Christmas. There are no other important functions then, but we'd better get the invitations right out. I'll see about those tomorrow. I've already made out the list. And it will be the perfect time to announce our engagement."

"Our what!" Baptiste wanted to leap up from the couch. As it was, all he could do was pound on the table, rattling the coffee cups and spilling the wineglasses.

When Catherine casually added that sentence, she was

prepared for a surprised reaction, but she didn't expect such a violent outburst.

"Well, naturally. I mean, I just assumed." No, she mustn't appear defeated. She must regain the upper hand. "After all, we have attended every function together, and certainly people are going to expect it."

"I don't give a damn what people expect. I lead my own life, Catherine. That is something you would do well to remember. And I have no wish to marry you or anyone else."

"Oh dear, this is all so humiliating." *I've not lost yet,* she thought. *He's so softhearted he can't bear to see anyone hurt. I'll work on his pity—yes, and his desire. He's wanted me since the first day I came here, and that wasn't loathing on his face a few minutes ago. You want me right now, Monsieur Fontaine, but you'll get me only on my terms, and those terms are marriage.* "I can certainly never attend another party with you. And when I think of all the invitations—and yes, the proposals—I've turned down." She released a deep sigh and dabbed at her eyes with a bit of lace. "I think you might have been a little more considerate than to insist on being my constant escort if—if you had no thoughts of marriage."

"Insist!" he stormed. *All right,* he admitted to himself, *I might not have insisted, but I didn't refuse either.* He looked at the beauty that could be his, and he thought about the news Pierre had given him.

Pierre had received a letter from Leah asking him to go into the house and send her a marked box of baby clothes.

"Did—did she send me any word?" he'd asked.

"Yes," Pierre said, "she told me to tell you that she is happy and she hopes for the same happiness for you."

The weeks since Leah'd left him had become months. He'd written more than a dozen letters to her but committed none of them to paper. Now, with a child on the way, she'd never return. He had to recognize that she was lost to him forever.

"All right, Catherine," he sighed and poured a fresh glass of wine. "If it's what you wish."

"Good," she brightened up immediately. "I'll tell Pierre he can make the announcement."

He saw the triumphant smile on her face. He'd forfeited

the game they were playing, but somehow he didn't care anymore. At least when he looked at Catherine's blond hair, fair skin, and blue eyes, he'd never be reminded of Leah.

"And there's time," Catherine said, "for me to go into the city and order a new gown. Pierre can like it or not, but I intend to stay with him."

In which case, Baptiste thought, Pierre had better be forewarned to find more suitable quarters for his mistress.

"Is that what the engagement means to you, Catherine? A new gown?" Well, did it really have any deeper meaning for him?

"To all women, darling. That is something most men fail to realize. Women celebrate great occasions with new gowns. But if it displeases you, I shall wear one of my old ones."

"No indeed, dress as fancy as you like. You've earned the right to the most expensive one in town," he added sardonically. "If Pierre is paying, that is. Because you'll have to be more frugal once you're under my roof."

Or so you say now, Catherine thought. *Well, women also know how to handle that.* She extended her hand in an invitation for Baptiste to kiss it.

"Oh no, sweetheart, we're not playing games anymore. I want you over here on the couch next to me."

For just an instant Catherine stiffened. Expecting him to put his arms around her or to lean over and kiss her, she moved the table to sit beside him. Instead, he reached for her hand and laid it on his lower left leg. Catherine winced. She was more disgusted and repulsed than if he'd thrown her down on the couch and attacked her.

"Feel that," he said. "Feel how natural it is, almost like the real thing. And look," he pulled up his trouser leg. "See that catch down there. See how I can bend my knee, or lock the catch if I want the leg stiff."

Catherine shut her eyes, swallowed hard, and tried to repress the shudder forcing its way through her. She abhorred imperfection of any kind, and the sight of the stark-white, linen-covered artificial leg with its catches and locks and straps was the ugliest thing she'd ever seen. Her delicate sensibilities were revolted at the idea of having to see this—this horror every day for the rest of her life.

Then she thought of having to live with Helene in Pierre's house for that same lifetime. In spite of what she'd said to Baptiste, there'd been no other proposals, nor were there likely to be any since the war had killed off most of the eligible men, and there was a wealth of younger, prettier belles for the survivors to choose from. She weighed her present condition against the likelihood of Baptiste's being really wealthy in the future, and she knew she could learn to tolerate his physical deformities. But, as with her insistence on marriage, it would be on her own terms.

"Yes," she smiled coldly. "I'm sure it must be an improvement over the old leg. Although you certainly learned to ride as well as walk with it."

"That wasn't the real reason I showed it to you," Baptiste said. "I want you to see it and this one, too." He raised his right trouser leg. He was not oblivious to her cringing or her reluctance to touch him. But if she had any hesitancy about accepting his infirmities after marriage, he wanted her to voice it now. "Do you think you can get used to them?"

Catherine looked straight at him and without a flicker of an eyelash to betray the lie, she said, "Yes."

"Then I think it's time we sealed our engagement." Before she could stop him, Baptiste pulled her across his lap. While he moved his hands up from her waist to caress her breasts, he kissed her so long and forcefully, she was gasping for breath. Almost before she could recover, he had opened the bodice of her gown and was kissing her breasts.

Through it all Catherine neither resisted nor responded. She felt neither pleasure nor revulsion at his touch. Cool and emotionless, she was completely devoid of any sensuality. She was ruled completely by her calculating mind and her rational will. Reason alone prevailed in her response to anything. She had a palate that appreciated food only as necessary for life; bland or highly seasoned, it was all the same to her. Her eyes saw beauty only as something to impress others. She had long since recognized her own sensual powers, and she used them to attract. Catherine was like a mare in heat used to attract and trap into an outer pen wild stallions unable to reach her. Catherine's aloof mien was her high fence. Her power lay in watching the emotional reaction of others and acting accordingly.

Thus, if Baptiste wished to caress her now, she accepted it as his due, but she felt no physical or emotional desire for him. She had never known what it meant to long for a man's touch or feel the throbbing in the loins that could be eased only by passionate embraces. Nor was this an attitude she had trained herself to maintain. She had been born lacking the most feminine of qualities: the soft, warm, generous desire to give oneself completely to a lover.

"Please, Baptiste, you're mussing my hair."

"Isn't that part of the game," he teased, and ran his fingers through the pale strands.

"I'd—I'd rather you didn't. And you're wrinkling my dress. Remember, I still have to go home, and I don't like appearing disheveled."

"You think Helene might guess what we've been doing? After all, you'll be telling her we're engaged. I'm sure she expects us to be doing something like this."

"I'm sorry, but I'd rather no one knew what occurred during our intimate moments. It's not the sort of thing I like to have others thinking about."

"Come off it, Catherine," he ranted. "You're no innocent virgin. You've been married before, and Helene is married now. Certainly it's no holy secret what married people do in private."

"In private, yes. But we're not married yet. Even though I've been married before, I'd prefer to keep things a bit more formal between us until we are. Is that really asking too much?"

"Then set the date. I don't intend to wait long. You wanted marriage and I wanted you. It's to both our advantage not to postpone it."

"I'll set the date when you put the diamond on my finger." A ring would make it official, and she wanted to be certain he didn't change his mind.

"I'll go to town tomorrow." The pain of knowing Leah was gone forever was still intense. The sooner he married Catherine, the sooner it might ease.

"A big one, Baptiste, not a little piddling stone like the one Lucy has."

"It shall be the biggest I can find, just to satisfy your

219

greedy heart." He found it easier to banter lightly with her than to get into a serious, emotional conversation. He could accept her honest expression of greed more easily than a false pretense of love.

"Not greedy, Baptiste, but proud to be your wife."

"Are you really, Catherine?"

"I really am," and for once she was being completely honest. To be his wife meant being mistress of Belle Fontaine.

As Baptiste promised, he went to New Orleans to choose the ring. While there, he dined with Pierre. For once he'd steal a march on Catherine and break the news himself.

"I guess that means congratulations are in order, old boy," Pierre said, stabbing his fork into a piece of flounder.

"Then why such a violent reaction?"

"Because I don't know whether the congratulations are for you or for Catherine. She set her cap for you, you know, beginning with the furnishing of your house."

"Sorry, Pierre, you're not telling me anything I didn't know. I'm no prey caught in a concealed trap."

"Are you sure?"

"And what in hell do you mean by that?" Baptiste was irritated by his friend's response. "Catherine's a beautiful and desirable woman. And since you told me about Leah—about having a child—I knew she'd never return to me. Catherine and I are going into this with our eyes open. We don't pretend to love each other, but she wants to be my wife and I want her."

"Look, Baptiste, Catherine is my sister, and I love her. But I also know her better than you do. You're my friend and I want the best for you. The marriage will be a mistake."

"For God's sake, why? I've told you how we feel. We're not children expecting an idyllic, never-ending romance. I need a wife. Leah said so and she was right. I should have children, for my pleasure and to inherit Belle Fontaine. Catherine will make an admirable mistress of the plantation; she knows how to run things and can take an awful lot off my back. And she's very beautiful."

"You asked me, and I'll tell you," Pierre said. "If you're

determined to go through with it, it's something you should know. Catherine didn't just love David, her first husband, she worshipped him. His memory has become an obsession with her. To her, he was perfect in every way, and if you know Catherine, you also know she cannot tolerate imperfection in anything."

"Then why——?"

"Because she wants a home of her own; more specifically, she wants Belle Fontaine. She'll be the ideal chatelaine, no fear of that, and everything will be immaculate and properly run to the nth degree. She'll supervise the household like a martinet, and nothing will ever be out of place. Meals will be served on time, and there'll never be a wrinkle in your suits. But be prepared. Whether vocal or tacit, she will be comparing you constantly to David. Can you live with that?"

"Wait a minute, Pierre, there's one thing you're forgetting. I'm no pushover myself. I can make demands, too. I never met David, but no one can say that Baptiste Fontaine is any less a man than he was. Don't think I don't appreciate your telling me this, because the first word from Catherine, the first time she mentions his name or hints at being displeased with me, she'll learn in short order she is now married to me, not to him."

"Keep that attitude, Baptiste, and you'll be all right. As I said, I'm fond of my sister, and I'm glad you're the man she's marrying. You're probably the only one who can get her over that fetish of hers."

Having returned to the plantation and eaten supper, Baptiste ordered the carriage and had Benji drive him to the DeLisle home. Alone with Catherine in the parlor, he took the ring from its box and slipped it on her finger. Instead of the glow of pleasure he expected, she turned to him in a fury.

"It's not a diamond!"

He looked at the opal surrounded by small diamonds. "I didn't promise you a diamond, just the biggest stone I could find. And this was it. I'm sorry you're disappointed. If you wish, I'll take it back and——"

"Oh, Baptiste, will you really? You would do that for me?" She was all smiles and dimples now.

"——and you can wait for the wedding ring."

Catherine didn't glower or fume, but the smile froze on her face. If he were trying to prove something, he'd soon find she could be just as contentious as he. But not yet.

"No, actually this is very unusual, and opals are rather rare. And they do have a mysterious beauty about them, like colorful flecks of fire glowing beneath ice."

"Very much like you, my darling. I hadn't realized it when I chose it, but it's your stone. I'll buy you a strand of opals and matching earrings to wear with it. They can be my wedding gift to you."

That pleased her. It was true: diamonds were so very common, and she could picture the iridescent opals coming alive against her pale skin.

The day after Christmas was the earliest date Catherine could choose since no marriages were performed during Advent. The morning wedding on December 26 was small, with only the priest, Pierre, and Helene in attendance in the DeLisle family chapel. Catherine, however, insisted on a large evening gala at Belle Fontaine, combining reception and Christmas party into one tremendous celebration.

Braced by the mantelpiece as well as his crutches, Baptiste stood beside Catherine all through the early part of the evening and accepted the congratulations of their guests. Catherine had spent days decorating the entire house, expending most of her effort on the long, wide hall, with its new Aubusson carpet she'd insisted on ordering and the furniture that Benji and his assistants had polished to a high gloss. Long garlands of smilax, decorated at carefully measured, regular intervals with red bows, festooned the fireplace and all the windows. Huge bouquets of magnolia leaves, red-berried pyracantha branches, and smaller clusters of nandina sat on every table and sideboard. The dining room was filled with a delicate but pungent fragrance from silver bowls of winter camellias and paper-thin, white Christmas narcissus. Remembering the story of the Greek lad Narcissus whose one flaw was self-love, Baptiste thought how appropriate it was that Catherine should surround herself with that flower. He wondered if she knew that such self-love ultimately destroys its object.

In a low-cut, emerald-green satin gown that perfectly

matched the magnolia leaves in the tall urn behind her, Catherine had never looked more beautiful. The opals that hung to the cleft between her breasts captured all the colors of the fire beside which she stood. Seeing the envious glances of the other men and receiving their congratulations, Baptiste felt a real pride that she was his wife.

"Congratulations, old boy."

"Thank you, George."

"You're a lucky son of a gun, Baptiste."

"Don't think I don't know that, Honoré."

"How did you do it?"

"My magnetic masculine charm, Charles, what else?"

"I'll be thinking about you later tonight, you lucky stiff."

"Sorry, Jean," Baptiste laughed, "but I'll certainly not be thinking about you."

And so it went. Everyone from plantations along the river and Vieux Carré society had been invited, and none had turned down the opportunity to celebrate the match of the season.

Soon after midnight the last guest left, the women with polite farewells, the men with more raucous and indelicate comments as to how Baptiste might want to spend the rest of the night.

"I don't suppose you'll be at the Ferriers' champagne brunch tomorrow," one of them suggested.

"I don't know why not," Baptiste grinned back. "I expect to be feeling especially fit by then."

"There is nothing that could keep me from one of their parties," Catherine added more seriously. "After all, we have accepted and one doesn't renege on one's obligations."

"Well, we'll see you there then."

Baptiste collapsed in his chair and asked Benji to bring him a brandy. He'd amazed himself by being able to stand throughout most of the evening, but now the effort was beginning to tell on him. He sipped the brandy slowly while Catherine moved around the hall pinching dead or dying leaves off the bouquets and garlands.

"Did you enjoy your wedding day, Catherine?"

"Very much. Just think, everyone we invited came. That means we hold a very important place in New Orleans society. Jessie outdid herself with the refreshments. Not a thing that wasn't just right. I shall have to commend Benji for his behavior. Usually he seems a bit too friendly, or forward perhaps, for a servant, but he carried it off quite properly tonight."

Baptiste raised one eyebrow but said nothing. He continued to sip his brandy. Once as she walked past, he reached out to draw her close to his chair and pull her head down so he could kiss her for the first time since they'd left the chapel. But she moved away too quickly. He knew she'd seen his hand go out. Had she deliberately walked away from him?

He set the liqueur glass down. "Wheel me into the bedroom, will you, Catherine? Even my arms seem to have given out."

"Certainly, darling." She used the term of endearment less with warmth than out of obligation: he would expect it when they were alone. "I can see you're tired. Perhaps you shouldn't have stood up for so long."

"Not so much that as weary of so many people. I don't remember knowing half of them."

"Then you must get to know them better," Catherine insisted. "They are all important people and ones you should cultivate. I worked on my list very carefully to make certain we excluded no one who should be here or invited any who shouldn't. And you *have* known them in the past. You simply let yourself get out of circulation while you— while the war was on." She didn't mention Leah's name, but both knew what she implied. "Many of them have vital connections. Certainly you don't always expect to earn your living just from the plantation. You must get back into the business world."

"I like the plantation, Catherine, and it's my home. I went into the brokerage only to prove to my father I could make it on my own."

"Well, we'll talk about that another time." She began turning down one side of the bed. "Do you—do you need any help? Shall I call Benji? By the way, I don't like his habit of calling you by your first name when he thinks no one is around. That will have to stop."

"It will not stop. He does it at my request."

Catherine turned around. She saw his hands curling into

224

fists and his face beginning to redden. Perhaps this time she had gone too far. "Well, I hope it is only when you two are alone. Do you want me to call him?"

"No, I've learned to manage very well by myself. You needn't worry. I'll seldom call on you for assistance."

"Well then, I'll say goodnight, and I'll see you in the morning." She still stood with her back to the bed, and Baptiste wheeled his chair up close enough to prevent her from moving. She put out a hand as if to push the chair aside.

"What the hell do you mean by 'in the morning'?" he fumed. "We're married now."

"Yes, I know, but—that is, I never thought—" It was not true. She'd thought about this moment many times and known it would come to such a confrontation. She'd considered every possible tactic to keep from sleeping with him and discarded most of them—fighting, crying, pleading—as unworkable. Finally she'd decided to pretend that she never believed him physically capable of consummating the marriage.

"To be my wife in more than name only? Is that what you're trying to say?"

"What else could I think since you were so badly injured. I—I heard stories about men who were wounded and could no longer—" She was growing whiter and fainter by the minute. She had to find some way out of her dilemma and keep Baptiste from making love to her.

"Dammit, Catherine, it was my legs I lost. *Nothing else.* You'll see I can be as satisfactory a husband as any other man." For a moment he really thought that had been her concern and she sincerely believed he was impotent. Given a few minutes to recover while she undressed, she'd be ready to welcome his embraces.

"Please, Baptiste, this has all been very upsetting. And I'm very tired." She put her hand up in an exhausted gesture. "If you don't mind, I'll leave you now."

Once again Baptiste saw the triumphant look on her face, and he knew she'd been planning all along to avoid him. Not because she thought he couldn't be a husband but because she did not want to be a wife. Let her think she'd won now, and she'd always have the upper hand.

"Where did you think to sleep, Catherine, if not with me?"

"I—I've fixed a room upstairs." His fierce look frightened her, and she was desperate to get away. He'd seen through her ruse, and unless she escaped from him now she'd never find a way to avoid his embrace. She had to have time to think and work out other plans. "If you'll let me by, I'll go on up."

"Upstairs!" He became more and more enraged. "To make certain I can't reach you, is that it? No, madame, you are my wife and will sleep down here. In this bed."

For once all her self-control gave way to despair. "No, Baptiste, I can't. I'll never be able to. It—it was hard even with David." Which was untrue. Even though she was left unmoved by David's caresses, she welcomed his embrace because it meant he loved her, and she loved him so desperately she would do anything to keep him all to herself. "Even so, it was different with him. I didn't find it easy then, but at least he was strong and whole." There, she'd said it. Maybe it would make him hate her enough to leave her alone.

"And I'm less than a man, is that it? Dammit, Catherine, you knew full well what I was when you lured me into marrying you. And you're going to be my wife—totally and completely." With his strong arms, he lifted himself up in the chair.

"You're not going to force yourself on me!" She was almost hysterical. "I'll not be made love to by a—a—"

"A cripple? Say it, dammit! It doesn't hurt much anymore." But it did. More than he'd admit to himself. He'd known Catherine didn't love him any more than he loved her, but he never dreamed it would come to this.

"Yes! Crippled and mangled and blemished. What other words do you want me to use?" She was screaming now. "You're hideous with those ghastly, unnatural legs."

"And my eye? You've said nothing about that." He reached up to pull off the patch.

"Don't! I'll be sick if you do." Her cheeks flushed a deep pink, and even in her vicious anger she was beautiful.

Aroused to a high pitch of both fury and desire, Baptiste lunged from the chair onto the bed and forced

Catherine onto her back. He ripped her dress from neck-line to hem and then tore off her undergarments. With fists and fingernails she hit his chest and clawed his face, but his arms were strong, and she was unable to prevent him from subduing her.

She'd no idea he was so strong or she'd never have let herself get into such a vulnerable position near the bed. Once he had her stripped, only the opals remained, glow-ing against her skin. He rose up just enough to look at her narcissus-white body against the dark green satin of her torn gown. Her disheveled blond hair lay in a tangled mass around her head. She was his now, and he meant for her to know it.

There was nothing gentle or loving about Baptiste's em-brace. He crushed her breasts until she could not keep from crying out, and he sunk his teeth into the softest parts of her body.

"Stop it, Baptiste," she pleaded. "You're hurting me."

"Shut up, Catherine."

He forced open her mouth with his, but in a momentary revenge she bit his tongue so hard blood spurted over both their faces. Maddened, yet even more aroused by her dar-ing, he entered her with such brutal force she could no longer fend him off and she went limp under the weight of his body.

When it was over, Baptiste lay exhausted. His conquest had been one of rape rather than seduction or love, and it left him less satisfied than disgusted. But at least he had shown Catherine that she was his wife and it would not pay her to resist him.

Neither of them moved the rest of the night. Catherine lay sobbing amidst the torn dress and underclothes. At first she felt completely defeated as well as soiled and disgusted and humiliated. She wanted to leave him immediately, but she could not move. Every part of her body hurt, and she knew it was covered with black-and-blue marks. She'd have to forego all the coming week's parties unless she wore a dress with long sleeves and high neckline like an old matron.

Then her own strong will took over. *All right, Monsieur Fontaine*, she thought. *You've won this time, but do not be surprised if you find that it's a Pyrrhic victory.*

Baptiste now knew that Catherine would never be a loving wife, nor could he hope to find in her the passion he thought lay deep beneath her cool exterior. They had been opponents in tacit combat from the beginning, and it now seemed they would continue as adversaries. Each sought what the other refused to relinquish. There would never be a truce, only a standoff.

In a quilted robe with a matching chiffon scarf around her bruised neck, Catherine joined Baptiste for breakfast at the small table in front of the library fire. The weather had turned bitterly cold, and the large dining room was difficult to heat. Every game has its rules, and both well knew the rules for this one. In front of others they would appear as a modestly happy couple. Since overt signs of affection were frowned upon, there was no need for them to do more than smile politely to each other occasionally. This they could manage. Both had too much pride to let anyone suspect theirs was not a genuinely happy marriage.

"Why did you marry me, Catherine?" Baptiste pushed aside his plate. Benji had just announced that Jessie was making a fresh pot of coffee and it would take a few minutes.

"I'm fond of you, Baptiste. I truly am." She reached for more butter for her biscuit. "After all, we grew up together as children, and I—"

"Don't hedge! At least be truthful, my darling. If lacking in other virtues, you at least are usually honest—or reasonably so."

"You really want to know? Or would you prefer to keep on believing I love you?" If she had to spend all her waking hours discovering his weaknesses, she was determined now to find every possible way to hurt him as he had hurt her the night before.

"I never thought that, Catherine. I know you too well. You've made a beguiling kind of *non*-flirtation into a fine art. No, I never believed you to be in love with me. But something about me had to attract you. Why marriage?"

"For position and security. There, I've said it. Does that make you angry?"

"No, not really. But I would have thought you had those already."

"Not in a home of my own, and certainly not the kind of things and pleasures I was denied for so long. After the war, after those years of flight and starvation and being deprived of the nice things that mean so much to a woman, I swore I'd never lack for any of them again. Do you know what it's like to wear the same dress day after day, to eat off broken china, to live like a beggar in someone else's home? I was tired of being a poor relation. Helene begrudged me every mouthful I ate and every cent Pierre gave me to spend on myself. I had nothing—do you understand—nothing that was my own. I need beauty and people around me. I crave them as others crave food. But where could I find them except in a home of my own and with a man who had enough money to supply them? Now you know why I married you. Does it disgust you?"

"No, Catherine, it doesn't. Surprisingly enough, it arouses a bit of admiration for you. That you would feel you could be that honest with me. Because, you see, I married for selfish reasons, too." He saw her start back and knew he had shocked her. He supposed it never occurred to her that he was not enamored of her. "I want children, to bear my name and to inherit this land. For that I need a wife. If you agree, we'll strike a bargain. You can do whatever you wish in and with this house. Yes, there's plenty of money, at least for the time being, and I think in the future as well. You can have all those luxuries you so ardently crave. I'll open charge accounts at the jewelers and what other shops you wish. If you begin spending beyond my means, I will so inform you; but as long as you're not too extravagant, I don't think you need worry about that. And you may entertain to your heart's content, though don't always ask me to be present."

"That sounds most generous, Baptiste." She could scarcely believe what he was saying. "And what do you require of me in return?"

"Don't try to act naïve, Catherine. You know perfectly well. In return, you will sleep with me willingly, not reluctantly, and you'll not try in any way to keep from having children."

He did not miss her expression of distaste as she spoke. "I'll try," she agreed, "but it will be hard. I told you, it was most displeasing even with David, and he was—"

229

"A whole man. I know. You made that perfectly clear last night. But I'm sure you'll find me a satisfactory lover once you learn to accept me. Leah never thought me repulsive."

"Leah!" Catherine leaped up from her chair. "Must I constantly be haunted by her? I'll agree to the bargain on one condition. You never mention her name again."

He nodded. That wouldn't be difficult. There was nothing in the house now to remind him of her. Catherine had seen to that. Even his sister's charming little bed, where he and Leah had known such joyous love, had been thrown out. Catherine had turned the small, cheerful room that overlooked the garden and river into her own private sitting room.

"You have the library that you use as an office and where you and Benji are always hobnobbing. If I'm to feel like an outcast in part of my home, I want a room of my own."

"Don't be ridiculous," he'd argued. "You know you're always welcome there."

"Welcome, maybe, but not comfortable. Except maybe in the evening. Surely you won't begrudge me one room." That was before he'd known about the bedroom she'd surreptitiously decorated and furnished on the second floor, and he agreed to her request.

No, he'd never mention Leah's name aloud. It would be securely locked away in his heart.

Chapter Nine

"HAND ME THAT garland of fir, will you, James?" Leah stood in front of the fireplace. "I want to drape it over the mantel. Be careful, it's stickly. I had quite a time putting it together."

"Stickly?" he laughed. "What sort of description is that?"

"A very good one. It's sticky from the sap and very prickly. So, it's stickly."

"Oh, Leah. I've a hard enough time with your accent, and now you begin making up words. How will I ever learn to understand you?"

"Not my words, maybe, but me, and that's what's important, n'est-ce pas?"

"See, there you go again. Understand you? I don't know. I just know I love you."

Leah leaned over for James's kiss and then took the garland from him. When she reached up to fasten it above the mantel, she had to stop midway with a stitch in her back. Then another one.

"James, I think you'd better go for Sarah and then Dr. Simmons."

231

"So soon?" He was alarmed that something might be wrong.

"I know. It's earlier than I expected. But I remember René's birth too well to be mistaken."

"How about Bridget? We'll need her, too."

"I don't think so. She'll be back in the morning, and this is her first night off. You and Sarah can do everything the doctor needs. But hurry. No, I don't mean rush, but don't waste any more time talking."

As soon as James left, flying off in the buggy in spite of her words that she didn't really mean for him to hurry, she went into the kitchen and put on water for tea. Both she and Sarah could use it. James would open a new bottle of whiskey to see him through the night. She remembered how drunk Baptiste had gotten when René was born, but it had been better than his pacing the floor outside the bedroom and his constant demands to know what was going on. It was the doctor who'd insisted he get a bottle and sit down in the parlor until he was called.

While the water heated, Leah went into the bedroom to check the pile of clean sheets and towels. There were soft receiving blankets and extra blankets for her on the dresser in case she needed them. She fingered one of the tiny gowns and sacques she'd so lovingly embroidered. At last she was going to be seeing them on her baby. She'd almost forgotten how hungry she'd been for another child after the death of René and the return of Baptiste from the war. Now that ache would be assuaged.

Another pain surged through her back, and she had to grab the footboard of the bed. As tempted as she was to lie down, she knew it would be better to stay on her feet until the last possible moment. She heard the water boiling. At least she could sit down while she drank one cup of tea.

While she poured the water, the pains became stronger. What was the expression she'd heard once? "They cut you down like a weed." She hoped James would hurry. She wasn't really afraid the baby would come before he returned, but she knew there were things Dr. Simmons had to do before she delivered.

Leah drank the tea—in which she'd forgotten to put sugar—in front of the fire. Seeing the garland she'd started to put up, she draped it across the nails James had already hammered into the mantel. Except for the tree, the house was ready for Christmas. Maybe she'd be able to lie on the couch and give James verbal support while he trimmed it. Feeling restless, she walked onto the porch to tuck more holly into the pine wreath on the door. While she was straightening the red bow, James drove into the driveway with Sarah, and she saw Dr. Simmons' buggy coming along right behind. She sighed with relief and admitted to herself she really had been frightened by the fleeting thought that they might not get back in time.

After Sarah helped her into a clean gown, Leah stretched out gratefully in the bed and rested her head and shoulders against three goose-feather pillows.

"There's tea in the kitchen, Sarah, if you'd like some. You needn't feel you have to stay here with me."

"Later perhaps, Leah." She pulled the rocking chair closer to the bed. "Right now I'm watching thee the way Dr. Simmons asked me to. Nod each time thee feels a pain."

"Where is Dr. Simmons? He should be in here."

"There's plenty of time. Right now he's persuading James to keep his pipe filled with tobacco and his glass with whiskey."

Leah laughed. "I rather thought that might be it." She tried to stifle a moan.

"Is thee uncomfortable?"

"A little."

"I've brought some lotion. I'll rub your back."

Leah began to ache all over, and she couldn't seem to get comfortable no matter which way she turned. "I'd like that, Sarah."

"Any feeling of pressure? An urge to bear down?"

"A little."

"Let me tell Dr. Simmons and then I'll massage thy lower back. That should help."

A cursory examination and Dr. Simmons said she had at least an hour to go. During that hour she sipped sweetened tea, let Sarah rub her back, and felt the pressure getting more and more intense. There was not as much pain as she remembered with René, but there was the tremendous feeling that she would explode if the baby did not come soon. Then she was gradually weaving in and out of consciousness, and she wondered if Sarah had put something in the tea besides sugar. Through a mist she saw Dr. Simmons at the foot of the bed, felt something being pulled out of her, and then drifted off.

"Are you awake, Leah?" It was Dr. Simmons. "Would you like to see your son?"

She looked at the tiny body in her arms. He immediately began sucking when she opened her gown and put him against her breast. His scalp was covered with fine black down, and his eyes were a deep blue. It was uncanny and frightening how much he resembled René. But he was not René. Just for a moment she realized he was Baptiste's son. Then she forced herself to remember that she must never again think of him as Baptiste's child. He looked like her, and he would be James's son. She brushed away the tears. They must be the last she shed.

"He's beautiful, Leah." She had fallen asleep as soon as the baby finished nursing, and now James was standing beside her bed but looking into the nearby cradle.

"He's a hungry little monkey, that's for certain."

James started to sit on the bed and then rose up again.

"Come up here and sit by me," she said. "You won't disturb me."

"Are you sure? How are you feeling?"

"A little tired, but fine."

In his cradle, the baby started fussing. "Maybe I'd better call Sarah," James said.

"Nonsense, just bring him over here. He's probably hungry again."

"Me?" James asked apprehensively.

Leah laughed. "You're not going to drop him. Just lift him up and hand him to me. Then hand me those diapers. I'm sure he must be wet, too."

While Leah fed the baby, James sat at the foot of the bed, and his heart was so full of love and gratitude he could hardly breathe. This was his child, and he would never think any differently. The love he and Leah had shared made the baby his as surely as if he'd been conceived between them.

"What do you want to name him, Leah?"

"Would you mind if I named him Jean-Paul after my

234

father? We can call him Paul. We'll name the next one after you."

"Paul he will be. It's a good name."

"Thank you, James. I loved my father. That may seem strange to you after all I told you about my earlier life. But he was always very good to me, and I knew he loved me. When I saw him just as New Orleans fell, I didn't know it would be for the last time. It's always haunted me that I didn't kiss him good-bye or let him know just how much I did love him. Somehow, I feel this will make up a little bit for that."

Leah was still half asleep when she heard Bridget return in the morning, but she woke up when the Irish maid brought her a steaming cup of coffee and a full breakfast tray.

To please James she'd agreed to hire a maid at the beginning of December to do most of the housework and then help with the baby. From the time Leah went with Mary Howard to take the enormous supply of desserts to the Irish immigrants, she'd been concerned about their almost squalid living conditions. She'd made four visits to the settlement with the women of the church, and each time she came back more disturbed than ever. If only there were some way to help them other than with occasional handouts. So when James insisted it was time to hire someone, she thought of Bridget, who was used to taking care of eleven younger sisters and brothers. Then the day before she was to arrive, Leah panicked.

"How am I going to manage her, James, and tell her what to do?"

"You never had a servant in New Orleans?"

"Yes, but she was a slave. How do I talk to a white servant?"

"The same way you would talk to anyone else, Leah, servant or friend. What do you think she is? An inferior to be kept in her place?"

Shocked at the stern expression on his face and his cross tone, she began crying. "I'm sorry, James, I guess I deserved that. I'm—I'm just not used to the idea of having a white girl working for me. Maybe I don't really need her. I'll feel so uncomfortable all the time."

"Do you like Bridget? Do you trust her to help you when the baby comes?"

"Oh, yes. She's always pleasant, and she keeps that small house spotlessly clean."

"Then think of it this way. You want to help her and her family, and this is the way to do it. She has too much pride to like accepting charity. She's here to make things easier for you, and you'll be paying her to do it. That is money badly needed by her family. How do you think she'd feel now if I went and told her you didn't want her after all?"

"Very hurt and very disappointed. Bring her here tomorrow. I'll have the back bedroom all ready for her when you return."

Bridget could not believe she was to have the pretty room overlooking the back garden all to herself. There didn't seem to be enough she could do for James and Leah. Up before they were, she had fires going in all the rooms and a hot breakfast on the table. The house was completely dusted every day, and laundry never stayed more than twenty-four hours in the hamper. Leah didn't know how Bridget did it all, but she was grateful James had insisted on hiring her.

Now Leah looked at her across the tray. "Thank you, Bridget, this looks delicious and I'm starved. Oh, this coffee is good." She saw Bridget glancing sideways at the cradle. "Would you like to hold Paul? If he's wet, maybe you should change him while I finish eating. Then I'll feed him. It must be about time for him to start crying. I think he's inherited his mother's appetite."

She watched Bridget lift Paul tenderly from the cradle. She'd be as good a nurse as she was a housekeeper.

Christmas Eve afternoon, Leah lay on the couch and directed James where to place each of the decorations on the tree. Bridget was rocking Paul before the fireplace.

"I think we'd better put the candles on last, James. Then we'll wait to light them later. They never shine so well as with just the firelight after dark."

James walked over to the window. "I thought I heard horses in the driveway. Wonder who it could be."

"Sarah said she'd come early for dinner, but I didn't

think she'd be this early. I haven't even changed my robe. Bridget, hand me Paul and get the red robe. Oh, and the shawl, please, at the foot of my bed. I don't need this heavy comforter."

"Leah, you're acting as if Sarah were company. She stayed with you the whole night Paul was born."

"I know, but she always looks so fresh and neat."

When James answered the door and Leah saw who walked into the family parlor, she was doubly glad she'd insisted on changing.

"How are you, Leah? And you, James?"

"Very well, thank you, Eloise," James said while Leah remained speechless.

"I hope I'm not interrupting anything, but I did want to bring the new baby something. And here's a little extra sweet for your Christmas table." Mrs. Rhinehardt handed Leah a beautifully wrapped package and James a linen-covered plate smelling of rum and spices.

"Why, thank you so very much, Mrs. Rhinehardt," Leah said. "Won't you sit down. We were about to have coffee and fruitcake."

"Thank you, I can't stay long, but I can't resist having a bit of cake."

"Bridget, please take Mrs. Rhinehardt's plate into the kitchen and then you can bring the coffee and plates for the fruitcake." Still amazed at the sudden appearance of Mrs. Rhinehardt and even more at the gifts she'd brought, Leah turned her attention to the package.

"May I?" Mrs. Rhinehardt walked over to the crib. "What a beautiful child, James. I believe he looks like you, Leah."

"Yes, yes he does," she said.

Eloise Rhinehardt sat down by the fireplace and took the coffee Bridget handed her. "My, but it does look homey in here. We've given up having a tree, and now I'm sorry. We closed up the fireplace when we put the large coal heater in the center hall, but I think I'll tell Mr. Rhinehardt that we must have a fire tomorrow morning. To make it seem more like Christmas."

Leah lifted an exquisite blue silk sacque and bonnet from the box. "Oh, Mrs. Rhinehardt, this is perfectly beautiful. And large enough for Paul to wear in the spring when it gets warmer. How very thoughtful."

Mrs. Rhinehardt nodded toward the cradle. "You've named him Paul? After someone in your family perhaps?"

"My father," Leah said. "Jean-Paul, but we call him Paul since double names don't seem to be as popular here as in the South."

"Oh yes, Jean-Paul Bonvivier. I understand he died during the war."

"Yes, he did. But how did you know?" Now the truth would come out. This, not the gifts, was the reason for her visit. Leah tensed. How much did she know? More important, how much would she reveal?

"I—I have a cousin in Louisiana. When I mentioned in a letter that you had moved here, she wrote that she was acquainted with the family and mentioned he was dead."

The lie did not come easily to Mrs. Rhinehardt's lips, and Leah wondered whether to probe for more information or wait to see what else the woman would say.

"Your cousin lives in New Orleans?" Leah asked. "I'm surprised you didn't mention her earlier, to ask if I knew her."

"No, not New Orleans—Baton Rouge. Actually she knows of your family through a mutual friend in New Orleans, a business associate of her husband's."

Leah could see that Mrs. Rhinehardt was trying to avoid saying she'd written for the information while at the same time she meant to indicate she knew a great deal about Leah. One thing seemed strange. If she did know all about her past and her being Jean-Paul's natural rather than legal daughter, why was she hesitating to speak out? In spite of the outcome, Leah had to learn what the woman knew.

"And your cousin merely told you my father was dead?"

"Oh, no, she said he was a highly respected and wealthy importer. You know, Leah, we up here really know so little about the South that I must confess I wrote back and asked her for more information. And, my dear, we are so pleased that you've come to Hickory Falls. Why, this town must seem like a stodgy backwater village after the rich, gay life you led."

Leah looked over at James, who merely raised his eyebrows and shook his head. He was as bewildered as she by what Mrs. Rhinehardt was saying.

"Yes," she continued, "you've been much too modest about yourself. James, you should have told us that she was married to the scion of a fine, old New Orleans family that had one of the largest sugar plantations on the Mississippi. Such a pity that your husband died trying to save New Orleans. My, the war was a terrible one for all of us—for both sides, I mean."

Leah breathed a sigh of amazement and relief that she feared Mrs. Rhinehardt would hear. Married to a fine plantation family? Husband dead? The fear was gone, but in its place was a dazzling mystery.

"Yes, the war was bad," Leah said, "and I suppose the best thing is for all of us to forget it. My husband's death was a great tragedy, but marriage to James and the birth of our son has made me feel life is worth living again." She paused a minute to watch the grin spread across James's face. "I—I don't suppose you know who it was your cousin wrote to. I mean, if he knows so much it must be someone I was acquainted with."

"Not by name, no. But my cousin's husband is a lawyer, so I assume he is in the legal profession."

Pierre! It had to be Pierre. Only now, when the threat was over, did she feel her heart pounding and her chest pulling tight. Out of all the people in New Orleans, why was she so lucky to have the cousin contact Pierre. And bless his heart, he'd realized why he was being questioned, and he sent exactly the right information. Now maybe all her fears could be laid to rest.

"We knew several lawyers," Leah said as calmly as possible, "so I've no idea which one it would be. Some were friends of my father's and some of my husband's." Best to stop now while she could still speak casually. "I see your cup is empty. Wouldn't you like more coffee? If I know Bridget, she's made a full pot."

"No, thank you, my dear. I must be going. But it's been such a pleasure visiting with you. You have a lovely family, James, and we're all very happy for you. By the way, Leah, after the Christmas holidays, there will be a number of quilting bees. Something to do when the weather keeps us inside. The first will be at my house, and I do hope you can join us. They're just informal gatherings, but we enjoy sitting around the quilting frame and chatting. And do bring Paul. There will always be someone to help you care for him."

"Thank you, Mrs. Rhinehardt. I'd be delighted to join you."

"I—I hope you won't mind if some of the women ask you about life in the South—before and during the war. They can't help but be curious."

"I'm sure I won't mind answering their questions. I may have a few of my own."

While Leah remained on the couch, James saw Mrs. Rhinehardt to the door. When he returned, he sat on one of the cushions beside her.

"I don't know whether to laugh or cry, darling."

"I know what you mean." Leah could finally release the big sigh she'd been holding back. "She was trying so hard to be nonchalant about it all."

"But she was bursting inside to tell us what she'd learned." James stood up suddenly, put both hands on his hips, threw back his head, and filled the room with his loud guffaws. "By God, it did me good to see that pompous stuffed shirt bowing and scraping to you. She loves to lord it over everyone else, but she finally met someone she considers her social superior. Who do you suppose it was? Pierre?"

"It had to be, thank God. Someone else might have glossed things over. Pride in the South and so forth. But only Pierre would add those convincing touches."

"You appreciate what her final accolade was, don't you?"

"No, I'm not sure what you mean." Leah looked up inquisitively.

"The invitation to the quilting bees. That little informal group she referred to is made up of what they think is the *crème de la crème* of Hickory Falls society. You have made it, my darling. You have been accepted."

"I'm pleased," Leah said. "Not because it's the inner circle, but because it means I no longer have to be afraid. I think I'll enjoy the quilting bees, but as far as friends are concerned—well, I guess I admire Sarah more than any of them."

James kissed her softly. "Know how you feel, darling, but there are others who would like to be your friend, too, and I think you'd like knowing them."

"You're right as usual, James. Maybe I've let my fears make me a recluse."

Bitter winter weather with deep snows and sleet had kept them all housebound for days at a time. There were a few visits with Sarah whenever the weather broke enough to hitch up the buggy and bundle Paul in a thick blanket cocoon. Leah also attended a quilting bee and thoroughly enjoyed the full day of sitting with nine others around the huge frame and learning to sew together the backing, filling, and patchwork face of the quilt. Eloise Rhinehardt had evidently spread the word about her fabricated past, for she was welcomed eagerly and several of the women, like Mrs. Jacobs and Mrs. Simpson, actually fawned over her as if she'd been royalty rather than the daughter of a wealthy Southerner. To her relief, Mary Howard, Elizabeth Benson, Martha Simmons, and Mrs. Peters treated her with the natural friendliness they always had.

She was amazed, however, at the amount of curiosity they all evinced about life in the South before and during the war. They were ready to believe that everyone—every white person—was wealthy beyond belief, but she could also see they were discarding as exaggerations what she started to tell them about the horrors of life under Federal occupation. She decided it was wiser to talk about life in Hickory Falls. It had not taken her long to realize two things: people will believe what they want to believe and the way to another woman's heart is to ask her advice about something.

Finding Bridget a real help, Leah didn't argue when James suggested she remain with them. One day while she was dusting in the bedroom and Leah was straightening the drawers, Bridget picked up Leah's rosary and stood holding it in her hand for a long time.

"That's a very precious memento, Bridget," Leah said. "It was given to me by a dear, dear friend, a nun in the convent where I went to school. Sister Angelique was a close friend as well as teacher. The rosary had been a gift to her from someone who'd been to Rome. It was blessed by the Pope."

"By the Pope, ye say!" Bridget fingered it as if it were a precious jewel. "Then ye be a Catholic?"

"Yes, I was brought up in the Catholic faith."

"But how then do ye go to the church here? 'Twould be a sin, I should think, a mortal sin."

"I suppose some would say that, Bridget. But we all worship the same God, and when there is a moment for silent prayer, I say my own prayers. I doubt that God cares which building we are sitting in."

"Oh my," Bridget sighed, "I wish me mum could hear ye say that. She is that distressed that we have no church and no priest to baptize our wee ones or give the last rites to the dying. And so many have died, all now condemned to Hell."

"No, Bridget," Leah insisted, "you mustn't think that. You must consider the circumstances. You've been here such a short time and no money to build a church or bring in a priest. Do you—do you get together and pray?"

"We do that. But 'tis not the same. Candles we have and a bit of holy water brought over from Ireland, but no priest." Bridget crossed herself and shook her head as if in mourning for all her family and friends.

"Bridget, let me tell you a story. It's a true story, and I want you to know what a priest told me once." Painful as it still was, she told about losing both Clotilde and René to yellow fever and having to see them buried without the last rites. "And then that young priest, so terribly exhausted and distraught, said to me, 'God in His infinite mercy will not condemn them during this time of sorrow.' You see, I too was certain they could not be saved, but since he told me that, I've never doubted for a moment but that they were."

"He sounds like a fine man, ma'am, but we've no sich reason as a grave illness."

Leah knew nothing could dissuade Bridget from her fears that all of her family and friends were doomed unless they had a church and a priest. "Have you contacted the bishop; have you asked him to send a priest to your homes?"

"How can we?" Bridget asked. "We none of us know how to write."

"That's easily remedied. I'll write to him myself. James mentioned his name once, but I can't remember it now. I'll find out this evening and send the letter off tomorrow. He can write back to me, but I must know the names of all the families. Come, we'll go back to the parlor. You tell me and I'll write them down."

She mailed the letter the next day, and within the week she received a reply from the bishop. Father Fitzgerald, a young priest who'd been born in Ireland, would be down the following Sunday to meet with the Irish community. Immediately Leah went with Bridget to talk to some of them and decide on a proper place to meet. The houses were nothing but shacks, but Bridget's cousin, Michael O'Flarety, thought his kitchen/parlor would be big enough if a bit crowded.

"Then get everyone here on Sunday, Michael," Leah said. "Father Fitzgerald won't mind if it's crowded. He'll be pleased to see so many needing his services."

"But we've no money to pay him, Mrs. Andrews."

"Nor have you need for any yet. This will be a mission sponsored by the bishop. I'm sure that dinner and feed for the horse is all he'll require. He's not coming from the cathedral, only from a town nearby, so you don't have to worry about putting him up for the night. Now, do you think you can have all that's necessary ready for Sunday?"

After Father Fitzgerald's fourth visit and his assurance that he would continue to ride over every Sunday, Leah sat in the parlor trying to decide how best to broach to James an idea she had. He didn't disapprove of her helping the Irish community, but then he didn't seem particularly enthusiastic either.

"James." She finally decided to come straight out with it.

"Yes, dear. What's on your mind? Something's been wrinkling your brow."

"James, I have some money of my own, and I'd like to see the Irish community have their own church."

"I thought it might come to that, seeing how involved you've become. But even a small church they build themselves will cost a lot of money. Are you sure it's wise to do so much for them? It's your money, so I won't say no, but you should think about it."

"Oh, I don't mean give it to them," Leah said. "I thought I'd offer to match what they save. Just enough for lumber and a roof, and they will build it themselves. They've had so little done for them, and they work when there are jobs available. It's not as if they want charity."

"It's what you really want, isn't it, sweetheart?"

"Yes, James, I really do." Not as an atonement for leaving the Church, not to seek forgiveness for past sins, but as a gift of self."

"Then go ahead," James nodded, "and I'll be as pleased as you when it's completed."

"Thank you, darling."

She told Father Fitzgerald her plan when next he came by to see her, and he said he'd be glad to hold the money for them. He always dropped by the house on his way to or from Michael's, and after the first visit he ceased trying to persuade Leah that she was derelict in her duty by attending the community church.

"If I'm an apostate, so be it," she said. "But I've reconciled my action with my conscience, and I have no intention of changing. You're here to minister to the Irish, not to me, so you'd do me a real favor by no longer being concerned with the condition of my soul."

"Have it your way, Mrs. Andrews. I've no intention of continuing an argument I can see I'm not going to win."

After he made the announcement of her offer, he came by to show her the fourteen pennies and two nickels he'd collected for the building fund.

"It's not much," she smiled, "but it's a beginning. There will be more next week, I'm sure."

On an unusually warm day in April, Leah pushed Paul to town in his wicker carriage. While she walked along, enjoying the warm sun on her back and the first real hint of spring in the tiny green leaves on the trees and the bulbs bursting through the ground, she thought about the Irish church. Each week she handed Father Fitzgerald exactly the same amount he'd received during the services. She also wrote to Sister Angelique, the one person in New Orleans she still corresponded with, and the nun offered to contribute whatever it took to provide simple stations of the cross around the inside walls. One of the elderly Irishmen was a woodcarver, and he was busy making the plaques, as delighted to be doing something for the church as he was to be earning money for the task. Only Leah knew that half of the money sent to him by Sister Angelique was going back into the building fund. Sister Angelique wrote again saying that someone had contributed a magnificent new Baptismal font to the convent church and she was having the old one shipped up for the new church.

The fund on this April day stood close to the halfway point of what had been estimated they'd need.

Leah reached over and tucked the blankets more securely around Paul's active feet. If he stayed asleep, she might have time to look at fabrics for a spring dress. In her haste to leave New Orleans, she'd left most of her wardrobe behind. She walked slowly by the courthouse and was surprised to see the steps and the benches under the trees empty of idlers. Usually a fine day like this would bring them out in droves. "Alamo" Jones was always to be found on the third bench where he whittled and told anyone who would listen about his exploits at the Battle of Jacinto under Sam Houston after the massacre at the Alamo. Whatever his first name, no one ever called him by anything but "Alamo" since his parting remark to everyone, friend or stranger, was "Remember the Alamo!"

Then Leah saw why the grounds in front of the courthouse were deserted. At the farther end of the square, around which the town was built, there was a huge crowd. Curious but concerned lest they jiggle the carriage and disturb Paul, Leah walked cautiously toward them. As she came nearer, she saw that the center of all attention was an enclosed wagon gaily painted with stripes and curlicues in brilliant red, yellow, blue, and green. Covering part of the huge sliding door on one side, a crudely lettered banner flapped in the wind: *See the Wild Man of Borneo!*

Leah moved in closer. A tall man wearing a high top hat that made him appear even taller stood on a rickety stage next to the wagon. He was well into his spiel, and Leah was fascinated by his raucous voice and the benefits he guaranteed were bestowed by the nostrum he was selling.

"You," he pointed to one man who'd taken off his hat to wipe the top of his bald head, "wouldn't you like your once-glorious head of hair restored? Look at mine." He took off his mildewed silk topper and ran his hands through a massive mane of oily black hair. "Not a hair did I have—lost it all during scarlet fever as a child—until I began drinking this wonderful magic elixir from an ancient Indian receipt. *El gae e kil!* Roughly translated, it means 'Fly like an eagle' and you'll know why when you drink it. You will soar above your ills and pains."

The victim of the barker's attack shuffled his feet and quickly put his hat back on.

"And how many of you suffer from ingrown toenails or itching piles?" Leah blushed to see some of the people squirming at the mention of these intimate afflictions. "Just apply a few drops of this magic elixir and your troubles will be over."

The barker looked at one of the women. "And you, madam, if you don't mind my getting personal—but after all, these are medical symptoms we're talking about and no one minds frank discussions if they can be cured—do you suffer each month from female complaints? Headache and vapors?" *Oh my,* Leah thought, *is nothing sacred?* Why, she wouldn't even speak to James about such things. "If so, madam," the barker seemed oblivious to the looks of embarrassment on many faces and the frowns of disapproval that greeted his words. "If so, madam, I urge you to take three tablespoons of this magic elixir every day for the next month and you'll feel like a girl again. Any of you men who are having problems, and you'll know what I mean, I'll see you behind the wagon after the show."

Flustered and upset, Leah started to leave; but having waited this long, she just had to see what a wild man from Borneo looked like.

"Now, my friends, I know you are all anxious to see the ferocious man I captured while on my many travels throughout the world. Captured him with my bare hands. Gave me a mighty tussle, I'll tell you, but by drinking this magic elixir," he held up a bottle, "I had the strength of ten. After an hour's struggle I had him subdued. So just come forward and purchase the elixir. You'll thank me forever after. Only fifty cents for the pint bottle, or my extraordinary special just for this day because you're such a wonderful group—a full half-gallon for only a dollar. Just think, that's enough for a whole family.

"Who'll buy first? Don't be shy. I can hear my friend in the wagon getting restless, and when he gets restless—well, look out. There's no tellin' what he might do. I think the bars are strong—yes, lady, they're strong, no need to feel you have to leave. But he can rattle them mighty fierce-like."

One man stepped forward and said he'd take two of the pint bottles. Leah'd seen him among the idlers at the courthouse, and she had no doubt he was a shill who'd be paid for his part in the charade. Who else would buy two pints when he could get a half-gallon for the same price?

"What you want it for, Luther?" someone called out. "You having trouble at home?"

"None of your danged business, Gerald. I just wants 'em, that's all."

"No need to get personal, folks," the hawker called out. "We all have little disturbances that need help now and then. Now, who's next to take advantage of my offer. Won't be around again for at least a year, so be sure to stock up."

I'll bet you won't be around again at all, Leah thought, *or you'll find yourself ridden out on a rail.*

Several more moved forward and shyly bought bottles. Then the crowd began to get restless and demanded to see the wild man they'd been promised.

"All right, folks, I'll open the big door and you can see for yourself how ferocious he is. But I'll continue selling for them what wants to cure their ills and improve their looks. Watch closely now and you'll see how he handles the tremendous serpents—all of them deadly. Can strangle a man in two minutes. But see how he keeps them in his power."

Snakes! Leah shrank back. She hated the dreadful things, but she forced herself to watch.

"Had the same show this morning," one of the women near her said. "My, I tell you, I never seen nothing like it. Had to come back this afternoon just to make certain I wasn't imagining it."

Inside the cage was the wild man. Only partially covered by a mangy leopard hide, the rest of his body was decorated with brilliantly colored stripes either painted or tattooed on his skin. His face was covered with a chalk-white paste to look like a mask, and an odd assortment of feathers was stuck in his shaggy black hair. Seeing the people staring at him, he began leaping up and down, gesticulating wildly, and howling like a madman. Worst of all, he held a long snake between his teeth and grasped two more in his hands. By his weird actions he seemed to be threatening to throw them out into the crowd, who kept moving forward and back like waves on a beach.

"Don't worry," Leah's neighbor whispered, "he never lets go of them. You'll see, he'll finally stomp on them, and then the barker gives him a bottle of the elixir to drink. That calms him down."

The barker was still telling how ferocious the wild man was and cautioning people not to get too near. "No, little girl, I wouldn't poke him with that stick, if I were you. No, madam, he doesn't eat the snakes, but he does feed on raw meat. He's really just a wild animal, no way to train him or civilize him."

Unseen by most, who were staring glassy-eyed at the savage, a boy approached the group from behind the railway depot. Standing at the outer edge of the crowd, Leah saw him and wondered idly what he had in the big burlap sack he was dragging along the ground. The boy inched his way through the spectators until he was right in front of the cage. Curious, Leah had followed him through the path formed as he made his way forward. Then, horrified, she jumped back.

In one quick second the boy opened the bag partway, threw it into the cage, and released two big rattlesnakes. As one, the people in front moved back, pressing against those behind them. For an instant neither the barker nor the wild man was aware of the new snakes. When he did see them crawling straight toward him, the wild man really began shrieking and darting from one corner of the cage to another.

"Do Jesus," he screamed, "get dem things outta here!"

All was pandemonium. The people outside were screaming for fear the rattlers would turn and come after them. Women lifted up their skirts and ran as they never had before. Several fainted and had to be carried to nearby stores to be revived. Men brought out revolvers but dared not shoot for fear of hitting someone in the crowd. The barker was furiously gathering up the money that he'd been piling on the stage beside him.

Leah kept her eyes on the "wild man." He was banging against a rear door and shouting, "Oh, Lordy, do help dis poor black man." He'd pulled off his feather headdress, and the sweat from his fear streaked the paint on his face and body. He finally got the door open and went rushing madly away between two nearby buildings.

Leah's first instinct was to follow him and see if there were some way she could help him, but a fear quite different from that engendered by the snakes deterred her. Was it her imagination or did she recognize him as a former slave, a coachman for the Lorraine family whom she'd often talked to in the Market. In the confusion, he might only have appeared to resemble the man, but she dared not take a chance, and she allowed cowardice to overrule compassion.

Too upset now to do any shopping, she started for home. She was distraught not so much at what the boy had done, though he'd endangered the lives of many, but at the degradation the former slave had had to endure. She was shocked to think that he was probably not the only one. To what depths had the newly freed been forced to descend? What humiliation must they suffer in order to remain alive? She walked slowly along, sorely beset by the turmoil in her heart and the conviction that her attitudes and responses would always be influenced by that part of her she had tried so hard to deny and an ever-present fear that part would be found out.

The weather remained warm and beautiful, and a few days later, she took Paul with her on a drive out to Sarah's. While they sipped tea and ate some of Sarah's brown-sugar tarts, they talked about the baby and the progress he was making.

"He's really grown these past weeks, Leah. Amazing how much they change from day to day."

"I know. Sometimes too fast, I think." Then she changed the subject. "Did you hear about what happened when the medicine show was in town last week?"

"I did," Sarah said quietly, almost too quietly.

"A great pity, scaring the poor man that way. Worse though, being forced to earn a living in that degrading fashion."

"Then thee knows that he was not really a wild man from Borneo."

"Oh no, I knew—that is, I heard him talk and thought he must be a Southern Negro." She could have bitten her tongue off, coming so close to giving herself away.

"Yes, a former slave," Sarah said.

"But how—how did you know?"

"I don't know how much of this area thee have ridden through, but it is honeycombed with caves. Two nights ago I let Rummy out for his evening romp before turning in, and when I called to him, he didn't return. I heard him barking in the distance. So I got my lantern and went after him. He sometimes chases squirrels up a tree and won't come back until I scold him. This time he was just inside the entrance to one of the caves. I could hear something farther in, and at first I was afraid. Then I realized it was someone moaning."

"And you went in?" Leah asked. "But you might have been attacked or killed."

"No, I had my lantern and God was with me. I'll admit I was frightened when I first saw the poor painted-up creature. Lordy, if he wasn't a sight. I thought he was hurt, then I saw he was just scared and hungry."

"And if I know you, you brought him back to the house."

"I did. Nor have I ever seen anyone eat like he did. He was pure famished."

"Well, according to the barker, he lived on raw meat, but cornmeal and water was probably more like it."

"And home-brewed whiskey in the bottle he was given after each show," Sarah added.

"So that's what kept him hopped up enough to handle those snakes," Leah nodded. "So what did you do with him then?"

"He spent the night sleeping on a pile of sacks in the shed. Said it wouldn't be fittin' to sleep in the house, though Lord knows he was too weak to do any harm."

"Did—did he tell you where he was from?"

"I don't know whether he did or not. He was first so frightened and then so grateful at being rescued, he could scarcely speak more than a mumble. He mentioned several places and one of them sounded like Louisiana, but I couldn't be certain."

So he was from Louisiana, but she now realized that it was only in her imagination that she had recognized him. In her terror, she had seen a danger that was not there.

"I wonder how he ended up with that vicious, greedy fraud of a medicine man," Leah said. "Selling stuff that isn't worth a penny, let alone fifty cents."

"Oh, it's probably worth that to some people. It's almost pure alcohol. And if one drinks enough or applies it on the right places, it's bound to ease the pain for a little while."

Leah started laughing. "You mean—you mean all those women who bought some—all those who shout against liquor in any form, will be drinking pure alcohol?"

"They will, and probably wonder why they feel so giddy."

"Oh, Sarah, that's almost worth seeing what happened. Now that the poor 'wild man' is safely away. I know you and I feel differently about alcohol—and I still insist a little wine every night would be good for you—but at least you keep quiet about it and don't rant and rave at us sinners. Where is the poor ex-slave now?"

"I sent him on to Friends in Pennsylvania who'll find work for him. Drove him in the buggy to catch the train in the next town."

"So you gave him money, too. It's well that James found someone to rent your farmland. You're too generous."

"The Lord's work never asks the price, Leah. Thee gives what thee must."

Driving home in the buggy, Leah berated herself. She knew at the time, standing there in the town square, that she should step forward and help the man. She should have followed him to see how she could help him. The shame of it made her shake all over, and she wondered if her life would always be dominated by the fear that someone would learn about her past.

Her convictions were put to the test a few days later.

The next quilting bee met at the home of Mrs. Jacobs, and before long all the talk around the frame was about the medicine show and how some of them had been duped by the owner.

"Why that stuff didn't do a thing for me," Cora Simpson said. "Just made me feel dizzy. Julius took it away from me and drank the whole thing in two nights. Said it made a new man out of him, but I didn't see any change."

"I didn't even get a chance to try mine," Mrs. Peters said. "George insisted on taking a sniff and then pouring it down the drain. I don't know why. Men! They've no idea how women need help at certain times. Now I'll have to buy more laudanum." She shook her head. "All that money wasted, too, that I could have used to buy new ribbons for my bonnet."

"What about the poor wild man," Mary Howard said. "Someone should take Jackie Brunner behind the woodshed and give him the tanning of his life."

"Oh, I don't know," Elizabeth Benson answered. "It was absolutely hilarious the way he really began screaming and yelling. If it hadn't been for the danger to all of us, I'd think the whole thing was terribly funny."

"Why, Elizabeth Benson," Mary said, "I've never known you to sound so cruel. What about the danger to that man. Trapped that way in the cage. It's a wonder he got away without being bitten."

"Oh, come now," Mrs. Shelby said, "look at how he handled those others."

"They were probably trained or drugged in some way," Martha Simmons interposed.

"Even so," Mrs. Shelby insisted, "those people are just savages anyway, and probably immune to snakes with that thick black skin of theirs."

Leah's face began to redden. Now was the time. Did she dare to speak up?

"Yes," Mrs. Shelby added, "you remember those escaped slaves we helped before the war. Could hardly speak properly. Their speech sounded like gibberish. Pure savages, that's all."

"Those people are human beings," Leah said in a low voice, yet not so quietly that all of them didn't stop and listen to her. "And their skin is no thicker than yours."

She should have said "ours," but if she corrected herself, the error would be even more evident. "Nor are they immune to snakebites. If you could not understand them, it was because they were afraid, or they spoke in a *patois* peculiar to their region. You were right to help them escape, but you are wrong to call them savages or make fun of them."

"Why, Leah," Eloise Rhinehardt exclaimed, "I never thought to hear you speak like that. Didn't you and your family own slaves and fight to defend slavery?"

"My father and the Fontaines owned slaves, yes, but— but I personally did not approve of the practice. Nor did the South fight to defend slavery. We fought for the right to secede from the Union and form our own nation."

"But of course Lincoln did free the slaves. It was an important issue."

"Yes," Leah said, trying hard to maintain her poise, "but only in enemy-held sections. New Orleans was under Union rule for four years, and the slaves were re-enslaved by the Federal troops. Even free men of color and Negroes who'd been free all their lives were enslaved to work for the Union on the plantations and on defense works."

"Oh my," Mrs. Jacobs gasped. "We never knew that."

"No," Leah said, "I expect there is much most of us didn't know about what was going on on the other side." She rethreaded her needle and bent her head over the quilt. The others went back to work and turned to more juicy subjects to gossip about. She had done it; she had defended the man as best she could, and her conscience felt somewhat clearer.

Chapter Ten

BAPTISTE SAT AT his desk working on the plantation
ledgers. If all went well, they could carry part of this
year's profit over to next year; and there would be more
cash money for him and the workers to jingle in their
pockets. He would need it, too, the way Catherine demanded more and more for the parties she gave and the
accounts she ran up at the stores. Each time he said anything to her about it, she gave him the same answer: "You
promised, Baptiste; it was part of the bargain." As long as
he could pay the bills, it wasn't worth arguing about.

Earlier in the morning he'd ridden around the plantation and was pleased to see the cane sprouting in the April
sunshine. Then he'd spent some time in the gardens. The
azaleas were past their first beauty and the dogwood had
dropped their blooms, but the lawn was lush and green
beneath the fragrant magnolia and bay trees. Yes, the
plantation had become the beautiful, fecund place he'd
hoped for. He had no complaints there. If his marriage to
Catherine wasn't what he'd envisioned, he couldn't ask for
everything to be perfect. All he wished for now was a son
to carry on his name, but Catherine gave no sign of being

pregnant. At least she kept up her part of the bargain, if reluctantly, and slept in his bed every night.

He looked up when he heard the carriage coming along the drive to the house. Catherine was back early from the city. She'd said she'd be spending the night in Pierre's townhouse, but evidently something had changed her mind.

He heard her walking determinedly up the outer stairs and through the hall. She never raced up the steps or stormed into the hall for fear of raising the color in her face or disturbing the hang of her gown, but he knew that purposeful walk boded no good. She was upset about something.

"Welcome back, my dear," he said without smiling. "How was your trip to the city? Did you order everything you wanted?"

"What you mean, Baptiste, is how high will the bills be next month. Not high enough, I assure you, to make up for what I endured today."

"You mean you couldn't find just the right colors to please your fancy? Or the milliner can't get the hats here in time for the garden parties?"

"Oh, you do enjoy making those snide remarks, don't you?" Her hands twisted the strings on her reticule, a sure sign her temper was rising. "You should be pleased that your wife wants to look her best at all times, to be an asset to you. You have no concept of how important the social amenities are. If you won't look out for your future, I have to."

"I have told you, Catherine, that I'm perfectly content with life here on the plantation and the way things are going."

"But I'm not. And I intend to live in the Vieux Carré, and not when I'm old and gray, either. There is no reason not to reopen your cotton brokerage after next year."

"I'm not going to argue with you, Catherine." He started to return to his books. "I thought you were staying the night with Pierre."

"I couldn't. Not after what happened today."

"Oh, yes, what did go wrong? You're usually in such high spirits after returning from the dressmaker. Things must have really turned out badly."

"To put it mildly, yes."

"Really bad, eh." He leaned back in his chair. He couldn't resist needling her because he knew how much it infuriated her. "Yes, you look like you've got the red ass from sitting in a briar patch."

"Really, Baptiste! When did you add vulgarity to your other vices?"

"Vulgar, perhaps, but true. Sit down, and I'll tell Benji to bring you a drink."

"Just a little wine." She collapsed on the sofa while Baptiste asked Benji to bring sherry for both of them.

"Want to talk about it?" She looked really upset, and he thought it wouldn't hurt to be nice to her for a change.

"Well, I went to that new dressmaker, the one I discovered after Christmas. Her name is Cecile and she does do beautiful work. We were chatting as women do in a fitting room, and I asked her how she happened to come to New Orleans."

Catherine paused, and Baptiste saw she was holding the wine glass so tightly she threatened to snap the stem.

"And do you know what she had the nerve to tell me?" Catherine's voice rose several octaves. "That she'd been urged to come here by a *charming* woman named Mam'selle Bonvivier who was being married to a Mr. Andrews. *Mam'selle* Bonvivier, if you please. And didn't she go on and on about what an exquisite figure *Mam'selle* Bonvivier had, and such impeccable taste." Catherine was almost screaming now. "Am I never to hear the end of that—that—"

"Watch it, Catherine! Maybe you've said enough."

"That whore—that colored whore of yours."

Baptiste immediately wheeled across the room and slapped Catherine hard across the face. "Enough! I'll hear no more of that."

More shocked and bewildered than hurt, Catherine rubbed her hand across her flaming cheek. "How dare you! How dare you hit me like that. So you don't want to hear any more? Well, you're going to. Listen to this. She was married to James Andrews in a blue silk suit. And for her wedding night? A pale-yellow sheer gown and peignoir. Picture her in that, Baptiste. Pale yellow against that skin you loved to touch. That's what you're doing, aren't you?

Imagining her in your bed. Do you close your eyes when you make love to me and pretend it is she you are caressing?"

"Go to the bedroom, Catherine." He was furious and aroused to a white-hot, passionate hate.

"Not now, Baptiste." She cringed. He was an animal, making demands like that when she was in such a state. "I couldn't. And it's only five o'clock."

"When I say go, you go."

"There's no need to anymore," she smirked. "I'm pregnant. I've done my duty as a wife."

For a moment Baptiste's heart rose. "How can I be sure?"

"You want all the intimate, feminine details? Or will you take my word for it?"

"It makes no difference. You're still my wife."

"My part of the bargain was to give you children." she reminded him superiorly, "and that I'm going to do. But that's all!"

"And to share my bed when I require."

"And if I won't?" There was nothing he could do to her now. He wouldn't hurt her if there were a chance she was pregnant.

"You want all those dresses paid for, don't you?"

"You bastard!" No longer caring how she sounded, Catherine screamed like a harridan. "You'd do it, too, wouldn't you?"

"Put on the green gown. I'll be there in a minute."

The green gown reminded him of their wedding night, and he wanted to hate her as he had the first time when he took her against her will. It was not his physical longing he would satisfy now, but the desire to humiliate and debase her. Then if she really were pregnant, he'd let her move to the room she'd furnished for herself upstairs. He had no more need of her until after the baby was born.

By May, it was evident that Catherine was pregnant; and in his elation at the thought of having a son. Baptiste willingly accompanied Catherine to all of the spring social functions and agreed to play the gracious host at the parties she had at Belle Fontaine. He paid the mounting bills with no complaints and accepted the congratulations of his friends on the forthcoming birth.

"Didn't take you long, did it, Baptiste," Henri chortled.

"That must have been some wedding night." Another slapped him on the back.

"You're a lucky bastard," one of the men bewailed. "Both a wife and a plantation that produce. My cotton doesn't look like it's going to do a damn thing."

"Told you to switch to cane, Jules. This part of Louisiana's no good for cotton. Especially with no slaves."

"I would, but Catherine said you were opening up your brokerage again, and I figured the way you always turned a profit, you'd see that I did, too."

Baptiste raised one brow and reached for another cigar. "Catherine is mistaken. I do not intend to leave the plantation."

"Well, then," Jules said, "if I manage to get through this year, it'll be cane from now on."

Baptiste looked around at the friends who had come to drink the finest champagne France could send over and eat Jessie's cooking. Among them, he and Catherine were considered an ideal couple, and he the luckiest man on the river. No one would ever know what it cost them to live up to their bargain.

In June a series of violent thunderstorms inundated southern Louisiana. The only tangible effect at Belle Fontaine was that Catherine moped around the house and complained that so many social events had to be canceled.

"It's better for you anyway, my dear," Baptiste said. "You shouldn't be gadding about in your condition. Most women have the innate modesty to remain secluded at home after they begin showing."

"Well, I'm not most women, and that's a ridiculous tradition. I'll be tied down enough after it's born. Since you refuse to agree I should hire a wet nurse."

"No stranger is going to nurse my child. That's a mother's duty. Or rather, it should be a pleasure." He thought of Leah with René at her breast. How beautiful she'd looked in the full bloom of motherhood. and how she'd enjoyed those moments of feeding their son.

"A pleasure! Having my body pulled out of shape. And

tying me down so I can't leave the house except for an hour or two at a time. It's barbaric." She looked down at her thickening waist. "I may never get my figure back again."

"No need to. Not if you keep having children."

"Oh, you are cruel, Baptiste." How she hated him. She'd married him for his money and for this house, and what good were they if she were going to be pregnant all the time. There were ways. She knew there were. If she could just find out how. She'd heard the men speak of Madame Broulé's and other places when they thought no one was listening. Those women had to do something to keep from getting pregnant all the time. She wondered if she dared disguise herself and visit one of them. During the daytime, of course. She'd think about it after this child was born. That would mean having to sleep with Baptiste all the time and not be able to retire to her nice private room as he was letting her do now, but it would be worth it.

At first, Baptiste welcomed the rains; then he began to fear the fields would be flooded. So far they were draining well, and if the storms ceased before long, there would be no real damage.

Late in the afternoon, he and Benji were sitting on the rear gallery, looking across the river and watching the lightning streak over the distant bayous. Although the skies were still dark with menacing clouds, there'd been no rain for twenty-four hours. Catherine was napping in her room upstairs, and Baptiste was enjoying one of his increasingly rare quiet hours with Benji.

"Crop's all right, boss," Benji said. "Maybe got their feets a little too wet, but that's all. They'll absorb the water."

"Feets! By God, Benji, you're spending too much time in the quarters and not enough with me. What's so pleasant down there that you don't stay around the house?"

"Ain't so much what's down there as what ain't up here anymore. Though I've been seeing a right good bit of Evalina."

"A right good bit is an understatement," Baptiste grinned; "you've been spending every night with her."

"Who been tattling on me?" Benji tried to frown but his mouth curled up in a matching grin.

"Your face, that's who. Look at you now. Beaming like a perfect fool."

"She's a sweet thing, boss, that's for sure."

"Then why don't you marry her and make an honest woman out of her. She could come in the house as a personal maid for Catherine."

"I'll think on it. Don't aim to rush things."

Suddenly, at the same time, they both heard the sound that filled everyone with dread. It was like a fantastic, giant locomotive thundering across the land.

"Tornado!" Baptiste screamed. His first thought was Catherine and the danger to the baby. He started to rise from his chair, and once again was smote with how helpless he was in situations like this.

"Benji, go wake Catherine and get her down to the kitchen."

"What about you, Baptiste? I can't leave you here."

"I'll manage. I'll slide down the steps like I've done before. I promise," he said as he looked at the expression on Benji's face. "But she can't lose the baby."

Benji ran into the house and up to the second floor. Baptiste eased himself out of his chair and made it to the steps just as he saw the giant funnel of wind approaching from across the river. With one strong push, he was on his way to the bottom of the stairs. On all fours he crawled onto the brick flooring of the lower level and through the kitchen door. He saw Benji carrying Catherine down the last of the inside stairs.

Within a minute—a minute of crashing trees, exploding buildings, and deafening roars—it was all over. *At least the lower part of the house is still standing,* Baptiste thought, as he looked around the kitchen and at the overhead beams.

It took only another few minutes for Benji to run upstairs and then come back down to tell them the house had completely escaped destruction. In its erratic path, the tornado had bypassed it.

"What else, Benji?"

"Most of the barns are torn up and blown all over the place."

"We can rebuild those. What else?"

"The fields, Baptiste." He was almost crying. "From what I could see, it looks like at least two-thirds of them are as chewed up as if we'd run a dozen plows back and forth across them.

"And the crop?" Baptiste asked anxiously.

"There ain't no crop."

"Can we plant again?" There had to be a crop! They'd made a good profit on last year's, but it was not enough to carry them another full year and more.

"Can try," Benji shrugged, "but I don't know how much of a harvest there'll be."

"Go tell Septimus I want to talk to him. How about the houses?"

"Not as bad as after the fire. Weird, though. Two or three, maybe four, completely demolished. The rest untouched."

"Well, that's one thing in our favor."

Baptiste had been slumped against the kitchen fireplace. Now he asked Benji to help him back upstairs.

"And how about me, Baptiste," Catherine called from across the huge room. "Do I just remain here?"

"You can't walk upstairs?" As gently as Benji had carried her, there was no way she could have been injured. "Are you hurt?"

"Not physically, no, but I've had a tremendous shock. I think I deserve some consideration."

"Benji, help Madame Fontaine to her room and then come back for me. Jessie, you got anything in that oven to quiet a growling stomach?"

"Sure thing. A cake I was baking for supper. Iffen that crazy wind didn't make it fall."

When finally he got upstairs, Baptiste stood on the front gallery and surveyed the damage the tornado had wrought. Septimus was waiting to tell him that several of the workers and their families had been injured when their houses collapsed. Baptiste shook his head. Benji hadn't mentioned that.

"Any of them seriously?" Baptiste was more concerned for their lives than for the damaged houses. Although with the threat of more rain, they'd have to be replaced as soon as possible.

261

" 'Fraid so, suh," Septimus said. "Josh, he done got struck by a tree and ain't waked up. And some of the chilluns got pretty bad cut up. Mos' of the other mens and womens all right 'cept for scratches."

We were lucky to come out so lightly, Baptiste thought. "Benji, tell Jessie to take what she needs to bandage up those that are hurt. Then take the fastest horse we've got and ride into town for the doctor to look at Josh. Now then, Septimus, about the houses and outbuildings. Organize the men into crews just like we did after the fire. Do enough to make certain the livestock can't get away. I suppose some of those were killed or injured, too."

"Yessuh," the foreman nodded.

"Then I'll count on you to do what needs to be done. For now, patch up the outbuildings and start on new houses. The families'll just have to move in together until they're finished." He looked out again at the fields he could see from the gallery. "Benji says most of the fields were wiped out."

"More'n half. Ain't gonna be much of a harvest come fall."

"Can we replant?"

"We can try," Septimus said. "Iffen the winter ain't too cold, could have a spring harvest."

"How about cuttings? Do we have any left from the earlier planting?"

"Some few. Mebbe for one field."

"So we were depending on this year's crop for cuttings, too." Baptiste shook his head. "I'll look at the fields themselves as soon as I can. And I think we'll replant what we have. Would be foolish not to try. May take a little longer to grow, but it will at least give us something."

"So what does we do first?" Septimus asked.

"The houses and the buildings. From the looks of that sky, we're not going to be able to do anything in the fields for several days. You might be checking to see just how much we have in the way of cuttings; no point in preparing more fields than we can plant. Tell Josh's wife the doctor will be here as soon as possible. And see that Jessie stays with those that are hurt as long as she's needed. Madame Fontaine would be doing that, of course, if it weren't for her condition."

"Yessuh, we understands, and we is pleased for you."

"Thank you," Baptiste said. "I'll count on you to check with me and come up here anytime you need to see me."

Before morning, the rains started in again, and it was another four days before the land dried up enough for Baptiste to mount his horse and ride through the fields to appraise the amount of damage done. Septimus and Benji had not been overly pessimistic. No more than a third of the land had been spared the wind's onslaught. There would be a mighty small harvest come fall. It wouldn't bring in nearly enough to carry them through the year, let alone put some aside for the future. In spite of Benji and Septimus's insistence that it would do no good to start over, Baptiste said they must at least try. Even if that made a second crop, the money in the reserve fund would have to be meted out sparingly for more than a year.

"What you should do," Catherine said, "is cut down on the amount you give the workers every month. No need to drain your own cash reserve."

"I'm not draining the reserve. We'll need that to get through next year. I'm paying them out of their own earnings for this past harvest."

"That's what I mean," she insisted. "Don't pay out all of it. Make them live for two years on what they earned this year. No one will know."

"You'd have me cheat my people! That's their money. They're my workers, and I owe them something. We'll just have to tighten our own belts in the same way."

"The workers! What about your wife? Don't I count for anything?" There was real venom in her voice, but there were times when it was impossible to reason with Baptiste.

"You're not going to starve, Catherine. Just have to stop spending so much."

"But I thought you had plenty of money," she said petulantly.

"Don't whine, Catherine; it doesn't become you. I had just enough to restore Belle Fontaine and live comfortably for several years. You—in a few months—have managed to go through that like—like that damned tornado went through the cane crop. The gowns you buy, the china service imported from France. And the extra help you insist you need for parties. I have to pay them. They're not slaves anymore."

"So I'm to live like a pauper, is that it? Well, I'll give you this one child, but no more. Unless you do what I ask and go into business again."

Baptiste had already given the idea some thought, but he wasn't going to give Catherine the satisfaction of reminding him she'd been right.

"If I can't have the things I want," she continued, "then you've no hold over me to force me into your bed. I'll stay here as your wife. I wouldn't shame you by leaving you at this time." She turned and walked toward her small sitting room, the one room in the house except for her second-floor bedroom that she thought of as hers alone. Baptiste never entered it. She didn't know why, and at first she was hurt after all the pains she'd taken to make it so attractive. Then she was glad it was a refuge when she was upset. Baptiste could be so hateful at times, in spite of all she did to be the kind of mistress a plantation should have.

She knew she'd never leave Baptiste. It was not he who would be shamed, but she herself. There'd be all sorts of questions and innuendoes. And the only place she could return to was Pierre's home and that dull life with Helene. Oh, if only they'd move to the Vieux Carré, with all the shops and Jackson Square and the continual round of teas and luncheons. Somehow she had to persuade Baptiste that it was the thing for him to do.

Baptiste opened the letter. He'd been surprised at the return address on the outside: Martinique. He was even more surprised at the signature: Claud Bonvivier. That could only be one of Leah's uncles, one of her father's younger brothers. He read the contents with mounting interest.

My Dear Monsieur Fontaine:

I have been meaning to write you since the end of the war. We were distressed to learn about the death of my brother, Jean-Paul. We know that his wife and daughters fled to France soon after New Orleans fell, but we have heard nothing about the sons who, we understand, fought in the Confederate Army. If you have any information about them, we would most appreciate hearing from you. We also have heard nothing about Jean-Paul's daughter Leah.

I am sure you are surprised to be hearing from me. However, I think it will interest you to learn that Jean-Paul wrote often about Leah and her relationship with you. Therefore, you are the one person we knew to contact. Is Leah still with you, and is she well?

I have another reason for writing. My brothers and I would like to re-establish the family import office in New Orleans. It did so very well under Jean-Paul, and we think the time is propitious to open it again. We know you were a successful cotton broker before the war, and, according to Jean-Paul, an excellent businessman. Therefore, we would like you to consider heading up the import branch in New Orleans. Unless of course you have returned to your brokerage firm.

Please give this matter serious consideration. I am certain we can arrive at terms that will be beneficial to all of us.

> Your gracious servant,
> Claud Bonvivier

Baptiste re-read the letter three times. At first stunned that Claud knew so much about him and Leah, he remembered her saying that her father loved her very much, and it would not have been unusual for him to write his family about her. But so much about himself. That was a shock. He'd heard nothing about the Bonvivier sons, but he felt certain he could find out. He would contact Pierre and ask him to begin an investigation.

Then he mulled over the offer Claud had made. There were a number of advantages to be considered. The import office and warehouse had not been destroyed as completely as his own, and they could be rebuilt in a matter of weeks. More important, the Bonvivier firm was still well established. It wouldn't mean starting over as with the brokerage firm. There would already be ships on the sea, and contacts had been maintained with exporters. Yes, the offer was worthy of serious consideration. There was one serious drawback. What if the Bonvivier sons were located and one or both wanted to re-establish their father's end of the business? They would certainly have the right to do so, and then where would he be? Consider it? Yes. But a quick decision, no.

Additional letters were exchanged between Martinique and the plantation, all of them brought directly to Baptiste before Catherine could see them. Pierre had had no difficulty in getting information about the sons. One of them had been killed at Antietam, and the other had married a girl from Charleston, South Carolina, and settled there. A letter to him elicited the information that he had no desire to return to New Orleans or to be a partner in the family firm unless an office were opened in Charleston. That, Baptiste thought, might just be a possibility, and it would reduce any claim the young man might have on the profits from the New Orleans branch.

Finally a letter arrived from Claud to say his ship would dock at New Orleans sometime during the first week in July, and he hoped to meet and talk with Baptiste then.

So far he'd said nothing to Catherine. She was still bemoaning the lack of money and the lack of parties. The tornado had damaged many of the plantations along the river, and social life had come to a peremptory halt.

While Baptiste stood on the wharf and watched the arrival of the ship from Martinique, he was amazed at how beautiful and modern she was. That meant the firm was on strong, stable footing. He was also surprised when he met Claud and saw how young he was. Then he remembered that Jean-Paul had been the eldest of a large family of children, and Claud must be the youngest. He was, in fact, not much older than Baptiste.

"Welcome to New Orleans," Baptiste greeted him. "I've made luncheon reservations at one of our finest restaurants. I hope you don't mind that we'll be joined by a friend of mine, Pierre DeLisle. He is also my lawyer, and I thought it would be good to have him with us while we talk." He purposely did not mention that Pierre was also his brother-in-law.

"Very wise, M'sieu Fontaine. Or may I call you Baptiste? I am a businessman, not a lawyer, and it is always wise to have one of the legal profession near at hand when agreements are being drawn up."

They joined Pierre at La Maison Blanche, and were soon chatting over their Pernod like old friends.

"I was distressed to learn of my nephew Armand's death," Claud said. "I met him once when I was here on a visit. But I am relieved to know that Henri is safe and well established in Charleston. Did you know them?"

"Oh, yes," Baptiste said. "The Vieux Carré is like a village. We know almost everyone. How long will you be in New Orleans?"

"Just a few days. Then I'm sailing to France to complete an inventory study of a shipload of goods from the Orient. It is a new firm we are dealing with."

"To Paris?"

"No, to Marseilles. I seldom get to Paris. Our father cut all ties with his family after he married our mother. She was Polynesian, you know."

"Yes, so Leah told me. I thought perhaps you'd be visiting your sister-in-law and your nieces."

"No, when they fled and left my brother behind to die, we wished to have no more to do with them. In fact, I believe my sister-in-law has remarried."

Once they got down to the reason for the meeting, Baptiste soon saw that although Claud might claim to be only a businessman with no head for legal matters, he was indeed a shrewd entrepreneur. He'd already written up the agreements, and Pierre immediately set about reading them carefully.

"This looks acceptable to me, Baptiste," Pierre said. "Your percentage seems like a fair one, and you're well protected against failure and responsibility for certain losses."

"And how much actual selling will I be required to do?" Baptiste asked. "And travel?"

"Very little," Claud said. "The contacts have already been made. We can, of course, see about expanding later. Right now your main function will be as middleman. To receive the goods from our ships, store them, keep an inventory, and then to transship to the places indicated on the manifests."

"And goods going out? Cotton, cane, and manufactured items from up north?"

"That, too. However, we're more interested right now in moving the imports. The places we sold to before the war are crying for our goods, and these are what we need to concentrate on."

"Very well," Baptiste said. "Shall we drive over to the old office and see what needs to be done?"

"Not a great deal, I hope," Claud said. "I'd brought along several crates and cartons on this trip. I'd hoped we could get started right away." He laughed. "You see, I counted on your accepting our offer."

"You're a man after my own heart, Claud. I like to come right to the point, too."

A cursory examination of the offices and warehouse indicated they could store the goods Claud had brought. Some of the warehouse windows needed boarding up for security, and Pierre said he would contact a carpenter for them. "You sure you're not trying to weasel out a share in this?" Baptiste asked him.

"No, I'm just damned glad you're going to be spending some time in town. I thought maybe you'd buried yourself out there on that plantation."

The office could be in good enough shape to open up within a week and more furnishings added as time went on.

After spending two nights in town, Baptiste knew he'd made the right decision. Weekends on the plantation would be enough to keep in touch with Septimus and Benji. No, on second thought, Benji would come into town with him.

At dinner the evening of his return to the plantation, Baptiste mentioned casually that he would be living in town during the week from now on.

"You mean it, Baptiste?" Catherine asked. "You really mean we're moving there?" She was elated for the first time since the tornado.

"I mean I am moving into town."

"Well!" she fumed. "You certainly don't intend for me to stay out here alone."

"That is exactly what I expect. For you to remain here

268

and behave like a woman who is having a child in a few months."

"You wouldn't, Baptiste," she wailed. "You couldn't do that to me."

"Aren't you going to ask what I'll be doing?"

"I don't give a damn what you'll be doing." Then she softened her voice. "Opening the brokerage firm, I suppose, as I suggested a long time ago. I think that since you've taken my advice, you could at least let me share some of the pleasures it will afford." Her tone became beguiling.

"I did not take your advice, Catherine, nor am I opening the brokerage office. I have told you before that I make my own plans and my own decisions. I've been in correspondence with Claud Bonvivier, Jean-Paul's younger brother, in Martinique, and he—"

"Bonvivier again! You didn't tell me you kept in touch with her family."

"What I do with her family is of no concern to you," he said sternly. "As a matter of fact, I was taken completely by surprise to receive a letter from him. I'm going to become a partner in their import firm and run the branch office in New Orleans."

"That's it! You refuse my suggestion to open your own business and then flaunt it in my face that you'll be connected with her family. That's really too much, Baptiste."

"If you will simmer down, Catherine, and stop being so touchy about everything having to do with Leah—who is now completely out of my life—I will explain why this is much more to our—yes to *our*—advantage than my starting all over again."

"I'm listening." Her pregnancy, the tornado, and now this had her so upset she wanted to cry. Nothing, *nothing,* was turning out as she'd planned when she inveigled Baptiste into marriage. Yet maybe this new venture in New Orleans would open the door to a better future. If she could just get into town.

Briefly Baptiste explained how and why he'd arrived at the decision to throw in his lot with the Bonvivier brothers. "And so, Catherine, there will be a guaranteed income from the very beginning with none of the worry I had before about cotton harvests and prices on the cotton market."

"There will be money again?" She brightened up once more.

"There will be money, even if our second cane crop doesn't produce too well. That's all your heart desires, isn't it?"

"It makes up for many things that are missing," she said.

"It's your fault, Catherine, not mine that we can't be a loving, happy couple."

"I'll try harder in the future, Baptiste, I promise. Let me come to New Orleans with you, and I'll be the loving wife you wanted." Once there, she would grit her teeth and let him share her bed again. It wouldn't be too hard, as long as she could entertain and go to the theater and the opera.

"I'm sorry, Catherine, but it's too late. I want you to stay here at least until after the baby is born. It would be too dangerous for you during the malaria and yellow fever season. You're safer out here. Then we'll see."

"Is that a promise?"

"It is a promise to talk about it again after the baby is born. No more. I'll spend weekdays in the city and weekends out here. I think it will do us both good to be apart for a while."

Damn! Catherine thought. She knew that meant being the loving wife when he was home, even though she was pregnant. The thought of exposing her swollen body to him and having him touch her was disgusting. But if it meant spending the social seasons in town—that's what she had to keep in mind.

"You may be right, Baptiste. And, as you say, with the fevers it could be dangerous."

"And you'll be busy from now on sewing for the baby." He remembered the hours Leah had spent on garments so tiny he couldn't imagine any being small enough to wear them. And the piles of blankets and sheets that mounted up in the spare-room-turned-nursery. Strange, he hadn't seen any of that around this house. "Do you need thread or materials from town? I'll bring them out when I return if you'll make a list."

Sewing! Always having everything made by the finest

couturiers in New Orleans, Catherine had never sewed a stitch in her life. Now she supposed she would have to prove she was a good wife by making the layette. Maybe she could bribe some of the cabin women to do it for her. No, she'd have to pay them well, and Baptiste would question her about the money. Maybe with his new position he'd understand if she told the truth.

"I—I hadn't planned to do any of the sewing myself. I've already sent an order in to Madame Duvalier. She has the finest seamstresses in town and turns out exquisite things. Everyone has their layettes made by her."

"Without consulting me?"

"Well, really, Baptiste, that was before the tornado changed everything. And how was I to know you'd object to having your child wear the finest that money can buy."

"So we must do like everyone else again, is that it?" Baptiste asked. "All right, if you've already placed the order, I can't very well rescind it."

"It was just a small order, just a few things to begin with. I'll need a great many more."

"Then you will make them, my dear, and there will be no danger of your getting bored this summer while I'm away. Ask Jessie who the best seamstress is in the quarters, and I'll pay her to teach you—but," he'd already seen that look in her eye, "not to make them."

Taught to sew by a Negro! Just one more humiliation he was forcing her to endure. It was the really important things she'd not yet ordered: the day gowns, the embroidered robes and, especially, the embroidered coverlets. Oh, and most important of all, the christening gown.

"I'll do it, Baptiste, if you will do one favor for me."

"I think I could do that. What is it?"

"Let Madame Duvalier make the christening gown, long robe, and bonnet. They should be perfect."

"Agreed. Now start the list of what you'll need, and I'll bring it back next weekend."

The first days in New Orleans were hectic ones for Baptiste. He had to find good assistants to supervise the offloading of the ships, carting the goods to the warehouse, and running errands. He spent hours interviewing young men, many of whom, to his dismay, were sons of his friends. He'd almost forgotten how many years had passed since he'd been in business for himself. While he was doing the interviewing, construction workers strengthened and refurbished the warehouse and office. He added more rooms to the latter for conferences and for his employees. He saw no reason for them not to have their own office space. Thinking back, he remembered how elegantly Jean-Paul had furnished his own office, and Baptiste set about to make his as handsome. He ordered a huge semicircular desk constructed of solid walnut, and he had Benji search through all the antiques shops for a large oriental rug. To avoid transporting his wheelchair from apartment to office, he had a more comfortable, better-cushioned one made for the office. He could then move around behind his desk with ease. Additional upholstered chairs were brought in for clients, a liquor cabinet built against one wall, and the outer reception room with its long counter made more attractive.

When the office opened for the first day of business, Benji walked in with a package.

"For you, boss, from me. It's not your office without it."

Baptiste grinned as he opened the handsome leather box. He was pretty certain what he would find inside. Sure enough, his favorite long, black cigars.

"Here, Benji, light one up with me."

"Don't mind if I do."

"They're still better than chewing." And they laughed together, remembering the days behind the stable when they were young.

"You want me to stay here and buttle for you as Madame Fontaine calls it?"

"No, I want you to go back to the apartment and fix me an especially fine dinner for tonight. Jessie's a good cook, but no one can turn out a meal like you."

"You're just saying that so I'll spend all afternoon over the hot stove." Benji pretended to frown.

"You're damned right, and I expect the best you can turn out. Come back for me at six."

Baptiste didn't see how merely checking imports and then transshipping them all over the eastern United States could keep him busy five days a week, but he soon learned there were never enough hours in the day to complete everything that had to be done. He had to check invoices against shipping manifests, keep up with the correspondence from dealers as well as the main office in Martinique, check into complaints when goods were not received on time, and follow up on insurance claims for loss or damage.

There were small local clients, like some of the dressmakers waiting for a few yards of Belgian lace and shoemakers demanding to know how soon the shipment of Moroccan leather would arrive. He'd no idea how many boxes of exotic feathers were used by milliners in New Orleans. He sometimes felt as if he were running a dry-goods store as well as an import house. Then there were dealers in Chicago, New York, and all the small towns in between who received dozens of crates or one small package. Nor had he realized that a Bonvivier ship would be coming into port every week. He began to have more and more respect for the company he'd joined, and before long he realized with a start that he was going to be as wealthy as Leah's father before the year was up. With that, he hired himself a secretary, lit up another cigar, and joined Pierre for a drink at Le Coq d'Or.

"How're things going?" Pierre asked.

"Splendidly! Far better than I ever dreamed."

"I assume you mean the business," Pierre said somewhat cynically.

"If you're referring to Catherine, things are all right there, too. We struck a bargain, and I've no complaints. But it will be good for both of us if I spend more time here in the city."

"You want me to make some introductions? The quadroon balls are *passé*, but there're still plenty of beauties around to add spice to your life."

"I don't think so, Pierre. Thank you. Maybe I'm getting old, but that life doesn't appeal to me anymore."

"As you wish."

Only one place in town did he avoid—the house where he and Leah had lived. Pierre still had the key and urged him to sell it. His answer remained the same—No!

One night Baptiste sat up later than usual, long after Benji had cleared the dinner table and gone to the rooms rented for him on Rampart Street.

"You sure you don't need me?" Benji asked. "I'll stay as late as you want."

"I know you will, Benji. No, I'm just not sleepy, but I can manage for myself. Leave something here on the table in case I get hungry and bring me a bottle of wine."

Baptiste poured himself a glass and then looked long at the bottle, remembering the night he and Leah had drunk to themselves and their future together. That was the night she'd become his *placée* here in this apartment. There'd never be anyone else like her. Pierre's suggestion had left him cold. If he took another mistress it would be only to satisfy a physical need, and that would be unfair to both of them. He'd always be comparing her to Leah, and she'd never be able to satisfy him in any way. During all his wild youth, going from one brief affair to another, he'd never thought of himself as a one-woman man. He'd have scoffed at any such suggestion. Now he knew differently.

He had loved just once. In spite of the war and in spite of his injuries, the years with Leah had been perfect. Those years had brought him more happiness than most men know in a lifetime; and if now he had to be content with only the memory of them, he could live with that, too. No, there was no point in trying to replace her. He had a successful business and soon there'd be the baby to whom he could devote all his love and affection. With those he would be satisfied.

He finished the bottle soon after midnight, made his way into the bedroom, and slept more soundly than he had in months.

Chapter Eleven

"YOU SEE, PAUL," Leah was explaining to the baby, who at seven months was sitting propped up against the pillows in his crib, "women are always needing new dresses and things in their wardrobe. It's the way women are. Last year, when I was expecting you, I wore very large, bulky dresses. Now I need some new fall clothes, and it's none too soon to start making them."

Paul reached for the teething ring hanging on a ribbon around his neck and stuffed it into his mouth.

"Oh, darling, are they hurting again? Here, let me take you out and you can crawl around on the rug."

She lifted him from the crib, ran her fingers through the soft black hair just beginning to curl like Baptiste's, and set him on the floor with a box of ribbons to play with.

"Now, as Mama was saying. I do hope you'll be good with Bridget, because I simply have to go to town and see about material and patterns. I promise we'll walk to the barn when I get back and you can pat the calf. And if your daddy's home, he'll take you for a ride on the horse."

Paul gurgled something incomprehensible and raised his arms to her. "All right, we'll go in the kitchen and find

Bridget. Maybe she has some of that good custard pudding left from lunch."

Leah carried Paul out of the bedroom and back to the kitchen.

"If you're ready to go, ma'am," Bridget greeted her, "I'm finished in here and can take care of Paul now."

"Paul wants to know if there's any custard left."

"Oh, he does, does he. The little darling. Sure and Bridget saved some for you. Ye go on, Mrs. Andrews. I've everything started for dinner, so stay as long as ye like. When the sun goes down a wee bit, we'll go out in the yard."

"Thank you, Bridget. I should get home before Mr. Andrews does. He's coming all the way from the county seat, so he may not return before dark. We'll keep his dinner hot if he's late."

Leah tied on her bonnet, kissed Paul good-bye, and went out to hitch her horse to the new buggy James had gotten for her so she wouldn't always have to walk to town when he was away for several days. With the whole afternoon to herself, she could look in all the shops and then have tea in Aunt Tabby's Tea Shoppe. While she rode in, she thought about what she needed to replenish her wardrobe. Her cape and bonnet from last year would do fine, but they did need new ribbons. Three dresses should suffice, one for the house and two for church and social functions. She'd better go by the bootmaker and see about shoes and a sturdy pair of boots for walking. James had hinted he wanted to teach her to hunt this year, not just go along and watch him. She doubted she could shoot anything wild, but if it pleased him, she'd try.

She headed first for Milady's Emporium, which boasted a large sign reading *Latest from Paris, London, and New York—Millinery a Specialty*. Tying Dobbin—surely James could have come up with a more original name for the horse—to the hitching post, she went in.

"Good afternoon, Mrs. Andrews, so nice to see you again."

"Thank you, Mr. Simpson."

"And what are you looking for today? Have some very fine hats in from Paris. Came up from New Orleans just yesterday."

"Oh really! From New Orleans, you say?"

"Yes, the importer we traded with before the war has recently reopened for business. We received one of the first shipments from abroad. Being an old customer, we received special treatment. I'm sure you'll find them very elegant."

"Yes—yes, I'm sure I will." An old import house—from before the war. Her father's was not the only import firm in New Orleans, but surely the others would have started up again before this. Could it be possible that one of her half-brothers, whom she'd seen from a distance but never met, had reopened the business? How ironic that she might be buying something from her own family and they not even know it.

"Tell me, Mr. Simpson, do you buy directly from New Orleans or through a wholesaler?"

"Oh, I buy directly. My father, who started this store, was one of their first customers. He always traveled to the importers himself, twice a year to New Orleans and New York, to place his orders. I've always done my business by mail, however. We place smaller orders than wholesalers, to be sure, but the Bonviviers never stopped dealing with the small retail outlets. I'm glad to see they are resuming the same practice."

"So am I," Leah said. "For your sake, I mean." He'd spoken the name with a strong Indiana, non-French pronunciation, but she still recognized it. It made her feel good to think that name was once more established in the Vieux Carré. Her father would be proud to know the war had not destroyed it.

"Yes, I've never had to return a thing they've sent me. Come, let me show you the hats." He started leading the way back toward the shelves on which they sat.

"In a minute. Tell me, which of the Bonvivier brothers do you correspond with?"

"Actually, I've not written to them at all. This first shipment was sent to me on approval, to see if I wanted to continue doing business with them. I wrote right back and said I would be happy to and placed an order for the kinds of imported goods I used to get in the past. However, the invoice was not signed by a Bonvivier. I can't recall the name. Wait, let me look it up."

277

"Oh, no, don't bother, Mr. Simpson. I remembered the firm and was surprised to hear the name again, that's all."

"Oh, no trouble at all. I'd forgotten you were from New Orleans. It might well be someone you know."

At least he didn't know she'd been a Bonvivier, or hadn't remembered if his wife ever mentioned it. That was just as well. She began looking at some dress goods while she waited.

"Here it is, Mrs. Andrews. The writing is hard to make out: people do scrawl their signatures so, but I think it is B. Fountain. You know any Fountains down there?"

She looked at the signature and nearly fainted. But there could be no doubt about it. It had to be Baptiste Fontaine. How—how in the world had he become associated with the firm?

"No—no, I didn't know any Fountains. Must be someone who just moved in or was brought in by the firm." Baptiste doing business again in New Orleans. How she wished she could drop by the office and surprise him. Instead she swallowed hard and concentrated on her list of things she needed.

"Now about the hats, Mrs. Andrews."

"If you don't mind, Mr. Simpson, I'd just like to look around. There's several things I want to buy."

"You go right ahead. If you need me, just call."

Upset by learning that Baptiste had been the one to send up the bonnets, and maybe other things too, Leah couldn't concentrate on anything. She looked at all the materials and then at the colorful pattern plates, but nothing seemed to be what she wanted. She was furious with herself. She finally had a whole afternoon to shop, and if she didn't get what she wanted today, she'd have to make another trip into town. Had he packed the hats himself? Or did he order someone else to do it? And always it came back to the same thing: How did he get into the firm?

She moved from the dress-goods counter over to the ribbons. Surely she could choose some of those, and then maybe she'd be able to settle down enough to pick out patterns and material. She was trying to decide between beige and green for her winter bonnet when the bell over the door rang, and she heard someone walk in. Good, another shopper would keep Mr. Simpson busy. He'd been looking at her and waiting for her to purchase something.

It wasn't a woman shopper; it was a man, and the voice sounded vaguely familiar. Probably one of the men in the church or someone she'd met in James's office. It wasn't anyone she'd seen often. The man had his back to her, and it bothered her that she couldn't place that voice. Funny, she had a strange premonition of danger. That was ridiculous. The repeated references to the Bonvivier name and the news that Baptiste was associated with it had made her jumpy. She had to stop getting upset every time there was a mention of New Orleans.

Yet, even as she looked at the ribbons, she kept listening. The man was a drummer, taking Mr. Simpson's order for pins, needles, and other findings. Each time he spoke, Leah felt as if someone were rubbing sandpaper up and down her spine. Then the men began speaking about how the dry-goods business was going and the drummer's orders in particular.

"Does the work pay well?" she heard Mr. Simpson ask.

"Fair, but better than what I did before the war. I'm still looking for more customers and trying to expand my territory."

"In the army, were you?"

"For more years than I like to remember," the drummer answered.

"Wounded? Too many men were wounded and killed."

Oh dear, Leah thought, *if they get started telling war stories, I'll be here all afternoon. Maybe if I settle on what I want, I can get Mr. Simpson to cut off the lengths and I can leave.*

"No," the man said, "I was lucky enough not to fight much. Stationed with the occupation in Louisiana. Nasty business. They treated us like hell down there, but at least it wasn't dangerous."

Louisiana again! Leah's premonition became tangible fear when she finally recognized the voice. It was Lieutenant Grimes, who'd worked in the same office she had after the war. Worse than that, he was the very man who'd accused her of murdering Major Charles Anderson, his commanding officer. It was Grimes's false testimony that nearly cost her her life. Anyone from New Orleans could be dangerous to her, but being recognized by Grimes would be fatal. He'd been her enemy when they were forced to work together, and she knew he really hated her after she'd been set free but he'd been found guilty of perjury. Even now, he couldn't be long out of prison.

Leah felt as trapped as she had in prison, and the situation was almost as desperate. There was no way she could get out of the store without his seeing her. There was a back door, but she knew Mr. Simpson always kept it locked, so that would mean summoning him and calling attention to herself. She would simply have to wait him out. She moved farther behind the bolts of material and slipped on the largest hat she could find, a hideous thing with lots of feathers and bows, and then kept her back turned to the men.

Now the talk between them came back to business, and she could only pray they'd bring things to a close. She was breathing so hard she didn't see how they could help but hear it. Then she stopped breathing altogether and her heart began pounding. Mr. Simpson was calling to her.

"Oh, Mrs. Andrews, will you come here a moment?" She couldn't very well ignore Mr. Simpson. He knew she was there. "We need your opinion on these silks."

Still wearing the large feathered hat, she tipped it forward and pulled down the veil so as to hide her face from Grimes. Somehow she would have to play out the farce and find some excuse to leave as quickly as possible.

"Mrs. Andrews, Mr. Grimes here thinks these striped surrahs and Persian prints will be popular with women this year. I don't know. They seem a bit gaudy to me, but then maybe I don't know female taste as well as I should. What do you think?"

Leah gave them a cursory glance, all the while concentrating on getting to the door. Thank goodness Mr. Simpson hadn't referred to her being from New Orleans, at least not yet.

"They're quite lovely. I'm—I'm sure I would like a dress of the ombre stripes. Now, if you don't mind, I'm in a bit of a hurry." Grimes had moved so as to block her way to the door. She would have to retreat to the yard-goods section again and wait for him to leave. "I—I want to go back there and select a bonnet." A bonnet! Why had she said that? She'd about decided that all she needed was ribbons and she'd forget about the material until another day, but she was too flustered to think clearly.

"Do take a moment to look at the prints." The voice of Grimes was the rough file against her nerves again.

She started backing away. "I'm not one for prints, but I'm sure many ladies will like them. The designs are most unusual."

She took three more steps. Then Grimes moved again, and she could finally see her way clear to getting out of the shop.

"You agree then," Mr. Simpson said, "that I should stock some of them? You have such excellent taste, Mrs. Andrews."

If he repeated that name one more time, Grimes might begin to put two and two together. He'd heard James's name often enough during the trial. But that was foolish. He'd no reason to think she'd married James or that he was from Indiana. She could get away now if only Mr. Simpson didn't ask any more questions, and she kept going toward the door as she answered. "Please, I'm no real arbiter of taste. Only what pleases me. Now, I'm afraid I must leave."

She walked straight toward the door. Then she remembered. The hat! Would Mr. Simpson call her back? Maybe he'd say nothing and just charge it to her. It was hideous and she'd never wear it, but any price would be worth escaping from Grimes. Bridget would love it and wear it every Sunday to the church that had at last been finished.

"I'm glad you found a hat you liked, Mrs. Andrews. Shall I just put it on your bill?"

Well, thank you for that, she thought. "Yes, please. And I'll come in another day to look at materials." She was nearly out the door.

"Wait," she heard Grimes calling to her. "For being such splendid help, you must accept a small gift. Pins? Needles? Anything you need?"

Still keeping her face hidden, Leah shook her head. Just a few more steps and she could run to the buggy and get away from there.

"Come, come, there must be something you need."

Grimes had walked to her side. "How about one of these new jeweled hat pins? They're the latest rage. The hat you have on will blow off in a minute without one."

Now he was standing right in front of her and blocking her escape.

"Also good for protection against mashers," he said. "A lady as pretty as you. Never know when it'll come in handy."

Grimes stared directly at her, and she felt as if he were looking right through her, watching her heart beat and seeing the fear she was trying to suppress. She knew the moment he recognized her. There was no concealing the shocked expression on his face. She was trapped for the moment, but she still had one card up her sleeve if the time came that she needed to use it. Grimes might try to cause trouble, and she knew he would if he thought he could get away with it, but she had the means to fight him.

"Well," Grimes smirked, "if it ain't Miss—"

"Mrs. James Andrews, and I don't believe we've met before." It was foolish but worth trying.

"Oh, but I think we have. How about joining me for a bite in the tearoom next door. Or would you prefer a drink at the hotel?"

"I do not take tea with strangers, and ladies are not allowed in the bar." Her calm voice belied her quaking heart.

"Oh, come now, you and I ain't strangers. As for being a lady—"

"I'll—I'll meet you in the tearoom." Although badly shaken, she didn't dare ignore the implied threat in his voice.

During this interchange, they had kept their voices low, but she could see the inquisitive look on the face of Mr. Simpson, who had remained behind the counter. Her own expression must have betrayed her fears.

"This man bothering you, Mrs. Andrews? Look here, Mr. Grimes, Mrs. Andrews is one of our most upstanding citizens, and her husband is a lawyer. We don't hold with strangers bothering our folks."

"It's all right, Mr. Simpson." Leah managed somehow to keep her voice steady. "Just a slight misunderstanding on Mr. Grimes's part, but I assure you, it's nothing I can't handle myself. Good day."

"Good day, Mrs. Andrews. My best to your husband."

Leah headed straight for the buggy. She'd no intention of sharing tea or anything else with Grimes. He'd be leaving Hickory Falls as soon as he finished his business with Mr. Simpson. No one else in town sold his line of goods. Let him tell the store owner whatever he wanted. She could always deny it by saying it was a case of mistaken identity. She began to loosen the reins from the hitching post. Then she saw that Grimes, evidently having finished his business in the shop, was coming out the door.

"Leaving so soon, Leah. I thought we had a date in the tearoom."

"And what makes you think I'll take tea with you? I'll see you in Hell first."

"Oh oh, just as peppery as when you worked in the office. Always did admire that hot blood you showed. Must come with being part—"

"What is it you want of me, Mr. Grimes?"

"Thought we'd drink a little tea, chat a bit."

"The afternoon train leaves in half an hour," she said; "aren't you afraid you'll be late for your customer in the next town? It would be a shame to keep him waiting for another whole day. Not very good for business."

"Oh, I'd already planned to spend the night and most of tomorrow in Hickory Falls. I have to rent a buggy to go to some of the towns not served by the train. So you see, I have all the time in the world." He took her arm. "Shall we go in? You can tell me what I should order from Aunt Tabby to go with my tea."

He grasped her arm so firmly she couldn't get loose. She knew now he could be extremely dangerous and meant her real harm unless she cooperated in some way.

Leah ordered only tea while he asked for tea and several small cakes.

"Do you come here often, Mr. Grimes?" She couldn't swallow the tea, so she might as well talk to keep from betraying her fear.

"Often enough to make it worth my while," he grinned. Again that latent threat. "And for pleasure. Like a sailor I have a sweetie in every town. I think you know Miss Jennie Sullivan. Fine seamstress. High-class clientele among the women here. And you know how women love to gossip during fittings."

"If you are trying to tell me something, Mr. Grimes, say it right out. I don't like innuendoes."

"Fascinating subject, the way colored people like to come North and pass as white," he smirked. "I'd like to discuss it with you sometime, find out just why they do it. Then there's always your husband—"

"My husband knows the truth about me. He was my lawyer; you certainly can't have forgotten that."

"Yes, yes he was. And I understand he has a very successful legal practice here in Hickory Falls. Be kinda rough on him if that truth, and certain other ones, were made known in town. I imagine he'd pay well to keep them quiet. Wife accused of murder. Affair with a Yankee major. Oh, yes, and mistress to a Southern soldier. Mustn't forget about that. My, my, that could keep this town talking for a long, long time."

"You would, wouldn't you? And I imagine you'd add some lies as well that I couldn't possibly deny."

"Then again," he said, as if he hadn't heard her, "I always had a yen to know you better. I'm getting a little tired of Jennie. But she wouldn't have to know. We'd keep it to ourselves. The hotel rooms aren't much, but the place is quiet. You could manage without being seen."

Her disgust at this suggestion rose like bitter gall in her throat. She had to get some tea down or she'd be sick. Never! Never would she submit to this man. He was like filth under her feet. The hatred she felt for him gave her the strength she needed.

"If you are thinking of blackmail," she said sternly, with no trace of the fear that had her shaking inside, "I might remind you that you served time in an army prison for perjury and false accusation. Does your employer know about that?"

Leah watched with extreme satisfaction when he blanched at her words. She knew she was grasping at straws. It might not be a real threat for him at all, but then again it might stall him until she could think of some other way to get out of his clutches. She waited for his next words. They'd tell her whether her threat were a shallow bluff, or if she'd hit him in a vulnerable spot. She was delighted to see him begin to sweat from more than the afternoon heat.

"There, there, Miss Leah, I meant no harm. Just wanted to be friendly." He almost fell over backward getting up from his chair. "I'll—I'll see you next time I'm in town, though."

He hurried out the door, and Leah noticed he'd left her to pay the bill. She'd upset him, but was it enough? His last words were less than reassuring.

Leah was having a second cup of coffee after supper when she heard the buggy drive into the yard. Bridget was bathing Paul prior to putting him to bed.

"Oh, James," she greeted him at the door, "I'm so glad to see you."

"Any special reason for all this affection?"

"Only that I've missed you very much."

"And I thought maybe you were going to ask me for something."

"I am," she whispered, "a whole night of love."

"That will cost you dearly. I'll expect just as much love in return."

In James's arms she could always forget the past, at least momentarily. She needed him tonight to erase the memories called up by the mention of Baptiste's name and the horror of seeing Grimes again. James must never know about that. Somehow she'd have to handle Grimes in her own way if he returned and continued to threaten her. She didn't know which made her suffer more, the fear that Grimes engendered or the longing for Baptiste. Just as she was beginning to feel she could really be happy in Hickory Falls, he reappeared in her life. It wasn't fair to James that Baptiste should still mean so much to her. But never would she let James know that her ardent response to his lovemaking was as often a result of despair as of desire.

Accustomed to making most of her own clothes, Leah had not yet sought the services of Jennie Sullivan, but she knew the young seamstress was highly thought of by many women in town. She often heard them speak about the careful work she did. It would cost more than she'd budgeted for clothes to have something made, but she decided it would behoove her to learn if Grimes had revealed anything to Jennie. Even a hint about her past could prove fatal.

As long as she was paying for it, she thought she might as well have Jennie make a tailored suit. She bought the material, selected the pattern, and took them to Jennie's house.

"This is very handsome fabric, Mrs. Andrews."

"I always feel it's wise to get the best for something that should last as long as a suit."

"This is quite a detailed pattern, too," Jennie said.

"Do you think it too difficult for you?" Leah was surprised. Was there some reason Jennie didn't want to sew for her?

"Oh no, I meant it will take longer than with most things. I hope you're not in a hurry."

"In this weather?" Leah asked. Then she remembered that she was doing all this to find out what Jennie might know, and she could tell that the girl was too busy finishing up a gown for someone else to talk now. "I wonder, though, if we could have the first fitting soon to see if I need any more material before Mr. Simpson sells the rest of the bolt."

"Let me see," Jennie said, "I could be at your house on Thursday. Will that be soon enough?"

"Fine. And I appreciate your being able to come to the house. With the baby, it will make it so much easier."

"Bridget is no longer working for you?"

Leah'd forgotten they both lived in the Irish community. "Yes, but I don't like to be away from Paul for too long at a time." She couldn't very well tell her that she thought the atmosphere at home would be more conducive to the kind of gossip she wanted. "And Bridget's very busy putting up fruit for the winter."

"Then I'll see you on Thursday."

"Thank you, Jennie."

Leah bustled around getting things ready for the fitting in the family parlor. She was as nervous as when preparing for her first tea. Jennie would surely bring everything she needed, but there was no harm in having extra pins and scissors handy.

Jennie came promptly at two, right after Bridget put Paul down for his nap, and Leah slipped into the basted skirt of the suit. It fit as perfectly as if she'd already had several fittings.

"How do you do it, Jennie?"

"I have a good eye for women's figures. You have thirty-six-and-a-half-inch hips, a twenty-four-inch waist—"

"Twenty before Paul came," Leah sighed.

"And a thirty-six-inch bust. I can measure later, but I'm certain I won't be far off. Now the sleeves may give us a little trouble. You're broader in the shoulders than I thought and your arms are longer and slimmer. But that's easily taken care of."

Jennie quieted down to slip a handful of pins between her lips and began pinning adjustments here and there.

"Tell me, Jennie," Leah said, when the girl sat back on her heels to survey what she'd already done, "why isn't a pretty girl like you married? I should think you'd have suitors flocking around."

"I have me a steady beau. But he wants to get well established in his business before we marry."

A steady beau, Leah thought. *Is that what he tells you? When he tells me he has a sweetie in every town. Poor Jennie.* But there was no time to be concerned about the little seamstress. It was her own worries she had to concentrate on.

"What does he do? Does he live in Hickory Falls?"

"No, ma'am. Frank's a traveling salesman, a drummer for piece goods and findings. That's how we met. In Mr. Simpson's emporium."

"Frank?"

"Frank Grimes."

"Really!" Leah hoped her feigned astonishment was not too exaggerated. "Why, I saw him in Simpson's myself just the other day."

"I know. He told me. Fancy you meeting here in Hickory Falls after knowing each other down South."

So he had told her that much. More important, what else had he said. "Only very slightly, Jennie. We worked in the same office, that's all."

287

"There, I believe the skirt is finished. Do you mind slipping the jacket on? I think I'll have to adjust the shoulder line a wee bit." Jennie laughed self-consciously. "When I pretended to be jealous of him having known you, he said the same thing. Said you were really enemies, what with him being from the North and you from the South. So I gathered you were never friendly-like, in a personal way that is."

"That's right, Jennie."

"Now, that should do it. Careful of the pins when you take it off." Jennie carefully folded the skirt and jacket and placed them back in the large box. "Will two weeks from now be time enough? I want to take special care with the lapels."

"Two weeks will be fine. Thank you for coming over here."

If that were all the information Grimes had given Jennie, then certainly it was innocuous enough. Yet, somehow Leah still felt far from secure. If he had so much as hinted he knew something interesting about her and that word was passed along among the women Jennie sewed for, it could be as damaging as the truth. Also, Grimes had said he would return. Was she never to be able to shed her past completely?

In spite of trying to console herself with the words of Sister Angelique, "You are who you think you are, not what others think you are," she knew that was not true. She could think she was white all she wanted to, but her mother's heritage was as much a part of her as her father's and grandfathers'. She'd never been particularly superstitious, except perhaps about certain Voodoo beliefs, but she began to wonder if such things as Mrs. Rhinehardt's cousin in Louisiana, learning about the re-establishment of the Bonvivier import firm in New Orleans, and the confrontation with Grimes were meant to tell her something. They had to be more than coincidence. From the time she was a child, Leah had been convinced she could make her own choices and determine her own life. Now she wondered if Fate were taking over and letting her know that no man can direct his own destiny. Or were these things telling her something else? That she belonged in Louisiana and had been wrong to come to Indiana.

Then her good sense took over. They were coincidence, nothing more; Hickory Falls was not far from the Ohio River, part of the vast waterway through the Midwest and South, and there were probably similar coincidental situations occurring in other states on the inland transportation system, too. She was just not as conscious of them. So far she'd come to no harm. If Grimes returned, she'd deal with him somehow. Neither Fate nor man was going to destroy the happiness she'd found with James.

"You want to go see something I don't think you've ever seen before?" James had just returned from another four-day court session away from home.

"That sounds mysterious and interesting," Leah said. "Will you go with me or is this another all-female event? I'm getting rather tired of those."

"I will. Not only that, but I'll be home now for several weeks, maybe months."

"You will! How wonderful. Oh, James, I'm so glad." When James was away, she felt her strength ebbing with every day he was gone. Not until she saw him again did she find herself strong enough to cope with all the worries that beset her. Especially since she hadn't mentioned to him either the meeting with Grimes or the news about the import firm. He'd be upset at the first and concerned about the second lest it had her regretting she'd come North.

"Yes, we've a very sticky—or as you would say stickly—case to handle."

"You're laughing at me again."

"No, that word is just right. It's very sticky and I know it's going to prove quite prickly before it's over. It's a land dispute, which is always difficult. Surveying in the past wasn't as accurate as it might have been, and to make it worse they referred to such landmarks as the old oak tree—now cut down—or a stream which has since shifted in its bed. It's going to take weeks to redetermine some of the boundaries."

"I hope it takes months and months, and you're on the winning side, naturally. Which side are you on, by the way?"

"That's another problem. The dispute is between two

289

branches of the same family. Two branches between which there is no love lost. I happen to be representing the ones who have farmed the land for three generations and have done very well with it. It's true, they did inherit the best farmland. The other side owns the property that is comparatively hilly and rocky. Filled with some of those caves Sarah told you about when she helped that ex-slave who'd hidden in one. Now they claim the river shifted over the years, and some of that fertile bottomland rightfully belongs to them. My clients claim that's not true. That in fact, if anything, the river shifted the other way and they've lost some of the land to their distant cousins."

"That does sound like a hard one."

"As I said, it means tracing deeds and doing a complete new survey of hundreds of acres to establish clear titles for both of the parties."

"Well, I'm not sorry if it will keep you here. Now what is this mysterious something you mentioned?"

"A good old-fashioned camp meeting and revival."

"A what?" The only camps she knew about were army camps during the war.

"I told you you'd never heard about it. An intinerant preacher or evangelist has set up camp just outside town, and he's holding revival meetings every night." He noted Leah's questioning look. "To revive your faith, to bring you back to God."

"Oh, a church service. What's so new and exciting about that?"

"Ah, but unlike any you've been to before. It's no ordinary church service. We'll go tonight, and you'll see what I mean."

More than amazed, Leah was stunned at the number of buggies already arrived and tied under the trees. In a nearby field, a huge tent had been erected, with three of its sides raised in the warm evening. The fourth side, or front of the tent, was almost completely covered on the inside by white sheets garishly painted with strange signs, fanciful animals, and at the exact center, a huge golden throne. In front of this sat three men playing a fiddle, a horn, and a drum. Leah didn't recognize the tune, but many already seated on the rough wooden benches were clapping their hands and stomping their feet. In her mind, Leah went back to New Orleans and her first visit to the House of Mystery, filled with clapping, singing, swaying people awaiting the start of the Voodoo rites. The painted sheets at the front of the tent and the mesmerized looks on the faces of the people around her, although white instead of black, were an eerie duplication of those she saw the night she followed her mother through the swamp and saw her in her role as Voodoo priestess.

In spite of the crowd, Leah and James found seats about midway down. Since the evening had not yet begun to cool off, Leah was thankful she'd worn a light gown and brought her fan. More people crowded in and pushed her tighter between James and the heavy woman on the other side who was sweating profusely. The only relief came from the slight breeze blowing in under the tent top.

"It's already well after eight," Leah whispered to James. "I thought it was to start at eight."

"It's not the clock that determines when it starts. It's something else. Just wait, you'll see."

Not until the benches were completely filled and people were standing around all three sides of the tent did the preacher appear. In his long, black swallow-tail coat and with his stern face, Leah thought he looked more like an undertaker than a minister.

The first thing he did was nod to several men standing near him, and they immediately pulled the ropes that let down the sides of the tent. The heat and smell from the kerosene lanterns hanging on the posts and across the front added to the heat and the stench produced by all the bodies packed so closely together. *I'm not going to faint, I'm not.* The first waves of nausea had her heart pounding. Gradually the queasy feeling subsided.

"Why did they close the sides?" she whispered to James. "As warm as it is tonight."

"So's everybody will get real hot."

"Well, that's for certain," she said. "But on purpose?"

"Easier to put the fear of Hell in them if they get an inkling of what it's going to feel like down there."

"Oh." She guessed she could stand it for an hour.

Now she focused all her attention on the preacher, who came forward and raised his arms in a combination benediction and victory salute. Stern and sonorous, his voice was hypnotically commanding.

"Have you come here tonight to be saved?"

"Yes!" The shouts came from all around her, and Leah cringed at the raucous sound.

"Have you come to give yourself to the Lord?"

"Yes! Yes!"

"And do you want to be reborn in the blood of the Lamb? If you do, say it! Shout it out. Let me really hear it."

Now the exuberant shouts were almost deafening.

"Then hear—hear what I have to say! Open your hearts and minds to my words." As quiet now as they'd been voluble before, everyone settled back on the benches. Women rearranged light shawls, hushed children, and nestled babies against their breasts while many men let their pipes go out and made no effort to relight them.

"The truth and only the truth will save you." Flinging his arms about or pounding one fist into the palm of the other, the preacher continued almost without taking a breath. "Put no faith in those who say we do not know what the future holds. But—but beware of false prophets. I will tell you what is in the future for all of you. I have searched for the truth and found it. The truth can be found in only one place, the Bible. The Book of Revelations. Revelations—to reveal. And tonight I will reveal to all sinners the true path—the one and only path—to salvation."

He paused, wiped his brow with a large handkerchief, and looked slowly around the assembly. Everyone waited expectantly.

"Who among you has sinned?" he shouted out suddenly. "Who among you has walked the path of abominations? Has a heart black with secret longings or unconfessed evil?"

The shouts and screams were as loud as before, as if they were proclaiming innocence rather than revealing guilt.

"That's it! Let it all out. Purge yourselves. Later you can come forward and I will absolve you of your sins. Now let us have these fine musicians lead us in song."

In the suffocating heat, the nausea and heart palpitations returned, and Leah found herself swaying on her feet. Only her strong will kept her from fainting. The verses of the song went on and on, growing louder and louder. She was not the only one swaying; all were moving back and forth in a kind of ecstasy. Finally the musicians stopped, and the people once again forced themselves back into the narrow spaces on the benches.

"And now for the truth I promised you." For more than an hour he quoted one chapter and verse after another. His voice deepened when he paused to interpret and rose menacingly when he exhorted the people to repent. Accentuating his words was a constant undertone of "amens" and "hallelujahs." Now and then someone jumped up shouting "I believe" or "I'm saved! I'm saved!" James sat unmoved but amused by what was going on around him.

"How much longer?" Leah whispered.

"It's just begun. Could go on all night."

"Well, I can't." She didn't know how much longer she could control the queasy dizziness. Beads of sweat covered her upper lip and coursed down the cleft between her breasts. Her armpits were sticky with perspiration. "How do we get out of here?"

"During the next song if you think you've seen enough."

The preacher stopped for a moment, reached into his pocket again for his large bandana, and began wiping the sweat from his forehead. Maybe, Leah prayed, he would now suggest more music and they could leave. Instead he began talking again.

"I have told you how John has revealed the means of salvation for all of us. Now let me warn you about the temptations that will be in your path. You must destroy those temptations if you are not to fall again."

Leah closed her eyes and only half-listened to him ranting on about those who worship false idols and speak in foreign tongues. Suddenly she heard him shout, "Beware! Beware!" Startled, she opened her eyes in time to see him pointing around the tent to one member of the audience and then to another. Then the finger was pointing at her. "Beware the whore of Babylon!"

There was a sudden intake of breath from everyone under the tent.

"Revelations, chapter seventeen: 'With whom the kings of the earth have committed fornication, and the inhabitants of the earth have been made drunk with the wine of her fornication.' And John goes on to say she is that city which ruleth over many kings of the earth. Seek her out and destroy her before she destroys you."

Leah leaned against James. The words had become only sounds drumming against her ears. Finally the preacher announced a song, after which those who wanted to be saved were to come forward and receive absolution.

"And while we sing, accompanied by our very fine trio," he announced, "I will send among you some who were saved at an earlier service. I know you will want to give generously to insure salvation for yourselves."

Slowly James and Leah began to ease their way out, but not before they were stopped by one of the earlier converts. James put some coins in the man's hat, and they continued moving toward the rear. "Wait just a minute," James said, "and you'll see something."

"I think I've seen all I want to." Leah was gasping for fresh air.

"Look up front."

While the people concentrated on singing and a few hesitantly walked toward the front, the preacher was swiftly counting the money collected so far. He shook his head and sent the men back out among the congregation.

"See what I mean, Leah?"

"Why that greedy old fraud. He's doing all this for money."

"Did you think he was doing it to save their souls?"

"But they do," she insisted. "Why he's no better than that medicine-show man."

"Same breed. Some go after the souls, some after the bodies, but all go after the money."

"Disgusting." She shook her head. "I've never seen anything like it."

"I told you it would be a novel experience."

Sometime around two in the morning, Leah and James were awakened by someone knocking violently at the front door.

"Who in the devil?" James mumbled as he turned up the lamp.

"Careful, James. Nothing good comes in the middle of the night like this."

Leah reached for her robe and slippers, but she was still in the bedroom when James returned.

"That was John," he said.

"John Howard? What in the world did he want?"

"The Irish church is on fire."

"Oh, no!" Leah couldn't contain her distress. "How did it happen?"

"He didn't know. He thinks it was set."

Now Leah was furious. "Who did it? Who would do a thing like that?"

"There are rumors it was done by some who'd been to the revival."

"The revival! But why?"

"God only knows!"

"That lovely little church," Leah cried. "And the pennies and nickels that went into its building. How badly was it damaged?"

James hesitated, but she had to know sooner or later. "Burned to the ground."

"Gone? All of it gone?" she moaned.

"Only the stone baptismal font remains. John said it was eerie the way it stood there starkly white among the rubble."

"It isn't fair, James; it just isn't fair," Leah wailed. "Those people never did any harm to anyone. All they wanted was their own church. This is a horrible town. And I don't think I like your Indiana very much."

"There, there, Leah, I know you're upset, but—"

"Upset! I'm furious and horrified, and you should be, too."

"What I'm trying to say is—those were only a few who did that. You can't blame the whole town for the actions of a few ignorant, bigoted, stupid people who took literally the words of a man who was trying to bilk them out of their money. It seems that somebody interpreted his words about worshipping idols and speaking with foreign tongues as referring to the Irish Catholics. And his quote about the whore of Babylon being a city as meaning the power of Rome."

"And then arouse them to an emotional pitch so they'd lose their heads," Leah nodded. "I knew I didn't like him when I saw him. It's his fault. Ranting on about people being sinners, when he's the worst of the lot."

"You're right. The sins of greed and a desire for the power he can exert over people."

"I don't know," Leah said. "It's all so bewildering. All we know for certain is that a church has been burned, and there's no more money for another one. They'll never save up for another. And those beautiful wood carvings on the walls. I'd be crying if I weren't so damned mad. I suppose someone will have to go out and save the font. It can't just stand there all alone. It's been consecrated and should be protected in some way."

James put his arms around her. "If I promise to go out there first thing in the morning and find a proper place for it, will you go back to bed now and try to sleep?"

"I don't think I can, but yes, I'll try."

In the morning, Leah insisted on going out with James. She had to see for herself. No matter how hard it would be to look at the dead and desolate site, the charred rubble and blowing ashes and acrid smoke. Instead, much to her surprise, the place was alive and busy with men and women working to clear away the remains. Charred timbers were being put into one pile; and as a patch of ground was cleared of the wood, others raked up the ashes. Leah saw Michael O'Flarety putting the baptismal font into a wagon. To one side were some of the undamaged stones from the foundation pillars. Three of the men were walking around the site and pointing occasionally to the stones.

"What—what are they doing, James?"

"I have a pretty good idea. I think I'll talk to Michael."

Sitting in the buggy, Leah was astounded by the energy of the people who'd seen their most precious possession destroyed. Mrs. O'Flarety saw her and came over to the buggy.

" 'Twas a sad, sad thing that happened last night," she said.

"Dreadful," Leah answered. "I would have thought you'd find it impossible to come out here today."

"In our hearts, maybe, but sure and there's nothing like hard work to take the sting out of sorrow."

"Where is Michael taking the font?"

"To our house. We'll worship there again until the church is rebuilt."

"You're—you're going to rebuild?"

"Oh my, yes. We've na' got a mind to be without a church after having sich a lovely one. 'Twill take longer than before, I've no doubt, but we'll get it done. The men will be laying the cornerstones later today, and we'll ask Father Fitzgerald to bless them when he comes on Sunday. Will you join us then? We'd be ever so pleased to have you."

"Thank you," Leah said, ashamed at having underestimated the will of these people. "I'll be here."

While they were dressing on Sunday, Leah asked, "You don't mind my going to the Irish community today rather than with you, do you?"

"Not at all. It's right you should be there."

"I can't offer to help them as much as I did before, but I can pledge something toward the new church."

"Whatever you think, my dear. And pledge something for me, too."

"Thank you, darling. I won't be extravagant, I promise."

When she returned, James met her with a gleam in his eye. "I've good news for you," he said.

"I could use some right now. They're going to lose Father Fitzgerald unless the church is rebuilt soon."

"And it will be. The whole service today—the sermon and most of the prayers—was dedicated to them. As a result, the congregation pledged to match them two dollars for every dollar they raise. It shouldn't take as long as last time."

"Oh, James, that's wonderful! I think I'm going to cry."

"And do you still think this is a horrible town?" He took her in his arms. "And do you still dislike my Indiana?"

"No, James, I'm sorry. I spoke in haste. But I was upset."

"You know, Leah," he said as they sat down to dinner, "I'm damned proud of this town myself. The church was packed this morning, and not one of them refused to sign the pledge sheet. I even heard little Joey Mitchell say he'd give up his nickel-a-week allowance for a month."

"And you signed that pledge sheet, too, I suppose."

"I did. If I can't match what my wife did last time, I'd be a pretty sorry person. You may be limited in the number of gowns you can have this winter, but I'm trusting this will go a long way toward saving my wicked soul."

"I know just how evil you are," she smiled. "You and your wicked ways. I love every one of them."

James reached across the table and took her hand. "If you say that for my giving a few dollars to the church, I'll give every cent I possess to hear you say it again."

"Put your money away, it won't do you any good in this establishment. Here we love for nothing or not at all." Yes, love was beginning. Not deep and passionate, but tender and fulfilling her present needs. She watched his eyes glow and soften.

"Where's Bridget?" He said it in an offhand manner, but she knew what he was leading up to. Let him say it, though.

"Michael came by for her in the wagon after I brought her home. She asked if she could go back for the afternoon."

"And Paul?"

"She wanted to take him and show him off."

"So we are alone?" His smile turned into a malicious grin.

"We are alone."

The word "love" had slipped out, but once she'd said it, she found it easier and easier to say it again and mean it. The important thing, she realized, was that loving James did not mean she had to stop loving Baptiste or try to put him completely out of her heart. They belonged to two different parts of her life; but not to two completely different women: an octoroon *placée* and a white wife. That had been her problem; she had thought she had to replace the one by the other. She had forgotten that in trying to destroy the *placée* she would be killing the wife. She snuggled into James's arms. The disparate halves were slowly coming together, and she was beginning to feel like a whole woman again.

Chapter Twelve

BAPTISTE STOPPED WHEELING his chair back and forth and looked down at the white figure on his bed.

"What in hell did you think you were doing, Catherine!"

"Killing myself. Isn't that what you'd like?" She tried to turn away from him, but the pain was too great. Why didn't he go away and leave her alone? He left her alone all week and then chided her for taking the buggy and visiting friends. He said he considered it indecent for her to be seen in public in her condition, but she knew it was to keep her a prisoner at Belle Fontaine. Even when they fought, he was at least someone to talk to. So she had actually looked forward to the weekends, to hearing all about what was happening in the city. But what did he do during those days? Rode over the plantation with Septimus and then shut himself in the library with Benji during the evenings. She could spend just so much time sewing or sitting in the gazebo and looking out at the river.

"I don't believe that," he said. "You think too much of yourself to deprive the world of your presence."

"That's cruel, Baptiste." She couldn't hold back the

tears, and for one of the few times in her life they came from real despair and hurt.

"No more cruel than your trying to get rid of the baby, which is what I think you were really doing. Were you that determined to seek revenge because I wouldn't let you go to New Orleans? You know how much that child means to me." As furious as she'd been with him, he found it hard to believe she'd commit such a despicable act as deliberately trying to lose the child.

"No, Baptiste, I swear I didn't think an easy ride would be dangerous. Hate me if you must, I'd never do anything to endanger my own child."

"The child you didn't want? How can I believe you?"

"I have some womanly instincts, though you may not think so. I couldn't kill something that was a part of me."

"Then why did you do it?" he demanded. He thought no hate could match what he'd felt on their wedding night. That had injured his masculine pride, but this—this destroying of a life that was a part of him—was a much more despicable act for which there could be no forgiveness.

"I was bored. I was miserable. I only wanted to get out of the house." *Why didn't the pain go away?*

"But you have the buggy," he said.

"Yes, and your hateful remarks when you know I've taken it out."

"But you still could have. It's much safer than riding." He watched to see how she would squirm out of this one.

"I don't know why I rode instead. It was just something I wanted to do. Moses assured me the horse was the gentlest one in the stable, and I am a good rider." He had no right to question her like this, but he continued to stare coldly at her and she saw him waiting for her to continue. "Surely a gentle walk couldn't hurt me. How was I to know a rabbit would run across the path and startle the horse? I lost my balance. That's it."

Baptiste looked long and hard into Catherine's face. Her eyes were filled with tears and her cheeks covered with those she'd already shed. Her hair was mussed and still tangled with briars.

"All right, Catherine." He reached over from the chair and took her hand. "I'll believe you." He'd rather believe her than think she was capable of intentionally destroying the baby. "Are you in much pain?"

"Not now. Just a dull ache. Dr. Verner gave me something, and he said I'll be able to sleep tonight."

"Good. He assured me you're not going to lose the baby, but you'll have to remain a semi-invalid until it arrives. Plenty of rest and eating everything Jessie cooks for you."

"But I can't be moved yet, Baptiste. Where—where will you sleep?" Dear God, would she have to give up the luxury of sleeping alone and share the bed with Baptiste again? Even if the doctor warned him against having relations with her, she cringed at the thought of lying beside him.

"Don't worry. I won't come near you. Benji will fix me a bed in the library." *No, Catherine,* he thought, *you won't be bothered by me for several weeks. Maybe never again.* He rolled his chair out of the room.

In spite of the medicine, Catherine found it impossible to sleep. She was in more pain than she'd admit to Baptiste, but she wanted to feel the pain. It meant she was still alive.

When she'd first felt the horse shy, she hadn't panicked. She'd thought she could handle it. When she realized she was falling, she was furious with herself for failing to know and do the right thing. If she scorned imperfection in others, she despised any form of it in herself. Then as she lay there, her whole body screaming in pain, she became terrified. Catherine was not afraid no one would find her; the horse had already headed back to the stables. But she had an all-consuming fear of death, and she was certain the pain she suffered meant serious internal injuries. Death to her meant going from life to nothingness, not to either Heaven or Hell, and it was that nothingness she dreaded, that end of everything vital and exciting.

Lying there in the grass beside the path, she knew she would endure any pain and suffering if she could just live. Live and destroy Baptiste. This was all his fault. He'd done this to her by forcing himself on her and demanding she have a child. In one way she almost wished the fall would kill the baby. That would be the most perfect revenge. In another way, she hoped the child would live.

She'd bring it up to be like her and to hate its father as much as she did. Baptiste wanted the child desperately, but she would see to it they were never close. Just as she had set out to marry Baptiste, she would devote the rest of her life to making him regret the way he treated her. So really it mattered little to her whether the baby lived or died; either way she would be avenged.

Moses and Septimus had finally found her and carried her back to the house. As gentle as they'd been, she feared that her injuries were worsened by the jolting.

Even now there were sharp pains in her chest and back each time she took a breath. And every pain multiplied her hatred for Baptiste. Had she ever thought she could be happy with him or learn to love him? She'd wanted his home and his money and the position marriage to him would give her. More than that, he was a challenge, and Catherine was never one to refuse a challenge. Her mistake had been in not looking beyond the wedding, of failing to see herself as wife to a cripple instead of thinking always about herself as mistress of Belle Fontaine. Even when she did dwell on the prospect of his claiming his rights as a husband, she'd been so sure she could have things her way. But no, he'd gotten the upper hand right from the beginning, and now look where she was. Lying in bed in such agony she was torn between wishing she were dead and afraid she was going to die. Only one thing gave her the will to endure: planning how to make Baptiste suffer as she was suffering now.

For a long time Baptiste lay awake on the mattress Benji prepared for him on the library floor. He'd tried the couch, but it was too stiff and narrow. Once on the floor, he could turn on the mattress more easily and there was no danger of his falling off. Sipping the brandy Benji left for him, he stared at the low-burning lamp. From time to time he heard weak, almost imperceptible moans from the bedroom.

Whether or not Catherine was lying about the fall being an accident, he would never forgive her if she lost the baby. Whatever her intent, the ride had been a foolhardy thing to do, and she must have known the danger. Dr. Verner said she'd broken three ribs and injured her back, but he was unsure about internal injuries. So far the baby was still alive, and they could only hope.

This baby had to live. Baptiste knew there'd never be another. Whatever the outcome, he doubted if he and Catherine would ever sleep together again. She'd completely destroyed the longing he once had to possess her, and somehow he couldn't see himself making love to her without feeling some desire. Time had dissipated his need to master her, and sexual relations with her had long since become routine and unsatisfying.

For a moment he thought about divorcing Catherine in spite of the fact it would be hard to establish sufficient grounds in the eyes of the Church. And since neither of them could then marry again anyway, it seemed pointless to go through the involved procedure. As long as she remained on the plantation and he spent most of his time in the city, they would be living as much apart as if they were legally separated.

It was the child he had to think about. To be sure that Catherine did not exert undue influence over him—or her—Baptiste would have to retain control of his offspring's upbringing. That meant being at Belle Fontaine considerably more than he would like. At least until the child was old enough to live in New Orleans with him. Catherine had indicated often enough that she didn't want to be burdened with the responsibility of a child, and he would be more than glad to take that duty off her hands. No, not a duty, a pleasure.

Jessie tiptoed past him on her way from the bedroom.

"No need to be quiet, Jessie. I'm awake. How is she doing?"

"Not good, suh, not good."

"Her condition's still pretty serious then." How soon would they know if there were any improvement? Hours? Days?

"Yessuh. She bad hurt."

"Broken ribs can be very painful, Jessie."

"It ain't the ribs or the back I'se worried about. It's her insides I'se frettin' over."

"What do you mean, Jessie? You were midwife for the cabins. Is there something the doctor doesn't know—or hasn't told me?"

"She busted up inside. Lessen the pain eases, she gonna lose that baby for sho'."

"She can't!" Baptiste put his head in his hands.

"We know in a day or two. Iffen the little heart stop, we know."

"And after a few days?" he asked.

"The baby should live. Then we jus' waits for the birthin'."

"And there's more danger then." In his despondency it seemed as if the child were his only reason for living.

"Always danger, suh. This only make it worse."

"Thank you, Jessie, for all you're doing. If Madame Fontaine has a successful delivery, I know you'll deserve much of the credit."

"Naw, suh, all any of us can do is jus' wait and see."

Wait and see. That's all he could do, too. He finished the brandy, but it was a long time before he fell asleep.

For another week Baptiste remained at Belle Fontaine, chafing at the bit to get back to the office but not daring to leave until he heard Dr. Verner's verdict. From a sense of duty he went twice into Catherine's room to see how she was feeling, but since she turned her head away and refused to speak to him, he never looked in on her again. He knew she was blaming him and his insistence on a child for the pain she was suffering. Perhaps it was just as well they didn't speak to each other. Any attempt at conversation would only end in ugly recriminations they could never take back. There was no need to make the situation any more intolerable than it already was.

Unable to pace the floor while Dr. Verner examined Catherine, Baptiste could only sit on the gallery and stare out across the river. The doctor seemed to be taking far too long to determine if everything were all right.

"Benji!"

"Yes, boss."

"For God's sake, come out here and keep me company. I'll go raving mad if I have to sit here alone much longer."

"You want me to bring you anything? Bourbon? Brandy?"

"No. I've been drinking too much this week as it is. Jessie come out of the room yet?"

"Far as I know she's still in there with the doctor."

"I trust her judgment in these things more than I do his. He may be all right for broken bones, but she knows babies."

"She does that, for sure," Benji agreed with a nod.

"You think she'll tell me the truth?" Baptiste wanted to be told everything was all right, but he tried to convince himself the truth would be better than false hope.

"She ain't one to lie, boss. She give it to you straight."

"That's good. I guess. I don't know what I want to hear."

"It won't be long now, Baptiste." The first name always slipped out when he was genuinely concerned. "Then you can rest easy."

"Rest easy? Or know it's all over?" He clasped and unclasped his hands. His total absorption in his fears over the baby was evinced by the lack of a cigar. Benji recognized the sign and was very worried.

At the sound of footsteps, they both turned toward the door that connected the gallery with the hall.

"Dr. Verner, how—how is she?" He wanted to ask about the baby, but it would be expected of him to be more concerned about his wife.

"Catherine is doing fine. The ribs are healing nicely, and her back injury, though very painful, was superficial. No damage there."

"And—"

"The baby is still alive."

"Thank God!" Baptiste released the breath he'd been holding since the doctor came through the door.

"Because the injury was to her lower spine," Dr. Verner said, "the delivery will be difficult, but there's every reason to think both she and the baby will come through fine. I'm going to recommend she stay in bed until then, just to make certain. But—it is merely a precautionary measure and no need for you to be alarmed."

"Thank you, Doctor. That's what I've been waiting to hear."

"You can go in now if you like. I've given Catherine a mild sedative, but she's still awake. And Jessie is a damned fine nurse. She'll follow all the instructions I've left with her."

"Yes, yes, she is."

"I'll come out once a week, oftener if she needs me. So don't hesitate to send word if she does."

Dr. Verner seemed to be waiting for something, and Baptiste realized it was for him to go into Catherine's room. It would be only natural he should want to see her, and together they could celebrate the good news. For him it was good. He hoped for her, too.

This time when he wheeled himself into the room, Catherine didn't turn her face away.

"You should be joyful, Baptiste. Where is the big grin I expected to see?"

"Because you're doing so well? I am glad for you. And happy that any danger to the baby has passed."

"I didn't mean that," she said sarcastically. "I meant because now I have to lie in this bed for the next few weeks and can't possibly escape from the house. That should really please you."

"My, we are bitter today, aren't we?"

"What did you expect? Shouts of joy because I'm confined to this room?"

"No, but at least some show of thankfulness that you're going to be all right, that your injuries aren't permanent."

"For that I am grateful. I should hate to be *crippled* from now on. It must be horrible and demeaning to go through life as a *cripple*."

Each time she accented the word, Baptiste cringed inside. "Only for those whose minds are crippled, Catherine. Not their bodies. We disgust only those whose minds are crippled. They're the ones to be pitied. Does it devastate you to have a crippled mind?"

"Oh, you are really hateful and repulsive. I wish now the baby had died just so I could enjoy watching you in total, abject misery. Get out of here! If I have to stay in here, at least let me stay in peace."

Catherine's words stirred up new fears in Baptiste. "Just to make certain you will continue to improve, I'll insist that Jessie stay in here with you every minute. Do you understand what I'm saying, Catherine? Every minute, day and night. You need never fear being left alone."

Instead of answering, Catherine turned her face away from Baptiste. She knew what he was implying. If she had

307

any thoughts of trying to endanger the baby, Jessie would be right there to see that she didn't. That showed how little Baptiste really knew her.

"Good-bye, Catherine. I'll be back in time for the delivery."

Driving into the city, Baptiste knew that Catherine's fall had ended forever any hope of even a pretense at marriage. In spite of their constant bickering, their union had afforded some relief from the overpowering loneliness that smote him now. It was a good thing the import firm kept him busy. By becoming totally engrossed in that, he might be able to forget how desperately he longed for Leah. He thought he'd suffered total despondency right after she left, but it was nothing compared to the need he had for her now.

Catherine lay on the bed and looked up at the ceiling. The pain had begun to subside, and she was filled with a strange new exultation. Now that Dr. Verner had assured her she was going to live and there would be no lasting effects from the fall, she could concentrate on the new strategy that had been fomenting in her mind. The irony of it pleased her. Baptiste would never know it was his words that had given her the idea.

Her plans had to be worked out very carefully to assure there would be no slip-up to prevent their completion and no clue to give her away. It would be a few days before she dared try getting out of bed, and that was good. She could spend the time plotting every move. Now Catherine was in her element. There was nothing she liked better than conceiving a complicated idea and working it out to perfection. Especially if it meant victory over Baptiste.

"Time for lunch, missy." Jessie walked in carrying a large tray. In her studied preoccupation with her latest scheme, Catherine had lost track of time.

"I'm not hungry, Jessie. Anyway, I'm too sore to sit up and eat." She must continue to complain of excruciating pain that made it impossible for her to move.

"I give you something for that jus' as soon as you finishes this tray. You know what de doctor say. You gotta eat."

"Nonsense. I need less than usual if I'm just lying here.

What I need is some of that medicine Dr. Verner left for pain."

"After you eat. You jus' lie there and let ol' Jessie feed you."

Catherine re-evaluated her opinion of Jessie. The old Negress would not be as easy to fool as she'd first thought. Best to go along with whatever she suggested, or at least appear to.

"All right, Jessie," she conceded with a smile. Jessie had been her staunch advocate since Catherine first came to the house and began wooing Baptiste. She would lull the cook into thinking she was following all orders. "What good things do you have on that tray?"

"Some gumbo, real easy to swallow, and soft rice. Now don' you move anything 'cept your head, and we manage."

The lunch was good, and Catherine had forgotten she hadn't eaten much since noon the day before. It was not hard to let Jessie feed her everything on the tray.

"Now for the powders," Jessie said. "I go mix 'em in water."

"Good. I really need them, and I think they help me sleep."

"They does that, missy. They put you right out."

For the next two or three days, Catherine took the medicine as often as she could get Jessie to bring it to her. Soon she'd have to devise a way to get rid of it while appearing to continue taking it. Three more days of rest and she should be ready to carry out the next step in her plan.

By evening of the third day, Catherine felt almost no pain when she moved, but she continued to let Jessie help her when she wanted to turn over. It was no problem to emit moans and small shrieks of pain each time.

"Poor lamb," Jessie murmured. "You sho' done suffered from that fall. I don' rightly see how you stands it."

"It's pretty bad, Jessie, but I'll endure whatever pain I have to as long as the baby is all right. It would break my heart if I couldn't give M'sieu Baptiste the child he wants."

"Don' you worry 'bout that. We gonna have a nice, healthy baby the way you bin eatin' for ol' Jessie."

Yes, Jessie was definitely on her side and would now do almost anything she asked. When the cook brought her medicine that night, Catherine managed to sip only a few drops and then pour the rest into the slop jar. From now on she had to remain alert and awake.

In the morning she repeated the same procedure.

"Jessie, will you do something for me?"

"Anything you wants, missy."

"Ask Abelia to come in here. She was helping me with the layette and now—well, you can see it's impossible for me to do any more sewing. I'd like to talk to her about finishing it for me."

"I go get her now."

The next problem was to get Jessie out of the room while Catherine talked to Abelia. The young woman was a vital link in her scheme.

Carrying an armload of tiny gowns and receiving blankets, Abelia arrived within a few minutes.

"Jessie," Catherine said, "I know I'm making a lot of work for you, but—"

"It ain't work to do what you wants, missy, it a pleasure."

"Then will you go to the kitchen and make some of those tiny frosted cakes only you know how to bake. I suddenly have a craving for them."

"You be all right alone?"

"I won't be alone, Jessie. Abelia will stay right here until you return."

That request should keep Jessie in the kitchen for nearly an hour, plenty of time to persuade Abelia to help her.

The young servant began spreading the things on the bed.

"Don't worry about those, Abelia. Although I do want you to finish everything up for me. But that's not the reason I needed you here. You know the Cat Man?"

"Cat Man! Do Lord, missy, don't mention 'is name."

"But you do know him or can get in touch with him?"

"No, no, I don' know him."

"Nonsense!" How exasperating these people could be at times. "Don't lie to me. I know perfectly well he's the high priest or Papaloi or whatever you call him of Voodoo. And I also know most of you sneak off at night to attend those Voodoo rituals of yours. Don't you?"

"Yessum, but I ain' never talk wid him. He mighty fearsome. He live way back in the bayou and nobody kin go near him. He got yellow skin and green eyes what glow in de dark."

"I don't need a description, Abelia. I just want to get in touch with him. Can you go to his place?"

"Lawdy, no, ma'am. Ain' no one gonna go there. Ain' you heerd 'bout Big Sam and Cat Man? Big Sam done walk up de road and him never heerd from since. The next day Jaybel found catprints on the road and ain' done say nuthin' for two days."

How stupidly superstitious these people are, Catherine thought. *Big Sam probably got drunk and walked straight into the bayou and drowned.*

"But you do have a way to get a message to him?" she asked. "I know he makes stronger Voodoo charms than any other witch doctor, and I need to see him."

"Do Jesus, missy, you don' wanna see him. He might put de spell on you."

"He's not going to put any spell on me," Catherine insisted. She was beginning to get irritated at Abelia's hesitancy. "He's going to sell me something, and he won't harm anyone who's willing to pay him. Now—how do I get a message to him?"

"You puts it in the holler of a big oak tree what's covered with moss."

"Not just any oak tree, though."

"No, ma'am, de one at de end of 'is road."

"He can read?"

"Oh, yessum, he read."

"Then get me paper and pen from that desk over there, and hurry." Catherine began to write. "Not a word of this to anyone—to anyone, you hear?—or I'll whip every bit of black skin off you."

"Yessum, yessum, I stays quiet. I do jus' what you say."

Abelia tucked the note down the front of her dress just as Jessie came in with the cakes.

"Thank you, Jessie. I hope you brought coffee, too."

"A steamin' potful, missy. You think you can sit up?"

"If you help. Oooh, it still hurts right back here. I'm not sure I'll ever be able to walk again. It's almost as if I were paralyzed."

"Not iffen you feels pain. You jus' gonna have to learn to walk all over again after being in bed so long."

Now she was sure Jessie wouldn't suspect her of being able to get out of bed and walk as far as the gazebo at the bottom of the lawn.

The following night Catherine was ready to carry out the next step in her scheme. She had asked Jessie to put the packets of painkilling powders in the drawer of her bedside table and said she would mix them herself anytime she needed them.

"Jessie, any of the little cakes left?"

"A few. You want one 'afore you goes to sleep?"

"Yes, and a little coffee. And, Jessie, bring a cup for you, too. As attentive as you've been, I think we should sit and have a cup together."

"Oh, Lordy, missy, that ain' right."

"It is if I say it is. Now, no arguments. Get the coffee and I'll pour. See, I can sit up a little now. These powders have really worked miracles." And they were going to work their greatest miracle tonight.

While Jessie was arranging the cakes on a plate and getting a linen towel to protect Catherine's gown, Catherine slipped the contents of three packets into Jessie's coffee and masked the slightly bitter taste with plenty of sugar and cream.

"There you are, Jessie. Now sit in the rocker and tell me how you learned to be a midwife."

Before Jessie could utter a fourth sentence, her head fell back against the cushion of the rocker. Catherine waited until she knew the cook was sound asleep. Thank God Benji was in New Orleans with Baptiste. The way he sneaked around, she would be caught for sure.

Slowly Catherine got out of bed and placed her feet on the floor. The tingling pain in them from days of not walking almost sent her back to bed. Again she put them down, one at a time, and gradually she was able to put some weight on them. At least there was little pain in her ribs or back. Still feeling giddy, she walked to the armoire and found her long blue cape. Anyone seeing her walking across the lawn at this time of night would take her for a ghost or a worker sneaking off to meet one from another plantation. Probably the former, given the superstitious nature of the Negroes, and that would help her plan.

It took more time that she'd originally thought to make her way down the stairs and across the lawn. A good thing she'd left early. Reaching the gazebo, she fell exhausted onto one of the seats. Only the lapping of the river against the bank disturbed the night. There was something eerie and haunting about such complete silence.

Suddenly Catherine sensed she was not alone, and she looked up to see a man standing in the door of the gazebo.

"Oh, you startled me. I didn't hear you coming."

"I knows. Be *je* Cat Man. No one ever hear me."

"Then you got my message all right."

"I here. What you want from Cat Man?"

Catherine looked into his green eyes that, as Abelia said, seemed to glow in the dark, and there was a faint trace of long whiskers on his upper lip. He wore a battered, mildewed top hat and equally greenish swallow-tail coat. From one ear hung a large gold ring. His yellow, desiccated skin clung to his prominent facial bones like tissue paper.

"I want you to make something for me," she said. He didn't frighten her, but he made her feel decidedly uncomfortable. She could understand why the darkies believed he was able to put a charm on them.

"A love potion? A Voodoo *gris-gris* to torment someone you hate? I make 'em all. For a price."

"I can pay your price, but I need something more potent and lethal than either of those." Quickly she told him what she wanted. "Can you get it for me?"

"I get anything. For a price." He reached out his hand, and as his long, clawlike nails touched her cape, she involuntarily shrank back.

"Here," she said, "is this enough?" Thank goodness she knew about Baptiste's lock box and had learned to open it without the key.

Slowly Cat Man flicked through the bills with his long nails. "It enough. When you want it?"

"Tomorrow. Can you put it in the oak tree? I can send someone for it."

"Tomorrow at sunset."

Catherine blinked once and he was gone. As quickly as

she followed him to the door, he had disappeared completely by the time she got there. Nor had she any idea which direction he took.

There, now to see Abelia again and have her secure the package. If they were careful, Abelia could give it to her right under Jessie's eyes and no one would suspect. Jessie was still snoring loudly when Catherine returned and crawled gratefully back into bed. The excursion had taken more out of her than she realized, and she reached for a packet of the powders. There would be no hiding it or throwing it away this time. She was really in a good bit of pain. But no pain was stronger than her elation that she had managed to pull off this most dangerous part of the scheme.

Chapter Thirteen

ON A THURSDAY morning in mid-September, Leah told James she wouldn't be home when he came in at noon for dinner. "I'm going out to Sarah's to help her put up cherry preserves. And there will be several jars for us."

"Tell Bridget not to fix anything for me then. I'll eat at the café. This land case is getting much more involved than John and I expected, and we can talk with the surveyors at the same time."

"That's why I don't like you having dinner downtown. You keep right on with business instead of relaxing while you eat."

"Maybe if there were more hours in the day, I wouldn't have to," James said. "But it's better than being gone at night, isn't it?" He tipped up her chin to kiss her good-bye.

"All right, but don't eat too fast. You always do when you're upset. I'll see you tonight."

By nine she had the buggy hitched and was on her way. She took Paul with her so Bridget could get started with fall housecleaning, and she let the horse amble along while she pointed out all the interesting sights to Paul, who was suddenly becoming very much aware of birds and flowers

315

and rabbits. She and Sarah spent a busy day preparing the fruit, boiling up the rich, red pulp, and pouring it into jars. All the while they chatted and watched Paul playing on the floor, they were blissfully unaware of the tragedy that had taken place in town and the threat of violence about to erupt a few miles away.

Having wanted to stay with Sarah as long as possible, Leah returned home later then she'd planned. She was surprised that James's buggy wasn't yet in the yard, and she walked into the kitchen to find Bridget sitting at the table and wringing her hands.

"What's the matter, Bridget? Where's Mr. Andrews? Has he been home at all?" As she talked, she put Paul in the high chair and began fixing him something to eat.

"Oh, ma'am, it's terrible. Mr. Andrews came home about an hour after you left and then rushed away in a frightful hurry. He hasn't been back since."

"What's wrong? What do you mean, 'terrible'? Something to do with Mr. Andrews?" All the while she forced herself to feed Paul, who was grabbing at the spoon and demanding more.

"No, no, it's Susan Price." Bridget shook her head and bit her fist.

"What does Susan Price have to do with Mr. Andrews? Come now, Bridget, calm down and tell me."

"Susan—Susan was attacked last night." Bridget broke into a fit of weeping.

"Stop that, Bridget! Is she dead? Murdered?"

"Oh, no. She was—she was—" Bridget found it impossible to go on.

"You mean she was raped?" Leah was stunned. She'd never dreamed of such a thing happening in a small, quiet town like Hickory Falls.

"Yes, ma'am. Oh, no decent girl is safe anymore," she wailed.

Before Leah could question Bridget any further, James walked in, looking as haggard and disheveled as she'd ever seen him.

"Here, sit down," she said. "I'll get you something to eat."

"Some whiskey, Leah. I need a good stiff drink."

Leah brought the bottle and glass. "Bridget told me

about Susan Price. It's horrible, I know, but why are you so distraught?"

"They had to question her this morning. The Prices thought there ought to be a lawyer present while she told her story to the police. She was bound to be incoherent, and they wanted me there to help keep her calm and try to get the true story. Arthur and Lucile are old friends, and Susan has been much like a daughter to me. Both of them were too wrought up to handle it."

"It must have been terrible for you. And for Susan, having to tell what happened."

"No, actually she hasn't been able to say anything. She's in a state of complete shock and can't even speak. Dr. Simmons has her sedated, says he doesn't know if she'll ever remember what happened."

"But that would be good, wouldn't it?" Leah asked. "For her to forget it all, as if it never happened. Maybe—maybe she need never know. Just wake up thinking she's been ill or something. Surely her parents could pretend that."

"No, it's all over town. Anyway, we have to find out who did it. Some other girl could be in danger or the wrong man punished for it."

Leah saw James's legal mind at work, and she knew he was right.

"Do they suspect someone?" she asked.

"Yes, and that's what really has me upset."

"Drink your whiskey, James, and tell me. You're trying to keep something from me, and I don't like it."

"I need something to eat. My stomach's been churning all day and those drinks didn't help. I needed them then, but now I need food."

"Yes, yes, of course." Leah opened the icebox. "It won't be a minute. Just have to warm something up. Have a cup of coffee. That will help settle you."

Once she had everything on the table and Bridget had taken Paul away to be bathed and put to bed, Leah sat horrified at the story James told her.

"Arthur and Lucile found Susan unconscious on the living-room floor when they came home from church last night. She'd been severely battered around the face, but it

317

didn't take a doctor's examination to tell what else she'd suffered."

"Oh, the poor child. Was she alone in the house?"

"Apparently. George Blackman, her fiancé, had been with her when the Prices left for church. He was almost as incoherent as Susan when we asked him what he knew. The shock to him must be fierce. He said he and Susan went out on the porch with her parents, and then he left almost right away. He knew it wouldn't be proper for them to stay alone unchaperoned. A bit too proper, perhaps, considering they are engaged, but the Prices have always been very particular where Susan is concerned. Now George is blaming himself for not staying. He feels, naturally, that it never would have happened if he'd been there."

"Does anyone have any idea how long after that it happened?" Leah asked.

"Couldn't have been long. George says he stayed maybe ten minutes, saw Susan into the house, and then left. Church service lasted less than an hour, and the Prices live only three houses away."

"Does he—do they have any idea who might have done it?"

"Yes, that's why I'm here, waiting for someone."

"I thought you had one ear cocked toward the outside while you were talking. Who're you waiting for?"

"George said he saw a Negro yardman working around the house next door earlier in the evening. He thinks the man must have seen him leave and come right over. George can't remember whether Susan locked the front door, so the man could have gotten in easily."

"But that doesn't answer my question," Leah said. "Who are you waiting for?"

"Ambrose." The name came out like a sigh.

"Oh, no!" Leah put her hand to her mouth. "Not Ambrose. He'd never do a thing like that."

"We know he wouldn't, but the town is in an uproar. The sheriff and John and I argued our throats raw against taking the law into their own hands. But it did no good. The men have organized a lynch mob and gone after Ambrose."

"And you expect him to come here." That could be as

318

dangerous for James as it was for Ambrose. Lynch mobs shot it out rather than listened to reason, and she knew that whether he thought the man innocent or guilty, James would not give Ambrose to them without a fight.

"I think he will if he's innocent. He trusts me."

"Don't act foolishly, James. We could all be killed if the men are as wrought up as you say."

"I wouldn't put you in danger, Leah, and there won't be any if things work out as I plan. I sent the men on a false trail, to a cabin miles on the other side of town where I told them Ambrose sometimes hangs out. That will give us at least another hour if he does come here. I think he'll tell me the truth."

Leah looked at the food on her plate. She hadn't eaten a mouthful. She thought she heard something in the carriage house and then scolded herself for imagining things. But James had heard it, too, and gotten up from the table.

"I'll be back in a few hours, Leah. Don't wait up for me. If anyone comes here, say—say I've gone to see John. He knows what I plan to do and will cover for me."

Leah locked the door after him and went into the parlor. There was no sense in James's telling her not to wait up. She couldn't possibly sleep until he returned. She called Bridget in.

"Is Paul asleep?"

"Sound asleep, ma'am."

"Then come sit down and we'll continue reading." Some months earlier she'd begun reading to Bridget and then teaching her to read. Thrilled at the thought of being the first in her family to read and write, Bridget was an eager student. While she listened patiently to Bridget sounding out words and then phrases, Leah thought of Rachael, her mulatto grandmother, who had taught herself to read with the newspapers that fish and meat came wrapped in. In turn, she had scrimped and saved to buy books to teach Clotilde, Leah's mother, to read and write. Those books had been her proudest possessions. Leah was the fortunate one. Her father had given her a convent education.

Tonight they were nearly halfway through Dickens's *Great Expectations*, and Leah was amazed at how quickly Bridget was mastering the difficult prose. They read through one chapter, then three, then five, and still James had not returned. Leah's one desperate fear was that the lynch mob had found James and Ambrose together. If they were in as surly a mood as James had suggested, they might take it into their heads to hang them both, or at least hold James at gunpoint while they strung up Ambrose. For the moment she felt helpless and all she could do was pray.

Closing the door behind him and waiting for Leah to latch it, James had walked slowly to the carriage house. If anyone followed him home, he wanted to appear as nonchalant as possible and wait for them to reveal themselves. Then he would merely recheck the horses, add feed to the stalls, and return to the house. He knew Ambrose was there. He'd heard the slight rustle in the grass by the house, and he could sense the frightened man's presence.

James paused halfway as if to check something in the flower border, and he listened carefully before walking on. If anyone were nearby they would soon make their presence known. Nevertheless, he took no chances. He spent several minutes going from stall to stall, testing the reins for cracks, rubbing them with a bit of oil, and then carrying more feed and water to the horses. Casually he took one set of reins and carried them over to his buggy.

Only now did he feel it was safe to crawl up the ladder to the hayloft. "Ambrose." It was no more than a whisper.

"Mistuh James, that you?"

"It is, Ambrose. And I'm alone."

"Oh, Mistuh James, you gotta help me. They gonna string me up for sure if you don't."

"Then you'll have to tell me everything. If you're innocent, I'll get you away from here. But if you're guilty, I'll take you in to the sheriff, make certain you're protected, and then handle your case. But I won't lie for you. And I won't make any guarantees."

"I didn't do it, Mistuh James, I swear it. You knows I wouldn't do nothing like that."

"I don't think you would either, Ambrose, or I wouldn't be here with you now. But tell me everything—everything—you know about last night. You can talk while we drive."

"Where you gonna take me?" Ambrose asked fearfully.

"Never mind about that. To a safe place, I assure you. Now climb down and get on the floor of the buggy and cover up with this blanket. I have to go back outside and make certain there's no one around."

James looked at Ambrose, whose hair and clothes were soaked with sweat. Ambrose had worked for him and for others in the town for over ten years, inside their homes and out. Now these same people were ready to turn on him and lynch him merely on the circumstantial evidence that he'd been seen next door to the Prices' shortly before the attack on Susan.

Coming out of the carriage house, he walked over to his vegetable garden and moved up and down the rows as if checking which should be picked the next day. He lit his pipe and looked up at the sky. Clouds covered the moon, and he felt certain it would rain the next day. He ambled back to one of the stalls. Now his movements took on greater urgency as he hitched the horse to the buggy, climbed inside, and took the reins in his hands. He moved as fast as he dared along the road leading out into the country. His buggy was identical to Dr. Simmons's, and he hoped anyone seeing him would think the doctor had been called out on an emergency case.

While they drove, he questioned Ambrose. "Were you working next door to the Prices yesterday?"

"Yessuh. Most of the afternoon and part of the evening. Mrs. Harrison had some plants she wanted transplanted 'afore I left, and it took longer than I thought to finish. I worked until six, maybe six-thirty."

"And then you left? Went home?"

"Straight home."

"You didn't see George Blackman come to call on Susan?"

"Yessuh, I seen him come to the house. I knowed he was there."

"Did you see Mr. and Mrs. Price leave for church?"

"No, suh. I was gone by then."

"Then how did you know they went to church?" James hated tricking him like this, but he had to get at the truth.

"I stayed home all day today, working in my garden. I didn't know nothing 'bout what happen till a friend came running up to the house to tell me they was a mob gathered and they was figuring to lynch me. I knowed I ain't got no chance at all lessen I gets to you, so I lit out."

"Why didn't you just keep running, Ambrose? You know I should turn you over to the sheriff."

"No, suh; no, suh! Don't do that. I wasn't nowheres near that place when that girl was hurt. You knows what'll happen. They'll string me up for sure. Take me outta the jailhouse and string me up."

Under the dirt and sweat, Ambrose's face was a study in terror. James tried to imagine how the man felt, knowing that at any moment he could be captured and have a noose put around his neck. He didn't know why the man hadn't panicked and tried to leave town.

"Ambrose, I'm going to take your word that you're innocent, and I'm going to get you away from the town."

"How, Mistuh James? They'll hunt me down no matter where I goes."

"A place where I guarantee you'll be safe. But you're going to have to give me your word you won't try to run away until all this has been cleared up. When Susan Price recovers from shock, she can tell us who her attacker was. But—and listen to me carefully. I'll be checking on you every day. And if I hear you've run away, I'll be part of the posse that hunts you down. Understand?"

"I understands. Thank you, Mistuh James, thank you."

There was no light on in the house when James pulled around to the back. He drove the buggy under the shed.

"Wait here, Ambrose. She's probably asleep, and I don't want to frighten her. She's had enough harassment these past few years. That's why I think she'll understand what I'm doing."

He walked around to the front porch and rapped gently on the door.

"Sarah. It's James. Can you let me in? It's urgent."

He finally heard the shuffling of slippered feet inside and began to breathe more easily.

"What in the world is thee doing out here this time of night, James? Is Leah ill? Or the baby?"

"No, nothing like that. Just let me in. I don't want anyone to see me on your porch. It wouldn't be safe for either of us."

"What's the trouble, James? I know it must be serious the way thee is talking."

Sarah lighted a kerosene lamp, but not before James made sure all the curtains were pulled across the windows.

"It is. The young Price girl was raped last night."

"Susan? Oh my, no. How dreadful."

"Right now she's in shock and can't tell us who did it. Her fiancé says he saw Ambrose working earlier in the yard next door. Now there's a lynch mob after Ambrose."

"I don't believe it," Sarah declared stoutly. "He's a good man. Why, he's worked for me, all alone out here, and I've never felt threatened."

"George claims he's often seen Ambrose eying Susan and was just waiting for the chance to find her alone."

"Does thee believe him or Ambrose?"

"At this point I don't know who to believe," James sighed. "All I know is Susan was attacked, and we have to find out who did it. There are certainly others who could have seen the Prices and George leave the house. The point is, until we know for certain, until Susan can tell us, we have to protect Ambrose. He's given me his word not to run away until we do know the truth."

"Oh, James, I'd love to help thee and Ambrose. But knowing how I feel about violence, this is the first house they'll come to. Neither he nor I would be safe."

"Nor would I ask you to keep him here, Sarah. But you're familiar with the caves around here. Isn't there one of them where he could hide and not be found?"

Sarah thought a minute. Others knew the caves, too, and would be sure to search them as the most likely place for Ambrose to hide.

"There is one, James, where he might be safe. It's one my boys discovered years ago, and then I had to forbid them to go in again because it's dangerous. But if Ambrose listens carefully to what I tell him, he could hide there undetected for weeks."

"Where is it, Sarah?"

"I'll have to show you. Let me get my shawl."

Within minutes they were in the buggy and resting their feet gently on the blanket that covered a quaking Ambrose. In another few minutes they had crossed the fields, circled a sinkhole almost hidden from view by tall grasses, and driven up to the place Sarah indicated.

"Now listen carefully," she said, as Ambrose clambered down from the wagon and took the lantern she handed him. "The first cavern is large and dry, but don't be tempted to stay there. Thee would be found in a minute. In the opposite wall is a small opening, but large enough for thee to squeeze through. Beyond it is a drop of about six feet. Hold the lantern in front of you, because just after thee drops down, thee will see an underground river a few feet ahead. It is deep and the reason I would not let my sons go back there. But thee can get across the river where it narrows, and beyond is another large cavern where thee can be dry and comfortable."

James saw that Ambrose was terrified of being left there in the dark and of the deep river he had to cross. He could almost read the Negro's mind as he debated whether to take this chance or let James turn him in.

"Ambrose, either Miss Sarah or I will check on you every day. No one will look for you in that farther chamber. You just have to be certain to remain absolutely quiet if you hear anyone but us in the outer one."

"Yes, Ambrose," Sarah said. "Thee will be fine. I'll bring food every day and leave it just inside the opening to the drop. Thee should be able to reach it without any trouble. If I should not come one day, it's because the men are searching the area and I dare not."

"Thank you, Miss Sarah. I trusts you like I trusts Mistuh James. I do just like you say."

James followed him into the cave and stayed until he was certain Ambrose had dropped down to the lower section and made it across the river. To his relief he saw that no light came to him from the lantern Ambrose carried. "Ambrose," he called, and he heard his voice echoing and re-echoing throughout the depths of the cave, "I'll bring more kerosene, too, for the lantern so you won't have to be in the dark."

He crawled back out, and he and Sarah made their way immediately to her house. "I thank you, too, Sarah. He may be as guilty as George says he is, but at least he deserves a trial, not a lynching. That cave was a good choice."

"For two reasons, James. I think he is innocent, too, but I also know he's terrified. He might reconsider and try to run away. The worst thing he could do. I don't say he couldn't scramble back up that drop, but he'll pause to think about it a long time before he does. And that may be what saves him from making a mistake. In the second place, anyone who knows the cave will never dream that Ambrose would go through that opening into the deeper cavern. They'll check the first chamber and leave."

"And you don't mind carrying food to him every day? I dare not be seen around there."

"Thee do not need to come out here at all, James. It's well known I take long walks, looking for wild fruits and herbs."

"Be careful, Sarah. Don't let anyone suspect what you're doing."

"Don't worry, James. I'll take a different route each time. Maybe take enough food to last two days, so I can skip a day. Once the posse has searched out here, they won't return."

James drove slowly back to the house, and as he knew she would be, Leah was waiting up for him.

"Oh, James, I am glad to see you. Where in the world have you been and what've you been doing?"

"Getting Ambrose safely away from here to a place where he won't be found."

"Can you tell me?"

"No, Leah. Not because I don't trust you, but I don't want you under any pressure. If anyone asks, you can honestly say you don't know where he is."

Tension in the town increased every day. Feelings ran especially high against those who might be in sympathy with Ambrose; Mr. Peters, the minister, and Dr. Simmons, as well as James and Sarah, suffered having their houses searched as thoroughly as if they'd been the culprit themselves.

Leah was terrified when she saw the mob approaching. It was too reminiscent of the searches in New Orleans during the Federal occupation. She'd never dreamed she would have to undergo such humiliation and cross-examination again. With James not at home, she had to face them herself.

"I have told you," she insisted, "that Ambrose is not here. You have looked through the house, you have searched the root cellar and the barns. Maybe now you'll believe me."

"Sorry, Mrs. Andrews, but your husband is known to be fond of Ambrose, had him working for him for a long time."

"As he did for many of you." In all their faces she saw the same expressions that had frightened her when she met up with Union soldiers on the streets of New Orleans and when she was arrested for murder. They were brutal faces, demanding blood, anybody's blood, to satisfy the wrong that had been done.

"We're gonna get that nigger," George Blackman said. "He raped my Susan and he's not going to get away with it." Leah tried to understand the young man's feelings. Someone he loved had been brutally attacked and perhaps ruined for life. But she thought that he, of all people, would want to get the right man and make certain it never happened again. "Where is he?" he demanded.

Leah saw a look in his eyes that made her wonder if he would marry Susan after she'd been defiled by another man. It was the look she'd feared to see in Baptiste's eyes should she ever tell him what had happened to her in the prison. Nor had she been able to let James know the hell she'd endured. A man's pride is a strange thing where his women are concerned. She saw no sympathy for Susan on George's face, only a determination to avenge the wrong that had been done—but to her or to him?

"I told you," she said. "I do not know."

"Now see here, Mrs. Andrews." This was a man she'd never seen before. "We know he came out here that night we were chasing him. Someone saw him. Either he's here or Mr. Andrews spirited him away, and you know where he is."

"And what makes you think he didn't just run away from here?" Now she was glad James hadn't told her where Ambrose was hiding. She'd be bound to give away at least the fact she knew about it.

"All right. So he isn't here. But we'll keep watching." He turned to the other men. "Let's go out to Sarah Toffer's. She was always helping those niggers before the war. It'd be like her to side against the law."

Leah tried to work around the house as if nothing had happened. There were more fruits and vegetables to be canned. James's garden had fed them well all summer and would continue to do so through the winter if she could get everything put up. She had three cotton bags of grape mash dripping into pans to be boiled up for grape jelly, and Sarah had sent her two bushels of tart apples. She needed to get them into the root cellar and covered with straw. It was good to have something to keep fingers occupied. If only her mind had something to think about other than the attack on Susan and the search for Ambrose.

Then she remembered with relief that it was time to stop and prepare the French lesson. She'd forgotten the girls would be coming at three. Leah had found it difficult to conceal her surprise when Cora Simpson asked if she would be willing to teach French to her daughter and a few of her friends.

"We do so want them to have an appreciation of the finer points of life," Cora had said, "and being able to speak French would put them above the common run of people."

Remembering the earlier comments about her funny accent, Leah was tempted to laugh. Accepted now as the daughter of a wealthy Louisiana importer and widow of a planter, she had achieved a unique position in the town, much like a cherished landmark: the biggest house, the oldest building, the tree under which the founder had smoked a peace pipe with the Indians, and the resident New Orleans import.

"We do hope we're not imposing," Cora had continued, "but we do want the girls to have a certain finish they can't possibly get from the school here. You know, in case they ever have the opportunity to travel abroad. To be real ladies."

"It will be my pleasure, Cora. But I'll need to see them at least twice a week if they're to really learn the language."

"Oh, my," Cora said, "I hope you're not going to make them work too hard. Just a smattering is all they need, a few phrases to impress—to speak."

"I think I understand," Leah said, sorely tempted to tell Cora Simpson just what she thought of her superficial attitude. "I'm sure they won't find it too tedious."

She was sorry she'd agreed when she realized what it was the women wanted for their daughters. Not a real study of the language, but merely enough to give them airs. Thinking they would be little snobs, she dreaded facing the girls that first day. She was delightfully surprised to learn the girls were much more serious about their lessons than Cora Simpson had led her to believe they would be. After an hour of intensive study, two afternoons a week, they listened avidly to her descriptions of New Orleans and its fascinating customs as well as to highlights of French history.

Leah left Bridget to finish the canning and changed from her fruit-stained cotton wrapper into a fresh afternoon dress. Then she looked over the books to see which one she would use for today's lesson. They had been concentrating on conversation; now she thought they might like to try reading a little. She put aside one after another of the classics, feeling they were too heavy going for the first venture into literature, and selected a volume of Jean de la Fontaine's fables. She looked at the frontispiece engraving of Fontaine. Was that why she'd chosen it, because of the name? *Don't be ridiculous,* she scolded herself. *It's because the fables are light and humorous and the girls may already know some of them.* The name had nothing to do with her selecting the book.

Promptly at three o'clock, four of the girls arrived. "Jennifer and Elizabeth won't be here," they said. "Jennifer is—is not feeling well and Elizabeth had to go someplace with her mother."

"I'm sorry they won't be with us," Leah said, "because I have a special surprise for you."

Engrossed in the stories Leah read to them and then had them take turns translating, the girls stayed an extra half-hour. To be sure, they knew only a few words, and she continually had to prompt them, but she sensed the thrill they felt at actually being able to read the foreign words.

During the course of the afternoon, Rebecca Morrow

asked if, since it was raining outside, she might use the commode in Leah's bedroom.

"Certainly, dear. Right behind the screen."

Rebecca returned with Leah's rosary in her hand. "This is a beautiful necklace, Mrs. Andrews, but why was it hanging around the bed post?"

"That's not a necklace, Rebecca. It's a rosary, and I use it when I pray."

"Jewelry when you pray?" Victoria Simpson was both curious and amused.

"Not jewelry in the way you think of rings and bracelets. Each bead represents a prayer. Would—would you like to learn about my church?"

The four girls leaned forward in their chairs. First she told them about Sister Angelique. "She was a wonderful teacher. There was no question, inside the classroom or out, she would not answer. She encouraged us by saying there was no such thing as a stupid question if we sincerely wanted to know the answer."

"I wish we had teachers like that," Rebecca said. "Ours just tell us to sit still and keep quiet. I'd never dare ask a question."

"Sister Angelique was rare. She gave me this rosary when I graduated from the convent—that's a school run by the Church. Now, each of these beads represents a prayer, and you can count them off with your fingers and still keep your eyes closed while you pray. Or, you can keep it in your pocket and pray while you're walking down the street or sitting in the park, and no one but you knows what you're doing."

"You mean you pray in places other than church and beside the bed at night?"

"Oh, yes, whenever I feel troubled or thankful for something."

"It's very beautiful," Victoria said, fingering the amber beads. "It must be very valuable."

"It is, but more because of the friend who gave it to me. I remember her every time I say my prayers."

"Could you—could you send to New Orleans for one for me?" Victoria asked.

"I don't think so, dear. Your church doesn't use them, and I don't think your mother would approve."

"May I hold it when I come here then?"

"Yes, if you're always very careful of it."

Leah smiled when the girls left. It had done her good to spend the afternoon with them. She had no thought of molding their minds in any dynamic way, but she did feel she was opening their eyes to the wider world around them.

A week went by and Susan Price was still heavily sedated. Each time she roused up she began screaming, and Dr. Simmons didn't think it wise to question her. Sarah faithfully took food to Ambrose. The searches for him had become less intense but had not been discontinued. James talked to the frightened man, now desperate to get out of the dank, lonely cave. He'd become convinced he was going to be left to die there, especially when Sarah had to skip two days when searchers returned to her house.

"They're not going to give up, James," she said, "not until Susan can talk to someone. Ambrose is going to go mad down there, and that will be as tragic as if he were hanged by mistake. There is no one else they suspect?"

"No one. But I have a hunch something is going to break soon. I've been watching someone very closely, and I think we'll see some positive action before long."

"My thee is mysterious, James. Care to share your feelings?"

"I'd rather not, Sarah, because if I'm wrong, what I'm thinking would be a terrible condemnation of an innocent person."

James returned to his office, conferred with John Howard, Dr. Simmons, and the sheriff, and then sat back and waited. Soon the word filtered into every home and store: Susan was awake and going to name her attacker. At James's suggestion, the sheriff stationed one of his men at the railroad depot. The word about Susan had coincidentally gone out just about an hour before the train for Chicago was due to leave.

Within that hour, James joined those same men in Susan's bedroom. Dr. Simmons had agreed they might be able to get something coherent from Susan without doing her any harm.

The story that emerged from her lips was not far different from what James had suspected. After her parents left for church, she'd said goodnight to George Blackman at the door. Earlier she'd told him she wanted to break the engagement; she no longer loved him. Instead of leaving, he became enraged and forced his way into the house. She fought him off as best she could, but he beat her brutally about the head, got her down on the floor, and raped her. All but Dr. Simmons left her room quietly, shaking their heads and wondering how this was all going to affect the innocent girl. Soon after James returned to his office, the sheriff sent word that George had been apprehended at the railroad depot just as James had foreseen. He confessed he'd stayed in town only because he thought Susan would never recover and he thought he'd look guilty if he left. For them the case was closed. Not so for Leah.

After Ambrose left the cave and insisted he could never return to town, Sarah told him she'd try to find work for him on her land.

"That's kind of you," James said, "but you know you haven't enough for him to do or—or the money to pay him."

"He can't go back to town, James. Thee knows that."

"No, but I can rent that last three acres from you, on shares the way they're doing in the South. I'll pay Ambrose and we'll split the crop."

"And thee tells me I'm too generous and kindhearted."

"Nonsense, they're getting a good price for corn at the market. It can be household money for Leah." James liked to play Lord Bountiful, but he hated to be accused of it.

The following Tuesday Leah waited for her students to arrive. Even though the weather was still warm, she baked the apple dumplings she promised them. Instead of the girls, five notes arrived from the mothers saying that with school starting their daughters would be too busy to study French in the afternoons. At three there was a knock on the door. It was Victoria.

"Have you come with a note, too," Leah asked, "or to continue with our reading?"

"Not with a note, but I can't stay." Victoria's face was smeared with tears.

"School has begun and you've too much to do, with piano lessons and everything. I understand."

"No, you don't, Mrs. Andrews. Oh, it's so unfair," and she started crying again.

"Now, now, it can't be that bad. Come in." She handed Victoria a clean white handkerchief. "You can at least share a bit of tea with me." Tea always seemed the perfect antidote for trouble.

Victoria sat at the kitchen table while digging into the apple dumpling covered with cream and sipping her tea. "I really shouldn't have stayed. I told Mama if she let me come over, I'd hurry right back."

"And why is it you can't stay?" Leah asked.

"Mama and—and the other mothers don't approve of you as a teacher. They say you are co—corrupting our morals."

"Because we read French literature." She nodded. All French books had the reputation for being risqué.

"No, because you helped Ambrose hide when the men were looking for him. They call you a—a— Oh, Mrs. Andrews, I can't say it."

"A nigger lover?" The irony of it struck her as absurd. When she first arrived in Hickory Falls she'd been scorned as a fine Southern lady who mistreated slaves.

"Yes, ma'am. And—and you worship idols."

"Worship idols!" Leah was horrified. "Whatever gave them that idea?"

"I told Mama about the rosary and how you pray with the beads and about the crucifix. And about the statues you said were in the cathedral in New Orleans, the ones in the little chapels you described. You know, the Virgin and some of the saints. Mama said it was wrong to pray to them."

There was no point in trying to explain to this child the difference between praying to a saint and asking for intercession. She was too young to understand. *My God*, Leah thought, *it's a good thing I didn't mention being a Voodoo queen. They'd have me tarred and feathered and run out on a rail for sure.*

"I see," she comforted Victoria. "Well, I'm sorry we won't have any more lessons, but thank you for coming around to see me. Now maybe it would be better if you went right home."

For a long time Leah stayed close to home, using the excuse of needing to spend more time with Paul, of being busy with the fall housecleaning, and getting the rest of the fruits and vegetables canned. She continued to see Mary Howard and Elizabeth Benson from time to time, but she felt that Sarah was her only real friend. Even James was more preoccupied in the evenings and less inclined to talk about events of the day, although he was just as loving and gentle as always. She knew what was bothering her, but she had to know what was disturbing him.

"You're so quiet, James. Problems?"

"In a way." He paused and reached down for Paul, who was trying to crawl up his leg.

"Something to do with Paul and me, isn't it?"

"Not what you're thinking, Leah. In spite of your fears, there's never been a hint that someone knows about your past. But it is something that could touch you both. I haven't wanted to worry you, but now you've brought it up, I think you should know. You know, of course, about the land case."

"Yes, I've been meaning to ask how it's going. Then there was all that trouble with Ambrose. I'd almost forgotten about it."

"It's a long way from settled. In fact, we won't even be going to court for several months. But I've been receiving threats from those opposing my clients."

"Oh, no, James!" Now she was worried. "What kind of threats?"

"Just general. Nothing specific. Saying I'd better drop the case or I'll be sorry."

"And now you think we're in danger of some kind?" Where could they go, what could they do to escape people like that?

"Not really. They're too cowardly to do any real harm, I'm sure. They're just trying to scare me off, and when they see I won't be scared, they'll stop."

"Yet you felt I should know. Why?"

"Just to be on the alert. If you see anyone around here

who doesn't belong . . . I think they might try to harass us. Enough to be annoying, nothing more."

"Then I think you should drop the case, turn it over to John," she insisted. "For all our sakes."

"No, it's not that serious. I probably shouldn't even have mentioned it. Now how about some of that coffee you said Bridget was fixing after supper."

In spite of his calming words, Leah sensed James was more worried than he wanted her to know. Somehow the peaceful small town she'd envisioned when she came to Hickory Falls had become anything but that.

Chapter Fourteen

WITH CATHERINE DUE at the end of October, Baptiste began making plans that would enable him to stay on the plantation for a week or more just after the baby came. There were other plans and decisions he had to make, too. Should he have Catherine remain on the plantation in complete charge of the baby, or should he bring them both into the city to make certain the baby received every bit of care and attention it required? He didn't particularly want to live in the same house with her, and he was certain she felt the same way. On the other hand, she'd been wanting to live in the city, and being able to attend all the social functions might make her easier to live with. Most important of all, he'd have the baby with him every day.

With that thought in mind, he began to look for a house big enough to devote an entire first floor to the nursery, his living quarters, and a room for the nurse. He'd give Catherine the rest of the house to do with as she pleased and for all the entertaining she longed to do. That should keep her happy and out of his way.

He was tempted to buy the Bonvivier house when the most recent occupant, a Northern lawyer in New Orleans to oversee elections, put it up for sale. Baptiste walked through the first floor and noted how little need be done to restore it to its former grandeur. Benji reported that the two upper floors were in equally good condition and just needed to be redecorated. At least the Yankees who had occupied it during and since the war hadn't desecrated it the way they had the plantation homes along the river.

It would be a proper setting for a soon-to-be wealthy importer, and it never hurt to keep up appearances among the business community. At the same time it was perfect for Catherine's grandiose style of entertaining. The design was such that each of them could have separate apartments without revealing that arrangement to guests.

Then he changed his mind. As beautiful as the house was, moving Catherine into it would only heap more coals on the already blazing hatred she had for anything to do with Leah. A bone of contention that would have them continually at swords' points. And a constant reminder of Leah he didn't need right now. He continued looking.

Bonvivier ships were coming in according to a regular schedule, and Baptiste spent several hours each morning going over the routine work with his assistants. He didn't plan to be gone more than two weeks, and he wanted everything in order so they could expedite the shipments as speedily as possible. They were good, competent workers, and he had no qualms about leaving the office under their direction.

Benji came in at noon to ask his plans for supper.

"You coming home, Baptiste, or planning to meet M'sieu Pierre for drinks first?"

"He's coming to the apartment. He's found some houses he wants me to look at with him tomorrow."

"It sure will be nice to have a house here," Benji said. "I'm tired of traipsing over to Rampart every night."

"In other words," Baptiste said, "I'm to make certain there's a room for you."

"Naturally. You can't get along without me. Not if Mam'selle Catherine's coming. She's got to have her butler."

Baptiste said nothing to Benji about the plans he had for separate apartments. There was time enough for that.

"And for Tabitha, too?" Baptiste couldn't resist joshing

Benji about the girl he now stayed with when on the plantation.

"I told you I wasn't one for rushing things. She'll come here when I'm good and ready to settle down."

"You're not getting any younger, Benji."

"Yeah, but I still got others to enjoy first."

"Now," Baptiste said, "as to dinner tonight. Any good fish in the market?"

"The prettiest pompano you ever did see. Want it cooked with wine?"

"How else? And stuffed with shrimp. Or crab. Whichever you can get. I'm not fussy about that, but—"

He was interrupted by someone banging frantically on the door. *Strange,* Baptiste thought, *we're not closed. Why don't they come right in?* He looked up and through the double panes.

"What in hell is Moses doing here?" Baptiste pointed to the door. "Go tell him to come in, Benji." He whirled around in his chair to face across the desk.

A panting, sweating Moses came shakily through the door and across the carpet.

"You look like you've ridden with a ghost on your tail, Moses. What for? Something wrong at Belle Fontaine?"

"It Mam'selle Catherine, suh."

Baptiste rose up from the chair as far as his arms would lift him. "She's had the baby? But she's not due for another five weeks."

"Naw, suh. But she mighty ill. And Jessie say baby come anytime. She say come and bring de doctor. Quick, she say. I runs de horse de whole way. She want you back same way."

"Benji, go get Dr. Verner. Find him no matter where he is. Then come back and get me. Moses, stable the horse behind the office. One of the men will show you, and you can ride back to the plantation with me."

Baptiste sat at the desk trying to concentrate on the books in front of him and the orders he was leaving for his assistants, but words and figures swam before his eyes. Catherine had been recovering so well, the danger now could only be to the baby. This was much too early for her to deliver. Premature births seldom survived, and Dr.

Verner had said the delivery would be a difficult one. That meant the baby was in serious danger.

Moses hadn't said how ill Catherine was. Could it be that she'd taken a turn for the worse and there was a threat of her dying? He hadn't considered that. As wide as the rift between them was, he didn't want her to die. For her sake as well as the child's, he hoped Moses had been exaggerating. Maybe it was just that Jessie thought it was time he came home, and this was her way of getting him there. Jessie could not be blind to the way things were between Catherine and himself, but she might think it was his place to be with his wife at this time.

"Dr. Verner's gone on," Benji said. "He said he'll meet us out there."

"Then get the horses moving. If Catherine's gone into labor, I want to be there."

All the way through town and along the river road to the plantation he kept reassuring himself that many premature babies did survive. Catherine might even have miscalculated and this was the normal time for the baby to come. If Catherine were really very ill, everything must be done to keep her alive until the baby could be delivered.

Dr. Verner was with Catherine when they arrived, so Baptiste had to wait to talk to him. Frustrated at not being able to walk the floor, all Baptiste could do was light one cigar after another and drink the thick, black coffee sent up from the kitchen.

When Dr. Verner came out of the room, Baptiste didn't like the concerned look on his face. "How is she?"

"She has a little fever, but that's not unusual. Especially since she's been forced to stay in bed and not move around. It's just a little chest congestion. What bothers me more is how violently sick to her stomach she is. Jessie says she's been vomiting since early this morning. Bound to be something she ate, and poor Jessie is distraught. Said she hasn't fed Catherine a thing to make her that sick."

"How about the medicine you left for her? The painkillers."

"A mild sedative, that's all. Even two or three packets would do no more than make her sleep for several hours. No, she's gotten ahold of a poison of some kind."

"Poison! How could she do that?"

Dr. Verner shook his head. "I don't know. But whatever it is has put her into labor. If it were earlier in her pregnancy, I'd say she was in danger of aborting. As it is, she'll simply deliver prematurely. More prematurely than I like."

"Then the baby is in danger," Baptiste sighed.

"To some extent, yes. It'll be very small and will require a lot of intensive care, if it is born alive. I'm more concerned about that than I am about Catherine. I don't like the erratic contractions. Jessie said they started about the time Catherine got sick. They should be stronger and more regular by now. It could mean the baby will have a hard time coming out."

"What can you do? There must be something you can do to save the baby." Baptiste was frantic now.

"Everything I can, I assure you."

Baptiste knew he would, but he found little comfort in the words.

Finding sleep impossible, Baptiste spent the night drinking black coffee laced with brandy. As usual, Benji stayed up with him.

"She gonna be all right, Baptiste."

"It's the baby I'm worried about. You don't know how much having that child means to me."

"I think I do. Remember, you told me about René, and—and I ain't blind to how things are between you and Mam'selle Catherine."

"So you see, there'll never be another child. This will be the only one to bear my name and inherit Belle Fontaine."

Just then Jessie ran out of the bedroom, into the hall, and down the stairs to the kitchen. In less than five minutes she returned. Her body was shaking with sobs and she held her white apron over her face.

"Oh Lordy, it terrible, jus' terrible."

"What is, Jessie!" What had Dr. Verner sent her downstairs for?

"Mam'selle Catherine all tore up inside, and the baby don' wanta come out. Everything all wrong. The doctor say it look like she been burn wid hot ashes."

"Dammit, Jessie, what are you saying?"

"Please, 'sieu Baptiste, don' blame ol' Jessie. I didn't know. I didn't know."

"Benji, calm her down. How in hell can we know what's happened if she won't calm down. Now, Jessie, why should I blame you for all the trouble in there?"

" 'Cause I done fell asleep and let her do that to herself."

"Sit down, Jessie, and stop wailing. Nothing you've done could be worth all those tears. Now—start from the beginning. What happened?"

Baptiste wanted desperately to wheel his chair into the bedroom and find out for himself what was going on with Catherine and the baby. But he'd only be in the doctor's way, and right now nothing must prevent his delivering a healthy child—if possible.

"Yessuh. I got it all from Abelia, the one helping Missy with the baby clothes. Missy done fool me by pretending to take the powders. So's I think she was in too much pain to move. Then she done got word by Abelia to Cat Man."

"Cat Man! Who the hell is he?"

"He's the local Voodoo high priest," Benji said. "He's supposed to have all kinds of magical powers. He scares the daylights out of everyone around here, that's for sure. Someday you'll have to see him for yourself. You wouldn't believe the stories otherwise."

"Shut up, Benji. Tell me your local ghost stories another time. Go on, Jessie."

"Well, Missy got word to him she want to see him. And she done put them powders in my coffee so's I fall asleep. That's when she went outta the house. He give her the ju-ju leaves."

"Ju-ju leaves! My God—Cat man, ju-ju leaves." Baptiste threw up his hands in despair. "Get to the point, Jessie."

"That it, suh. Them leaves brings on the baby too soon."

"You mean she did that to bring the baby early on purpose?"

"Yes, suh, she done that."

"I'll kill her! If the baby dies, I'll kill her."

"Take it easy, Baptiste," Benji said. "The baby may be perfectly all right."

"Dammit, Benji, don't you dare tell me to take it easy. That she would—would dare do something like that. I

340

knew she hated me, but treachery like that— I didn't really think her capable of it. Well, that settles one thing." He paused for a moment as if thinking something through. "Jessie, go back in there and let me know exactly how things are going."

But it was Dr. Verner who came out some time later. "You have a daughter, Baptiste. She's very tiny, but she seems healthy in every other respect. Catherine did more injury to herself by taking that Voodoo concoction. Her uterus is badly burned and ruptured. It's going to take a long time to heal. And—"

"And she may never be able to conceive again. Is that it?"

"That's it. I'm afraid the damage is permanent. Also, you'd better find a good wet nurse in a hurry. The baby will require plenty of nourishment, and with all those infections, Catherine won't be able to nurse her."

"Can I go in there and talk to Jessie?"

"Yes, and see your daughter, too. But Catherine is sleeping."

Baptiste wheeled himself through the bedroom door. "Jessie, is there a good wet nurse nearby?"

"On Saint-Beuve plantation. Her baby is nearly a year old, but she got plenty of milk."

"And she'll come over here?"

"She be glad to," Jessie said. "She jus' waitin' to be asked. Missy sent word over there some time ago."

"Oh, she did, did she?" How like Catherine to disregard his wishes that she nurse the baby herself. For his own plans, he was now happy to fall in line with hers.

"Benji, ask Moses to ride right over there. Tell him to take the buggy and bring—what did you say her name was?"

"Melissa," Jessie said.

"And bring Melissa right back."

He wheeled over to where Jessie was rocking the baby on her lap. "Can I see her?"

"You most surely can. She a pretty little thing. Mighty tiny, but mighty pretty."

"She going to be all right, Jessie?"

"She got a long way to go to get up to birth weight, but we gonna make it, ain't we, honey lamb?"

Baptiste looked at his daughter. Was it possible that this tiny bit of humanity was actually his child? And could she possibly live? She had to live. No matter what she needed, he would provide it for her. He'd thought only a son who could carry on the name would satisfy his urge for an heir; but looking at his beautiful daughter, he knew he couldn't be happier.

By midafternoon, the wet nurse had arrived and fed the baby twice. "Don' you worry, suh," Melissa said, "she know how to suck and she getting every bit she need."

"That's great. You want your little boy here with you, too?"

"No, suh, he do fine with his gram. I jus' keep nursing to be ready for this one. And my milk good and rich." She chuckled to herself. "You see my boy and you knows what I mean. He fat as a dumplin'."

For the first time in twenty-four hours Baptiste dared to hope his little girl was going to live.

Sometime before supper, Catherine woke up and Baptiste wheeled in to see her.

"How could you do it, Catherine, how could you? Do you really hate me that much?"

"Baptiste, you will never know how much I despise you. I'm only sorry I couldn't see the look on your face when you found out what I'd done. My one regret is that I didn't succeed."

"Well, look at my face now because you'll see there the hate you say you feel. If the baby had been born dead, I would have found some way to punish you. Killing would be too easy."

"Don't gloat, Baptiste; she's not out of danger yet."

"You lay a hand on her, and I'll throw you out of the house no matter how sick you are."

"Oh, I don't intend to touch her. She's all yours."

"You're damned right she is!" His fury mounted as he looked at Catherine. How could she feel that way toward her own child? There was something monstrous about her. No animal rejected its offspring as she was rejecting her daughter. But it made his plan that much easier to carry out.

"I won't have to do anything," Catherine said men-

342

acingly. "She's very weak. Don't be fooled by those lovely pink cheeks."

"You—you she-devil! She's going to live. And from now on, she's not just 'the baby.' She's to be named Lisette after my mother."

Shaken by Catherine's words that Lisette wasn't yet out of danger, Baptiste knew there was something that had to be done immediately. And for one last time, he and Catherine had to appear together as doting parents. He wheeled out of the room and called for Jessie and Benji.

"Benji, go get the priest. We need to have Lisette baptized right away. Just in case. Jessie, you know where the christening clothes are I brought out from New Orleans?"

"I got them all ironed and ready."

The priest arrived in time to share supper with Baptiste, and then the small group gathered in the bedroom. During the service, Catherine was all maternal smiles and Baptiste wondered again at what sort of devil he'd married. No, she was more like a succubus that fed on the souls of those who came under her spell. Well, she would never have the chance to work that spell on Lisette. He had already seen to that.

For more than two weeks, Lisette held on to life by a slim thread. She ate greedily but often lost the milk immediately afterward. Dr. Verner said maybe it was *too* rich, and he ordered that Melissa's nursing be alternated with water. He also checked carefully on Melissa's diet, to make certain she wasn't eating anything that could get into the milk and harm Lisette. When finally she was able to keep it down, she became jaundiced, and her pale pink cheeks turned a pasty yellow.

"Don't be too alarmed, Baptiste," Dr. Verner assured him. "Babies often go through a spell of jaundice, especially premature ones. Every day she lives increases the chances of her survival. She's just having a damned hard time adjusting to this world."

"How soon can she travel? I want to get her out of this house as quickly as possible. I don't think it's any secret that Catherine and I are estranged, and my wife has—has no desire to keep Lisette with her."

Dr. Verner's brows arched, but he made no comment.

"There's no reason why Lisette can't go with you to the city. That short distance won't upset her. The only question is if Melissa and Jessie will go with you. Melissa's milk is the best I've seen in a long time, and Jessie is a wonderful nurse. Then, too, I'll be right there in New Orleans, close by if you need me."

"That's what I wanted to hear."

Melissa was immediately agreeable to the move. There was no question of her letting anyone else nurse her Lisette. Then Baptiste called Jessie out. "Jessie, you're a darned good cook, but would you like to become a nursemaid, too?"

Jessie put both hands over her round, smiling face and laughed. "How you guess? I been teaching Julia at the stove. She make a fine cook and I sho' would like to stay with little Lisette."

"It won't be here, Jessie. I'm leaving tomorrow for the city and taking Lisette with me."

"I ain' surprised, 'sieu Baptiste. I 'spected it after what Mam'selle Catherine done. She don' love dat baby like she oughta. It ain' natural."

"Then you don't mind leaving the plantation?"

"Lordy, no. You got us a fine place to live in the city?"

"A mighty fine apartment, Jessie, and right near the park where you can take Lisette for walks every nice day."

The apartment. He hadn't thought about its being too small for all of them, but he'd manage until he could locate a house. He remembered he was supposed to look at several with Pierre. For now he'd turn his large bedroom over to Lisette, Melissa, and Jessie, and he'd manage very well in the smaller one.

Once more, and for the last time he hoped, he went in to see Catherine.

"We're leaving this afternoon for New Orleans, Catherine. I thought you'd like to know."

"I assume by 'we' you mean you and Benji."

"And Lisette," he said.

"Don't be ridiculous, Baptiste. She'll die without the proper care."

"You trying to tell me you want her here with you? I'm surprised." Baptiste wondered at this change of heart but

344

felt it boded more of vengeance against him than maternal love.

"Her place is with her mother, at least until she's older and stronger." Since Lisette had been born alive and was probably going to live, Catherine had decided to put her other tactic into play: to bring Lisette up to hate her father as much as she did. She would not have Baptiste thwarting those plans.

"I don't think so," Baptiste said. "And she'll get the care she needs. Melissa is going with me."

"You're only threatening me. You wouldn't dare expose yourself to what other people will think by taking Lisette away from me."

"Have you forgotten, Catherine, that I don't give a damn what other people think? By the way, in case you're really worried about Lisette, Jessie is going, too, as her nurse."

"So I'm to be left out here all alone, is that it? You *are* cruel."

"No, not alone. Jessie has trained Julia to be a good cook, and there are plenty of others around."

"Yes, all darkies!"

"And your friends. Now you can entertain to your heart's content. I'll leave enough in the lockbox for you. And this time I'll leave it unlocked. I don't want it forced open again."

"How—how did you know?"

"Knives leave easily identifiable marks, my dear. I assume that's where you got the money for Cat Man. How much did he charge you?"

"Who told you about Cat Man?" She'd sworn Abelia to secrecy on the threat of whipping her senseless. Now she'd have to carry out that threat.

"Jessie learned all about it. Oh, and if you're thinking of punishing Abelia for spilling your little secret, she's already gone into New Orleans to work for the wife of Pierre's partner."

"Good riddance to both of them!" But, oh, how she'd like to see her under the lash. She knew how to use one, too. "Is there anything you haven't thought of?"

"Only this," Baptiste said. "I'm not going to reveal what

you did, although there's a stiff penalty for attempted murder or abortion and enough witnesses to convict you. But—if you do one thing to humiliate me while you're living out here or make one attempt to get Lisette away from me, I'll sue you for divorce before you can bat an eye. That will put you beyond the pale of decent society, and you know it."

"Get out!" she screamed. "If this is my home now, I don't ever want to see you here again."

"That, my dear, will not be possible. I'll have to come out from time to time to check with Septimus about the crop and the general running of the plantation. You are not to interfere with that in any way. The house, yes, that is yours to run; but nothing else. And now—I bid you a fond adieu."

Once established in New Orleans, the small household settled into an easy routine, and Lisette seemed to thrive on the new regimen. It was as if she'd been disturbed by the unease and hatred infecting Belle Fontaine. Every day she grew plumper and rosier. Before long she had a halo of soft, blond hair, and her cheeks took on a natural pink glow.

Seldom a day went by that Baptiste didn't bring something home for her—an embroidered silk bonnet or dress, quilted coverlets for walks in the park, and even a new carriage.

"M'sieu Baptiste," Jessie scolded, "iffen you don't quit toting things home, we gonna run out of space to put 'em. She gonna outgrow half these things 'afore she ever gets to wear 'em. You spoil her like this now, what you gonna do when she grow up?"

"She's mine and that gives her the right to be spoiled. Isn't that so, Lisette? Oh, Jessie, there's never been another little girl as beautiful as she. Don't you agree?"

"Beauty ain' all on the outside. We gots to see she be pretty on the inside, too."

"That's your job, Jessie.

Just before Christmas, Baptiste received a startling new proposal from Claud Bonvivier. From the time they'd met in New Orleans, their correspondence had been limited to brief notes about the business. Now Baptiste opened a longer letter.

My dear Baptiste:

It was indeed a great pleasure to meet and talk with you in New Orleans. I feel most gratified that our business arrangements were concluded so swiftly and on such an amicable and satisfying level. My brothers share with me the assurance that the Louisiana branch will prosper under your direction.

I was extremely disappointed not to be able to meet my niece Leah, but pleased to learn that she is happily married and living in Indiana. Perhaps sometime you will be so good as to inquire about her address and send it to me so that I may write to her.

Now to the main reason for this letter. As I indicated, my brothers and I have been highly pleased with the success of the New Orleans branch. It is our thought that it might be to our advantage to have an office in France. This would expedite not only goods exported from Europe, but also those from the Near and Far East coming by way of the Mediterranean. If it would be agreeable with you, we would like you to go to Paris, locate a suitable office, and hire a competent staff. We will supply the list of names of those we wish you to interview as well as letters of introduction to business acquaintances and people of influence who will assist you in every way they can.

This would require you to be away from New Orleans for no more than two months—three at the most. We would also want you to make an annual visit to the Paris office of one or two months' duration.

All expenses will, of course, be assumed by the firm. In addition, your shares in the firm will be increased proportionate to your new responsibility.

Please give this proposition serious consideration. We would want you to leave as soon after the New Year as possible. You will sail on one of our ships, with a stopover in Martinique to become acquainted with our family and to clarify all details.

Hoping to hear from you soon,

I am your obedient servant,
Claud Bonvivier

Once again, as with the first letter, Baptiste read it over several times. It was true his branch was prospering beyond what any of them had hoped. He knew, too, what Claud was implying but not stating in the letter. Much of the success was due to the young men he'd hired as his assistants. Otherwise, Claud would not have suggested he could leave for three months. Nor would he have asked Baptiste to hire the staff for the Paris office. The expansion would no doubt also mean smaller, two-man branch offices at the major ports of LeHavre and Marseilles.

Yes, the entire enterprise was a real challenge, and Baptiste was proud that Claud thought highly enough of his business acumen to suggest he undertake the task. It would also mean getting away from Louisiana for a few months and the pall of horror that still hung over the plantation after what Catherine had done. He still had violent headaches every time he had to go out there to talk with Septimus, even though he never set eyes on Catherine.

Then he thought of Lisette. He'd never be able to leave her for two or three months and probably longer. These things were never completed as quickly as one thought. He wheeled over to the glass doors that opened onto the balcony overlooking the street. He could see Jessie pushing Lisette's carriage toward the park. He had no qualms about leaving Lisette in the capable hands of Jessie and Benji, but if he sailed soon after the New Year and was gone for several months, Lisette would be sitting up and crawling by the time he returned. He was haunted, too, by the memory of that summer he went abroad and returned to find that René had died during the yellow fever plague. No, he could never bear to leave Lisette for even a week.

Yet, how could he refuse Claud's offer? It was not the additional money he was considering, but the loss of esteem in the other man's eyes and perhaps even the loss of the office in New Orleans. Sentiment should play no part in a business relationship, and Claud could easily buy him

348

out, close the office in New Orleans, and open one in Charleston, South Carolina, under the direction of Leah's half-brother. Charleston was as fine a port as New Orleans and as eager to re-establish its prewar reputation.

For two days Baptiste considered and reconsidered the alternate suggestion he contemplated sending to Claud. He'd reached a compromise with his desire to keep Lisette with him and his wish to accept Claud's offer.

My dear Claud:

As you requested, I have thought over your offer very carefully. I would indeed be pleased to go to Paris and establish an office there. I am certain that all of us will benefit from closer contacts with the exporters.

I have one request to make. For personal reasons which I would rather not mention in a letter, my wife and I have been estranged since the birth of our daughter, Lisette, who is living with me. Would it disrupt your plans to too great an extent if I postponed the trip until March when Lisette will be six months old and able to travel with me? Even though her nurse will accompany us, I hesitate to subject her to an ocean voyage while she is still so young.

Meanwhile I can be making everything ready here for my extended absence.

I will be awaiting your reply.

> Sincerely,
> Baptiste Fontaine

Within two weeks Baptiste received the reply he'd hoped for. They would indeed be happy to comply with his request to postpone his departure until March. As if it were spring instead of midwinter, Baptiste was filled with a new sense of well-being. He had Lisette to lavish all his love and affection on and a new business venture to keep him occupied. He managed to subdue if not entirely erase his hatred for Catherine; and if he longed for Leah in the evenings, he at least was tired enough after a full day's work to go right to sleep and then wake to another busy day.

He asked Pierre to forward Leah's address to Claud. He

preferred not knowing it himself. As it was, he knew only she was somewhere in Indiana, beyond his reach. If he could pinpoint the location on the map, it would bring home to him with too great a finality the fact that she was married and settled down with James. And he might be tempted to write to her. No, it was better that she remain in some faraway, nameless limbo.

Chapter Fifteen

GRADUALLY LIFE IN Hickory Falls returned to normal.
People were too busy with preparations for Thanksgiving
and Christmas to concern themselves long with even such
a violent tragedy as the brutal attack on Susan Price. The
Irish church was rebuilt; the quilting bees resumed; and
the community church had a bazaar to which Leah contributed jars of the first jelly she'd ever put up herself.
Frank Grimes never returned with his threats of revealing
her past, and Leah began to feel secure that her bluff
about his own prison record had scared him away. The
town was once more the small, placid community James
had described to her before they were married.

"Mama—Mama—Mama—" Sitting in his high chair,
Paul sang and kept time by beating on the wooden tray
with his spoon.

"Mama, Mama, yourself," Leah responded with a smile.
"And when are you going to start saying something more?
Not that I don't like the sound of it, love, but it is time
you expanded your vocabulary a bit."

With that Paul broke into baby laughter and pointed
gleefully at the table where Leah was carving a face on a

351

pumpkin. Earlier she'd scooped out the insides and put them in a dish to cook up later into pumpkin pies.

"This is a jack-o'-lantern, Paul. And when it's finished, we'll put a candle inside, set it in the front window, and scare your daddy when he comes home."

The sound of someone at the front door interrupted her studied concentration on the jagged mouth she was trying to carve.

"Now who in the world can that be?" She looked down at her dress, covered with pulpy bits of orange pumpkin and seeds. Somehow, when deeply engrossed she frequently forgot to put on an apron. "Oh, and don't I look a mess. If it's Eloise Rhinehardt or Mrs. Jacobs—well, there's no help for it now. Stay right there, Paul, and don't go trying to climb out. I'll be right back."

When it wasn't any of the women, she couldn't have been more surprised if it had been the President of the United States.

"Why—Victoria, come in. And Deborah, and Rebecca, and Polly. Please, come in. This is a very lovely surprise."

The four girls, still silent, followed her into the family parlor.

"If you'll excuse me," Leah said, "let me get Paul. He's in the kitchen where I've been making a jack-o'-lantern for him."

"Oh, please, Mrs. Andrews," Polly asked, "may we go in there with you and see it?"

"Why, certainly. Paul will be delighted to see you again."

"Oh, you're nearly finished," Rebecca said, when they were all in the kitchen. "I've always wanted to carve one, but Mama says they're too messy."

"You never had one for Hallowe'en?" Leah asked.

"Yes, but the cook always does it."

Leah looked over in the corner where James had stacked the pumpkins from the garden that he planned to sell at the market. One or two were all she needed for pies, so she'd agreed he should sell the others. However, there were four small ones that she could easily use or cook up and give to Bridget for her family.

"Would you each like to carve one and take it home?"

"May we, Mrs. Andrews?"

"Oh, yes, do let us!"

"What fun. Will you show us how?"

"All right, but first you have to put aprons on." She looked down at her own skirt and knew what the outcome would be if the girls returned home as messy as she was now. From a drawer she took four aprons that Bridget had carefully washed, starched, and ironed.

"Now," she said, "I'll show you how to cut off the top and then you must clean out the inside just as thoroughly as you can."

The four girls worked assiduously, vying with each other to have the neatest pumpkin, while Leah held Paul and tried to keep him from getting up on the table and playing in all the beautiful orange pulp as it piled up. Finally, she gave up, set him in the high chair, and let him squish his fingers through a handful she put on the tray.

"And what brought all of you here this afternoon?" Leah finally asked. The girls were now concentrating on cutting the most hideous faces their imaginations could conjure up.

Through lips clenched to help her get just the right sneer in the mouth she was carving, Victoria answered. "We want to continue with the French lessons. We talked to our mothers and they agreed we could."

"Yes," Rebecca added, "Mama said I should resume them in order to prepare myself for the trip abroad she's promised me next year."

"And," Polly said a bit haughtily, more to impress Victoria than Leah, "I'm to go on to finishing school after I graduate, and Mama feels I would be most inadequately prepared if I could not speak and read French."

"The truth is," Victoria whispered to Leah, "we nagged them until they said yes, and then they came up with the reasons why we should. Mamas are funny that way, aren't they?"

"I guess they are," Leah whispered back, "but I'm glad you're here. So," she said aloud to all of them, "we will have to work hard to catch up. I expect you'll need some reviewing before we can go on."

"Not very much," Deborah grinned. "You remember those books you lent us?" In all the distress during the past weeks Leah'd forgotten she'd lent them some of her precious books. She would eventually have missed them and then worried over getting them back. "Well, we got together ourselves when no one was around," Deborah continued, "and kept on with the reading. As well as we could, that is."

"Yes," Polly said, "whichever mother was going to be away for the afternoon—well, we just all went to that house."

"I'm proud of you," Leah said. "We won't do anything today, but we'll start in fresh next week, two days a week as before."

The four left later in the afternoon, their jack-o'-lanterns clutched proudly in their arms.

"*Bonjour, madame.*"

"*Adieu,* Paul."

"*Adieu, mesdemoiselles,*" Leah smiled. "*Bonjour, mes amies.*"

Paul grinned and waved. It would be good to have them coming to the house again. She enjoyed teaching them as much as she loved having someone to speak French to.

Thanksgiving and Christmas were festive occasions, both shared with Sarah. Late Christmas afternoon, after Sarah had gone home and Paul was curled up asleep before the fire with his arms around his new stuffed animals, Leah looked over at James. In spite of the long hours of work he was putting into the land case, he looked more relaxed than usual.

"Things must be going well with the case," Leah said. "When does it come up for trial?"

"End of January or first of February. I think we'll have it pretty well sewed up by then. John and I've been studying the surveyors' reports carefully and some old letters our clients found. There seems to be no question they have a valid claim and the decision will be for them."

"And then you go back on the circuit?"

"I'll have to. There's a number of regular clients I've neglected shamefully because of this one case. I'm going to have to see some of them even while we're preparing the arguments for the trial."

"I hate to think of you being away again," Leah sighed. "It's been so good having you home every day."

354

"Only two or three days a week. But that's how I make my living," he reminded her. "The town just isn't big enough to keep me busy."

"I know."

"And those people need us. Isn't every town or crossroads that has a lawyer either."

"At least," Leah said, "it means this case will soon be over. I didn't like what you said about receiving threats. Have they stopped?"

"Nothing for the past several weeks. I guess they finally decided I wasn't going to get off the case and knew it was pointless to keep on."

"Well, that makes me feel better. I've been afraid you were keeping something from me."

In spite of James's comforting words, Leah continued to keep a wary eye peeled for strangers around the house, and she never let Paul out of her sight unless Bridget promised to remain inside with all the doors locked. Her greatest fear was for James. There was nothing she could do to protect him, and when she accidentally discovered he was carrying a gun, she knew he was worried. Nor did she reveal that she'd found it. If he left it at home to ease her fears, he'd be completely vulnerable to attack.

In the middle of January, James came home for dinner more worried and upset than she'd ever seen him.

"All right, James," she said. "I know you haven't wanted to frighten me, but something has you scared. And I think I have the right to know what it is."

"You do, and I intend to tell you. The threats have begun again, much more serious than before. They are now directed against you and Paul—very specifically."

"Oh, no! What do they want?"

"Not just for me to get off the case now. They know my clients will simply turn it over to someone else. They want a settlement—the right settlement—out of court before it comes to a trial."

"And what sort of threats are they making?" She had to know the truth, no matter how bad, even though she was aready shaking at the thought of being threatened at all.

"They're still vague, but the implications are there that you'll come to some real harm."

Leah's first thought was to return to New Orleans with

Paul until the case was settled, but that would mean James would be the sole target of the threats.

"What do you think we should do?" she asked. It was no time to get hysterical but to think of the safest alternative.

"I want you and Paul to go out and stay with Sarah. Ambrose is there, and he'll make certain no harm comes to you. It shouldn't be for more than two weeks, because the trial is set for February second. But I want you to take everything you are going to need—everything. There will be no coming into town for any of you. There must not be a hint where you are. The word will be spread around town that you've gone to New Orleans for a visit. Very plausible this time of year."

So James had had the same idea as she but had figured out a way to use it and still keep her and Paul nearby.

"And you think it will work?"

"Yes. We're going on the train together toward Louisville, where ostensibly I'll be seeing you aboard a riverboat. However, we'll only travel three towns down the line. I'll stay long enough to come back on a later train, but you and Paul will return with John in the buggy in a roundabout way to Sarah's. He has clients down there, and it will be perfectly plausible for him to make such a trip out of town. There should be no way anyone will know where you are."

"I'm frightened. Do you really think it will fool them?"

"It will if you help. Tell your students and any of the women you see in the next couple of days about your trip, how you've looked forward to it, and so forth. You know how to do something like that and make it sound believable. Be excited, talk about the shops. Whatever it is that would make you eager to go. Above all, don't act apprehensive about anything."

"That shouldn't be hard." Leah laughed in spite of her fears. "I'd love to be going into some of those shops again." She thought about the importing firm and her heart sank for just a minute. New Orleans meant more than shops; it meant Baptiste, and she preferred not to be reminded of him just now.

"Even Bridget is not to know the truth. She might say something, some little thing that would reveal it. So let her help you pack. John will pack the buggy with food and other supplies you'll need." Then he paused. "The worst part, Leah, is that I won't be able to see you during all that time."

"Surely you can come out there some nights."

"No, we can't chance it. Anyway, I'm going to be out of town much of the time while John handles the final details."

"There've been no threats against him?" Leah asked. "All are aimed at you?"

"He's had his share, and Mary is going upstate to visit her family. So—the decks are cleared for the final showdown."

"And—and," Leah hesitated, "you think we'll be safe once it's over?"

"No reason not to. There'll be no cause for threats once it's too late to change the decision."

"You haven't said anything about yourself, James. Don't try to hide from me the fact you're in danger, too."

"I'm not, Leah. But I promise you I'll be on the alert for trouble every minute. And I had plenty of practice in that while I was in the West."

"James, can you at least send some kind of word to me that you are safe? How can I go two weeks not knowing?"

"No, Leah, something like that would tip off our plan for sure. You'll just have to have faith."

Though she dreaded being out of touch with James for two weeks, Leah looked forward to spending the time with Sarah. She was good company and always had a way of keeping things cheerful. Paul would be thoroughly spoiled, and they'd all eat more of Sarah's good cooking than they should. She actually found herself singing while Bridget helped her with the packing, including some sewing Leah had begun and could finish while sitting before Sarah's fire. She was determined it would be a good visit, and she wouldn't let worries plague her.

Frank Grimes got off the train from Louisville and headed straight for the hotel. He had a lot to think about. He'd squared his prison record with his employer by passing it off as punishment for the kind of minor peccadillo that soldiers get involved in. So now he was ready to approach Leah again, and this time on his own terms. He planned to stay several days in Hickory Falls, watching and waiting until he could meet her casually, as he did before. Women always came to town at least once a week. If not—well, he didn't really want to go to her house, but if he had to, he would. Then there was always Jennie. Maybe she could lure the proud Mrs. Andrews into town.

Then something happened to change his mind. He'd stopped off in one of the small towns on the way north to make a quick sale. Returning early to the depot, he saw a number of passengers get off a southbound coach. He paid no attention until he saw the face of one of the women. What in hell was Leah doing in this out-of-the-way place? Buying a paper, he sat on one of the benches where he could watch and listen without being seen. He saw Leah, accompanied by an older, auburn-haired man, walk toward a buggy. That was James Andrews, her lawyer at the trial and now her husband. He'd never forget that face and build.

"Remember, darling," he heard Andrews say, "don't try to get in touch with me for any reason. I don't even want Ambrose coming into town. Sarah will take good care of you, and Ambrose has promised to protect you with his life."

Grimes's mind recorded the names "Sarah" and "Ambrose," though he had no idea at the time how important they'd be to him later.

"I promise, James. I'll wait right there until you come to get us."

Grimes's keen mind was already alert to the fact there was something odd in their seemingly natural farewell—a husband kissing his wife and son good-bye as they departed for a visit somewhere. But why from this depot? Could be just that it was closer to where they were going. But Grimes didn't think so. There was fear and concern on Leah's face. Something else to tuck away and remember.

The buggy drove away, and Grimes assumed James Andrews would get on the next northbound train, the same train that he planned to take. Instead, he heard the man ask for a ticket on a later train; and Grimes knew there was something highly unusual going on. He, too, stayed behind in the town, ate something in its one small restaurant, and then boarded the later train, all the while keeping an eye on Andrews. *That man is worried about something*, Grimes thought, *and whatever it is may just be to my advantage in some way.*

After watching Andrews alight from the train, Grimes checked into a hotel and then headed for the Corner Café. It didn't take him long to learn that Andrews was involved in a serious land suit and that Mrs. Andrews had gone to New Orleans for a visit with her late husband's family. *Or so they believe*, Grimes thought. Now why would such a tale be told unless it meant she didn't want anyone to know where she was? All of this was worth looking into. There might be much more in it for him than a hurried rendezvous with Leah in a shabby hotel room. That could always come later.

After two more days of nosing around, Grimes learned the details of the case and about the threats to James Andrews and his family. He hired a buggy and drove out into the country. The house he approached was shabby, but he didn't hesitate a minute to knock on the door. He didn't much like the looks of the man who answered it or the two others sitting by the fire, but after a few introductory remarks, he came right to the point.

"I know about the land case," he said, "and about the threats to the Andrews family."

"And what do you have to do with them," Will Lederer growled. "You trying to say you want us to leave them alone?"

"Oh no, not at all. I'm just wondering what it would be worth to you to learn where Mrs. Andrews and her son are."

"They're on their way to New Orleans. We know that. So, what else can you tell us?"

"That they are not on their way South but are somewhere near here."

"The devil you say!" One of the men by the fireplace jumped up.

"Just that. And I know where they are." Grimes had earlier found it easy to learn who Sarah and Ambrose were and where Sarah lived in the country.

"Then you'd better tell us," George Lederer growled.

"For a price." Grimes didn't like the way the men were

staring at him, but greed gave him the courage to go on and say, "I also have an idea you might like, but it will cost you a whole lot more."

"And what if we don't like what you're charging?" Will asked.

"And how do we know you're telling the truth?" George said.

"You want the case settled in your favor?" Grimes asked. "Then listen to me." He repeated what he'd seen and heard in the depot, omitting only the names of Sarah and Ambrose. "Now what I propose is this. I'll kidnap Mrs. Andrews and send a note demanding the case be settled in your favor."

"And they'll come right after us," Will snorted. "That don't sound so good to me."

"No, that's just it. We'll choose a specific time, and you—all of you involved in the case—will be in town where people will see you. You won't even have to know where she is. And she won't know you're involved or why she was kidnapped." Or so he told them now. Once he had his and was gone, he didn't care what happened to them. "Then once the case is settled in your favor, I'll release her and get out of town. There won't be any danger for any of us."

"And the price?"

"I want enough to take me to the West Coast and set up a saloon. Half before I kidnap her, half when it's over."

"Fair enough," Will nodded. "You want to tell us how you plan to do it?"

"No. You leave all that to me. You'll know she's been taken when the note is delivered to Andrews. Now, is there any kid in town you can trust to lie with a straight face?"

Leah stood looking at the calendar on Sarah's wall. The trial was due to start that day. That meant only a few more days until James could come out and take them home. She'd enjoyed the visit with Sarah, but she wouldn't feel really safe for herself and Paul, and especially for James in town, until it was all over and they were back home together.

Startled by the knock on the door, she started to answer

it, not remembering until the last minute that no one was supposed to know she was there. In fact, it was strange that there should be visitors at all. She hurried into the bedroom while Sarah went to the door.

"Why, Timmy, what is thee doing here?"

"I came to tell Mrs. Andrews her husband wants her to come back to town."

Before she could think what she was doing, Leah came out from the bedroom. "Mr. Andrews sent for me?"

"Yes, ma'am."

"What—what exactly did he say, Timmy?" Sarah was more cautious than Leah.

"He said to tell Mrs. Andrews that everything is perfectly safe now, and she should come home."

"Then why didn't he come for me himself or send a note?" Leah had caught the alarm in Sarah's voice.

"He just dashed out of the courthouse and pulled me up off the steps. Then he went right back in." Timmy had learned his part well and was proud he hadn't forgotten a word of it. His fingers gripped the two fifty-cent pieces in his trousers pocket. He'd never had that much money before in his life.

"How can I know you came from my husband and not from someone else?"

"I wouldn't lie to you, Mrs. Andrews." He felt the sweat beginning to form on his forehead, and he was glad there was a blaze in the fireplace to account for it. He was glad, too, the man had told him she might ask this question. "Mr. Andrews said to tell you that he's missed you since he left you at the depot in Churchville. He said you'd know what he meant."

"You see, Sarah," Leah said, all smiles now, "it has to be from James. No one else knows about my leaving the train there except John."

"I don't know, Leah. I don't like it. Go in if thee must, but at least take Ambrose with thee."

"No, Sarah, if this should turn out to be a ruse, I tend to think they'd want to harm Paul rather than me. After all, it's still daylight, and I'll go straight to the courthouse in the buggy. But I want Paul protected when it gets dark, and there'd be no way for me to warn you before then.

Don't worry about me. I won't stop for anything until I'm in town."

"God go with thee then. And I'll look for thee and James to return in the morning."

It was not without a quaking heart that Leah climbed into Sarah's buggy and clicked her tongue at the horse. Timmy had already left on his horse, saying he was going out to his grandmother's place before heading back home. Leah knew his grandmother lived just beyond Sarah, and it was logical for him to visit her when he was so near.

Leah was at least relieved that it would remain light until she got to town. If the message had come any later, she would have sent back word to James that she'd wait until morning. There'd been nothing urgent in his message, just a request that she return home. She'd probably have been more suspicious if there had been. As it was, it seemed like a perfectly normal wish to see her now the trial was underway and things seemed safe for them.

She saw the other buggy approaching about a hundred yards down the road, but still she was not alarmed. This was a well-traveled road between Hickory Falls, the many farms around it, and another town some ten miles distant. The other horse was ambling along at a leisurely pace, as if the driver were in no particular hurry to get to his destination. Leah resisted the temptation to urge the horse into a canter, but she looked down at the floorboards in order to hide her face as the buggy approached. She was still wary of anyone recognizing her. The horse knew the road well enough so she didn't have to watch where they were going.

It was therefore a decided shock when Leah felt her buggy jerk to such a sudden halt she almost fell off the seat. She looked up to see Frank Grimes leaning forward and leering at her.

"My, what a pleasant surprise meeting you like this," he said.

"Is it? A surprise, I mean." Something cautioned her not to say too much. He must have been in town and overheard James tell Timmy to go out to Sarah's.

"You mean I should confess knowing you were coming into town, and I drove out here just to meet you? Would that be so unlikely?"

"I don't know. That depends on a number of things. But I've no time for a game of questions and answers. My husband is waiting for me, and I need to hurry along."

"My, my, you always seem to be in a hurry when we meet. Am I to assume you find me unattractive?"

Leah was beginning to feel a desperate, forboding sensation crawling up her spine.

"I don't like you, if that's what you mean. But I am in a hurry. If you have some new proposition to put to me, I'll meet you tomorrow at the tearoom. Now, if you'll excuse me—and let go of my horse's bridle—I really must go. Or my husband will begin to worry about me. He's expecting me to meet him at the courthouse."

"Oh, he'll worry about you," Grimes said, "but not just yet. Nor is he expecting you at the courthouse."

"What do you mean? Of course he is." Now Leah was really frightened, but more for James than for herself.

"He thinks you're still safely under the protection of Sarah and Ambrose. Meanwhile, you're coming with me."

"Oh, no, I'm not." She reached for the buggy whip to send Grimes on his way, but when she looked up again, it was into the barrel of a pistol. "What do you want with me and how—how did you get me away from the farm?"

She knew now, beyond any doubt, that Grimes was behind the message delivered by Timmy, that somehow he'd learned where she was, but that was a puzzle she'd worry about later.

"I told you. I want you to come with me."

Almost faint with fear, Leah managed to get down from her buggy and into his. She'd faced desperate situations before, and she hoped that if she flattered Grimes into thinking she'd be no trouble, she could put him off guard long enough to get away. She had no idea where he'd take her, but surely it was someplace from which she could escape. Grimes had said earlier all he wanted was a brief affair with her, and even if it came to— But no, she wouldn't think about that now, either.

The only thing she really feared was that Sarah wouldn't become worried until the next day when they didn't return to the farm for Paul. That meant no one would know for several hours she was missing. Damn, why had she fallen into the trap so easily! If only they'd questioned Timmy longer. He was lying, and if they'd thought at all, they could have gotten the truth out of him. But, no, she'd been too anxious to return to James.

Unable to move, she watched while Grimes took a note from his pocket, threw it on the seat of her buggy, and urged the horse to continue along the road into town.

Why the note? And why send the buggy on in? That would mean James would know right away and come looking for her. As frantic as she was, she couldn't make sense out of Grimes's actions. She'd thought he wouldn't want anyone to know this soon.

"What—what was in the note?" Her mouth was so dry she could hardly speak.

"Just a suggestion to your husband that if he wants to see you again—alive—he'd better settle the land case out of court and in favor of the right people."

"The land case! How did you get involved with that?"

"Well now, there's plenty of time to explain. We're going to be together for a long time."

Grimes made no attempt to tie her up, gag her, or cover her eyes, so Leah felt he must think there was no danger of her trying to warn someone. That meant they were headed away from any populated area. Leah was puzzled. The winding road led past several farmhouses, including Sarah's, and there was no turnoff, except for side roads to the various houses, until they got to the next town.

The sun was just beginning to set, and the brilliant red sky presaged a beautiful day tomorrow. Leah felt a chill run up her spine; a rabbit running over her grave. Would she still be alive to see the sunrise? Strangely, Grimes kept the horse trotting along, as if in no fear they'd be pursued as soon as James got the note. So, Leah thought, they must be near their destination. But what was it? She knew of no deserted houses in the area, and those were the first places a search party would look, anyway.

"I think you might as well tell me how you knew where I was and how you got involved with the trial?" It was all she could do to keep her voice from quavering, but she wouldn't let him know how really frightened she was.

"So," he grinned, "your curiosity's eating at you. Well, no harm now. We're almost there."

Almost there? Leah looked around. She saw nothing but

harvested fields and houses nestled among the low hills and narrow outcroppings of rock. Beyond, in all directions, circled the horizon of higher, deep-blue ridges, bearing capes of feather-light mist on their shoulders.

"I was in the depot when you got into the buggy and so fondly bid your husband farewell in Churchville."

"In Churchville? I didn't see you there."

"No, I made quite sure you wouldn't. You never know what interesting information you'll pick up when you're invisible."

She should never have underestimated Grimes in his desire to gain control over her. She could understand he might be foolish—or crazy—enough to kidnap her. He had been furious when she thwarted him before with her counterthreat to reveal he'd served time in federal prison, but that still didn't answer the question of what he had to do with the land case and the trial.

Before she could ask him again, he stopped the buggy, stood up, and looked all around as if trying to get his bearings. The road was still running the length of the valley between forested hills. Just beyond the hill to their left, part of the land originally owned by James's father, was Sarah's house and her acres of cleared land. To think they were this close and yet Leah was helpless to reach her.

To their right was another valley, just wide enough to be planted with about a dozen rows of corn. The crop had long since been harvested, but several dry stalks caught the last rays of the sun, and their shadows danced eerily on the bare ground. To Leah's surprise, Grimes sat back down, turned the buggy off the road, and headed through the field. At one point, about a third of the way along, they had to swerve around a small marsh or sinkhole masked with reeds as crisp and sere as the field. Leah knew the land belonged to a farmer whose house they'd already passed, and now she thought they must be headed toward some storage shed or outbuilding.

Once more Grimes stopped and shook his head. Whatever he was looking for had not appeared, and he turned the buggy around, retracing their route through the field. This time he crossed the road, found a narrow path leading between the base of a hill and a marshy area, and nodded his head, satisfied that at least he was headed in the right direction. Leah caught her breath. They were not more than half a mile from Sarah's house. In fact, she and James had walked this very path when berry hunting in the summer.

Suddenly Grimes stopped the buggy and ordered her to step down.

There was not a building or shelter of any kind within sight. Now Leah was very, very frightened. He'd not brought her out here to attack her but to kill her. The note, the business about settling the land case, were only a ruse to get her to come quietly. She should have screamed and fought when he first stopped her buggy or found a way to jump out while they were riding along. Even if she'd injured herself, even if he'd shot her, it might not have been fatal, and the sound of the shot would have brought someone to her rescue. Instead, she'd been so certain she could escape once they got to their destination she'd followed him like a lamb following the Judas goat into slaughter. Grimes pointed to some bushes and told her to precede him between them.

In spite of her fears, in spite of the pistol Grimes held cocked in one hand, she screamed as loud as she could and began running. She was not that far from Sarah's that her voice might not be heard echoing through these hills. And if Grimes shot, that would be heard, too. It was a desperate chance, but she had to take it. Breathlessly, her heart pounding, she waited for the gun to go off. Instead, all she heard was the sound of Grimes crashing through the underbrush in pursuit.

Her only thought was to lose him within the thick shrubbery and woods that covered the hillside. There was no way she could outrun him on the narrow path, and the marsh on the other side was filled with sinkholes that would trap her in a second.

She heard him cursing, not fifteen feet behind her, as she darted this way and that around trees. A painful stitch in her side almost brought her up short, but she bent over to ease the pain and, clutching her stomach, continued on. She knew it was inevitable that he would catch up with her, yet she refused to give up. Her one chance was to elude him until it became too dark for him to see. Then she might be able to hide within a hollow log or beneath an outcropping of rock. She did not believe that Grimes was a man to outwait her through a long, cold, dark night. Why he wanted to kill her was a question that could wait to be answered. Right now, she had to concentrate all her energies on remaining alive.

If darkness were her ally, it also proved to be her enemy. Once the sun had set beyond the hills, none of the purple twilight penetrated the woods. To her relief she no longer heard Grimes moving behind her. She needed to find a place to rest until morning and then she would make her way back to Sarah's. Grimes might still be a threat, but one she could be constantly on the alert for. While groping along a fallen tree in hopes of finding a comfortable spot to lie down, she twisted her ankle. There was no way she could suppress the shriek of pain or prevent herself from stumbling. The last thing she remembered was the blinding fire that seared the inside of her head after falling and hitting something sharp.

Chapter Sixteen

LEAH AWOKE SHIVERING in the damp cold. Every part of her body ached; and when she tried to turn her head, the pain was so intense, she could scarcely control the nausea that welled up into her throat. Wherever she was, she'd never known such total darkness as surrounded her now. She moved one hand and discovered she was lying on hard stone lightly covered with dirt. Yet her head was resting on something soft. Slowly she moved her hand up and realized it was her own cape. Surely once her eyes became accustomed to the darkness, she'd be able to see something. She blinked once or twice, but it did no good. All was black.

She was shaking all over now. Not with cold but with a new fear. She was blind!

Vaguely she remembered falling. She knew blindness could result from a severe blow to the head, and she remembered the terrible pain she suffered just before passing out. Blind! This was a terror she'd never known before. Alone in a strange, damp place and blind!

Had Grimes brought her here after the fall? If he'd meant to kill her, why not do it in the woods and get it

368

over with? Why carry her here to wherever she was? Then came the horrible realization. He'd carried her someplace to die. Maybe he thought she was nearly dead, and it would be safer for him to leave her than to shoot her. Left alone to die, maybe not found for days or weeks, and who would know he'd been involved?

She mustn't panic. That would surely result in death. No, she had to force herself to think clearly about her situation. She was still alive, and nothing seemed injured except her eyes. She had to get up and move around. As hard and painful as it was, she must force herself to learn something about where she was and figure how she might get someone's attention. Was she inside someplace or was she outside? There was no wind and she didn't feel cold. Therefore, she assumed she was in a shelter of some kind. That meant figuring a way to get out. If only she knew whether it were still night or now daylight.

There was no point in screaming until she could be certain someone might hear her. The way sounds carried through these hills, there was a good chance she would be heard if she were outside. She remembered sitting on Sarah's porch and listening to the hunting dogs baying along the ridges as far as two miles away. Rock under her could mean she was in one of the small sandstone hollows in the side of the hill. Last night she'd run without thinking, up and down the hill as well as through the woods. Now she would have to proceed more cautiously and try always to move downward toward the road or a path. It would be far more difficult not being able to see, but if she crawled along the ground, she'd know when she reached flat land. Then, if she felt the sun on her back, she'd know it was daylight.

But not yet. Just lifting her head brought on another attack of dizziness and nausea. The horror of her blindness smote her once more. Was she never to see again? No, she wouldn't think that way. It was only temporary. It had to be. *Don't think about it. Don't think about that anymore. Think about getting back to James and Paul.*

If Grimes had left her to die, there was no hurry. She could wait until she felt well enough to begin the dangerous trek to freedom. She needed to rest. Maybe even sleep for a few hours. Her body ached as much from being in one position as from the cold. Not until she tried to turn to find a more comfortable position did she realize her ankles were tied together.

She'd been so concerned with her blindness, the general aching all over, and the fear of where she was, she hadn't felt the rough touch of the ropes against her legs. In spite of the pain that knifed through her head, she sat up. She followed the ropes with her fingers and discovered they were tied securely around a jagged outcropping of rock in a wall next to her. Once again she gave way to panic.

For a long time she lay there, all hope consumed by a despair as dark as the world around her. Nor could she stop the tears coursing down her cheeks. Gradually the crying dissolved into heavy sobs that left her completely exhausted. Only then did she balance the desperation of her situation against the chances of survival. Now was not a time to give up and allow herself to lie there and die. She had to think.

If someone had tied the ropes that meant they could also be untied. Her head had cleared and she was able to move without the awful sensation of wanting to throw up. She felt the ropes at her ankles. They'd been wound around several times, but there were no knots. She had to struggle only with the one—or more—securing her to the wall. It turned out there were several, but the rope was thick enough for her to get a firm grip on it. She counted the knots again, four, one right after the other. If only they were granny knots. But no, someone had tied them very expertly and pulled them very tight.

Then she had to endure the new pain of fingernails tearing below the quick. She sucked the salty-sweet blood, but one knot was almost loose.

She was well into the second knot when something caused her to look up. For a brief second she thought she'd seen a flicker of light, but she forced herself to realize that the blind often suffered from such hallucinations. She remembered one such case while she worked in the hospital during the war. The soldier had been blinded by a shell fragment, and he often woke up screaming from nightmare flashes of light and color that tormented him and actually made him physically ill. He kept insisting he could really see, he wasn't blind at all, that someone was persecuting him by keeping him in a dark room and then taunting him with colored lights. He often worked himself into such a frenzy they had to keep him strapped to the bed. Well, that wasn't going to happen to her. As long as she knew what it was, she could keep her sanity.

There it was again! A single flickering glow, like a candle or a lantern. And it was coming closer. Not just a light, but reflections off something shiny in the rocks. She stopped working on the knot and looked around her. Only one thought possessed her at first. She could see! She was not blind. The rock formations and the absolute darkness gave her another clue. She was in a cave. More than that, the light coming toward her meant she was no longer alone. Someone was coming to save her.

She called out, and the footsteps came closer. More than one pair of them. A hard, pounding set followed by lighter ones shuffling or sliding along. She could see the shadowy body of a man now, but the lantern held up in front of him obscured his face, and for the moment she was blinded again by the glaring light after so many hours of darkness.

"James? Sarah?" She was shouting now. "I'm over here, just keep coming."

But it was not either of them who answered.

"Don't you wish it was James," Grimes chortled. "Sorry, my dear, but he has no idea where you are."

Letting go of the rope, Leah fell back against her folded cape. He'd not killed her nor left her to die, and with his return, escape seemed impossible. He could not help but notice she'd been untying the knots, and he'd make certain she wouldn't be able to do that again.

"I believe you are acquainted with Jennie." Leah saw the seamstress step out from behind him. "She's going to remain here to keep you company and see to it you don't try to work the rest of those knots loose. Of course, just to make sure you don't, we'll have to tie your hands as well. I'd no idea you'd wake up so soon. That was a nasty fall you took."

Leah said nothing. She wouldn't humor Grimes by either pleading with him or trying to defy him. At least now it seemed evident he was not intending to kill her.

"What, no more curiosity about why you're here?" He

turned to Jennie. "Now we know she's awake and well, take your lantern and go back to the entrance for those things we brought."

"Please, Frank, I'm scared to go all that way by myself."

"Quit whining and do as you're told. Besides, there's nothing to be scared of."

"Yes, there is. That narrow passage where I almost got stuck and that deep pit we had to go around. What if the lantern goes out?"

"Just make sure it doesn't. If you fell in the hole, nobody'd ever see you again."

"I'm scared, Frank. You said I'd just have to sit here with her."

"Shut up, Jennie, and get going, or I'll toss you in that bottomless pit myself. You'd just keep falling and falling and falling until you hit water and drowned. Now—scat!"

Jennie was gone a long time, and even accounting for her moving slowly because of her fear, Leah knew they were very deep inside the cave. No hope of being heard if she screamed.

Grimes unstrapped a rolled blanket off his back, laid it on the ground, and stretched out.

"Might as well be comfortable while I wait for Jennie to bring the supplies."

"You are without a doubt—no, I won't say it," Leah said. "You'd consider it a compliment." She thought about the word *supplies* and wondered how long she'd be kept prisoner. Surely she'd be freed as soon as James got the note and came to an agreement with the opposition or forced them to tell where she was. Then she remembered that Grimes had never answered her question about how he was involved with the trial. Nor did she really know what was in the note—or even if it were more than a blank slip of paper. She was back to being frightened that all this was just to kidnap her for his own reasons, and those could mean anything from keeping her here or taking her away with him. If so, she'd have to count on James finally learning she was gone from Sarah's and starting a search. With the hundreds of caves in the area, a hopeless search.

James walked out of the courthouse and looked up at the sky. The brilliant red of the sunset augured a beautiful day tomorrow. Maybe it also forecast a decision in his clients' favor. So far all the evidence he and John had presented—the deeds, the old letters, the bills of sale—indicated a legitimate claim for them. He didn't see what the opposition could do to refute it.

"What do you think, James?" John came down the steps beside him.

"I think it should be over tomorrow, next day at the latest, and then I can bring Leah home. You going after Mary?"

"No, I think I'll wait a few days. She hasn't seen her mother in a long time, and I want to make certain the Lederers are well out of town and back on their land—their own land."

"They'd have no reason to threaten once the verdict is in."

"You forgotten how long these Indiana feuds go on? What about the Carltons and the Ramseys? Three generations and they're still at it."

"Maybe so. But the house is mighty empty without Leah." James walked over to unhitch his horse.

"What about staying here and eating at the Corner Café. If you're lonesome for Leah, no point in going home to an empty house and a solitary meal."

"Thanks, but I have the feeling I should. Anyway, I saw the Lederers go in there, and I've no inclination to be in the same room with them any more than I have to."

"Good night, then. See you in the morning."

" 'Night, John. I'll bring those extra copies you wanted."

James rode through the purple-gray twilight. In the houses he passed along the road, lights had been turned on; but when he approached his own drive, there was only darkness waiting for him. Why hadn't he thought to leave at least the hall jet burning? He hated going into a darkened house. It intensified the feeling of loneliness that swept through him. It would be good to have Leah home again. He didn't care what John said. He'd be staying in town for the next two weeks, preparing briefs for the cases on the circuit. He might even bring Ambrose in to help him clear the additional land. He could sleep in one of the rooms over the carriage house. Leah would be perfectly safe from the machinations of the Lederers.

Circling the house, he drove straight to the back and stopped just outside the carriage house to unhitch his horse and lead him into his stall. Suddenly his ears caught the sound of something behind the stable. A scuffling and then a whinny. Reaching up into the buggy for his rifle, he pushed the lever down and saw the round slide easily into the breech. He pulled the lever back. He checked the hammer. It was in *on* position. It was ready to fire.

Instead of going directly around the stable, he went into a stall from which he could look out between the boards without being seen. Quietly he knelt down and squinted through the one-inch space. What he saw had him on his feet immediately. It was Sarah's horse, still harnessed to the buggy, cropping some hay dropped when he'd unloaded the latest bales. In three rapid movements he reached for the lantern hanging by the door, lighted it, and ran outside. The first thing he saw was Leah's string bag on the seat.

His intuition immediately told him something was wrong. If she were home, there would be a light in the house. Nor would she have left her bag in the buggy. Maybe Paul had taken ill and she'd brought him to Dr. Simmons and somehow the horse had gotten away and wandered here. No, that was a fruitless thought. She'd not have gone anywhere without the bag, and she'd have gotten word to him somehow. No, something had happened to her.

When he picked up the bag, he noticed a slip of white paper under the seat. It had probably blown in there while the horse was making its way here, but it was worth looking at. James unfolded it, but he had to read it twice before he was fully aware of the message's meaning.

"If you hope to see your wife alive, see to it the Lederers win."

Nothing more. No signature. Just the flat statement that Leah would be killed unless he flouted justice, betrayed his clients, and reneged on everything he stood for as a lawyer. That was what the writer of the note expected him to do, knowing he'd do anything to have Leah safely back in his arms.

But the person who wrote that note had seriously underestimated the man he was dealing with. James was never one to be intimidated by threats, implied or overt. Instead he got mad, and he was madder now than he'd ever been in his life. He was not a red-headed Scotsman for nothing, and now his Highland blood was boiling.

James was neither a fool nor a coward, and he went into the house to get his pistol and more ammunition. Furiously he stormed around the house, alternately cursing and slamming doors. Leah had better not be harmed or there'd be hell to pay. Just let him get his hands on the Lederers and they'd learn what it meant to threaten James Andrews. By the time he found what he needed, he finally cooled down enough to realize that losing his temper in front of the enemy would gain him nothing. He hitched up his buggy again and drove first to John's house.

"John, I need your help," he said as soon as his partner came to the door. "Read this." He handed him the note.

"Damn!" John swore. "You mean they've got Leah? I don't believe it. They wouldn't dare. Not when we have them right here in town."

"That's what I thought, too. Only one thing to do. They might still be in the café."

The two of them climbed into James's buggy and headed toward the main street.

"They were still there when I left," John said.

"We've got to find her, find out where she is." James was frantically running his fingers through his hair and gripping the unlit pipe between his clenched teeth.

"You think they'll tell us?"

"They damn well better."

"And if they don't?" John asked.

"I'll get great pleasure out of strangling their filthy necks. There's more than one way to get information out of someone."

As outraged as James, John was still rational enough to realize that killing the Lederers wouldn't help them find out where Leah was. He had to calm James down and make him think before he acted.

"You could always give in to them. We could come to some kind of a compromise between the Campbells and the Lederers. I'm sure the Campbells would be willing when they learn the situation."

"Damned if that's so. Not unless I have to. I have to remember I'm not the only one involved. It would be different if I were. But there's you as well as the Campbells. And the evidence. How can I ask them to consider a compromise or settlement out of court when it would mean they'd lose what is rightfully theirs?"

"They can always bring a countersuit against their cousins."

"With more lawyers and more expenses? Even if I take no fee, I can't ask you to donate months of work. And how about the title and survey expenses? No, we've got to find Leah, and the Lederers are damn well going to tell us where she is—or face charges of kidnapping." He wiped his brow. "How in hell would they dare do such a thing? Or know how to find her? That's what has me puzzled."

They pulled up in front of the café to see the three Lederer brothers still seated by the front window.

"There they are, James. What now?"

"Face them and have it out. Call their bluff. Because I think that's all it is. Just to throw a scare into me. But I don't scare that easily."

"Well, leave the guns in the buggy. A shootout isn't going to help."

"Give me credit for some sense, John. I had to do something, and bringing them along made me feel better."

The three Lederers looked up when James walked in, then went back to their food. They looked up again when he came to stand by their table.

"Whatta ya want, counselor?" George Lederer asked. "Or should you even be talking to us?"

"Read this and tell me what it means." James handed the note over, and all three scanned it.

"So, maybe you'd better tell us what it means," said Will Lederer, the oldest of the three. "I've never seen it before."

"You're lying! Where is she?" It took all of James's willpower to keep his hands at his sides.

"How the hell should we know. We haven't taken her anyplace."

"Are you trying to tell me," James said slowly, his temper seething, "you had nothing to do with this?"

"Where did you get the note, Andrews?" George Lederer asked.

"In Sarah Toffer's buggy. Her horse found his way to town from someplace."

"Then ask the horse," Will sneered. "We've been in court all day and came right over here for supper. We've got witnesses to prove it. YOU!" and he pointed right to James and John.

"He's right, James," John said.

"By God, that doesn't mean they don't know something about it." He lunged for Will Lederer's throat. "Tell me, you bastard, where is she?"

"Get your fucking hands off me, Andrews. I told you, I don't know nothing about it. Prove I do, or I'll have you arrested for assault."

But James couldn't stop. He pulled Will off the chair, landed a single punch across his face, and sent him sprawling. Will shook his head to clear his brains and came right back at James. John caught James after Will landed a solid punch, and at the same time ducked the blow aimed at his head by George.

"All right," John yelled. "Break it up! Nothing's gonna be solved this way."

"Then tell him to keep his hands in his pockets," Will spat out between his bloodied lips.

"He's right, James. Take it easy. Even if they do know, you'll never find out this way." John managed to get him moving toward the door.

"So what do I do?" James asked. "Leave Leah out there someplace, God knows where, until I decide to throw the case? My God, we don't know who has her or what he's doing to her. She could be—oh, God, what's happening to her!"

"We'll see the judge and ask for a forty-eight-hour recess. Then we begin searching. The Lederers will be kept under surveillance."

"My God, John, how can you stand there so calmly and make such logical suggestions?"

"Because I want you to find Leah alive and unharmed."

He turned back to the Lederers. "If you know anything—anything at all—and are not telling us—"

"Honest, counselor, we got no idea where she is."

It wasn't the answer John wanted, and he had the feeling they knew more than they were saying, but he had to be satisfied with it.

Within an hour the judge granted the recess and the men who once formed a mob to lynch Ambrose organized a search party for Leah.

"Where do we start, Andrews?" one of the men asked.

"God only knows. She must have been coming into town in the buggy, so that means she had to have been waylaid between here and Sarah Toffer's house. She could have been taken anywhere, but we can start combing that area. Others can form search parties around the outskirts of town. I'm going on out to Sarah's and start from that end. She'll surely know why Leah left the house and maybe have some idea where she was going."

"I'll come with you, James," John said, getting into the buggy. "You're in no condition to ride out there alone."

Jennie finally returned with baskets of food and kerosene for the lanterns. At least it was no longer dark in the cave. Ropes now bit into Leah's wrists as well as her ankles. The rocky floor was getting increasingly wet from a trickle of water oozing through the wall and down the sloping ground from a hole just beyond her head. She'd asked for a blanket to lie on, but Grimes had merely laughed and said he'd brought just one—for his own comfort. She refused the food he offered; her stomach would never hold it. Instead she had to listen while Grimes and Jennie gorged themselves and drank from the bottle of whiskey he opened. He was drunk, and Jennie was giggling hysterically at his sodden efforts to open the buttons of her blouse.

Earlier Leah had listened to the recital of his clever plan. How he'd learned about the trial, had approached the Lederers with his scheme, and been promised a large reward when the trial was over. Jennie, the foolish little idiot, had cooed ecstatically when he described how he was going to take her to California and buy her the finest

378

house overlooking San Francisco Bay. He might buy a house, all right, but if Leah knew Grimes it would be to set her and a number of girls up for his own profit. More likely he'd dump her along the way or take off without her.

Leah wished she could cover her ears or go to sleep. Anything to keep from hearing his voice.

"That's right, lovey, the biggest house there is," he was bragging.

"Oh, Frank, you're too good to me." Leah heard the girl's rapid breathing.

"Yes, indeed, you be good to Frank and Frank will be good to you."

"I'll do anything you say, you know that."

Now Leah wished she could shrivel up and disappear into a crack between the rocks. With the grunts and heavy breathing coming from the blanket, she needed neither eyes nor much imagination to know what was going on. At least Grimes was leaving her alone, and for that she should be thankful. Maybe if he got his fill of Jennie, he'd go away and somehow she'd persuade the girl to set her free. If only she could convince the little ninny not to believe a word Frank was telling her. As infatuated as Jennie was with Grimes, that would be hard to do, but it was worth a try.

"Pull your skirts down and button your blouse," Leah heard him order. "I'm going to sleep for a while." Grimes rolled the blanket around him and left Jennie to sit and shiver on the cold floor of the cave.

Hours passed—Leah had no idea how many—with no sound save their breathing. Occasionally she dozed off, too, for short naps, but pain from the ropes cutting into her wrists and ankles kept her from falling into a deep, soothing sleep. Finally she heard Grimes stirring.

"I'm going back into town to see how things are coming along."

That must mean it's daytime, Leah thought, *but morning or afternoon?*

"You're not going to leave me here—alone—with her," Jennie whimpered.

"Why do you think I brought you along? Just for fun

and games? And you damned well better not let her get loose."

"But I'm afraid here in the dark."

"Then don't let the lantern go out. And quit whining. You're beginning to get on my nerves. You want to go with me, don't you?"

"Oh, yes, Frank. I'm sorry. I'll stay here just like you say."

"Then hand me the blanket."

"Why? You're not taking it with you, are you? I'll freeze to death if you do."

"No, you can have it back. Just a little something I want to do first." He walked over and stood beside Leah. "You don't like me, do you?"

"Does it make any difference?" She hated even having to talk to him. "Will it get me out of here any sooner?"

"No, but it might make things a little more pleasant for you." He stood with his hands on his hips and his legs apart, trying to intimidate her by his massive presence.

"Do you want me to smile and say pretty things, or do you want me to grovel at your feet?" As frightened as she was, she still managed to keep a sense of pride in her voice.

"Neither," he spat out with a glare. "I just want to have a little pleasure with you, and I want you to be an exciting and willing partner."

So it does come to this, Leah thought. *He's postponed it until he's sure I won't refuse or try to resist.* "That I will never be. You try to touch me, and I'll claw your eyes out. The only way you'll have me is if I'm bound and gagged, because I can bite and I can kick."

"If that's the way you want it," he snarled, "that's the way it will be. Jennie! Get over here."

"Why? What—what do you want?" Jennie'd begun whining again.

"Tie her hands to that rock behind her head, while I loosen these ropes around her ankles just enough so she can't kick but not enough to prevent my having some fun with her."

"You—you bastard!" Leah spat out.

"No, Frank, you can't," Jennie begged. "Not—not here in front of me. After all you've said to me about—"

380

"Shut up and get those ropes tied. And as for you," he leered down at Leah, "this should take care of that sassy tongue of yours." He pulled a dirty handkerchief out of his pocket and stuffed in into her mouth.

Leah prayed she would faint, but she didn't. Minutes seemed like hours, and she had no idea how long she must endure the humiliating, degrading, abusive actions of Grimes. She thought she'd suffocate from the gag in her mouth, but when she tried to spit it out, it just lodged all the more securely farther back on her tongue, but not far enough to make her retch. She wished she could, just to show him how really vile he was. When he was finished, there was no part of her body not bruised from his lust and cruelty. At least he finally took the cloth out of her mouth and loosened the ropes around her legs. He also pulled the blanket out from under her and tossed it over to Jennie, so Leah was once more lying on cold, damp stone.

"Now," he said, "maybe you'll be a bit more cooperative next time. I've only half begun with you."

"Will you—will you untie my hands," she asked, refusing to give him the satisfaction of crying aloud; but her insides were wracked with the sobs she choked back. "It's very painful having them pulled above my head like this."

"Jennie, let down her hands, but keep the ropes around her wrists."

Jennie began working on the ropes, all the while crying piteously. "How could you, Frank? You said you loved me and no one else."

"Love you? Why, you little slut, you mean no more to me than the women in the cities. Less even. At least they get paid for it and I get you for nothing. And that's what you're worth to me. Nothing!"

"But—but, what about California, and the big house you promised?"

"Do as you're told and I may take you along. You could be useful to me out there."

Leah turned over in time to see the rage mounting in Jennie's tear-stained face. When Grimes bent over to pick up his jacket, Jennie brought her right arm from behind her back and hit him savagely on the side of the head with a rock. With a single sharp cry he slumped to the ground.

"Oh, God, I've killed him!" Jennie screamed. "I didn't mean to. I've murdered him and now they'll be after me."

Jennie picked up the lantern and began to run. Then she turned around and reached inside Grimes's coat pocket for the money he'd shown her.

"Wait, Jennie!" Leah screamed. "You can't go off and leave me like this. Where are you going?"

"As far away as I can get."

"But you'll tell someone where I am," Leah said desperately.

"Not likely. I'll be held for murder then."

"But Grimes is dying and no one knows where I am. At least untie me and let me go with you."

"Oh, no. You'd turn me in. He's dead! I killed him. I don't want to be hung for murder." Jennie was all panic now. "I've got to get away. I've got to run!"

Leah watched in desperation as Jennie and the lantern disappeared around a bend in the tunnel leading from the deep recess of the cave.

Now no one knew where she was. Even if James had already begun a search, it could be days, even weeks, before anyone would think of this cave. Nor, having been brought in while she was unconscious, did she have any idea of how to get out. Once more she was in total darkness, and her future seemed just as dark. Without wanting to, she gave way to complete despair.

Then she thought about Grimes lying there, maybe already dead, and the horror of it restored her reason. At least she was alive, and she'd fight to stay alive as long as she could. More than that, she'd try to make her way out of the cave. But she had to plan her moves carefully. She remembered Jennie referring to a very narrow tunnel and to a deep pool of water. With no light, her only safety lay in making her way on hands and knees so she could constantly feel ahead. To make any progress at all, she'd have to have at least her feet free. And her hands, if possible.

She began working on her ankles first. With her hands still tied, it was a long, slow process, but she was finally able to loosen the ropes enough to slip her feet out. She waited a few minutes to let her legs and feet recover from the numbness that had set in. She couldn't take a chance on another fall when she stood up, as awkward as she'd be with her arms restrained. She reached out and finally felt the wall beside her. There were a number of jagged rocks protruding. Maybe she could cut through the last bonds if she were careful. As she started to work on the ropes, she discovered that when Jennie released her arms from above her head, she'd loosened the knots enough that Leah could now work the ropes open and pull her hands out. It was good to be able to shake her arms and restore the circulation.

Slowly she crawled over to where Grimes had fallen. He was still alive, but barely. He'd never recover enough to get her out of this grave. She also found one of the baskets he'd brought in, and she took time to eat some of the bread and meat it contained. She forced herself to drink several mouthfuls of whiskey. It was potent, and she shuddered as each swallow went down, but she knew it would help her through the forthcoming ordeal. Finally getting her courage up, she crawled until she touched the wall, paused just long enough to get her bearings, and then began moving in the direction Jennie had taken. Always she stayed close to the wall and put her hands well out in front of her before inching ahead even the least bit.

"What do you think, Sarah?" James asked.

"I think it is the most abominable, most despicable thing I've ever heard of. Holding that lovely woman hostage just to win a case."

"Then you do think the Lederers are behind it?"

"I do indeed." The calm, quiet Sarah came dangerously close to losing her temper. "They've never been known to tell the truth in all their three miserable lives. They may not know where Leah is, but only because they got someone else to do their dirty work for them."

"Then we have to find her ourselves," James said. "So what do you think? Where could she possibly be hidden around here? We know what time she left you, and the buggy was there when I got back to the house."

"Then I agree," Sarah said, "it seems most likely she's hidden in this area."

"Any deserted buildings? Anybody who'd be on the side of the Lederers?"

"No to both of them. I'm certain no one around here

would cooperate in something as vile as this. As to the buildings—there might be some I don't know about. Thee'll just have to start searching. And in all these wooded hills that won't be easy."

Ambrose came in the back door bringing a load of wood for the fireplace. "I just heard, Mr. Andrews. It's terrible, terrible. That pretty young woman stolen like that. Let me help look for her. I knows the area mighty well."

"Are there any old buildings? Either here or around the outskirts of town? I know she's not in the Irish section, and we've already sent men out to the Lederers' own land."

"How about the caves, Mr. Andrews? They's a most likely place."

"The caves! Of course. Why didn't we think of that? But how many are there? Hundreds at least."

"Means only one thing," John said. "You'll have to wait for daylight to begin looking."

"I can't wait that long," James said. "I'll go crazy. There must be something we can do."

Ambrose looked at the man who had helped him when no one else believed him innocent. He had to find some way to ease James's distress.

"If you want to, Mr. Andrews, we could start going from one to another and holler inside. The way sounds carry in them—"

"You're right, Ambrose. Get some lanterns. It's better than sitting around here waiting for light, and we might just find her that way."

"You want me to go with you?" John asked.

"No, why don't you stay here. Then if she's been found by some of the other men you can come out and get me. We won't be so far away that you can't see our lights. Sarah, I'll count on you to pray."

"Thee knows I will, James, and God go with thee. May thee find her soon."

His legs aching and his hands torn by brambles, James followed Ambrose from cave to cave. Each time they stopped and called Leah's name until they were hoarse. They entered caverns where they could stand up, and crawled through others on their bellies. Both James and

Ambrose finally became so exhausted they could scarcely move.

"Mr. Andrews, suh, I think we better go back to the house."

"And give up, Ambrose? No, not until I find her. I'm convinced you're right that she's hidden in one of these caves."

"No, it's 'most daylight. You need something to eat. I knows I do. We'll start out again on the other side of Miss Sarah's house."

"All right. I could use some of her strong coffee."

Slowly they trudged back to the house. Sarah had both breakfast and coffee waiting for them.

"No word from anyone, John?"

"Not a word."

Neither James nor Ambrose said anything else until they'd finished a second cup of coffee. "You know, Mr. Andrews, I think now it's light, we might see some tracks. Maybe signs around an entrance of someone going in. I been doing a mighty lot of huntin' lately, and I knows that even a rabbit leaves tracks. People gonna do the same."

"Tracks, tracks," James mumbled. "Where did I see buggy tracks where they shouldn't have been? A field. Now, I remember! There were two sets, as if coming and going. Let's go, Ambrose. I think I might have a clue, and I'll need you with me again. Fill up those lanterns. If we find her where I think we might, we won't be long."

In another minute Ambrose climbed up beside James in his buggy. While James urged the horse into a gallop, Ambrose filled the lanterns and got them ready to light.

Leah found that the only way she could move at any speed at all was to rip off her skirt. It no longer dragged her down, but now the rough floor of the cave cut through her drawers, and her knees were badly bruised and bleeding from the sharp rocks. But she dared not stand up and walk. She had no idea how far ahead was the narrow tunnel or the deep pool of water. Inch by inch she moved along, making her way around corners where the cave opened or narrowed. She felt as if she were in a labyrinth with no exit, only interminable, twisting passageways. Was she even in the right one, or had she taken a turnoff that was leading her deeper and deeper inside rather than toward the exit? Staying close to the wall, she could get no idea whether there was just one route into the depths or several leading off the main one. Yet, somehow, she felt as if she'd been moving ahead in one direction. If only she could see for just a minute, she'd have more faith in the possibility of eventually getting out.

Every few minutes she had to pause. As frightening as the darkness was the acute silence. It seemed to her this must be what Hell was like, a complete absence of light and sound. Or maybe she was in Hell. Maybe she'd died from the fall and all that had happened since was death.

No, she told herself, *I must not think like that or I'll go insane before I get out of here.*

She didn't know how long she'd been crawling, but she was painfully tired. When she came to another turn, she stopped. She couldn't see, but she had the feeling the passage had widened out. She didn't feel as closed in. Here was the greater danger of another passage going off in a different direction. She knew she had to go on but she also knew she should conserve her strength, and she sat down and leaned against the wall for a few minutes. Now was a time for thinking out her next steps very clearly and logically. The first thing was to learn if this were a chamber or just a widening of the passage. Then she must ascertain if there were one or more routes leading away from it. That would mean making her way around the entire circumference, a waste of time perhaps, but an inner sense told her it was imperative she do so.

Leah started to crawl, always keeping the wall to her left. Then she stopped again. Unless she had some way of marking the spot she left, she could go round and round for hours. Taking off one of her shoes, she placed it carefully against the wall and then started out again. As she moved, she could feel a slight curve in the wall, so she knew she'd been right to think it was a large, open vault in the cave. Then she came to a sharp turn to the left. Was it something jutting out into the room or a turn into another passage? With nothing to guide her, she crawled straight ahead and came to another corner. She then continued on, feeling again the curved wall to her left. She'd been right. There was more than one exit.

After another few minutes, she touched her shoe. She'd circumnavigated a large inner recess in the cave. More important, there were two exits and somehow she had to determine which led to the outside world. She fell back exhausted, and the dark, silent world began reeling around her. After all the twists and turns, she was now completely disoriented. For a while she'd been so certain she could trust her sense of direction, but now she was bereft of that security, too.

Two exits. Which was more likely to lead up and out of the cave? That was it! That was her clue, the upward slant of the cave's floor. At first she thought that would mean making her way all around the large chamber again, but when she reached the first passage, she realized it definitely sloped upward. This had to be it. If she were wrong? Well, she'd just go back and start all over again. To mark the chamber, if she did have to go back, she left the shoe. She crawled along a little faster now, always remembering there was a deep pool of water somewhere ahead and the narrow tunnel Jennie had referred to.

At the very moment that a new confidence restored her strength, she heard the sound. In the abysmal silence, the low moan was like the roar of a cannon. She stopped and listened. The moan was accompanied by a scraping sound, as if someone or something were crawling along the ground. There was something else, too. From time to time a bright, quick flash of light, gone almost as soon as she saw it.

Grimes! He must have come to, and he was striking matches as he moved along. He knew the cave better than she, and he had light to guide him as he made his way. Nor was he crawling cautiously along. She knew now the shuffling was from his feet moving across the dirt-covered floor. If she could see the light from the matches, that meant he was close; he'd begun following her, or at least making his way out, not long after she started. He was approaching steadily from behind her, as malevolent and inexorable as a tidal wave. He could catch up to her within minutes. Now haste was as important as caution. If he reached her, he would kill her.

When she came to the narrow, constricting tunnel, she knew why Jennie had been frightened. The very walls seemed to close in and trap her. But it had one advantage. She could touch both sides at the same time, and walk standing up. The shuffling sound was getting louder, and with each footstep, her breathing became more rapid and her heart pounded more wildly. He had a gun and the light from the matches. There was no way she could stop him from shooting her if he got close enough.

The walls widened out, and she had to start crawling again, but she was no longer afraid. She'd seen what she'd been looking for during the whole long trek—a pale suggestion of light ahead. She still could not see anything in her immediately vicinity, but there was definitely light ahead. She came to the deep pool and made her way easily around it. A few more yards and there it was. Daylight! Real daylight no more than fifty feet in front of her. She got up to walk those last few feet just as she heard Grimes's voice calling to her. Just her name, but enough to send rasping chills up and down her spine. But he could no longer hurt her. She was free from him. Forever. He'd never dare come near her again.

Leah reached the mouth of the cave and stopped. She was outside at last. She saw someone holding a lantern before she collapsed on the ground.

"Leah! My God, Leah. Here, Ambrose, hold this." James handed him the lantern and bent over to raise Leah up and cradle her in his lap. He wanted to weep over her bleeding hands, the deep cuts in her knees, and the bruises covering every part of her body. Who had dared do this to her! What clothes she still had on were hanging from her in tatters, and her hair was matted with dirt. He held her close, murmuring her name over and over while brushing her hair away from her face and rocking her back and forth like a baby.

"James? Is that you, James?" she whimpered. "I hurt all over. Please put me to bed. I think I fell. Why am I so cold?"

"What's wrong with her, Mr. Andrews?" Ambrose hovered over them. He was crying, tears streaming down his dark-brown cheeks.

"She's out of her mind from what she's been through. We've got to get her to Sarah's, and then you can go for Dr. Simmons."

Suddenly the quiet of the dawn was shattered by a single, terrified, agonizing scream, followed almost immediately by the sound of something large and heavy falling into water. The splash, coming from deep beneath the floor of the cave, echoed and re-echoed throughout the dark, hollow chambers and burst like an explosion from the entrance.

"What was that!" Ambrose jumped back.

"Something or someone fell into one of the underground lakes. I rather think Leah can give us that answer when she comes around."

For three days Leah lay in a stupor in Sarah's large, comfortable bed. With one soft down comforter under and another over her, she at last began to feel warmth seeping through her body. For a long time she thought she'd never be warm again or free from aches in every bone and muscle. Sarah kept plying her with cups of tea generously laced with soothing herbs and rubbed healing unguents into her skin. For more than twenty-four hours she had no idea where she was or what she'd been through. She knew only that James was sitting beside her, holding her hand, and assuring her that everything was all right now. Patiently he waited for her to speak, never urging, never questioning until she could remember and wanted to talk.

Finally she spoke, saying only that she wanted to go home, and James carried her out to the buggy. Once she was in her own room and surrounded by all that was familiar, her memory returned; but now she was tortured by the nightmare of reliving—over and over again—what she'd suffered in the cave.

"Talk about it, Leah," James said lovingly. "That's the only way you'll get rid of it and be able to put it out of your mind forever."

"Oh, James, it was horrible. It will take time, but I'll tell you everything."

"Those cuts and bruises didn't all come from crawling out of the cave."

"The cuts, yes, but not the rest."

"There was someone in there with you, wasn't there? Did he do that to you?"

"Yes." She could barely get the word out.

"The bastard! I'd kill him with my bare hands if he weren't already dead."

"Dead! Did you see him die?" Leah couldn't believe it. That meant all her fears that Grimes could still reveal her past were laid to rest. He could have used it as a threat to keep her from telling it was he who kidnapped her.

"Who was it, Leah? Did you know him?"

"Yes, Frank Grimes. The same one who accused me of murdering Charles Anderson. He's been threatening to reveal what he knows about me. I met him in town some months ago, and he's been making demands ever since. But didn't he come out? He was following me."

"No. Right after we found you, we heard a scream and then a heavy splash."

"The deep pool. He knew it was there, but he must have lost his balance. Thank God. No more harassment from him."

"How did he know where to find you? Or about the land case?" James was still puzzled.

"Give me a little time, and I'll tell you all about it."

While Leah was recovering, the trial had resumed and been brought to a speedy conclusion. The claim of James's clients was found to be genuine; the land was theirs. The Lederers left town, and James was certain they would hear no more from them. Then came Leah's revelation they'd been the ones behind her kidnapping.

"They told me they had nothing to do with it," James said.

"They lied. They paid Grimes to kidnap me and send that note to you. I saw the money. He bragged about how much more he'd get when you forced the decision their way."

"But how did they think they could get away with it?" James's temper flared up again.

"Simple. You said yourself they had the perfect alibi—you and everyone else in court—when I was taken. Then Grimes would leave town and no one would know. My word would be only hearsay. Actually, that's why I was so certain he meant to kill me before he left. He'd been a fool to tell me—or else he never meant for me to live from the beginning. I was the only one who could testify to the truth. He'd have the money, plus he'd get his revenge on me for the time he spent in prison and my refusal to submit to him."

"There's only one problem, Leah." He shook his head. "When it comes to accusing the Lederers. You *are* the only one who can testify, and it will be hearsay evidence. All you can do is repeat what Grimes told you, but he's dead. The Lederers can continue to deny any part in your abduction, and no one will be able to prove they're lying."

"I don't care anymore, James. I'm free and I'm alive. That's all that counts now. I don't ever want to hear their names again. Do you think they'll cause any more trouble?"

"No. The case is closed, so there's no reason to fear them now. They'd threaten only when they thought it would be to their advantage."

"I wonder," Leah said. "I'm still afraid, but maybe that's natural after what I've been through. Will they give up that easily, or are they still dangerous?"

"Not to us, my love. You can rest easy about that."

Gradually, during the first two weeks after the trial, with James home every night and coming home most days at noon, Leah began to regain some peace of mind. It had taken a long time, however, for her to lose the physical feelings of terror, the shaking and sweating every time she heard a sound in the house or saw someone walking past outside. Only with James by her side did she go downtown, and even then she clung to his arm for fear of being snatched away. She knew he was right to make her get out of the house and resume a more normal life. It was strange; she was more frightened since she escaped from the cave and found herself held close in James's arms than she had been during any part of the terrible ordeal.

With the case closed, it was time for James to begin riding the circuit again. After his first three-day absence, Leah began to relax and feel more secure. Bridget returned from her family, and James insisted on having Ambrose remain with them to protect the house during the day. Even at night, in his room over the carriage house, Ambrose was alert to any unusual sound. Leah's rational mind told her she was safe, but her emotions refused to believe it for a long, long time.

Finally one day she forced herself to put Paul in his wicker stroller and walk to town by herself. As cold as it was, below freezing, she was covered with perspiration by the time she got to the tea shop. Nor could she stop shaking. It took all her strength to hold a cup and help Paul with the bun she'd ordered for him. When Elizabeth Benson came in, she finally relaxed enough to be able to carry on a somewhat intelligent conversation.

It was now Wednesday, and James had promised he'd try to return from the circuit that night rather than the following afternoon. He was closing out a case, and since the town was only some twenty miles distant, he thought he would come right on home rather than wait overnight as he did when farther away. He'd be late, and she was not to worry if he didn't get there until sometime after supper.

While Bridget washed up the dishes, Leah played with Paul in front of the fire and asked Ambrose to bring in more wood so she could stay up until James got home.

"I do believe you're feeling better, Mrs. Andrews," Ambrose said. "You getting some color back in your cheeks."

"Thank you, Ambrose, I am. There's nothing so frightening as being frightened. Maybe that doesn't make sense, but it's how I felt."

"I knows what you mean." He laid the logs down and poked the fire.

"Yes, I guess you do."

"Them caves is mighty scary places. I don't know which is the worst feeling—waiting to be found or fearing you ain't gonna be found."

"Well, it's behind us, Ambrose—for both of us." She turned to help Paul with one of his toys.

"Little Paul sure do like that train." Ambrose pointed to the three wooden cars hitched together with screw eyes that Paul was propelling across the rug.

"Indeed he does. You did a beautiful job of carving it. And sanding it so smoothly. I'll bet you could earn money selling them if you wanted to."

"You really think so? I does love to whittle, and trains

is as easy as sticks. I do whistles, too. I got some in my room."

"Well, bring them down here sometime," Leah suggested. "I'll bet Mr. Siokos could sell them in his candy store."

"I'll do that, Mrs. Andrews. I sure will do that. You think you got enough wood now?"

"Plenty, Ambrose, thank you. Mr. Andrews may be late, so if you hear a buggy, you'll know it's him."

Bridget finished with the dishes and walked into the parlor at the same time that someone knocked on the front door.

"Please see who it is, Bridget, and I'll try to get Paul to put his toys away so you can take him to bed." She reached over to grab him by the seat of his britches as he tried to crawl under the couch with his train. "Come on, honey, time to pick things up."

She heard the voices from the front hall. "Is Mrs. Andrews here?" It was John Howard.

"In here, John. You come to tell me James won't be home tonight?"

"Not exactly, Leah." He turned and whispered to Bridget, "Go in and get Paul."

"Well, come in by the fire," Leah called. "It's freezing outside."

"Leah, James has been hurt." John looked over to Bridget, saw the knowing look on her face, and nodded.

"Hurt!" Leah leaped up from the rug. "What do you mean, 'hurt'?"

"Come with me. He's at Doc Benson's. I'll tell you while we ride over there."

Leah grabbed her hooded cape off the hall rack, saw that Paul was already in Bridget's arms, and followed John out to the buggy.

"How was he hurt, John?"

"On our way home. His buggy was ahead of mine. Someone stepped out from a grove of trees and shot him. I got him into my buggy and right to Doc's."

"Was he seriously hurt?" A shot could mean anything from being grazed slightly to a fatal wound.

"Yes, he was."

"He's dead, isn't he? You didn't want to tell me until I got there, but he is dead." Leah didn't have to wait for an answer. She'd known the minute John said James had been hurt. It wasn't that John didn't lie very well or that his face had revealed it. She'd simply known in her heart that James was gone.

"Yes, Leah, he is. He died almost immediately after I got him into town. He never regained consciousness."

Leah said nothing more during the short ride to Dr. Benson's. She sat rigid and unmoving in the buggy. Her mind and emotions were in the same frozen state as her body. The world was a void, and she was the only one in it, alone and cold. She didn't even have the warmth required for tears. Everything about her had ceased functioning.

When they drove up to Dr. Benson's house, Leah got down from the seat as obediently as a child. She moved in a dazed vacuum up onto the porch and into the front hall.

"Where is he?" She looked from Dr. Benson to Elizabeth.

"In our bedroom. Do you want to see him now?"

"Yes." Once more she followed where she was led. The Bensons walked with her over to where James lay on the huge double bed.

"Will you please go out and close the door after you," Leah said in a calm voice that might have been requesting a glass of water. "There are some things I need to talk to James about. Some advice I need from him."

"But he's—" Elizabeth started to speak, before Dr. Benson shook his head and took her by the arm.

Leah looked down at James. In the interim, before she arrived, all traces of the fatal shot had been removed. He looked as if he might simply have fallen asleep on the bed. There was even a trace of a smile on his face. Slowly she walked over to a side chair, pulled it up beside the bed, and sat down.

Only then did she collapse into tears. "Oh, James, why did you have to leave me now. Now of all times when I need your strength to face this. What do I do without you? How do I go on?" She took his hand, usually so warm and vital but now cold and bloodless, in hers.

She sat there crying quietly for a long time; then she began to speak in a normal, conversational tone. "I do love you, you know that don't you? I wanted you to believe it when I finally said it. I'll try to be strong, I promise." She wiped a tear away. "Paul was playing with his train tonight. He made believe there was a tunnel under the couch. It won't be long before he'll be too big to crawl under there. He's going to miss you terribly. Do you want me to stay here? We've such a lovely house, and it will be good for Paul to grow up here. I promise I'll see that he studies law if that's what you want for him.

"Oh, God, James, why can't you answer me? Don't you see I need someone to tell me what to do. It's not fair of you to leave me now."

She leaned over and touched his forehead. "You really need a haircut, you know. Why do you always wait until it gets so long it won't stay back?" she sobbed. "And your jacket's all mussed. What a lovable, comfortable person you are. We must see that you wear your best suit for the—for the—" She couldn't get the word out. Brushing a lock of hair away from his eyes, she ran her hand around the side of his head. Her fingers touched the bullet wound, so carefully covered by Dr. Benson before she arrived, and she heard the scream as if it were coming from someone else.

"Come, Leah." John was lifting her off the bed. "Doc wants you to lie down in the guest room. He has something for you to take that will help you sleep. That's what you need now."

"No," she said quietly but firmly. "I want to stay here. You take care of whatever has to be done, but I'm not leaving his side until—until it's all over."

Nor did she. Bridget pressed James's best suit and sent it over by Ambrose. Leah looked at it, shook her head, and sent him back for something else. With his help, Leah removed James's soiled clothes, bathed him, and dressed him in a neat pair of tweed trousers and the beautiful suede hunting jacket he'd bought just before they were married. That was James as she wanted to remember him.

When the wooden coffin arrived, she helped lift him into it and, with the top open, she rode beside him in the hearse to their house. Only then did she ask to be alone with him again until it was time for the funeral. For nearly an hour she talked with him and said her final good-byes. Then she ordered that the coffin be closed. She would have no morbid, curious faces looking down at him.

Many who came to the house were shocked and distressed that she flouted custom by not having the coffin open for them to look at James. Some said she'd always seemed strange to them, and this last peculiar act just proved it. Others nodded and said they understood. She brought more wrath upon her head when she refused to go to the cemetery. She wanted to say good-bye to him at the front door, not in the cold, barren air of the graveyard. She watched as the coffin was lifted once more into the hearse. There were no tears, only an empty, desolate feeling. She walked to the kitchen, passing the dining-room table laden with plates and dishes filled with food from their friends, and poured herself a cup of coffee. If she had to begin planning a new life without James, it was always good to start with a cup of coffee.

Chapter Seventeen

After Claud Bonvivier agreed that Baptiste could wait until March to sail for France, additional letters between them led to the conclusion that Baptiste should plan to stay there for a year to make certain all was going smoothly. As long as Lisette could be with him, it would be a real pleasure to do some traveling and spend more time with the friends he had over there.

Such an extended visit, however, involved extremely detailed instructions about the plantation. He had no qualms about leaving it in the capable hands of Benji and Septimus, but he wanted to make certain they felt easy about assuming such a responsibility. As he surmised, Catherine made no objection to his suggestion that she move into New Orleans and live in the apartment during his absence. While going through some papers in his father's desk, Baptiste came upon one that both startled and delighted him. It was a short but extremely informative letter.

He was sitting before the fire in the library at Belle Fontaine. For the past two months he and Catherine had been following the routine of letting her go into the city for a few days whenever he had to come out here to talk over plantation affairs. It meant they never had to see each other, and both could get things done they needed to do. Supper was over, and he invited Benji to sit down and join him in a drink. It was a nightly ritual. Benji knew he'd be asked, but he always waited for the invitation.

"Think you're ready to take over running this place for a year, Benji?"

"Don't know why not. I've been doing it now for a long time."

"Don't act so pompous. I mean without my telling you what to do."

"And you think I don't know what you're likely to tell me next? If you're so all-fired afraid I'll do something wrong, just say so."

"No," Baptiste laughed, "I know you can handle it. I think Septimus can manage the fields and the workers. They have confidence in him. All you have to do is see that the house doesn't fall down. Or go selling it to someone behind my back."

"What makes you think I'd do something like that?" Benji tried to look hurt, but he was laughing inside. He knew how hard it really was for Baptiste to leave, even with the prospect of a year in France.

Baptiste said nothing, only leaned back in his chair and puffed on his cigar.

"Benji, you ever see your father?"

"Never knew him and Mama never say. Why you ask?"

"He was a mean man, Benji. Handsome but god-awful mean."

"How you know?" Benji pulled himself forward and poured himself another drink.

"I heard talk," Baptiste said.

"I mean, how you know who my father was?"

"I told you, I heard talk." He stared long and hard at Benji. "He was my Uncle Jacques."

"We—we're cousins! The hell you say." Benji was so stunned he dropped his glass and then covered his embarrassment by hurriedly picking up the broken pieces.

"Right," Baptiste nodded. "You're a lot blacker than I am and not nearly so handsome, but you're a Fontaine all right."

"The hell you say," Benji repeated. "How about that!"

He slapped his knee. "How long you known this?"

"Not long. I've been going through some papers. I wanted to make certain everything was in good shape before I left—taxes all paid, and so forth. You know that old chest I keep things in?"

Benji nodded.

"Well, when I was sorting everything out—some to leave with you, some to give to Pierre—I discovered it has a false bottom. It took me a while to pry it up, but then I saw it was full of letters. Out of boredom and curiosity I began to read them. Most were meaningless, but I kept on. It was a good thing I did. That's how I found out about you. I should have known though. Close as we've been since we were boys."

"So—why tell me now?" Benji asked with the natural suspicion of his race toward a white man, even a white friend and relative.

"Because half the plantation belongs to you. Uncle Jacques was killed digging for gold out West. That's why I seemed to be the only one left to inherit this place. But half is rightfully yours. The letter from Uncle Jacques clearly states that you're his son. My father would probably have told me if he'd lived until after the war. Maybe he thought I knew. His will stated 'heirs'—but that's just legal talk."

Benji was too astonished to say anything. He just sat there shaking his head. Then he got up and walked around the room, as if looking at it and the things in it for the first time.

"Now, sit down, Benji, and quit staring at me like an idiot. We've got things to discuss."

Benji moved back to the chair but sat perched on the edge of the seat. "I can't—I can't believe it. You mean I own half this beautiful place?"

"You do, and that's why we have to talk seriously. I'll be leaving in a month, and we've got some decisions to make. Not just me—but us."

Benji frowned. Following orders was one thing; making the decisions was something else again. The idea was still too new to feel comfortable with.

Baptiste saw he needed to inject some humor into the

situation. "You were going to be in charge anyway. Now I know you'll do a good job since you'll be sharing in everything."

"Well, damn! You didn't really trust me before, did you?" He looked chagrined.

"Benji, I'd trust you with my life. But—my money, that's a different matter." Baptiste laughed and clapped him on the shoulder. "So let's get busy. There's not much time for all we have to do."

"Like what? You already got everything worked out. Why can't I just do what you've already planned?"

"Because it means we have to get Pierre to draw up some legal papers, naming you as half-owner. The letter will be the basis for them. But I want to make sure everything is just as it should be so you can sign in my absence—checks, orders, things like that. I was going to give Pierre power of attorney, but now I won't have to."

"Mam'selle Catherine ain't gonna like that."

"She has nothing to do with this. She'll be living in New Orleans and have her own allowance from a trust fund. The plantation will be under your complete charge."

"Is anybody else gonna know?"

"What do you mean, Benji?"

"I mean people like Septimus and the workers."

"I don't see why not," Baptiste said. "It's a fact. You *are* half-owner of Belle Fontaine."

"I don't think so." Benji shook his head. "They'll take orders left by you, but I ain't so sure how they'll take them direct from me."

"Oh, I see what you mean. By God, Benji, they should. It should't make any difference to them whether the boss is colored or white."

"But it does, and you know it."

"No, dammit, there'll be no hiding behind outdated tradition. If you're an owner, you're going to act like one. Assume all the responsibilities. Live in the house."

"If you say so, Baptiste."

"Not because I say so, Benji, but because we're equals now, and don't let anyone forget it."

"I'll stay in the house, but in my rooms next to the kitchen." Benji wanted to move slowly, to have time to absorb his new status in life, not rush headlong into it.

"You will sleep in the master bedroom."

"I can't. It's Mam'selle Catherine's room."

"There you go again with *Mam'selle* Catherine. If you act like something less than you are, you'll be treated the same way. You're going to have to command the respect of the people here. It won't be easy, but you can start before I leave for France so's they'll have time to get used to it."

"And when you leave, they'll refuse to follow orders. Probably quit and run off."

"That's another thing. You have to start taking a positive attitude toward things. The workers aren't going to run off. Where would they go? They need work and there aren't that many jobs around now. Remember this. Free men of color had plantations before the war and worked them successfully."

"Yes, but they had slaves who had to follow orders, who were afraid not to."

"Then you know what you have to do: earn their respect. If you can't hold them by fear, then show them you're the kind of proprietor they want to work for. Give them their due, and a little more if they earn it, but don't ever let them slack off. Some will try to test you, see how far they can go or how little they need do because of your once being one of them, but don't let even one get away with it."

Benji sighed and looked off into the distance. "Then I'm no longer one of them. They can't be my friends anymore. I won't be welcome among them. Sounds like I'm gonna be mighty lonely up here."

"How often did you go down to their cottages except to sleep with Tabitha? Did you think it wasn't lonely for me up here? Of course you'll still have friends, like Septimus, among them. By the way, we'll talk to him tomorrow. If I know him, he'll be your first strong supporter."

"He's a good man. I'm glad we've got him here."

Baptiste smiled to himself at the change from "you" to "we," not just in Benji's words but in his new proprietary tone. He'd always loved Benji like a brother, and being a cousin was just about as good. If anything should happen to him, Benji would see to it that the house and land were maintained for Lisette. Nor would the Fontaine name be lost now that he'd no son to carry it on. He sometimes allowed himself to dwell on the idea of finding a way to divorce Catherine on grounds that would allow him to marry again, but he immediately forgot about it. He hadn't been too successful as a husband, and certainly marriage was not the perfect panacea for either loneliness or a desire for children. No, he'd devote his time to the business of being a father to Lisette.

"Well," Baptiste said, "that should about take care of things here. We'll talk to Septimus tomorrow, and then when we go back to the city, I'll make certain all those legalities are taken care of before I leave for France."

Benji leaned over and reached into the silver box on the table beside Baptiste. Taking his time, he carefully selected a cigar, struck a match, and lit up.

"What in hell are you doing, Benji?"

"Smoking a good cigar. Isn't it one of the perquisites of being a Fontaine?"

Baptiste threw back his head and roared with laughter. "Where did you get that word? And what makes you think you can smoke my cigars?"

"I heard Mam'selle Catherine use it, and when I tried it, it rolled around so nicely on my tongue I thought I'd save it for just the right time." At the same time he twisted the cigar between his lips. "You said everything in the house was ours now."

"Not my personal things. You want all my clothes, too? Go ahead, strip the closets, see if I care. There's not much I could do about it if I did."

"I don't want your clothes. Your taste's too conservative for me. I'll order my own."

"Damn, if you're not beginning to sound like a white man. Well, order your own cigars, too."

Benji chuckled to himself. At least Baptiste was beginning to come out of his gloomy state.

"So tell me, Baptiste. Why're you staying away a whole year? Seems to me you could get the work done in a few months."

"I could, but I've friends over there, and I thought I'd make it a pleasure trip, too."

"A whole year? Come on, Baptiste, what's the real reason?"

"You're right, Benji. I've got to get away from here for a while, not just from the plantation, but from Louisiana. Too many memories. I don't know which hurt worse, the bitter ones or the happy ones. Out here, it's Catherine and all our problems. It's no better in the city. Everywhere I go, I'm reminded of Leah. Dammit, Benji, how does one get over loving someone who's gone forever?"

"I don't know. I didn't know her till just before she left you. I hated her for hurting you."

"The only woman I've ever loved." Baptiste put his head between his hands for a few minutes. Benji got up to settle another log on the fire and refill their glasses. He wished there were some way he could get his cousin out of the despondent mood he'd been in for the past months.

In another minute Baptiste raised his head and grinned. "You should find someone like her for yourself, Benji. At least you could marry her. You've got a lot to offer some beautiful mulatto or octoroon. Hell, they'll be swarming around you once they find out."

"They don't want someone like they are. They want a white man who can set them up."

"Don't kid yourself. Anyway, that was before the war. Now, you've got as much to offer as any white man—and more. They can be married. That's what they really want. Why do you think Leah left me? Because she loved Andrews? Hell, no; she wanted to be a wife, and I can't blame her. And have legitimate children. Now you can, too."

"Speaking of that, what can you tell me about my father?"

"Don't be in such a hurry to change the subject. It's time you quit whoring around and settled down." Baptiste looked into the fire. "About your father, I don't remember much. I loved him because he was always such fun to be around, but that wasn't often. I never saw him out here, always in New Orleans, when he'd returned from some wild escapade. He was always going to make a million dollars but usually returned broke. The plantation was never enough for him."

"Sounds like someone else I know." Benji grinned.

"Maybe that's why I was so fond of him, just like him myself. Anyway, he was always very gentle and generous

403

with me, but not so with others, from what I heard. He had a vile temper and a vicious cruel streak in him. Woe to anyone who riled him. He had to leave town several times after fatal duels, and he raised some of the most murderous fighting cocks in the South. Horses and game-cocks, those were his two loves. But he always brought me presents and took me to the finest restaurants. Sometimes just the two of us, and he treated me like a man, not a child. Yet I was only eight when he left for good."

"I wonder why I never saw him," Benji mused, "or why he didn't bring me presents."

"I got a hint of that from the letter. I'll give it to you; you should have it. I think he really loved your mother, but he knew it was hopeless. So he couldn't bear to see her. He must have sent money with the letter, to make certain you had what you needed. And he did give you something. He made certain my father knew you were his son. That's why I think Papa must have encouraged our friendship. He must have thought he told me at some time. Papa was a kind man; he wouldn't have purposely kept me ignorant of that to deny you your heritage."

"M'sieu Fontaine was always good to me, that's for sure. I wonder why my mama didn't tell me, though."

"I don't know, Benji. She must have had her reasons, but we'll never know what they were."

The fire died down, and each was quiet with his own thoughts. Benji had a lot to think about. He was the son of a white man and part owner of a plantation, a long way to come from being born to a slave in the quarters on that same land. Baptiste hadn't had to tell him. No one would ever have known. But Baptiste wasn't that kind of man, and he, Benji, would make certain his cousin would never regret revealing the truth.

Baptiste knew he was leaving the plantation in good hands. He'd told Benji about his paternity for two reasons. One, because it was right to do so; the inheritance was his by law. Two, because he wondered if he'd ever return to Louisiana, at least in the foreseeable future. Right now he wanted to run as far as he could go, and the proposal to go to France fulfilled that need. After a year, he might want to return; but if he didn't, he knew suitable arrange-ments could be made for the office here. At least this gave him time, and in France, away from the places filled with specters of his past, he could sort out his feelings.

"What are you doing here!"

"Having a small sherry before supper," Baptiste said. "Care to join me?"

"I do not." Catherine pulled off her gloves and slapped them against the palm of her hand as if she intended to strike Baptiste across the face with them. Then she threw them onto a chair. In the same frantic manner, she yanked off her bonnet and cape. "You're not supposed to to be here. You were to leave by noon. That was part of our agreement, that I would never have to see you either here or in New Orleans."

"I trust you had a pleasant week in the city," he said without bothering to answer her question. "How many bills did you run up? I know that's a good barometer of your mood."

"Forget about that. I want to know why you're still here." She looked around and started toward the bedroom.

"Don't look for her. Lisette has already gone back with Jessie and Melissa. What I want to talk about with you has nothing to do with her."

"I really don't think we have anything to talk about. Unless it would be to increase my allowance. I'm having a dreadful time living on it."

"That's impossible. You don't have a damn thing to pay for except incidentals. You have charge accounts at every store in the city, and I haven't complained about those—so far."

"What do you mean—so far?" He wouldn't dare cut those out.

"I mean that when I leave for France I'm going to establish a trust fund for you with a stipulated monthly allowance that will have to cover everything."

"Is that necessary? I should think you would leave all of the financial affairs in my hands. After all, I am your wife still. I assumed I'd be in charge of the plantation as well as the apartment in town."

"There is a very good reason why I'm not leaving you in charge of the plantation. Only half of it belongs to me,

405

and the other owner will take care of things here while I'm gone."

"Half-owner! What have you done? Sold half of it?" What in the world possessed Baptiste to do a thing like that?

"No, I did not sell it. I found a letter and learned that I have a cousin, the son of my father's brother, who should have inherited his half when my father died. My uncle died some years earlier. So I've informed him of his inheritance, and he will be living out here while I'm gone. You've already agreed that you preferred to live in town."

"And just who is this cousin? Am I to meet him?" This was impossible! To be stripped of half of what rightfully belonged to her. It was monstrous! If she didn't know how scrupulously honest Baptiste was, she'd think he was making all this up just to infuriate her.

"Oh, you've already met him. It's Benji."

"Benji!" This she couldn't believe, yet she knew by the look on Baptiste's face that he wasn't teasing her. "You mean—you mean half this plantation—half this house belongs to that—that—"

"Don't say it, Catherine."

"How could you! How could you humiliate me so. Leaving me here to share this place with him." She knew she'd been right to hate Benji. Her intuition had told her never to trust him.

"I? All I did was tell Benji who his father was. It was my uncle who sired him and my father who left me the letter."

"But you didn't have to tell him. You fool! There was no need to let him know. We could have kept all of this for ourselves. He was a slave, the son of a slave. What gives him the right to think he can inherit a plantation?"

"Because, my dear wife, it is his right. He is also the son of my Uncle Jacques."

"A by-blow of a one-night frolic! And that makes him half-owner." Catherine was near to tears from fury and frustration, but she'd be damned if she'd let Baptiste see them. How could she possibly live this down—half-owner with a Negro!

"It was not a *one-night* frolic as you so charmingly put it. But that's not the point. You will accept the fact that

Benji is my cousin with all the rights of a Fontaine. You will never have to see him or have anything to do with his responsibilities. As I said, I will establish a generous trust fund for you, and Pierre will handle any financial problems you have. If there's nothing more, I'll go into the city for supper. I think I'll find more congenial company there."

He waited for Catherine to say something, but she merely stood by the fireplace with her back toward him. He wheeled out into the hall and told Benji he was ready to return to the apartment.

Chapter Eighteen

LEAH FINISHED HER coffee, set down the cup, and looked out the window at the cold and desolate landscape. So different from New Orleans where the camellias, the azaleas, and the live oaks kept their green leaves the year 'round and there was always something blooming. The bulbs would be up, the dogwood ready to flower, and the azaleas just on the verge of bursting into riotous color. She felt as desiccated and barren as the skeletal fruit trees in James's garden and as cold as the wind soughing through the branches.

Both Elizabeth Benson and Mary Howard had wanted to stay with her when the funeral cortege left for the cemetery, but she felt a desperate need to be alone with her pain. They meant well, but Leah always found it easier to come to grips with tragedy and grief by herself. Early in her life she'd forced herself to learn emotional self-control, to remain seemingly unmoved and seemingly untouched by either great joy or sorrow. For this reason, many, including her own mother and father, thought her cold and distant. But each time she was made aware that being a free woman of color put her beyond the pale of social acceptability, the intense moments of pain she felt gradually piled up one upon another until they formed an impenetrable wall of disdain.

If to others she seemed totally self-sufficient, no one knew the agony she endured inside. She had a great need for comfort and reassurance, but never would she ask for either. Although she presented a bold, indomitable face to the world, she was often frightened and easily intimidated. Only two people—Baptiste and James—ever really understood her, and now they were both lost to her.

That was why she had to grieve alone. The kind of sympathy others would offer was not what she needed right now. Her communion with James and her memories of him had to remain private. She was not ready to talk about him with anyone else, or be comforted by words that were sincere but had no meaning for her: "It's better than if he spent the rest of his life paralyzed"; "His time had come"; "The good are taken young"; "It was God's will."

No, they were all wrong, every one of them. It was wrong that James should be shot. It was man's will, not God's, that the gun was aimed and the bullet shot at James. She alone could wrestle with her tragedy and not be defeated by it.

Strangely enough, she felt more joy than sorrow that she had come to love James before he died. She would miss him more because of it, but at the same time it gave her a strength she sorely needed right now.

The afternoon shadows were lengthening. She'd sat there long enough. It was time to be up and doing. There were certain decisions about her future that had to be made, but they could wait. What she needed now was something to do to keep her from thinking. For Leah, the panacea for trouble of any kind was hard physical work, especially if it benefited someone else.

Leah got up from the table and walked into the dining room. Struck by the irony of what she saw there, she began laughing, not the hysterical laugh of one bereaved but the deep, spontaneous laughter in response to something that is really funny. It was well she was alone, because no one else would have understood, and they would have thought her unfeeling or crazy.

Spread out on the table were plates and dishes of cakes, pies, puddings, casseroles, glazed ham, fried chicken, and heaven knew what else. Yes, there was even the bowl of Mrs. Shelby's special rice pudding with its accompanying glass jar of custard sauce. Just like the day all the women came around to welcome her to Hickory Falls. The room looked ready for a party or celebration of some kind. Why did people think that death made you especially hungry?

She supposed that it was expected of her to ask everyone to come back for supper after the funeral, but Leah held the rather unorthodox and peculiar belief that she had the right to invite to her home only people she really wanted to see. At any time that numbered only a few, and right now it was no one. Maybe Sarah. If Sarah drove in from the country she'd love to see her. In her own way she was a very private person, too. She'd not come to the funeral, but Leah knew Sarah was waiting for her to go out there, waiting until Leah felt the need to see her. In a few days she would go, taking Paul with her, and the gentle older woman would supply the sustenance she needed to go on living without James.

She was still in the dining room when Bridget came in with Paul. Then she went into the parlor and got down on the floor to play games with Paul. Better than any sighs of pity or words of sympathy, it was just what Leah needed.

"And you know what," Leah finally said to Bridget, "I'm hungry. When I first saw all that food, I thought I never wanted to eat again, but I think I'd like to try some of it."

"Very good. What would you like me to heat up?"

"I know. We'll try a little bit of everything we want." She looked again at all the plates and dishes. "No, I've a better idea. Give me a bit of that chicken and fix something for yourself and Paul. Wrap everything else up carefully. Tomorrow's Sunday. We'll go out to your church and then invite everyone back to Michael's house afterward."

"Oh, ma'am, do you think you should?"

"Yes, I do. It's just what I need. We won't allow any long faces or mournful conversation. When I grieve, I grieve by myself. But with others I don't want to be re-

410

minded of my loss. That's what I can't do with James's friends. They mean well, but they just make it worse."

The visit with her Irish friends was a tremendous success, and Leah returned more ready than before to take up her life without James. It would be a long time before she could become completely reconciled to her loss, but she tried to begin leading a normal life.

Knowing that black was *de rigueur* for anyone in mourning, Leah dutifully wore the heavy, black wool dress, the small black hat with the widow's peak, and the long, ribbon-edged veil whenever she went into town. For church on Sunday, she donned the black poplin that rustled as she moved and made her feel all the more conspicuous. She'd been stunned when she walked into her bedroom after bringing James back from Dr. Benson's and saw the garments lying on the bed.

"We knew you'd want them," Mrs. Rhinehardt said, "and have had no time to order them made." She implied but didn't need to say that most women spent the time between the death and the funeral buying appropriate clothes rather than sitting with and dressing the deceased. "They belong to Mrs. Jacobs, who we felt was about your size. She had them for the death of her first husband, but you are to keep them for just as long as you wish."

Since Mrs. Jacobs's first husband had died some fifteen years earlier, before the war, the clothes were decidedly out of date; but by omitting the full crinolines Mrs. Jacobs had worn under them, Leah managed to make them look a little less old-fashioned.

The minute Leah got back into the house, she took them off. James had hated her in black, preferring pastels and bright colors all year 'round.

Leah purposely put off going out to see Sarah, because she knew how easy it would be to become too dependent on her. She had to make her way alone first. Then came the day some two weeks after the funeral, when the first shock was over and the realization that James was actually gone forever surged through her like a stabbing pain. Only Sarah could help her through this period of agony.

As was her way, Sarah greeted her as if nothing was amiss. She found a toy for Paul, who sat contentedly playing with it on the floor and munching an oatmeal cookie still warm from the oven. Then she and Leah sat down with a pot of steaming tea.

"Nothing like a good cup of tea to cheer one up on a blustery day like this. I've been hoping thee would come, but I never expected thee when the skies are forecasting a blizzard."

"Then maybe you'll have to keep us for the night, Sarah."

"And I'd be pleased, thee knows that. But that's not why thee came today."

"No, it's not, Sarah. I had to talk to someone, someone who'd really understand what I'm going through. And you're the only person who can."

"I'm not the only one who's lost a husband, Leah."

"No, but you're the only one who's had to make the decision I'm faced with now. Do I stay in Hickory Falls or do I go back to New Orleans? Over and over I've wrestled with the problem of whether James was my only reason for being here, or should I stay for Paul's sake. Where do I belong? I feel so terribly lost."

"That's natural. I felt the same way. Don't think the decision was an easy one for me, especially after the boys wanted me to go with them. Then I realized there was one advantage to being alone. I could do exactly what I wanted to do, not what someone else desired. I stayed here because this was my home, and I loved it. I didn't want to be anywhere else. So give yourself time. Don't make a hasty decision."

"It's not that easy, Sarah. There are considerations you don't know about. I don't feel at home here. Oh, I love the house and have made friends, but it's not as if I'd be happier here than somewhere else. But then I must think about Paul's future."

"If thee thinks it better for him here, thee can make a place for yourself. There are many who would be your friends, but—if I may say it—thee has kept too much to yourself."

"I know you're right, Sarah. And life would be quite different for Paul in New Orleans."

"Give the people here a chance, Leah. And thee has much to offer them, too."

Leah stared at the teapot, wanting to speak yet fearing

to. What would Sarah think of her if she knew the truth? What would be her advice then? Yet that was what was really tearing Leah apart, the knowledge she was living a lie without James's support.

"Look at me, Sarah. I mean really look at me. What do you see?"

"A very sad young woman who's lost someone she loved more than she realized."

"How very right you are."

"Thee didn't love James when thee married him."

"How did you know, Sarah?"

"I know how newlyweds should behave. Thee both acted as though married a long time. Something just didn't strike me right. Why did thee marry him?"

"I'll tell you in a little bit. What else do you see?"

"A good and honorable woman who's carrying a burden much too heavy for her shoulders alone."

How wise and observant Sarah was. But how did she know so much?

"That's just it, Sarah, I'm not—a good and honorable person, I mean."

The time had come when she could keep it in no longer, and Leah broke down, crying with the need to release all the pent-up frustrations and fears.

"Tell me, Leah. Tell me what it is that has thee so distressed. It's not just the loss of James, is it?"

"No, and once I tell you, you'll know why the decision is so hard for me. I came here under false pretenses, and there are many who would call me a wicked sinner. I am not white. I am an octoroon."

Leah waited for the look of shock and horror on Sarah's face, but there was none, only the same calm, placid smile. "I was born a free woman of color. My mother and father were not married. I didn't live in that big house Mrs. Rhinehardt delights in describing to her friends. My father's legal white family lived there. I am an octoroon, and I met Baptiste Fontaine at a quadroon ball. I was his mistress, Sarah, not his wife all those years. Nor is he dead. He is very much alive. And Paul is his son."

She continued to tell Sarah all about the murder case and the trial. "So that is how I met James. He fell in love with me and, even knowing about the baby, wanted to marry me. It was the chance I'd waited for all my life, to come North and pass, to be married to a white man. So now you see why it could be wrong to take Paul back to New Orleans. He'd never have the opportunities he'll have here."

"I thank thee for telling me, Leah, for feeling I was the one person thee could confide in."

"Yes, I knew you'd understand, but that doesn't solve the problem of what I should do."

"Thee has relieved some of the burden by telling me. No one else need ever know. Nor should thee chide yourself for keeping it a secret. The important thing is to give yourself time. The biggest mistake people in mourning make is to think everything must be decided at once. I've seen women give up their homes and move in with their children right away, and then rue it for the rest of their lives. Thee will know what to do; thee will get a sign of some kind."

"Do you really think so, Sarah?"

"I do. Don't laugh at a foolish old woman, but does thee know what made up my mind for me? A tree in bloom. I walked out and saw the apple tree. It had burst into white blossoms overnight, and I knew I could never leave it."

"And you've been happy with your decision?"

"No, not always. I'd be lying if I said I were. But happier than if I'd left. No decision can guarantee happiness, but—what would the alternative bring us? That's what thee must consider."

"I will, Sarah. I'll take time and consider all the alternatives."

The promised snow came. Leah and Paul spent three days with Sarah, and just knowing there was someone with whom she didn't have to keep up pretenses did her a world of good.

"Now I know where to come," Leah said, "when the pressures get too much for me."

"And I'll take a stick to thee if that's the only reason thee drives out here."

"No fear, Sarah. You'll see more of me than you want to."

"Never, Leah. Thee and Paul cheer me up like the first sign of spring. Thee is always welcome."

For over a week Leah did as Sarah suggested. She got involved in a flurry of activity, as much as her widowhood allowed. She drove the buggy downtown and met some of the women in the tea shop. She attended church and met with the missionary circle, but all of it seemed false. She was acting a part, not really living. Then she decided to start spring housecleaning early. In spite of Bridget's protests, she scrubbed floors and washed windows, which did more for her than chatting over a cup of tea or sewing on layettes.

She put off cleaning her bedroom until last. All of James's clothes had been given away to the needy, but now it was time to go through his personal things. Still postponing the heartrending chore, she decided to clean out her own dresser first. In one box were some ribbons and gloves that were soiled past cleaning and should have been thrown out long before. She was about to put them all in the discard pile when she felt something in a finger of one of the gloves. Reaching in, she pulled out a key. For a minute she was puzzled. Then it dawned on her. It was a key to her home in New Orleans. She thought she'd lost it long ago; but it must have been there, in that glove, when she was packing to move to the plantation. And it just happened to be in the suitcase she grabbed up to bring with her to Indiana.

Why had she found it now? Was it, like Sarah's apple tree, trying to tell her something? The longing to return to the Vieux Carré swept over her like a flood, and she knew she could never stay in Hickory Falls. Somehow she would find a way to assure the future for Paul that she and James had visualized. Things *were* different now. He could return North to school. It would be wrong to deprive him of his complete heritage. She'd bring him up to be proud of it, and to be mature enough to make his own decisions when the time came. It would be wrong to deprive him of that privilege.

The first thing she had to do was find out exactly what her financial situation was. She knew James had left her enough to live comfortably in Hickory Falls, but she needed to know more precisely what her position was. To that end, she went to see John Howard the next day.

"John, I'm thinking of returning to New Orleans."

"I think the visit would do you good. Mary and I were saying that very thing last night."

"Not just for a visit, John, but to stay."

"We'll miss you, Leah, but I can understand why you'd want to go back home."

"Yes, so now I need to know exactly what James left."

"The house and land, of course, though not as much as there once was."

"Do you think you can sell it?"

"No trouble at all. Are you sure you don't want to lease it for a while, just in case?"

"No, John, I won't be returning."

"All right. I can send the furniture down as soon as you find a place to live."

"I want it sold furnished. I have a home in New Orleans." If there were nothing left in the house there, she'd buy new things. She wanted to take nothing from Indiana.

"That will be fine," John assured her. "Should be no trouble at all."

"So that," Leah said hesitantly, "and the bank notes are all I have."

"Indeed not," John said. "James made a number of investments that pay well. He didn't tell you? You're quite a wealthy woman."

"No, he didn't tell me. I guess he felt there was no need. He didn't expect to die so suddenly." She had to fight back the tears at the unfairness of his death.

"Well, at least you have no financial worries. I can wait for a good price for the house."

"I'll leave that up to you. Here's my address in New Orleans." As she handed over the slip of paper, she was struck with a pang of memory of the day Baptiste took her to the house and told her it was in her name. For a moment she was assailed by doubt over whether it was still waiting for her. But, no, he couldn't possibly have sold it without getting her permission. Pierre would certainly have contacted her if such a sale were in the offing. Empty or not, the house would be waiting for her.

She spent one more day with Sarah.

"I'll miss thee, Leah."

"And I'll miss thee, but it's your advice I'm taking. To go where the heart is."

"Then thee is doing the right thing and will not regret it."

"That's what I'm hoping. I've never been one to mourn over the past or let regret ruin my life. It's not worth it."

"You're strong, Leah, but don't be ashamed to admit you're also in need of stronger arms sometimes. We all are."

"More than you think I am, Sarah."

"Then I'll pray that thee find that strong arm in New Orleans. Thee is young yet; don't turn your back on life."

"Oh, Sarah," Leah laughed, "you're a romantic at heart and don't want to admit it."

"I'm not afraid to admit it," Sarah said. "I'm just too old to find romance for myself. But thee is not." Her eyes twinkled in spite of the tears in them. "And thee must let me be the first to know."

"I promise, Sarah." She threw herself into the older woman's arms, loath to part from her. "If I find that strong arm you speak of, *thee* shall be the very first."

"Now go," Sarah said, releasing her, "go and don't look back."

After a tearful good-bye to Bridget, Leah left Hickory Falls much more quietly than she'd entered the town. By train to the Ohio River and then by steamboat, she and Paul traversed the route that less than two years earlier she'd taken with James. Once again she was filled with mixed emotions. On the trip North, she'd had to shed one skin; now she was having to shed another. The minute she set foot on Louisiana soil, she would become the person she'd been born; for the first time since she left, she felt like a real human being again. Rather than dreading, she welcomed the chance to think and feel like what she was—an octoroon, not a mechanical doll playing a part.

The boat rounded a bend, and she saw the first hazy pink lights over the Delta. Gradually they grew brighter, and the crescent of lights that was New Orleans glowed in incandescent splendor. She was home. At the first sight of the levees and the familiar buildings, Leah couldn't control her tears. Paul was standing beside her at the rail, clutching her legs and dancing up and down; but when he saw her crying, he became upset.

"It's all right, honey, just the wind in my eyes. Here, let me tighten your cap. It's colder than I remembered."

She'd left the borrowed black clothes in Indiana and selected a gray suit to travel in. The bonnet with the white ruching around the hairline indicated her status as a widow out of first mourning, and she was able to get a cab immediately. She leaned back against the cushions and by pointing out the sights to Paul managed to calm the beating of her heart and the pangs that assailed her.

"And that's Jackson Square. We'll go there for walks. And to the Market for buns and strong coffee. You won't like the coffee, but you'll love the buns." She saw a praline seller and asked the cabbie to stop. "Oh, you'll love these, Paul. We'll get all sticky before we get home, but I don't care."

When the cab finally stopped, Leah got down and approached the house like one in a trance. She looked at, without really seeing, the plain glass pane replacing part of the stained-glass window in the door.

"Come, Paul, let's see what condition it's in. We may not even have a bed to sleep on, and I'll have to do some shopping."

Leah slipped the key into the lock, turned it slowly, and opened the door. She turned up lights in the hall and parlor.

Everything was exactly as she'd left it when she walked out. She might have been gone only a few minutes instead of nearly two years, and once again she had to fight to keep back the tears when she relived that evening. Returning to the present, she was overcome with a new emotion—the relief of a great weight removed from her heart. It was as if she'd slipped out of a tight, stifling dress into comfortably old and familiar clothes.

With Paul holding tightly to her hand, she wandered among the packing boxes, rolled-up carpets, and leather suitcases. Baptiste had taken nothing with him. In the dining room the table was still set for the last supper they did not share. Dust covered the plates and begrimed the crystal goblets.

"Oh, Baptiste," she whispered, "I didn't know. I'd no idea the pain my leaving would cause you. I hope you're married again or—or at least have found someone else. But I'm glad you didn't give her this house. Thank you for saving it for me."

"Mama, Mama—look." Paul had let go of her hand and was bouncing up and down on one of the rolled-up carpets.

"Careful, honey, you'll fall. Do you want to see your room?"

Paul nodded, and she led him into the nursery right off the dining room. The thought that Baptiste might have found someone else gave her something new to think about. After long deliberation, she had decided not to let him know she'd returned. After what she'd done to him, she had no right to think he would want to see her. At the same time, her feelings toward him were still too tremulously ambivalent. On the one hand, she longed to see him again and admit how much she needed him; on the other, she feared a renewal of their earlier relationship. After marriage to James, it could never be the same as before. Now, she knew, she must do all she could to stay away from the places he frequented in case there was someone else. If there was, she didn't want to know about it, and the best way to avoid that was to avoid him.

Paul immediately indicated he wanted to climb up into the crib that had never been removed from the room, and in there he happily bounced up and down while she stripped the single bed to air out the blankets and wash the sheets. One thing for sure, there would be enough work straightening the house to keep her busy for a long time.

At least she didn't have to worry about where they'd sleep tonight. Or have to think about buying new furnishings. She lifted Paul out of the crib and walked into her bedroom. The clothes in the suitcases and trunks had best be given away. Once she stripped this bed, she'd look in the boxes for clean sheets and blankets. Then she'd unpack the suitcases and see if there were anything worth saving.

"Hungry, Paul?" They'd eaten only a light supper on the boat, and she'd welcome something before retiring.

Paul nodded.

"Well, let Mama put a few things away so they won't get any more wrinkled than they are, and we'll see about something to eat."

Walking to the dressing table, she was surprised to see a velvet-covered box still on top. She opened it slowly, all the while knowing what she would find inside. No longer able to control the emotions that had been growing wildly inside her, she knelt by the bed, held the pearls in her hands, and counted the beads like a rosary. Each one brought back a memory she'd tried to stifle through the past months.

"Mama!" Paul cried, distressed at seeing his mother weeping.

"It's all right, Paul." She took him into her arms.

"Mama hurt?" He started kissing her as she did him when he fell down or bruised himself.

Only in my heart, she thought. Without realizing how desperately she was clutching the necklace, she broke the string, and pearls fell onto the bed and scattered on the bare wooden floor. Frantically she started picking them up, searching the floor around her and under the bed. She felt compelled to find every one of them. None must be lost.

When she had them all in a pile on the bed, she turned to see Paul looking very upset. His chin was trembling and his eyes glinted with unshed tears.

"It's all right, honey. Mama just stumbled and hit her chin on the bed. Will you kiss it for me again? And now look what I've done. Broken these pretty beads. But I know what we'll do. I'll put them back in the box, and we'll go out for a late supper. Would you like that? Then tomorrow I'll show you all the places I went to when I was a little girl. Can you get your coat?"

Paul started to run into the living room; then, seeing something on the floor, he stopped and picked it up. It was another pearl.

"Thank you, darling. I couldn't bear it if I lost a single one."

During the next few days, Leah felt as if a whole new world had opened up for her. James had never really been a part of her life in the Vieux Carré, so while she missed him, acutely at times, there were few things to remind her of him. It wasn't the same as when she was still in the house where they'd lived together, and she knew she'd been right to come back if for that reason alone. There were times when she knew Paul was missing him and wondering where his father was and why he wasn't with them, but he was not old enough to comprehend the truth. Nor did she lie to him. She simply told him that his daddy was no longer with them. Gradually he seemed to become reconciled to James's absence.

Almost every day she pushed Paul to the Market in the magnificent pram her father had given her when René was born. Imported from France, it was made of soft leather and could be converted into a stroller. It didn't take long to get the house back in order, and then she turned to the garden. Although she no longer needed to, as she had during the war, she planted a few vegetables just to have something to do. Paul pulled weeds as vigorously as she, and soon she had several neat rows.

"I think I'll buy some chickens, too. How would you like to have some biddies, Paul? You know, like the ones in your storybook."

"Biddies—biddies—biddies," Paul sang and ran for the book to point out the picture.

"That's right. Little chickens, and you can help me gather the eggs from the mamas."

Late in the afternoon nearly three weeks later, Leah sat in the parlor and watched Paul playing on the floor. She listened to familiar, long-loved sounds on the street outside. A vendor was hawking crisply fried crawfish, a woman sang of the sweetness of her pralines, pedestrians hurried home from shopping and work. The cathedral chimed the hour, and in the distance, two loud blasts from a steamboat heralded its imminent departure. Nearly two years ago she'd listened to the steamboat and, like the children after the Pied Piper of Hamlin, she'd followed its captivating, bewitching music into an unknown world. Now it was the chimes that enchanted her; they were her music, the music of the city she loved.

"Time for supper, Paul, and then to bed."

"No." It was the newest word in his now vast vocabulary, and she wondered if he were going to have as stubborn a temperament as his father. Every day he grew to look more and more like Baptiste, and was in fact almost the image of René who'd been about Paul's age when he died. Paul was not René; he was his own person, but he completely filled the void that had remained after her first son's death.

"Sweet potato pie and baked chicken. If you eat it all, we'll walk to the park in the morning, and I'll take you into that big church again. You know how much you like that."

"Wead." He came running with a book.

"After supper. I'll read two stories and then tell you another when you're in bed. And I think Mama is going to bed early, too. I worked too long in the garden today."

She picked him up and held him close while she walked to the kitchen. The warmth of his body in her arms flooded her and helped to dispel the chill she felt each time she faced a long evening alone. It was the one time of the day when the loneliness was almost more than she could bear. She hoped she was tired enough tonight to go to sleep almost as soon as Paul did.

Chapter Nineteen

FOR THE FOURTH time in less than an hour Baptiste went through all the papers on his desk and then organized them again into two neat piles. After several *bon voyage* drinks with Pierre, he'd returned to the office for a last-minute check of orders that had come in and the instructions he was leaving for his assistants. Having had a final meeting with them earlier in the day, he knew they were capable of handling anything that would come up. But none of this activity alleviated a nagging, restless frustration. Damn! If only he could get up and walk it off. In spite of what he'd accomplished since losing his legs, he still felt trapped in the chair most of the time. No one would know how often he came close to putting a pistol to his head and ending it all. It was a good thing he was leaving for France in the morning. If it weren't for that and for Lisette, he'd reach into the drawer for the gun right now.

"Ready to go, Baptiste?" Benji stuck his head in the door. In spite of his new station in life as part owner of one of the largest plantations on the Mississippi and cousin to Baptiste, he insisted on remaining valet and aide until Baptiste sailed. "You can't get along without me, Baptiste,

423

and you know it. Not here anyway. Where you going to find someone else who'll put up with your tantrums?" This would be the last night in that position, and it was all he could do to keep from letting Baptiste know just how miserable he was at the thought of staying behind and watching Baptiste sail away. "You want to go right home for dinner?"

"I guess so," Baptiste said.

"You in one of those blue moods again?" Benji asked as he helped him into the carriage.

"Just restless. Always am the night before starting something new."

"Want to go back to Le Coq d'Or? Saw some of your friends going in there."

"No," Baptiste said, "I've had enough to drink."

"How about Madame Broulé's," Benji suggested. "That always perks you up."

"Hell, no. I'm in no mood for that. What do you mean 'perks me up.' I haven't been there in months."

"Maybe that's what's wrong with you."

"Shut up, Benji, and get moving."

"How about a drive along the river? It's a beautiful evening."

"No, I can't sit still long enough."

"Through town then?" Benji had to think of something to stir Baptiste out of his lethargy. "See what's going on along Canal Street? Lotsa changes on some of the streets you ain't seen since you been back."

"No, just drive to the apartment." He didn't want to drive along streets that still held too many memories. The restaurants where he and Leah had dined, the theater she loved so much, Canal Street where they'd celebrated Mardi Gras. Except for the evenings he dined at friends' homes, he seldom went anywhere except the apartment, the office, and Le Coq d'Or. It was good he was getting away. He was determined to stay a full year, and then he'd think seriously about remaining permanently in the Paris office.

Absorbed in his own thoughts, Baptiste didn't realize that Benji had been driving up and down the streets of the Vieux Carré until it dawned on him they were near the block where he'd lived with Leah.

"Damn your sorry hide, Benji, what're we doing here? I told you to go straight home."

"I'm going, I'm going. Just thought it would take your mind off your troubles."

"Well, stop thinking. You're no good at it. Just follow orders."

"I thought we were equals now," Benji insisted. "You might not have wanted to go for a drive, but I did. All right, all right," he said when he saw Baptiste raise his crutch and aim it at his head.

"We can be equals after I'm gone, and then you can drive around to your heart's content."

The route to the apartment crossed a street just half a block from the house. Baptiste tried to close his eyes, but something forced him to keep them open.

"Benji!"

"What is it?" Afraid something was seriously wrong with Baptiste, Benji turned around so fast he nearly fell off the seat.

"Is there a light in the house?"

"I don't know. Looks like there might be."

"Drive past slowly," Baptiste said. "I didn't give Pierre permission to let anyone live there." *But then,* he thought, *it was not my place to do so. That would be up to Leah.*

As they got nearer the house, the light brightened and Baptiste thought it must be in the parlor. He would see Pierre tomorrow before he sailed and ask him to check on it.

They were right in front of the house now.

"How about that, Baptiste," Benji said. "It fooled both of us. That ain't no light inside the house. It's a reflection of the street lamp."

Baptiste slumped in the seat. He didn't know what he'd hoped a light in the house meant, but he felt as deflated and washed out as when he'd been recovering from malaria. "Let's go, Benji, and this time no more detours."

Like an automaton, Baptiste ate the supper Jessie'd prepared for him, but he scarcely tasted any of it. Then he held Lisette while she took her evening bottle. Since Melissa would not be going to France with them, she'd been weaning Lisette away from the breast during the past few days. Holding his daughter, feeling her nestle into his arms, and hearing her suck greedily at the nipple was the only really pleasant occupation of the day. She was his reason for staying alive. Already, at six months, she was so very different from the tiny baby he'd held right after her premature birth. Her hair was tiny golden ringlets instead of a faint halo, and her big eyes had turned from blue to brown. She was going to break a lot of hearts, and he wanted to be around to watch each stage of her growth.

"You're Papa's little darling, that's what you are. And no man will ever be good enough for you." He started to croon the lullaby his mother had sung to him and that he'd completely forgotten about until the night Lisette had colic and couldn't go to sleep.

"M'sieu Baptiste, you gonna wake her up again for sure with all that caterwallin' racket."

"Whatta ya mean 'racket,' Jessie. You dare to call my singing 'racket'! Papa's singing you to sleep, isn't he, honey?"

"You got a lotta talents, suh, but singing ain't one of 'em. Now I'm gonna have to rock her until she fall back to sleep."

"No you don't. Any rocking to be done, I'll do it. You make sure everything is packed. We don't want to get on that ship and find we've forgotten anything she needs."

"I done packed four trunks with onliest her things. We ain't goin' to the moon. I 'spect Paris has clothes for babies."

"Well, go check anyway. I'll call you when she's asleep. And," Baptiste said when he saw Jessie's finger go to her mouth, "no more singing, I promise. I know when I'm licked."

After Lisette was in bed, Baptiste wheeled his chair to the open double doors and looked across the balcony into the city. He remembered the night Leah had stood there and despaired of ever knowing any real happiness. He'd told her never to look down. Now he tried to tell himself the same thing. He had a whole new future awaiting him in France. Once he was away from New Orleans, he'd feel more like his old self again. Among former acquaintances and the new friends he was sure to make, he'd soon be rid of the gloomy fog that encompassed him here in Louisiana.

Baptiste sailed at noon on Wednesday, and on Thursday afternoon Catherine moved into the apartment. She lost no time in hiring a number of personal servants and redecorating all the rooms.

Since the Market was not crowded, Catherine was surprised to feel herself jostled from the side. Then something was tugging at her skirts, and she looked down to see two sticky hands, one holding a praline, the other clutching her dress.

"Go away, you nasty little boy. You're getting candy all over me." Where was the nurse that should be taking care of him?

"I'm sorry if Paul has mussed your gown." The soft, apologetic voice came from behind her. "I reached in my bag for something to wipe his hands, and before I could stop him, he dashed away. I really do apologize."

"Mussed my skirt? He's ruined it with that sticky praline."

Catherine turned around to face the woman who'd spoken to her. "There's no possible way it can be—" Her voice stopped in mid-sentence. It couldn't be Leah. She was supposed to be in Indiana. But Catherine knew she'd never forget the face of the woman she hated so violently, and she had no desire to talk to her. "Never mind. It's an old dress. No real harm done."

No matter that it was one of her newest. It was a good excuse to buy another. What pleasure it gave her to think of Baptiste having to pay for it. What irony that Leah's child should be the cause. She might even write and tell him just so she could picture him squirming as he read the letter. She snatched her skirts around her and backed away as if fearing Leah's nearness would contaminate her.

"You're—you are Catherine Fouché, aren't you?" Leah asked. Leah had seen her only once after getting out of prison, but there was no forgetting the pale-blond hair, alabaster-white skin, and deep-blue eyes.

"Correction, my dear. I am Catherine Fontaine— Madame Baptiste Fontaine."

"Oh." If Leah hadn't been holding Paul's hand, she

might have turned and fled right then. She had no wish for Catherine to see the tears welling up in her eyes or hear the rapid beating of her heart. In spite of trying not to believe it, she'd known all along—ever since returning to New Orleans—that Baptiste had married Catherine. But as long as she didn't have to hear the truth, she could pretend he was still alone. Now here she stood face to face with the woman she herself had encouraged him to marry.

"And I'm Leah Andrews. But I guess you knew that already."

"Yes, one doesn't forget the face of a notorious murderer—or suspect, I suppose I should say."

The words stung, but Leah forced herself to ignore the sneer behind them. She'd been right to ask Pierre not to tell Baptiste that she'd returned. But what she would give to know how he was and how he happened to join the Bonvivier import firm. Would she dare ask Catherine about him?

"I—I was just going to have some coffee," Leah said. "Would you care to join me?"

Why, the nerve of the woman! Catherine thought. Then she had second thoughts. The idea of sitting across a table from Baptiste's former *placée* was so *gauche* it was positively appealing. After all, it would be a pleasure to rub in the fact that Baptiste now belonged to her.

"I don't know," she said haughtily, "I've never considered eating with an octoroon before, but then we do have much in common, don't we?"

Leah was immediately sorry she'd suggested it. Catherine was showing a side she'd never dreamed was there when she thought Catherine would be an ideal wife for Baptiste. On the other hand, she probably shouldn't have been surprised at her attitude, only the way it was worded. After all, this was still the South. No, that was wrong. She would have met the same response from many in Indiana.

"Of course, I'd forgotten. Well then, I'll bid you *adieu.*" Leah turned on her heels, grasped Paul more firmly by the hand, and began walking home. She had no wish now to stay at the Market for the desired coffee. She'd make some at home.

Catherine was shocked when she realized it was Leah who was rejecting her. Instead of such calm and poised self-assurance, she'd expected Leah to stammer and repeat her invitation. She really wanted to talk to Leah, to find out how long she'd been in New Orleans, why she had returned, and if she'd seen Baptiste since coming back. It was the last she burned to know. She might hate Baptiste, but she'd be furious if he were finding consolation in the arms of someone else, most especially in the arms of the woman she knew he really loved. The thought of it made her furious. The only way was to swallow her pride and make the next overture.

After a few small purchases, Catherine got into her carriage and gave the driver directions to Leah's house. She assumed she still lived in the house where Catherine had gone two or three times to see Baptiste while Leah was in prison.

"Wait here, 'Sephus. I shouldn't be long."

When Leah answered the door, Catherine was amazed to note the lack of surprise on her face. Had Leah expected her to come here? Or was she always this cool and unruffled?

"If your offer of coffee still stands," Catherine said, "I'd be delighted to share it with you."

"Come in," Leah said. The interval between meeting Catherine in the Market and her appearance at the door had given Leah enough time to bring her antipathy toward the woman under control. "Please sit down, and I'll bring you a cup. Then if you'll excuse me, I'll put Paul down for his nap, and we won't be disturbed."

Catherine took the opportunity to scrutinize the house where Baptiste had lived for so many years. She'd forgotten how charmingly it was furnished, and she wondered whether it was Leah's taste or his. Grudgingly she admitted that it was probably Leah's. She also looked suspiciously around to see if there was any evidence of Baptiste having been in it recently. She saw none, but that didn't prove he hadn't visited here before sailing for France.

Returning with a fresh pot and a second cup, Leah sat down in a chair next to the sofa where Catherine had settled and spread out her skirts.

"I'm afraid I was a bit curt when I saw you earlier," Catherine said. "But you'll admit it was easy for me to be surprised to see you when I thought you to be in Indiana."

Was Catherine always this mercurial, Leah thought, changing from rudely domineering to obsequious and sugary-sweet? *Beware, she is out to cause trouble in some way.*

"I think I can understand that," Leah said, without answering the question she knew was on the tip of Catherine's tongue. She would make her ask.

"How—how long have you been back? And is your husband with you?"

"No, my husband is dead, killed in a tragic accident. I returned here soon after, just a few weeks ago."

Only a few weeks, Catherine thought, *but time enough for Baptiste to see her and renew their former relationship.* For the moment she'd avoid a direct question. Something Leah said might reveal what she wanted to know.

"I'm sorry," Catherine said. "I would have thought you'd prefer to stay in Indiana, to bring up—Paul, is that his name?—as—as—"

"As white? Is that what you're trying to say?"

"Yes. After all, that is the reason you married and went North, isn't it?"

"Among others." Leah was not about to discuss with Catherine her reasons for marrying James. "But New Orleans is my home, and after his death, it seemed most natural for me to return."

Why didn't she stay? Catherine thought. *Why has she returned here to haunt me?* Thank heavens Baptiste went to France. Maybe he'd stay over there as he said he might do. She couldn't bear it if he took up with her again.

"Yes; yes, I'm sure it was," Catherine said.

After that there was silence while Leah poured them each a second cup. How should she ask about Baptiste? Straight out, that was the only way.

"And how is Baptiste?"

Did she really want to know, Catherine wondered, or was she asking to throw her off the track? "He's fine. Very busy as manager of the Bonvivier Import Firm here. But, of course, that would be of special interest to you, claiming as you do that you're related to the family."

Leah longed for the right words to strike back. Instead she continued speaking as if she hadn't understood the implication behind the sentence. "Yes, I knew he was with them. One of the stores in Hickory Falls bought goods from the firm and I saw his name. Naturally I was curious to know how he became involved with them."

"Then you don't know? How strange." And how delightful that she should be the one to tell her. "An uncle of yours wrote asking him to manage the office here. In fact, Baptiste is in France now to open another office in Paris."

"In France!" Leah's heart sank. As much as she'd fought against letting him know she was home, she'd hoped they'd meet accidentally. Not until this moment did she realize how desperately she needed to see him.

"Yes, he left just two weeks ago. Oh, this is delicious," Catherine gloated, "to think you've been here since before then, and he left without knowing it." Her lips that could smile benignly curled into an ugly sneer. "You might be in France with him. And he's to be gone for at least a year; may stay over there permanently."

"And you're not with him?" Leah couldn't help but be surprised.

"We're what you might call estranged. Nevertheless, I hope you will remember, should he return, that he is still my husband."

"That is something I am not likely to forget. And I'd rather you didn't mention when you write that I've come back."

"Have no fear on that score, my dear. That's the last thing I want him to know. Do you think I want him hightailing it back here to take up residence again in this—this hovel." She looked around the room that she'd characterized as charming only moments before and knew that its appeal for Baptiste lay in that very informality she now considered primitive. "And think about this. When he does return you are not going to get him back. I will not tolerate your being his mistress."

"I would not consider it." .

"You did before when he was married to Marie-Louise."

Leah chose not to answer. "I think maybe you'd better leave now. I think we've said enough to each other." She paused. "And learned what we wanted to know."

Spring turned into summer without Leah seeing Catherine again. Gradually she became adjusted to the fact that, even if Baptiste returned from France, they could never be lovers again. Nor could she answer for herself the question Catherine had put to her. Why she could be his mistress when he was married to Marie-Louise but not now. As long as Baptiste was in France, she need not try to answer it. She knew Catherine would not tell him about her return, and she swore Pierre to secrecy as well. He raised one eyebrow, but he didn't question her.

In September, Leah casually purchased a copy of a daily paper to read while Paul played in the park, and she began to skim the headlines. When she reached one of them, she headed for the nearest bench to sit down before she fainted. Her stomach was churning, and she was afraid she'd be sick. It took her a moment to calm her shaking hands and hold the paper still enough to read it:

PROMINENT NEW ORLEANS CITIZEN
KILLED IN PARIS RIOTS

Below that were smaller headlines: "Body of Baptiste Fontaine to be Returned to New Orleans for Burial." Then came the story. "Baptiste Fontaine, proprietor of Belle Fontaine plantation and manager of the New Orleans branch of the Bonvivier Import Firm, died after being brutally attacked during the infamous September riots in Paris. A memorial mass will be held in the St. Louis Cathedral on Thursday. Further plans will be announced after the body is returned."

The news story went on and on, telling about his life, his heroism during the war, and his assuming the management of the firm. But no more details about his death.

Even as she wanted to destroy the paper and the words on it, as if by doing so she could put the lie to them, she read every sentence. She alternated between grief and fury. With his death went the last small hope she'd cherished that they might, just might, someday be together again. For James she had not wanted to wear black, but she would be in mourning for Baptiste for the rest of her life. Slowly she returned to the house and took the gray suit and gray widow's bonnet from the closet. She had bought them only to wear on the boat so she would not be bothered by unwelcome advances. Now she wondered if she had not given them away because she had a premonition she would need them again. There were those who would look askance at her daring to mourn Baptiste in public, but she cared not for their opinion.

On Thursday she made her way tearfully to the cathedral and entered one of the side pews where she once sat with her mother, away from the center section where her father and his family always sat. After the service she made her way along the crowded aisle, stopped now and then by small clusters of people in no hurry to leave. Leah *was* in a hurry. She wanted to get home where she could break down and let out all the grief and tears she'd managed to keep under control during the mass. She was detained again by a large group surrounding someone they were all consoling. Then by ones and twos they broke away and Leah saw who'd been standing among them.

"What are you doing here?" Catherine's shrill voice, shockingly, blatantly raucous among the muffled voices, startled her. "How dare you show your face at a mass for him!"

"I have as much right to mourn him and do honor to his memory as anyone here. Maybe more so." Leah would not let this woman antagonize or intimidate her. Not now—now that Baptiste was gone.

Then Catherine began laughing hysterically. "How ironic. How beautifully ironic. Baptiste is dead, and you and I are left to live out our lives in the same city. When I get bored, just the thought of that will renew my spirits."

"I'm flattered to think that I'll be the one to alleviate your boredom," Leah said. "I had no idea I played such an important part in your thoughts."

"You—you bitch! Flaunting your affair with him like this." It didn't seem to disturb Catherine that she was screaming so loudly everyone nearby had turned to look at her.

"I loved him, Catherine," Leah said quietly. "Can you say the same?"

"Get out of my sight! You defile me and his memory with your presence. If I ever see you again, I'll—I'll—"

"Scratch out my eyes? That would be the appropriate gesture for someone as catty as you. By the way, you should continue to wear black. It is a most becoming color. Or is that the real reason you chose it? That and the fact it matches your heart."

Leaving Catherine sputtering and speechless, Leah turned and walked off. The words hadn't dissipated her deep feeling of loss, but they had given her a great deal of satisfaction.

For Leah, Baptiste's death was a sorrowful loss and tragedy, but it did not dramatically affect her life. She would continue to squander all her love on Paul and devote her energies to rearing him toward the day when he must decide for himself whether to return North for his later years of formal education or go to France, as did many children of mixed parentage. She considered writing to her uncle in Martinique and exploring the possibility of having someone maintain the import office in New Orleans until Paul was old enough to take over. That, however, would be many years in the future, and she'd no idea it was what he would want to do.

From later news stories she learned that Baptiste had been found dead on a Paris street after being bludgeoned to death. No one seemed to know whether he had been the victim of an attack by the rioters or the military. Since he was dead, it didn't really seem to matter who was responsible. When she went to see Pierre DeLisle to ask his advice about some investments after John wrote that her property in Hickory Falls had been sold, she learned that Pierre had sailed for France immediately upon hearing the news of Baptiste's death and would be bringing the body and Baptiste's daughter, Lisette, home with him.

The news that Baptiste had a daughter not only shocked but distressed Leah. Being with her father could only mean that Baptiste did not consider Catherine a proper mother. And now the child had to return to her care. Then again, Leah thought, maybe she was being unfair. The estrangement between Catherine and Baptiste did not necessarily mean Catherine was unworthy to be Lisette's mother. But oh, how Leah would love to see another child of Baptiste's.

For Catherine, on the other hand, the death of Baptiste flung wide open the door to the cage in which his miserliness and restrictions had confined her. Just as soon as

Pierre returned from France, she would demand that the trust fund be set aside immediately and she be allowed complete control of her inheritance. Challenging the letter giving half the plantation to Benji would take longer; but if the legalities lasted for a dozen years, she was determined to wrest from him every inch of the land, every last item in the house that he claimed as his own.

To all who saw her in public, Catherine was the bereaved widow, and she accepted all offerings of sympathy and aid with a sweet smile and soft voice that contained just the hint of a sob. Admiration for the way she was holding up in the face of such tragedy was the topic of conversation in homes, restaurants, and theaters.

In private, Catherine assumed quite a different face. As a widow in mourning, her home was her refuge and no one would think to come calling without sending a card around first. In the apartment, she entertained a special coterie of guests who kept her amused in ways that would have astonished Baptiste.

The one most affected by Baptiste's death was Benji. Not only did he mourn the passing of the only person he really loved, but he had to prepare to assume vast new responsibilities. Although he'd been carrying the burden of running the plantation along with Septimus since Baptiste left, he always knew Baptiste was really the master hand behind it all. Wrapped in a cloak of unmitigated gloom, he paced the floor when in the house or rode the fields by the hour. At night he sat in the library and tried smoking one cigar after another to see if that would alleviate his misery. Nothing did any good, and when he thought of the saying that time would ease the pain, he wondered how long that would take.

Sometime before midnight, a ship pulled up to the levee. Among those debarking were a man breathlessly descending the gangplank and a plump Negro woman carrying a sleeping child. The man gave orders about luggage and cargo, signaled for a hansom, entered it, and then held the child while the woman took her place next to him.

In a few minutes the cab drove through an archway and stopped at the foot of a wrought-iron stairway leading to a second-floor apartment. Slowly the three passengers made their way up the steps, and the man opened the door.

Wrapping her robe loosely around her, Catherine walked out of the bedroom to see if she'd really heard something in the living room or if it were her imagination. Lately she'd been disturbed by unusual sounds in the courtyard. Sometimes she awoke screaming in the night from a terrifying nightmare. It was always the same: Baptiste threatening to kill her because she had harmed Lisette in some way.

First she was startled and then terrified to realize the lights in the living room had been turned up. She'd purposely turned some off and left the others burning low in hopes anyone coming by would think she wasn't at home. She definitely did not want to be disturbed. When she heard voices in the small bedroom, she put her hand over her mouth to keep from screaming and started back toward her room. Before she could move more than a few feet, a figure emerged into the living room.

"Baptiste! Oh, my God, no!"

Before Baptiste could reach her, she fell unconscious to the floor.

"What in hell's going on out there, Catherine?" The voice came from the bedroom. "It's just your imagination again. Come on back to bed so we can continue with what started out to be a delightful evening. This is the third time you've left me feeling like I needed a cold bath."

"Whoever you are," Baptiste shouted, "get the hell out here yourself."

A man in partially buttoned trousers, an open shirt, and a face gone white with shock, walked from the bedroom. "Who—who are you?"

"More to the point, I think," Baptiste growled, "is who you are and what you're doing in my apartment and in my wife's bedroom?"

"Your—your wife?" he stuttered. "You're Baptiste? But, my God, man, you're dead!"

"Dammit, sir, do I look dead?"

"No—no, indeed not."

Baptiste looked down at Catherine who still lay unconscious on the floor.

"How about putting Catherine on the couch and," he

said, pulling her scarlet chiffon robe back over her naked hip and legs, "in a more modest position."

"Yes, of course. I'm George Bordeaux. I—I came here to help console Catherine in her grief."

"Console?" Baptiste looked from George to Catherine. "That's a new way to describe it."

"You have no right to condemn her, Fontaine. She was informed you'd been killed in the Paris riots; and if I could help her in her sorrow, I saw nothing wrong with it."

"I'll bet you didn't," Baptiste said quietly. "Now get the hell out of here, because she's no longer a grieving widow."

George fled without returning to the bedroom for the rest of his clothes.

Baptiste asked Jessie to bring wine and glasses. He sat on a chair and waited for Catherine to come around.

"Ooh," she moaned and raised one arm to cover her eyes. "I'm sorry, George, but it was another nightmare, only this one seemed so real."

"Have some sherry, Catherine," Baptiste said. "It may cushion the shock and help you tell me what the hell's been going on around here while I've been gone."

"Baptiste? Then it's really you. And you're alive! How wonderful. You don't know what it means to see you after all we heard." She rose from the couch and held out her arms to Baptiste.

Baptiste ignored her feeble attempt at reconciliation and motioned her back to the couch. "Are you quite certain you're glad to see me? It would seem I returned at a rather awkward time."

"I can explain that, Baptiste, really I can." It would take more than soft words to calm the fury she saw in his eyes.

He leaned back in the chair and sipped his wine slowly. "Go ahead, I'm listening."

"I don't know how to begin." Catherine was shaking inside. Unless she could make Baptiste understand, he'd have every right to sue for divorce. At the least, he would send her back to exile on the plantation and reduce her to the role of pauper.

"Just start at the beginning," Baptiste said coldly.

"Well, we received word you'd been killed during the riots in Paris. That's all we knew, nothing more. It was all very mysterious. Pierre said he would sail over right after the memorial mass—oh, yes, we did have a lovely service." There was no change in his expression. "He'd see about bringing your body back and make certain that Lisette was all right. Oh, Lisette! Where is my baby?"

"She's alseep. You can see her later. That is, if you're really concerned about her."

"Oh, I am, I really am. I've been frantic!"

"So frantic you stayed here to mourn my passing. Is red chiffon the newest style for mourning?"

"You do like your snide little digs, don't you?" Catherine snarled. "I didn't go because Pierre thought I should stay here in case some additional information came after he left." He had to believe that lie or she was completely undone. "And I can't stand to wear black all the time."

"I'm surprised. I should think it would go well with your coloring. And George. Has he proved to be a real comfort?"

"What did you expect me to do after you deserted me? Go into a convent?"

"I would have thought after your apparent abhorrence of lovemaking that it would suit you better than what I saw tonight. When did you acquire a taste for this more seamy side of life? Maybe I should congratulate George Bordeaux for being the man I wasn't."

"I accepted his advances at first to humiliate you. You might not know what I was doing, but I did and so did others, and that was satisfaction enough. Each time I said, 'This is for you, Baptiste, just so you'll know how much I hate you.' "

"And you suffered the violence of his embraces just for my sake? How very difficult that must have been. I admire your stamina."

"I'm afraid you misunderstand, Baptiste. I've come to enjoy making love. Does that surprise you? And the more violent or the more passionate, the better. It might surprise you even more to learn there were times I found it desirable with you, but I was damned if I'd let you know. However, I find George much more exciting. After all, he is not just half a man."

438

"All right, Catherine, you've gotten in your last word. Now I'll put in mine. *Get out!* Now. Right this minute."

"You're not going to divorce me, are you?" At first Catherine was quivering. Then she reasserted herself in an attempt to regain the upper hand. "Because if you do, I'll demand *all* of the plantation in settlement. Not half, but all. Or I'll fight you until I completely destroy you."

"Only half is mine to give, Catherine. But, no, I'm not going to divorce you—not yet. Just get out of this apartment."

"Baptiste, you wouldn't dare put me out of here like that." She waited for him to say something. "Yes, you would. But where do I go?"

"To Pierre's or to Hell. I don't care which. But I don't want to see you again. I'll make some financial arrangements, but as of now, all charge accounts are canceled. You and I are through—for good!"

Baptiste spent breakfast trying to decide whether to send word to Benji or hire a cab and go right out. By the second cup of coffee he knew which he really wanted to do.

"Jessie, stay here and wait for our luggage. I'm going out to Belle Fontaine to see how things are going, and then I'll be back before night."

"With Benji?"

"Do you think I could leave him behind? It's been a shock to learn I was supposed to be dead; it may be even more of a shock to Benji to learn I'm alive. But at least I think I'll finally see someone who's genuinely glad I am."

"Don't be bitter, suh. You knowed how she felt 'afore you left."

"I know, Jessie, but it's still pretty hard on a man to come home and find his wife was more elated than grieved at his demise."

The reunion with Benji was far more emotional than the one after the war. During the interim there had formed between the two men a tie that was more than friendship, more than their newly discovered relationship as cousins. In many ways, each not only admired the other but was what the other wanted to be. They were again the ten-year-old boys who had cut their wrists and mingled their blood to become brothers.

"I wouldn't believe it at first, Baptiste." Benji was still shaking with relief and shock. "No matter how many times I was told. First Pierre sent word, then he came out and told me about it himself. He—he knew how upset I'd be. I appreciated that. You scared the living hell out of me, you know that, driving up just now the way you did."

"I'm sorry. I started to send word, but I just couldn't wait to see if you'd turn white when you saw a ghost."

"Damn you, Baptiste. Just for that I have half a mind not to offer you one of your cigars."

"And my whiskey? Any of that left?"

"All of it; it ain't my brand."

"Not your brand," Baptiste mimicked. "You've really taken your new status seriously. Well, get some of both and tell me how things are going."

Benji brought out the two bottles and glasses. "We can talk about the plantation later. First you got to tell me exactly what did happen in Paris. Obviously someone was killed and was taken for you. Who was it?"

"That I don't know. I can only tell you what happened to me. Yes, I was caught in the riots. But not in the crossfire. I was attacked by a street rowdy who wanted my wallet and then struck me over the head when I resisted him. The next thing I knew I was lying in a hospital recovering from a concussion and mutiple bruises. I can only assume it was my attacker who was killed, and evidently mutilated enough he could be identified only by my wallet and papers he carried. I'd been admitted to the hospital as 'Monsieur X,' and when I recovered and got the money from the firm's office to pay the bill, it never occurred to me there was anything to be straightened out."

"Then what brought you home? You'd planned to stay for a year at least."

"Just some business matters here that needed to be taken care of by me personally. Nothing serious, but I actually found myself homesick for New Orleans and thought I'd come home for a little while. While I was in the hospital, things went very well in the Paris office, so I knew it would be all right for me to get away for a while.

I'll probably go back in another few months, but I've given up any thought of staying there."

"So what's going to be home?" Benji asked. "Here or the apartment?"

"I don't know. I'm not ready to decide that yet. For now, the apartment. Ready to return with me?"

"Think you could keep me away." Damn, it was good to have him alive and home.

Baptiste was standing on the dock when Pierre's ship sailed up the river. Earlier Baptiste had sent a smaller boat out to meet the ship and apprise Pierre that he was still alive. He didn't want any more startling confrontations.

"By God, Baptiste, it's good to see you standing there, alive and all in one piece."

"Even if some of those pieces are removable?"

"Haven't lost your sense of humor, either. By the way, that story of your death wasn't your idea of a joke, was it?"

"No, God's own truth. I'd never pull a stunt like that."

"I know you wouldn't," Pierre said. "Benji here with the carriage?"

"He is. And we're heading straight for *La Maison Blanche* for dinner."

"Sounds good. By the way, you didn't need to send word to me on the ship. Your office in Paris told me you'd left for home."

"I thought you'd probably get in touch with them, but I couldn't be sure."

Pierre put down his fork and placed his napkin beside his plate. He'd made a promise to Leah, but it wasn't fair she shouldn't be told that Baptiste was still alive. And was it right that he not know she was here? Especially now that the estrangement between Catherine and him was total.

"Baptiste, I'm going to betray a confidence, but there's something I think you should know."

"More about Catherine? I think I know all I care to."

"No—about Leah."

"Leah?" Baptiste put down his glass to concentrate more completely on whatever Pierre had to tell him.

"Nothing's happened to her, has it? What have you heard from her?" Just the mention of her name brought on a surge of desire that made him realize how lonely life was going to continue being without her.

"No, she's fine. She's here in New Orleans."

"Here?" He didn't dare believe what he'd heard. Then he had a second thought. "She and James have moved here?"

"Not exactly. James is dead. He was killed by an embittered loser in a court case. Leah has been here since before you sailed for France, but knowing you were married to Catherine, she asked me not to let you know."

"Then I did see a light."

"What?"

"Nothing. Just that the night before I left, I thought I saw a light in her house. It turned out to be a reflection of the street lamp. Now I wonder. To think I was that close to her and didn't know it."

Why didn't she want him to know she'd returned? It couldn't be only because he was married. Maybe she no longer felt anything for him and didn't want to be bothered by him.

"She may still think you're dead," Pierre said. "I think you should see her and let her know you're alive."

"I imagine she knows. There've been stories in the paper while you were gone. She hasn't tried to see me."

"You sound as if you're not going to see her either." Pierre ran his fingers through his hair. "Remember, she has no idea you and Catherine are separated. That could be the reason."

"I'll think about it." Baptiste tried to remain cool and unmoved, but he knew exactly what he was going to do. Just as soon as they dropped Pierre off at his apartment, he was heading straight for the house. He didn't care why Leah had asked Pierre not to let him know she'd returned or why she hadn't tried to see him after learning he was still alive. He had to see her. She had come back to their house in New Orleans. And to him that meant only one thing. She still loved him, and he was determined to convince her he still loved and needed her.

Chapter Twenty

It was reassuring to see lights on all over the house, and to know for certain that this time they were not multiple reflections of the street lamp.

Baptiste opened the gate slowly and walked along the path to the gallery. As he walked up the three steps, he saw that part of the stained-glass window in the door had been replaced by a pane of clear glass. Who in hell! Then he remembered. He'd broken it himself with his crutch.

Through the clear glass he saw Leah stooping over and talking to a little boy. He paused just long enough to control his shaking hands and then knocked on the door, when what he really wanted to do was break it down and call out her name. He saw her start toward the door, then hesitate. But of course, it was late and she'd be afraid to open it.

Leah looked toward the door. Paul had awakened from a nightmare, and she was trying to get him back to bed. His only serious reaction to James's death was frequently waking up in the night with a need to be comforted and reassured she was still there, that she hadn't left him, too.

443

She looked toward the door again and saw a tall figure silhouetted by the street lamp. Overcome by memories of the searches during the war, she was suddenly afraid. *I'm being foolish,* she thought. *They don't do that now.* But living alone in the house, she knew how unwise and dangerous it was to open the door to strangers this time of night. Whoever it was knocked again, more determinedly.

"Stay right here, Paul, and don't move. Mama just wants to see who's at the door." He stuck one finger in his mouth and moved behind a chair by the fireplace.

While trying to determine if the man were alone, Leah started slowly across the rug. Then she saw something else. Her heart pounded and her hands were so clammy and cold she had to rub them on her skirts. It couldn't be him. But it was. The man was supporting himself with crutches.

In another moment she had the door open and was in Baptiste's arms.

"Oh God, Leah, I never thought I'd hold you like this again."

"Don't talk, Baptiste, just hold me tight so I know it's really you and that you're alive." She'd read about his return in the papers, but until this moment, she had not dared to think he would return to her.

"You're crying," he whispered. "Why the tears?"

"You should remember," she sniffed. "I always cry when I'm happy. And maybe some tears left over from when I thought you were dead."

"And you don't have a handkerchief."

"Did I ever?" She reached into his pocket where she knew she'd find one.

"Are you going to invite me in, *chérie*," Baptiste asked, "or must I stand here all night?"

Chérie. Only Baptiste ever called her that, and she was filled with long-dormant flutterings of anticipation. "I'm sorry. It's just that I can't believe you're really here."

She helped him over to his favorite chair. "Ah," he said, "this feels better." More than that, he felt he'd come home.

"Let me put Paul to bed, and I'll be right back." She had to have time to get her emotions under control.

When Leah left, Benji came into the room from the gallery. "I think you've found what you really came home

444

for, Baptiste." He returned to the carriage wondering if Baptiste had even heard him.

When Leah came back, she sat on the couch opposite Baptiste's chair. After their first impassioned greeting, she was unaccountably uneasy at being with him. What did he feel for her now? How wide a gap had two years' separation created between them?

"You look well, Leah."

"Thank you, Baptiste, so do you."

"Why didn't you let me know you were here? I had to learn it from Pierre."

"I don't know. Now that you're with me, I don't know."

"You have a very handsome little boy." How was he going to break through that cool, impersonal wall she'd suddenly thrown up?

"Jean-Paul, after my father, but we called him Paul. The French name was out of place in Indiana." Should she tell him or would it hurt him more to know that Paul was his son? She'd wait to see how things went between them.

"He looks much like René." *Almost a perfect image,* Baptiste thought.

"Yes, yes, he does." No, Baptiste must not guess, not yet. She changed the subject abruptly. "The house was dusty but someone took care of the garden. Everything was just as I left it, just as it was—"

She could go no further, talking like this as if to a stranger. She ran to Baptiste's chair, sat on the floor in front of him, and put her hands on the arms. When he put his hands over hers, the pain was crushingly intense. She had to say something, but her heart was overflowing and she could not say what she wanted to.

"Oh, Baptiste, I broke the pearls. I didn't mean to, and I found every one of them."

"What?" For a moment he was puzzled. "There, there, *chérie,* it doesn't matter. I'll buy you a dozen more strands."

With his strong arms he lifted her into his lap, crushed her against his chest, and smothered her face and neck with kisses.

"I love you, Baptiste. I didn't know how much until I

445

saw you through the door. You don't know how much
I've needed and longed for you."

"But you didn't let me know."

"I learned you were married, and I didn't know whether
you'd want to see me."

"Want you! Dear Lord, *chérie*, not a day passed I didn't
want you. I'm here to stay if you'll let me."

"Oh, Baptiste, I couldn't let you go now." How had she
ever been able to leave him?

"And you'll stay?" he asked. "You won't slip away
again?"

"Does your shadow ever leave you?"

"At night, yes."

"No, love, you just think it does," she said. "It becomes
a part of you. I'm a part of you and you're a part of me.
That's why the pain was so great when I left."

"Leah, your logic never ceases to amaze me, but if it's
brought us back together, that's all that's important."

Leah stretched out on the bed, and a single, low flickering lamp highlighted the dusky ivory of her skin. Baptiste
lay on his side while his fingers traced the curves of her
firm breasts, her flat stomach, and her beguiling thighs.

"Touch me all over, Baptiste; don't miss a place. I love
the feel of your fingers."

"Whatever you want, *chérie*. Your wish is my desire.
It's enough just to be able to lie here and look at you."

She reached for one of his hands and brought it up to
her breast. With a single gasp, his mouth was on hers, and
her body was welcoming him urgently and rapturously.
Flooded with his love, she relaxed beside him, no longer
feeling empty and hollow.

Throughout the night they lay in each other's arms.
There were calm moments, suffused with the joy of redis-
covering each other. Then soon their very closeness
aroused new urgencies and brought them together again
until, exhausted and sated with love, they slept.

Leah awoke when Baptiste turned over and threw his
arm across her stomach. He was mumbling something, and
she didn't know whether he was awake or asleep.

"You saying something, darling?" she whispered.

"Um, I think I said I loved you. Am I awake or dreaming?"

"You're awake now, but you can go back to sleep."

"And you won't go away if I do?" he asked. "And leave me alone?"

"No, love, I won't go away. And you won't be alone. In fact, we may have a visitor early in the morning."

"Who?" Who would dare to disturb any of their moments together?

"Paul. He crawls into bed with me when he wakes up. He's done that since James died. I think he needs to be reassured that I won't leave him, too."

"I know how he feels. You have a habit of running away when you're needed most."

"I'm sorry, Baptiste." She leaned over and kissed him. "I won't do it again."

"I can't get over how much Paul looks like René." Baptiste shook his head. "He could almost be his twin."

Now they were together again, Leah thought, it was time Baptiste knew the truth. It was right he should know. Paul was his son. But not the whole truth. She wouldn't hurt him by telling him she'd known before she left with James.

"He should look like René, darling. He's your son."

"What!" Baptiste sat as straight up in bed as he could. "My son! Is that what you're saying, *chérie?*"

"Yes, Baptiste. I—I realized I was pregnant almost as soon as I left. But by then I'd committed myself and I couldn't return." It was a lie but far better than the truth.

"James knew?"

"Yes, but, Baptiste, he loved him as much as if he'd been his own son. Paul was his son."

"But he's mine? I have a son?"

"Yes, love, he's all yours. And more than in looks. He has your stubborn streak, too. He'll take a strong hand."

"A daughter *and* a son!" he shouted. Then he lowered his voice. "And you, *chérie.* Come show me how lucky I am."

In the morning they sat on the gallery and watched Paul playing with Benji in the garden. "We'll go out to the

447

plantation in a couple of days," Baptiste said. "It was a dream once, and now we can see it come true."

"No, Baptiste, I can't." She wanted to live the dream, too, but there was something holding her back. "As much as I long to, I can't. I'd rather remain here in this house."

"Why not, *chérie?* It's our home. The one you made possible for me."

"I could have once, Baptiste. I thought of it as home. But—it's Catherine's home now. I don't belong there."

"I need you, *chérie*, and I told you, Catherine and I are completely estranged. She has no part in my life any longer." Baptiste reached over and took her hands between his.

"This can be your home when you're in town," she said quietly. She was tired of trying to be something she wasn't, and here in this house she felt comfortable.

"No!" he stormed. "It reeks of memories best forgotten—the war, the occupation, the degradation you suffered. I don't want you living the life your mother did."

Leah thought of Clotilde waiting for Jean-Paul to come to her. "I am my mother's daughter, Baptiste. That is something that cannot be changed. I tried, remember, and you'll never know the torment I suffered. The fears I would be discovered. I was happy with James, but not with the life I had to lead. Would it be so different on the plantation? There were happy memories here as well as sad ones."

"Then we'll take those with us," Baptiste insisted. "I want us to spend some time at Belle Fontaine, and we'll have the wonderful times we used to dream about."

"I don't know. We—we each have a part of life away from the other. A chasm separating our past from the present."

"Bridges can be built, Leah. Those very memories you spoke of keep us joined together." He was not going to lose her now that he'd found her again. He could not bear the thought of even a day away from her side, and he knew she was talking about more than just the move to Belle Fontaine.

"Maybe," she nodded, "if what we meant to each other before is strong enough."

"And now, *chérie?* I've never stopped loving you."

Leah could not bring herself to answer. She loved Baptiste, but she was not quite ready to shed the protective cloak of isolation she'd wrapped around herself after James's death, to become totally dependent on someone else's love. She needed a little more time.

"Is the plantation doing well?" she asked. "I know the business is." She'd told him about seeing his things in Hickory Falls.

Although disappointed at her response, Baptiste sensed her need to keep an emotional distance between them for the time being. "Very well. Production is higher than ever."

"And do you sometimes sit under the big oak to supervise the work?"

"At times. But it brings back other memories. I usually ride through the fields with Septimus when there's any supervising to be done."

"You ride?" She was stunned. She'd never thought he'd be able to mount a horse again.

"Yes, didn't I tell you? Benji fixed up a special saddle for me. It took a little while, but I can even manage a good, fast gallop now."

"Or an easy canter with someone on the saddle in front of you?"

"I haven't tried that," he said, "but do you know any charming young ladies that need rescuing from kidnappers?"

"No, but I'd love to ride with you across the fields and along the river. Is the gazebo still there?"

"It is, and waiting for you to sit in it."

Leah closed her eyes and envisioned the lawn sloping down to the river, and she remembered how she'd pictured her child playing there.

"I'll—I'll go out there with you for a while, and then we'll decide."

"That's all I ask, Leah. And you'll see you can be happy there, happier than we've ever been before."

Happy? She didn't know, but she'd be with Baptiste, and he'd have a better chance to get to know his son. Maybe that was more important than any feelings of her own.

Two days later, with Leah nestling Lisette in her arms and Baptiste holding Paul on his lap, they drove out in the carriage.

"She is beautiful, Baptiste," Leah said, adjusting the ribbons on Lisette's bonnet.

"She needs a mother, Leah. Jessie is a wonderful nurse, but she's not her mother." He didn't mention aloud that Catherine never had been nor would be.

"So that's why you lured me out here," she smiled. "And I thought it was because of my charming, irresistible personality."

"No, it's really because of your fascinating body. Didn't you know that."

"Hush, Baptiste! What will Benji think?"

"He'll think just what I do; that it's time you returned home as mistress of Belle Fontaine."

"I thought Jessie would be jealous and not ready to accept me because—because of what I am—but she seems pleased."

"She is," Baptiste said. "The more people she has under her wing, the happier she is. She'll take care of you just as devotedly as she does Lisette and me. But beware, she'll boss you around just as much, too."

"Well, I know why they feel that way," Leah said. "It's not because of me, but of you. They love you, you know that."

"They're good people and we understand each other. I've told you about Benji. He's still to live in the house."

"Of course. It shouldn't be any other way. We can fix up the whole second floor as an apartment for him. Until another large house can be built, that is. And you need to find another valet. Benji will go on being yours until you replace him, you know that."

"You're right," Baptiste agreed. "Now that I'm not going right back to France, I'll take care of that immediately." As to the house, Baptiste had some ideas of his own, but it would take a little time to put them into effect. He'd tell Leah when the right time came.

Throughout the late fall and winter, Leah knew what Heaven must be like. About one out of three weeks they spent in the city. Baptiste worked at the office and Leah either went to the park with Jessie and the children or shopped the stores for things needed on the plantation and to replenish the wardrobes of her fast-growing children.

They had no guests when they were at Belle Fontaine, but that was not surprising. No one was expected to call on a man's mistress. Certain that Baptiste was missing the companionship of his friends along the river, Leah suggested she go into town alone for a few days from time to time so he could entertain, but he assured her that wasn't necessary. He saw his friends often enough when they were in town together, and he occasionally went to a stag poker session or hunt breakfast.

Finally spring burst the garden at Belle Fontaine into full bloom, and Leah couldn't help but admire all the work Catherine had put into it—the curving paths that led to statue-filled niches, the miniature falls where the stream tumbled over rocks on its way to the river, and the perfectly shaped beds of camellias and azaleas. Three men kept the lawn clipped to carpet smoothness, and she never ceased to delight in walking down to the river or playing on it with the children. Their favorite time of day was late afternoon after they awakened from their nap. Lisette, now a year and a half, toddled beside Leah, and Paul lugged blankets for them to sit on. While Leah chased Lisette across the grass or rescued her from the flower beds, Paul threw sticks into the stream and did his best to tumble in so Leah would let him take off his shoes and play in the falls.

"You fall in one more time, young man, and we won't come back here. And, no, you cannot take your shoes off, so stop tugging at them."

"Why not, Leah? It's hot today." Baptiste looked down laughing from his seat on the horse.

"Oh you, how am I going to discipline him if you constantly disagree with me?"

"Little boys are supposed to take their shoes off in the spring and go wading in the stream. Just ask Benji. We used to do it all the time."

"And what if he heads toward the river?" she asked. "What then?"

"Then you have my permission to spank him."

"Well, thank you for that. No, no, Paul, not out of my

451

sight. Come here and Mama'll take off your shoes, but you have to stay right where I can see you. Or I'll cut a keen switch and you know what that means."

"Come help me down, Leah," Baptiste said. "You and Lisette look like you're having an especially wonderful time. The fields can wait."

He leaned back against an old dogwood, clasped his hands behind his head, and stretched out his legs. "Oh, that feels good. My thighs get mighty cramped from gripping the saddle."

"I still can't believe it, Baptiste. That you can ride as well as you do. Or even ride at all. When I—when I saw your damaged legs tossed up on that discard table, that was the first thing I thought about—you'd never be able to ride again. I think that undid me more than the thought you might die."

"And so here I am, almost as good as new," he said. "Look out! There goes Lisette again."

"What am I going to do?" Leah fussed. "She's even more active than Paul, if that's possible."

"You don't mind playing mother to her?"

"Mind? I love her. And what do you mean 'playing' mother. I am her mother. Do you think I could ever give her up now? You have a family, Baptiste, whether you want one or not."

"Thank you, *chérie*. That's what I've been waiting to hear. Then you are happy here?"

Yes, I'm happy, Leah thought. Only one thing kept it from being perfect. If only she could get over the feeling she was living in Catherine's house, not her own. There was nothing in it of hers, but it was so beautifully decorated and furnished she hated to ask Baptiste to let her change anything. She would simply have to get over the feeling that Catherine might someday insist on returning.

During their next week-long visit to town, Baptiste came back to the house almost as soon as he left.

"What is it, Baptiste?" Leah asked. "You look really upset. Something at the office?"

"I think Catherine is dead."

"What do you mean, 'think' she is dead!"

"A boat was washed up on the shores of Lake Ponchartrain this morning. Friends said she and George Bordeaux were boating yesterday, had gone out just before that thunderstorm came up, and no one has seen them since."

"Oh no!" As much as Leah wished Catherine had never been Baptiste's wife, she did not wish her dead. As long as she and Baptiste could not marry anyway and Catherine was no longer important in his life, she had begun to feel the woman was no real threat to her. "They've checked everywhere?"

"Her apartment. His house. His wife was used to his not coming home at night so she hadn't been alarmed. Also my apartment. It can be presumed they drowned, but until—until there is proof—" He couldn't bring himself to say until the bodies were washed up.

"They must be presumed alive, is that it?"

"That's it. For all we know, they could have gone on a trip or run off to live somewhere else. Except that if they did, they took nothing with them."

"So, what does that mean for you?"

"Nothing really. As far as I'm concerned, she's been dead since she tried to destroy Lisette."

"Either way, it makes no difference as far as we're concerned," Leah said. "I know it's harder on you, because it leaves things in an unsettled state."

"My only concern all this time has been Lisette. If Catherine ever wanted to, she could demand her rights as a mother to have Lisette with her, and in turn the control over Lisette's share of the plantation and business."

"You couldn't invoke the laws of primogeniture and leave it all to Paul with the exception of a large trust fund for Lisette?"

"You're right, I could. All I have to do is acknowledge Paul as my son, which I should have done legally months ago. I'll talk to Pierre about it tomorrow. At least about Paul. Since Catherine is Pierre's sister, I'd better wait to discuss the rest with him if she's still alive. She's given him enough sorrow. I don't need to add to it right now."

For several days, spring thunderstorms roiled the waters of Lake Ponchartrain, and those who watched and waited on the shores saw no sign of the bodies. More pieces of the boat, picnic supplies, a shawl, and a parasol washed up, and no one believed that Catherine and George could possibly have survived. But stranger things had happened, so they could not be declared officially dead.

"I know it doesn't make any difference to us," Baptiste said one night. They had stayed in town until there was some kind of definite news. "But there is something about this waiting that is driving me crazy. I feel so damn sorry for Pierre. He's scarcely slept since the accident. He rides out, walks along the shore, examines everything that's been found."

Another week went by with no news. Then some fishermen found George's body trapped beneath the branch of a fallen tree in a small cove. The search for Catherine reintensified in that area. Four hours later she was found. Her full skirts had snagged on the sunken remains of an old dock. Her body might never have been found if George's had not been discovered.

"It's all over, Baptiste. Did—did you have any feelings left for her at all?"

"I guess I did at one time. Now all I feel is relief, and a new, light-headed sense of freedom." More than that he didn't say at the moment, but he had a very special reason for wanting to shout with joy.

It was a golden morning. The sun, shining through a pale-yellow haze, suffused the countryside and the river with a delicate, almost palpable shimmer, as if Midas had blessed the whole world with a faint golden touch.

Leah and Baptiste had gotten up before anyone else to go riding along the river. They stopped to watch a steamboat churn its way up the Mississippi and to wave to flatboatmen poling their way toward New Orleans.

"Everything seems so alive today," Leah said, arching her back and stretching her arms to ease the unaccustomed aches from riding. She'd learned how only since coming to the plantation, and as much as she enjoyed it, she still found herself getting sore after an hour or so. The sidesaddle Baptiste had had made for her was as comfortable as a chair when she first started out, but now she felt the strain in her back and legs. Not for the world, however, would she let him know she was uncomfortable. These rides were among the most pleasant times they shared together.

"Admit it," he said, riding up next to her. "You're glad you came out here to live."

"It's easier now that Catherine is gone. I just wonder about whether it's right for Paul. He's yours, but—he's also mine. That's going to make a difference when he's grown."

"It needn't. He has my name now and someday he'll have all of this." Baptiste swept his arm around to embrace the plantation lands.

"But he'll always know what he is," Leah said quietly, "and so will everyone else."

"Leah, that's twenty, maybe thirty years from now you're talking about. Things may be different then."

"I doubt it," she sighed.

"Would it be better for him in the Vieux Carré? Look what he has here while he's growing up."

"You're right, Baptiste." She looked out across the river. Another steamboat approached, its crowned smokestacks billowing smoke and its decks filled with passengers. "It's hard to believe it was almost three years ago that I said good-bye to all this and sailed up the river."

"I missed you every day of the years we were apart, *chérie*. It's still like a dream to have you with me."

"I came to love James before he died. You have to know that."

"I can understand," Baptiste said. "He was a good man, a fine man."

"Yes, he was, but there were times when— Oh, yes, Baptiste, I needed you, too. The night I left, I told you I loved you. Leaving was the hardest thing I'd ever done, but I had to go. I had to find out what I really wanted."

"And now?"

"I came back, didn't I? And I don't want to leave again."

Just a touch of a frown swept across Baptiste's face. "Do you love it here that much? Would you miss it terribly if—if for any reason you had to leave?"

"The plantation? I suppose so, but it was you I meant when I said I'd never leave again."

Baptiste suddenly turned his horse around and headed back for the house. Leah followed him until he stopped on the lawn, next to a large oak that leaned out over the riverbank.

"Give me a hand, will you, Leah. I'd like to sit here for a little while."

In another minute she was on the grass beside him, her knees tucked up under her skirt while he lounged against the tree. There was still a golden glow in the sky, but the leaves and grass were now a brilliant green and the flowers startling shades of pink and purple and red. Baptiste seemed lost in thought, and Leah was content to sit quietly beside him. When he reached for her hand, she thought there was nothing that could make the day more perfect. She was wrong.

"Leah," Baptiste turned and looked into her eyes. "Will you marry me?"

She was so startled she dropped his hand and started to move away. "Please, Baptiste, don't be cruel." The words were like a knife in her heart. "That's impossible; you know it."

"Do you love me, *chérie?*"

"More than I ever thought I could."

"Then trust me." In spite of her attempts to pull away, he took both her hands in his. "Remember when, after I lost my legs, you wanted a baby? I was so sure I was impotent I was afraid to let you near me, ashamed to have you learn my fears. But your love was strong enough for both of us. Now—let my love do the same for you. Just say you'll marry me."

This is only a game, she thought, *with him making the rules. It's a bit of make-believe, of play-acting. It can't be real. We're going to pretend we're husband and wife, as if that will make any difference.* But she'd play along.

"Yes, I'll marry you." *If only it were true,* she wept inside. It was what she'd wanted since she became Baptiste's *placée.* She'd fled North with James not so much because she still wanted to be white, but because she could no longer bear being only a mistress to Baptiste. "If only there were a way."

"Ah, but there is." And now he was grinning like a child who knows what's under the Christmas tree. He reached into his pocket. "I have here, madame, a magic envelope that will make it possible." He pulled out a large envelope and then withdrew from it a smaller one. "Here are reservations for a suite on one of the Bonvivier ships sailing to France. And here," he pulled out a packet of letters, "are letters of introduction to social leaders in Paris and other delightful cities on the Continent."

Leah took each one in her hand and looked at it as if she'd never seen anything like a letter before.

"And here, my love, is a lease for the new, larger offices of Bonvivier and Fontaine, Importers. Read it and be impressed. You are now in the company of one of the partners. By the way, you are also one of the partners. I've not been entirely the idle country gentleman the weeks we were out here. Some very interesting correspondence has gone on between me and your uncle Claud. Also, I did a bit of shopping the last time we were in the city."

Leah was more and more amazed as Baptiste handed each of the items to her. He'd given her all the details about joining the firm, but now to be a partner. And she, too. How she'd love to meet all of her father's family in Martinique.

But she was not prepared for the next item Baptiste pulled from his pocket. When he slipped the diamond engagement ring on her finger and then showed her the plain gold band nestled in the velvet box, she broke into tears.

"Oh, Baptiste, can it really be true?" She was in his arms, crying and laughing at the same time and trying to wipe her eyes on his shirtfront.

"No handkerchief, *chérie?*"

"No—no," she was half-choking, half-sobbing.

"Here." He tried to sound stern. "Remind me to buy you a dozen lace-edged ones when we get to Paris. Then I'll pin one on you the way Jessie does with Paul and Lisette."

"Thank you." She let him wipe her eyes and then she looked at the rings. "The diamond is magnificent, Baptiste. But—but it's not nearly so beautiful as the gold band."

"I know, *chérie.* Will you mind leaving all this? Will you miss it very much?"

"At times, yes. I'd be lying if I said I wouldn't. But I've always wanted to go to France."

"It means living there permanently. Not returning to Louisiana," he reminded her.

"I know. But think what that means. In France it won't matter whether I'm colored or white. I can be one or the other; no one will even ask or care. I'll simply be me. And the children. They'll grow up without even knowing there's a difference. Oh, Baptiste, we will be happy there, and I'll be a good wife."

"I hope you won't be sorry."

"Why should I be? Don't you know this is what I've wanted since I met you?"

"I'm just afraid there's a curse on me," he frowned. "I haven't been very good as a husband in the past."

"Nonsense, that's just because—you—had—the—wrong—wife—each—time," she told him between kisses. "Did you know I wanted to kill Marie-Louise?"

"When I had to be gone during the yellow fever epidemic?"

"Well, yes, but more so that day she left you in the hospital. Until I realized she did me a favor. If you'd gone with her, I'd never have seen you again."

"And what makes you think I would have?"

"She was your wife; she had the right to have you discharged."

"And you think I would have just lain there and let her? No, *chérie*, my body might have been wounded but not my will."

"Well, anyway, I thought her a cruel, heartless woman."

"She was, but that marriage was arranged, and being a dutiful Creole son, I didn't argue. Catherine was a mistake, too."

"But a different kind," Leah said. "And she gave you Lisette."

"That reminds me," Baptiste moved so suddenly he almost dumped Leah off his lap. "Oh, sorry, but I just realized. We have to tell Jessie to get ready to sail again. She won't like it, but I think we need her. Don't we?"

"If she'll go, I'd love to have her." Leah stood up and smoothed the skirt of her riding habit. "Do you want me to get your chair?"

"Please. My legs are cramped from holding you on my lap."

"Well, thank you, sir!" She tried to look cross.

"Sorry," Baptiste grinned, "but you are putting on a little weight."

"And you know why, don't you?" She knelt down again beside him. "You haven't lost your fertile touch, my love."

"Another one! I'll really have to work hard once we get to France if I'm to support this growing family."

"And so long as you find me so irresistible, it will probably continue to grow. Sorry?"

"Never! We'll find a house big enough to hold a dozen if we have to."

"Speaking of houses and France, we'll have to wait until we get there to be married, won't we?"

"Yes, do you mind?"

"No, but I'd like to go into the city and order a trousseau. Like any woman, I've nothing to wear on a ship or to impress the ladies of Paris."

"Then by all means, go in today if you like, because we'll be sailing in little more than two weeks. There's a very good dressmaker, new since you left, that I meant to mention to you. One that Catherine— Oh, but you already know Cecile, don't you? You sent her here."

"Cecile? Yes, I did, but how did you know?"

"She mentioned your name to Catherine." He didn't tell her how Catherine had taunted him with descriptions of the gowns she'd bought for her wedding to James. He just hoped she wouldn't buy a pale-blue suit or a yellow night-gown.

"I certainly shall go to her. I'd no idea she took my advice. It'll be good to see her again. Good-bye, love. I'll think of you with everything I order."

Within an hour Leah was on her way to town. As she rode along, she felt as if the carriage were a golden chariot and she was floating through Heaven. She went from looking at the diamond on her left hand to dreaming about what life was going to be like in France. No more having to hide behind a mask as she did in Indiana or be afraid every day that someone like Grimes or Mrs. Rhinehardt would strip it off and reveal her as an impostor. No more living on the edge of a world she could covet but never really be part of, as she had in the Vieux Carré.

Oh, Papa, she thought, *I wish you were still alive to see how really happy I am. I loved you and I hated you. I*

*think you knew that and understood. Your mother was an
outcast, but she found a good life far away from her own
home. Now I can do the same.*

"Can you believe it, Cecile, I'm back for another trousseau." Leah looked around the well-appointed shop and
listened to the busy sounds coming from the back room.

"*Oui*, madame, I can see it in your face. Such sparkle!
Such color! And to be a bride again."

" 'Bride' hardly seems the appropriate word after being
a mistress and a wife." She'd already told Cecile about
James's death and her return to New Orleans.

"Ah, but this is the man you love, *non?*"

"Is it that obvious?"

"*Mais oui*. You cannot hide feelings like that. You
marry in the cathedral?"

"No, we're sailing for France. We'll be married there."

"Ah, *oui*, I understand." Cecile had been in New Orleans long enough to recognize what that meant. "You will
like it in France. It is quite different from here. And Paris!
What a perfect place for a honeymoon. You will be staying there, *non?*"

"I think so, or a small town nearby."

"So beautiful," Cecile sighed. "But I shall miss you.
Now—as to the gowns. What do you need?"

"What can you finish in two weeks?" It was evident Cecile was doing well and had a large clientele.

"As many as your heart desires. I have five seamstresses—all very good—working for me now. Thanks to
you I come here and find much success. For you, I will
stop all other work."

"No, Cecile, you can't do that."

"Yes, the others can wait." She fluttered her hands as if
a dozen orders were of no importance. "They are in no
hurry."

"I'm happy for you, Cecile. I wondered later if I were
wrong to suggest it. Women are funny about their dressmakers, hate to change from what they're used to. But I
can see you've done well."

"Oh, yes, and I find a wealthy patron, too. Not a husband, but I can't complain. I do not have to give up my

shop, and at night—ah, that is worth any slight unhappiness because he cannot marry me."

Now the two of them bent their heads over the latest fashion plates from Paris, with Leah suggesting a slight change here, and Cecile nodding and describing other alterations to make the designs suitable for Leah. Then over to the bolts of silk, satin, gauze, dimity, and linen. Gradually the pile of colored plates depicting suits, gowns, retiring robes, and lingerie increased, and two tables were piled with the mounds of fabric and trims they selected.

"Cecile, you'll never be able to finish all these. And Baptiste will have a fit when he learns the number of trunks I'll have to buy."

"You need them," Cecile said, "I will finish them. And which is to be the wedding dress?"

"The rose brocade? No, the white satin. No, not white. The ashes-of-roses silk. It's not so heavy as the brocade."

"Perfect," Cecile agreed. "And I'll make silk roses of a little deeper tone to wear at the waist. And the lingerie?"

"All colors. I want a rainbow of colors—except for yellow. No yellow, Cecile."

The seamstress nodded. "And for the very special set of gown-and-peignoir?"

Leah ran her hands through all the sheers trying to decide."

"May I suggest this delicate mauve?" Cecile picked it up and laid it across Leah's arm.

Just right, Leah thought. *A hint of the amethyst that Baptiste said was like my eyes but enough pink to make it soft.*

"Yes," she said, "that's exactly what I want."

"Very good," Cecile was all business now. "We'll get started at once. You order the trunks and have them sent here. I'll have everything carefully packed for you and ready to go on the ship."

"And fittings?" Leah asked. "When should I come in again?"

"Have you forgotten so soon? Cecile doesn't need fittings."

"Then," Leah hesitated, "will you make them with wide seams. Some of them will have to be let out before long."

"Ah, *oui*," Cecile smiled. "I shall make the very special

seam that can be opened easily with no additional sewing. You will see. Three times you can let them out. A design of my very own. No wonder there is such a sparkle in your eyes."

"Yes, and we have two others. I had a son in Indiana, and Catherine—you remember her—left a little girl."

"Such a fine family," Cecile nodded her Gallic approval of large families. "Come by before you leave. I want to bid you *adieu*."

Shoes, boots, and hats were all ordered with dispatch before Leah got back in the carriage to return to the plantation. She was exhausted but blissfully content with all she'd accomplished. And she'd seen to the children's wardrobes, too. Now it was just a matter of enjoying her last two weeks at Belle Fontaine.

"We won't be back, Benji," Baptiste said. "Belle Fontaine is all yours now." They were sitting on the gallery while Leah was in town.

"Don't say that, Baptiste. Half still belongs to you, and I'll send you an accounting every six months."

"I won't argue, but only after you've kept back what you need to run the place. That shouldn't come out of your share."

"If you say so," Benji said. "But don't say you won't ever be back."

"I'll probably return from time to time, after we've been over there for a few years. But Leah can't. We'd be arrested if she did. I'm not even sure I'll be safe coming alone."

"I know. It's a damned shame. I've half a mind to come to France with you."

"Why don't you? Sell the place, I mean, and come on over. You'd have no trouble finding a buyer. There're at least a dozen Yankees in New Orleans panting to own a place like this on the river. And they've got the money. Charge them double what it's worth and they'll never question the price."

"You think so?" Benji asked.

"I know it. There'll always be a place for you in any business with me, and you've never seen anything like Paris. Bring 'Toinette with you."

"How did you know?"

"You think I haven't seen you sneaking off to the city every night." Baptiste laughed. "I told you you'd have beauties swarming around you. And she really is one."

"How am I going to have all that fun you talk about if she's with me?"

"Treat her like most Frenchmen treat their wives—leave her pregnant and at home. Or love her the way I do Leah."

"You may be joking, Baptiste, but don't be surprised if you find me knocking on your door someday."

"And I'll greet you with open arms. Seriously, you get a good price and we'll invest it in France and make a fortune. I love this land, but I'm not married to it. That's something I learned a long time ago—when I lost the cotton brokerage during the war. It never pays to get so attached to something you can't bear to see it go, at either a loss or a profit."

"Well, I ain't married to this land either, and not that fond of growing sugarcane that I can't leave it," Benji said decidedly.

"No, you became a city dude in a hurry. You'll feel right at home in Paris. Bonvivier and Fontaine—how do you like the sound of that?—have ships sailing every month. And you have one advantage going for you I haven't. You can marry 'Toinette before you leave. So she'll know you're making an honest woman of her."

Benji chuckled. "An advantage for me or for her?"

Once more Leah stood on the deck of a ship that was pulling away from the levee. Last time she thought she was bidding a final farewell to New Orleans; now she was certain. But this time her emotions were less confused. Instead of a hard knot in the pit of her stomach, she felt an excited flutter of anticipation. She was giddy and light-headed from the champagne they'd drunk with Pierre just before embarking and from a sense of complete freedom she'd never known before. Freedom from the shackles of custom and tradition. She was escaping from that dreadful limbo of being neither white nor Negro. She was free of all stigma, of all labeling of any kind. She'd had no idea until this very moment that she'd lived with one kind of fear or another all of her life. It was as if she'd never taken a single breath before without feeling a tightening in her chest. A watching, a waiting for someone to say something that would hurt or humiliate or destroy. She inhaled and exhaled deeply, and the fresh air seemed to be cleansing and purifying her soul.

"What in the world are you doing, Leah?" Cautiously, Baptiste made his way along the deck.

"Be careful, darling, you could so easily fall. Why didn't you call me or send Jessie out?"

"If I fall, I fall. I'll be damned if I'm going to restrict my movements during the whole voyage. No ship is going to get the better of me." With that he lurched toward the rail.

"There, see, you might really hurt yourself."

"But I didn't, did I?" Baptiste fumed.

"Not this time. At least stay close to the rail."

"I think you're right," he agreed, as one crutch threatened to slide out from under his arm. "Now what were you doing, panting like a dying calf?"

"I was breathing. Nothing more. It made me feel good."

Baptiste adjusted the crutches so he could lean his arms on the rail. "Finding it hard to say good-bye?"

"Not really. I was thinking about Paris. Wondering if it will look the way I've always imagined it would."

"Do you want to live there or out in the country?"

"The country, I think. I'll know better when I see it, but I think a country place would be better for the children. And with most rooms on one floor so you won't have to worry about stairs."

"A small château," Baptiste nodded. "That's what I think I'd like. A small château with a bit of farmland. Near Choisy or St. Denis."

"We'll go together and find just the right spot. I'll know it when I see it. Will you be able to take some time before returning to the office?"

"I think so. I'll talk to Claud about it when we get to Martinique."

Leah paused a minute. "I'm excited, Baptiste, and scared about meeting my family. My uncles and their families. Mama always said it was important to know one's people, but I never thought I would. I'll be terribly nervous."

"Nonsense. Claud is easy to know. And you're so beautiful, they can't help but love you." He managed to get one arm around her and still grasp the rail.

"Then I shall have to choose just the right thing to wear."

"Speaking of clothes—I've just been counting the trunks. Where did all those extra ones come from?"

"Well, you're a real comfort! Telling me how beautiful I am and then asking me about trunks. Your romantic bones can certainly turn practical in a hurry."

"Just curious, *chérie*. Don't get in a huff. I want to see what's in them."

"All in good time. They are my trousseau and not to be opened until after we're married."

"That long, eh? Well, I guess I can wait." But already his mind was churning with an idea.

The swift, sleek clipper ship, built for trade in the highly competitive import business, made good time across the Caribbean. The seas were calm and the sun shone every day. Leah's only concerns were keeping Paul from sliding through the rail and out of the crew's way. Jessie took complete charge of Lisette. For Leah the days were not long enough to enjoy the exhilaration of the tangy salt air and the ever-changing views of the sea around her. Nor were the nights any less rapturous. There was nothing to make her regret having said she would marry Baptiste and go to France. Only actually being married to him would be more perfect.

They sailed into St. Pierre, a city glittering against the massive, overpowering grandeur of Mt. Pelé, just at dusk. The first, formal introductions were soon lost in a welter of joyous embraces and hearty welcomes. Leah felt almost smothered in Claud's friendly arms that were so like her father's.

"Oh, Leah," he said, standing back, "let me look at you." He stared so long and hard she began to feel something was wrong. "I can't believe it. I really can't believe it."

465

"That I'm here? That we're meeting after all these years?"

"Yes, that too. But you look so much like my mother, your grandmother."

"Lei-lei?" How often she'd heard her father speak of his beautiful Polynesian mother. Yet he'd never mentioned the resemblance.

"So like her. Don't you think so, Denis?"

"Yes, yes, she does." Leah hadn't been told he was a priest, and she didn't know whether to call him Father Denis or Uncle Denis.

So she looked like Lei-lei. She'd always known that she in no way resembled her mother, who was petite and pretty. But she'd always assumed she was a mixture of all her antecedents. It pleased her to know she was like the courageous woman who'd dared to brave the wrath of her husband's parents and the long ocean voyage from the South Seas to a strange land to be with the man she loved. Leah hoped her children would speak of her with the same love and admiration as Lei-lei's four sons spoke of her.

The evening was gay with laughter and everyone talking at once. The three aunts and their families had joined the uncles and their families in the big house that the first Claud Bonvivier had built for his immense family. Paul and Lisette had to be admired before Jessie could put them to bed.

"Jean-Paul. He should be called Jean-Paul now," Claud said imperiously. Although the youngest of all the Bonviviers, he was the acknowledged head of the family since Denis was in the church and Raoul, next oldest to Leah's father, was badly incapacitated with rheumatism. "He'll no longer be living where there are such provincial customs as calling a man by a single name if he has two good ones. All of us have Jean as a first name, after our grandfather. Our father never spoke about him, but nevertheless respected him. Jean-Paul, as the eldest, was of course privileged to use the two names. Now his grandson should do the same."

No one spoke, but all heads nodded around the mammoth, crowded table. Leah looked over at Baptiste, who was grinning. It was evident that when Claud spoke there was no argument, no discussion.

"Jean-Paul it shall be," she said. "I've always loved the full name."

"And you, Baptiste? What is your full name?"

"Just Baptiste. My parents were those provincials you referred to. Of course I have a saint's name—Louis, naturally, for the good French saint—but I've never used it."

"Louis-Baptiste," Claud nodded approvingly. "I like it. You might consider using it on your letterhead. So," he turned to Leah, "how do you think you'll like Paris?"

"I don't know. I've never been there. But I'm looking forward to seeing it for the first time."

"You'll like it," he said as if ordering her to do so. She'd been a bit intimidated at first by his abruptness, especially when she tried to thank him for all he'd done for Baptiste and herself. But when he shrugged off her words with a deprecating wave of the hand, she knew he was easily embarrassed by any form of gratitude, and she began to understand him better.

"Now if you'll excuse us," Claud rose from the table. "Baptiste and I have business to discuss. He insists he must leave within two days."

With the aunts and cousins clustered around her, Leah walked through the beautiful tropical gardens, lighted by a full moon and the flambeaux placed in sconces among the trees. It was like paradise, and if it weren't for going on to France where she could be married to Baptiste, she would happily stay right there the rest of her life.

"There's going to be a garden reception for us this morning," Baptiste reminded her after he'd gotten up and she was still relaxing in the big bed draped with mosquito netting.

"I know. I think I'll breakfast here in the room so I won't have to dress twice. I'll just wear my morning robe and sit out on the balcony. You don't mind, do you?"

"Not at all. Claud wants to take me to his office before the party. He's very proud of some modern improvements. Speaking of dresses, I want you to wear the very prettiest one you have. Open one of those secret trunks if need be. I know you must have some very special things in them, and I understand there are going to be a number of very important people here this morning."

"Why such a gala levee in the morning? Why not in the afternoon?"

"Because it gets very hot late in the day, and it often rains. Mornings are for work, afternoons for rest, and evenings for pleasure. A good regimen, I think. I'll be back at eleven."

So, what should she wear, Leah thought, as she lingered over coffee and croissants. One of the gauzes? Good for this climate and very pretty. But were they elegant enough for what seemed to be like a morning *soirée*. She thought about the ashes-of-roses silk she'd bought for her wedding. She really wanted to save it, but why not wear it today? It was not as if it were her first wedding, and she wasn't superstitious about Baptiste seeing her in it before then. Yes, it was the most beautiful she had, and he would be pleased.

She called for a servant and sent Jessie with him to open the trunk and bring the gown and accessories back from the ship. Then she bathed and spent two hours dressing and fixing her hair in a more elaborate style than she was accustomed to wearing. Claud and his family— her family—would be proud to introduce her to their friends. She looked in the mirror and thought about Claud's statement that she resembled her grandmother. Was this how Lei-lei looked when dressed like a French matron rather than in the native tapa-cloth garment she wore when the first Claud fell in love with her? Did she ever wish she could go back to that free, unfettered life on her own island? *Well, Lei-lei, I'll never know, will I? But thank you for coming here. Thank you for loving my grandfather enough to leave one tropical paradise and come to another. Thank you for making it possible for me to be alive on this beautiful day.* At the last minute she slipped the strands of pearls around her neck.

When she walked down the long staircase, she saw her Uncle Claud waiting for her at the foot.

"Come, I'll take you out and introduce you. Almost everyone is here."

"Oh, am I late? I'm sorry."

"No, people here have a tendency to come early."

"Where is Baptiste?" She never felt completely comfortable unless he was nearby.

"In the garden. Very busy talking to someone about our methods of harvesting sugarcane here. And the tobacco crop. He seems very interested in tobacco and the best qualities for cigars."

Leah laughed. "He would. You seldom see him without one, a long, black one, in his hand."

They walked across the long verandah and down the steps into the garden. There was a much larger gathering that Leah had expected, even after Baptiste's words that everyone of any importance would be there. Seeing Claud and Leah, they smiled and began to separate, as if to make a path for them. She finally saw Baptiste just ahead, talking to Uncle—Father Denis. She still didn't know what to call him.

"Here you are, Denis, the guest of honor has arrived. You may now begin."

"You're sure we have your permission, Claud?" Father Denis said with a half-grin. But Claud only coughed a bit and stepped back a few feet.

"Now, Leah," Father Denis said gently, "if you'll take Baptiste's arm, we can indeed begin."

Leah didn't know whether she were dreaming or about to faint. She only knew she clung to Baptiste's arm to keep from falling when everything around her began to swirl in a mélange of color and sound. She heard the words and she knew she responded, but not until Baptiste slipped the ring on her finger did she really believe her uncle was marrying them in this beautiful garden with all these people in attendance.

First she was in Baptiste's arms. "Oh God, you're beautiful, Leah. And now you're really mine." He was kissing her as if they were all alone. Then she was being embraced by the uncles and aunts and kissed by people she hadn't even met yet. But it was her wedding day, and she loved the whole world. Paul came running up with a bouquet of flowers, the stems almost crushed in his sweaty palms. While Claud's wife coached him, word for word, he said, "For you, Mama and Papa."

"Thank you, my darling. They're the prettiest I've ever

gotten. And did you pick them yourself?" He nodded and ran off to hide behind Jessie's skirts. And Jessie, holding Lisette in all her embroidered finery, beamed with a smile that stretched from ear to ear while tears poured down her brown cheeks.

The fête continued throughout the day, with food and wine and music and dancing, until midnight.

"When did you plan all this, Baptiste?" Leah asked, after they escaped at last to their room.

"Last night after dinner. I'd thought about it on the ship, and I knew it was right when I saw Father Denis on the wharf. I knew then you should be married among your family. The garden party had already been planned, the guests invited, and it all seemed so perfect."

"It was, Baptiste, even if you did give me the shock of my life."

"I hope I didn't spoil anything for you. I mean, if you'd bought a special dress for your wedding."

"That's just it," she smiled. "This is my wedding dress, the very one I chose. I wore it today only because I thought it would please you when you said to wear my prettiest."

"It is and you did." Leah had put on the mauve gown and peignoir she'd sent Jessie to the ship for during the afternoon. "Now, come here and turn around. I have another surprise for you."

She felt him place the necklace around her throat, and then she looked in the mirror.

"Amethysts! Oh, Baptiste, they look almost exactly like the ones you gave me before."

"They should. They are an exact duplicate. M'sieu Thibedeau made them up for me from his original design."

"I think I'm going to cry again. Between laughing and crying all day, I'm feeling like someone who's drunk too much champagne."

Baptiste started to reach into his pocket for a handkerchief. Instead he took her in his arms and kissed away the tears. "It's forever now, Leah. No more running away."

"Never again, I promise."

"Now, look in the mirror again." She moved to the long pier glass. "Who are you?"

"I am Leah Fontaine. Madame Baptiste Fontaine."

If for years she had searched for her identity, now the search was over. White or octoroon, it no longer mattered. In Baptiste's arms, she knew who she was—his adored wife.

**THE EPIC ROMANCE
OF KING ARTHUR
AND HIS UNCROWNED QUEEN!**

A Novel By
Barbara Ferry Johnson

The untold saga of Lionors—a beautiful young girl whose passionate love for a young knight, Arthur, grew into one of the great secret romances of history. At last her magnificent story is revealed, in a novel ablaze with the color and adventure of Arthur's Round Table and Camelot . . . and the timeless human secrets of love and loss, triumph and sacrifice!

3611/$1.95

AVON ◆ THE BEST IN BESTSELLING ENTERTAINMENT

☐ Homeward Winds the River		
Barbara Ferry Johnson	42952	$2.50
☐ Tears of Gold Laurie McBain	41475	$2.50
☐ Always Trevor Meldal-Johnsen	41897	$2.50
☐ Atlanta Milt Macklin	43539	$2.50
☐ Mortal Encounter Patricia Sargent	41509	$2.25
☐ Final Entries 1945: The Diaries of Joseph		
Goebbels Prof. Hugh Trevor-Roper	42408	$2.75
☐ Shanna Kathleen E. Woodiwiss	38588	$2.25
☐ Self-Creation George Weinberg	43521	$2.50
☐ The Enchanted Land Jude Devereux	40063	$2.25
☐ Love Wild and Fair Bertrice Small	40030	$2.50
☐ Your Erroneous Zones		
Dr. Wayne W. Dyer	33373	$2.25
☐ Tara's Song Barbara Ferry Johnson	39123	$2.25
☐ The Homestead Grays James Wylie	38604	$1.95
☐ Hollywood's Irish Rose Nora Bernard	41061	$1.95
☐ Baal Robert R. McCammon	36319	$2.25
☐ Dream Babies James Fritzhand	35758	$2.25
☐ Fauna Denise Robins	37580	$2.25
☐ Monty: A Biography of Montgomery Clift		
Robert LaGuardia	37143	$2.25
☐ Majesty Robert Lacey	36327	$2.25
☐ Death Sails the Bay John R. Feegel	38570	$1.95
☐ Q & A Edwin Torres	36590	$1.95
☐ Emerald Fire Julia Grice	38596	$2.25
☐ Sweet Savage Love Rosemary Rogers	38869	$2.25
☐ All My Sins Remembered Joe Haldeman	39321	$1.95
☐ ALIVE: The Story of the Andes Survivors		
Piers Paul Read	39164	$2.25
☐ The Flame and the Flower		
Kathleen E. Woodiwiss	35485	$2.25
☐ I'm OK—You're OK		
Thomas A. Harris, M.D.	28282	$2.25

Available at better bookstores everywhere, or order direct from the publisher.

AVON BOOKS, Mail Order Dept., 224 W. 57th St., New York, N.Y. 10019

Please send me the books checked above. I enclose $_____ (please include 50¢ per copy for postage and handling). Please use check or money order—sorry, no cash or C.O.D.'s. Allow 4-6 weeks for delivery.

Mr/Mrs/Miss _____

Address _____

City _____ State/Zip _____

BBBB 5-79

IN HOLLYWOOD, WHERE DREAMS DIE QUICKLY, ONE LOVE LASTS FOREVER . . .

"I love you," she said. "I've loved you since the sun first rose. . . . My love has no shame, no pride. It is only what it is, always has been and always will be."

The words are spoken by Brooke Ashley, a beautiful forties film star, in the last movie she ever made. She died in a tragic fire in 1947.

A young screenwriter in a theater in Los Angeles today hears those words, sees her face, and is moved to tears. Later he discovers that he wrote those words, long ago; that he has been born again—as she has.

What will she look like? Who could she be? He begins to look for her in every woman he sees . . .

A Romantic Thriller by TREVOR MELDAL-JOHNSEN

AVON

41897
$2.50